Joe's Place

Jan Matthews

For

Jules, Ben and Jono

1

February 1919

The road that curved away from the busy London Road was quiet and long, edged now with pebble-dashed frontages and pleasant modern villas although a few old farms and open fields could still be seen. When it reached the clock tower the road ended, delivering its responsibilities to the High Street.

The railway station on the London-Brighton line lay right beside the road but Joe had to climb from the train carriage on to the bleak February-morning platform, make his way up the echoing steps, out of the station, past the coal-merchants' shopfronts and around the railway-yard corner before the road was under his feet. He felt its familiarity seep up through his boots.

The sight of his army greatcoat was no novelty and the few people in the cold streets were bent with purpose but almost every one of them paused to quickly scan his face. He turned up his collar and lowered his head; a woman reached out to touch his sleeve and he looked up in spite of himself, but she was gone.

He thought about an alternative, but in the end took the direct route from the station even though he was more likely to meet someone he knew on the familiar road. It seemed that his feet would not allow a deviation from the tracks they had traced all his life.

The morning was still. The remains of light snow made the footpath treacherous and he trod carefully. His breath clouded as he trudged the half mile that he had to travel, carefully keeping his thoughts neutral in the way he had learned to do, concentrating on each step, clamping down on the bubble of pleasurable anticipation that swelled inside him again now, pushing the other thoughts aside. Despite his concentration he slipped and almost fell. He steadied himself, then suddenly a sob caught in his throat.

He swallowed hard and coughed, but the tears began to flood his cheeks and his sobs increased.

He was racked with a painful yearning for Sam's presence. He shuffled back against a fence to get back his breath and his composure, trying vainly to be unnoticed.

"Joe Barlow!" He turned towards the sound of the voice with a hand raised to hide his face, then lowered in defeat.

"Joe! Oh, Joe!" Stumbling in her eagerness, a woman came running from inside the house.

"Joe, Joe, Joe" she repeated, the name becoming a crooning mantra.

"Mrs. Wishart" He rubbed his eyes quickly and sniffed hard.

"Joe love, when did you get back? No, of course I can see that you've just this minute come. Oh Joe, I'm so sorry. So sorry. So sorry. You poor boy." The woman's eyes were filled with tears.

Joe patted her arm vaguely. Despite the fact of his own tears, her anguish seemed excessive.

"It's alright" he said, unable to find more suitable words.

"You dear brave boy" she sobbed and dug her fingers into his arm. "Your Ruthie will be so glad to have you home."

Joe nodded. "Yes." Then "yes" again as he prised the hand off and backed away, confused by such intensity, eager to escape. With a spurt of determined haste and without looking back, he continued up the road as his mind cautiously crept to the home-coming he had yearned for for so long.

Oak Tree Place was a quaint feature on the suburban road along which Joe made his way and it was his destination. On the top of a small bump on the road hardly deserving to be called a hill, a surprising cobbled forecourt revealed the venerable Oak Tree Public House, squatting under the boughs of the huge oak tree that gave it its name, or perhaps had been planted to baptise it.

The most visible and striking feature of the forecourt, however, was the row of cottages; a neat and picturesque row of six small dwellings that edged its left-hand side. The first one huddled side-on to the road, the next three crowded against it and each other, then two larger houses had been added at the end of the row with proper upstairs windows where the first four cottages boasted only a small dormer to light their single upstairs rooms. Past the six houses of Oak Tree Place a narrow laneway ran down the side of the pub's disorderly outbuildings to the next street. Joe's waiting bedroom in the last house in the row had a small window that looked out over that laneway.

He was coming up to Beulah Road and was almost within sight of Oak Tree Place when puzzlement pierced his thoughts. Old Mrs. Keily, known to him since babyhood, had popped out of her house ahead of him, and instead of greeting him, or even waiting for him to reach her, had cast a startled glance in his direction then scuttled away from him towards Oak Tree Place, as fast as her arthritic old frame would allow.

He was distracted by the Major, the upright soldierly relic of some other older war, who glanced at the unfaded patch on Joe's greatcoat sleeve where his stripes had been and snapped "Corporal!" in almost-respectful greeting as he passed. Joe smiled thinly.

He was almost there when Auntie Alice came running towards him out of Oak Tree Place.

◆

She flew towards him, arms open and waving up and down, whether preparing to envelop him or to keep her balance it was hard to tell. She was upon him before he could open his arms in response, but the expected embrace was in fact a furious attack, as she beat her clenched fists and her head against his chest with all her strength. He dropped his bag and attempted to put his arms around her.

"Where ... have ... you ... been? Where ... have ... you ... been? Where ... have ... you ... been?"

Auntie Alice was beating him in time with her words.

Despite his bemusement at her unexpected antagonism and its intensity, he felt a spurt of indignation.

"Sam ... " he began.

"SAM!" Alice almost screamed "Sam, Sam, *SAM*?" She resumed her attack, and the question to which she apparently did not want to hear the answer.

"Where … have … you … been … Joe, where-have-you-been-where-have-you-been?"

With rising anxiety, Joe began to realise that his aunt's very public display of distress meant something that he was sure he didn't want to know. He backed away, stumbling over his bag on the ground and almost falling.

"What?" he asked, still backing away from her, "What?" Then the question he had been asking reluctantly over the past four ghastly years came automatically.

"Who?"

His aunt seemed to crumple in front of his eyes. The human whirlwind was all at once a sagging body with a cloth-doll face. He stepped forward again to support her.

"We've been trying to find you." And again the question "Where have you been?" But this time the question was a whimper.

"Auntie Alice" his voice had risen in pitch. "What is it?"

"I sent telegrams. Charlie telephoned for me."

"Auntie Alice!"

She attempted to speak clearly. "I have to tell you"

"Tell me what?"

" ... before you get there ... "

They were only yards from Oak Tree Place. He could see the end house. Home and solace and an end to all the horror was only steps away. His mind skittered away from his growing dread and echoes of his childhood crowded. Oak Tree Place. Chants. Private jokes. "Place and chips!" "A Place in history!" Peter and Bill and Lizzie and Jim ... He shook his head against the creeping cold certainty that something was dreadfully wrong.

"Auntie Alice, I want to go home. Please."

Alice cupped her downturned face with her hands and stood sobbing helplessly in the street, but as Joe pushed past her she caught his arm with both hands.

"Your Mum."

Joe tore her hands from his arm with a viciousness that made her reel backwards and he began to run awkwardly towards the Place. Her voice carried after him.

"And your Dad."

He could not have heard her right.

◆

It looked the same but different. Smaller. Shabbier. The pub was not yet open and it looked squat and sad. He floundered across the Place, his boots clattering on the cobbles. There seemed to be people in his way, standing like sentries. He stabbed and twisted. The bayonet seemed solid and real; the bodies backed away. There were voices but they were unintelligible as the blood pounded in his ears. His legs weren't working properly, but it only took a few shuffling steps to reach the house at the far end of the row.

The door was closed. It should have been open, his Mum and Dad and Ruth spilling out with open arms and light and smiles and an end to it all. But he didn't try to open the door.

Alice had caught up with him and pulled at his greatcoat.

"Come away Joe. Come to my house."

"Where are they? What's happened?" Stupidly he yelled "Mum! Dad!"

"Joe!" said Alice sharply "come away."

"No," he snarled "Tell me!"

"The flu," she said simply. "Saturday and Sunday. One after the other. Sudden. Sudden."

Joe sat down quickly on the doorstep as the breath left his body. His question was almost inaudible.

"Ruth?"

"Oh Joe she's well. She's bonny. She's indoors. Come and see her. Come and see her"

"Wait a minute. Wait a minute."

Everyone seemed to be repeating themselves. He said again "Wait a minute".

He hung his head between his legs and sat for a moment on the doorstep. He looked at the V of the step, worn and scrubbed, which showed between his legs. There was a scuff mark—Mum wouldn't like that. Mum would be rubbing at that mark … No she wouldn't. Numbness pervaded his body and sang in his head. He looked up heavily.

Concerned and sympathetic faces surrounded him. Faces from his childhood, some as familiar to him as his Mum and Dad. But not his Mum and Dad. Not his Mum and Dad. Not his Mum and Dad.

There was the bang of a door and a whisper on the cobbles. The faces turned, the bodies parted and a small girl hurled herself at Joe, winding her arms around his neck. Joe wrapped his arms around her and they rocked fiercely together. After almost a minute she drew back to look into Joe's face.

"Joey," said Ruth gravely "Mummy and Daddy are dead and gone to Heaven."

"I know sweetheart."

"I'm very sad."

"I'm home to look after you now."

"I still want my Mummy. And Daddy."

"Yes ducky, I know."

"Are they really never coming back ever?"

Joe looked helplessly at his little sister.

Alice stepped forward. Her eyes were pink but she was Alice again.

"Come and have a cup of tea, Joe."

With difficulty he rose from the doorstep, Ruth still in his arms. Someone collected his bag from the footpath and brought it to Alice's door. As he made his way past the sympathetic faces the effort of acknowledgement was too much. He managed a nod or two.

Alice's kitchen was as familiar to him as the one he was brought up in. He would not have recalled every item, but they sprang readily from his memory. The plates on the dresser, particularly the green one with the tomatoes embossed on it. The cup and saucer of infinite fineness and painted yellow roses that was never used. The copper kettle, polished to a pearly lustre, the ladder-backed chairs with flabby cretonne cushions concealing their sagging rush seats.

The familiarity was at once comforting and alienating; he felt a rising panic that he quelled with a physical effort.

As Alice made the tea, Ruth on his lap examined minutely the buttons on his shirt, then went on to examine his face, his hair, his hands. She seemed to be engrossed.

Joe was looking at her vacantly but spoke carefully over her head to Alice.

"Tell me."

"Two of the customers at the Oak Tree died of the flu last week. One was Mr. Arland, Peter's dad. The other was Mr. Caudwell from around in Bensham—he used to be a regular at the Lord Napier until there was a case of the Spanish flu there. Your Dad and Mum could have caught it from one of them—or somewhere else. It's everywhere. It was very quick—just over a day from being poorly to ... to ... "

Alice struggled to recover herself. "The doctor said they didn't suffer." She looked quickly at Joe.

Joe exhaled as if ridding his lungs of every scrap of air and drew it in again slowly. He rose carefully and put Ruth on the chair. Deliberately, he opened the back door and went into the tiny back yard. He stumbled the few paces to the coal shed and carefully placed his hands on the raw brick wall. He leaned forward and began to beat his head against the bricks. Thud. Thud. Thud. Thud. Blood flowed down his face and dripped on the wall as he increased his intensity.

When Alice pulled him away he could not see for the blood in his eyes. Ruth watched warily as Alice led him inside and mopped his wound. She used some of the water from the kettle to pour into an enamel dish, cooled it with cold water and added disinfectant. She bathed the wound, her gaze avoiding Joe's eyes. The bleeding took time to stem. In the end Alice wound a strip of old sheeting around his head and tied it tightly. She said it looked raffish and Joe smiled weakly. After a few minutes he reached up to remove the bandage; the bleeding had stopped.

Finally Joe spoke. "Sorry Alice," he said.

He had dropped the "Auntie" and would never use it again. "It's just ... It's just—"

"It's alright Joe. I understand."

"No you don't!" he cried painfully "No you don't!"

"Hush Joe. Not in front of ... "

"Sorry."

"Joe?"

"Yes?"

"We'll talk in a little while, alright?"

"Alright."

Joe held the hot teacup in both hands, warming his numb fingers, relishing the pain of the returning blood. Concentrate on the fingers, Joe. Don't let the other stuff in. Contract the muscles in your belly, Joe, it stops you from crying like a baby. Talk to someone, Joe, don't let the thoughts in.

He asked about the funerals.

"Yesterday." said Alice.

"I must go to the cemetery."

"Yes." Then "Joe, where were you? We tried so hard to find you."

"Not now."

Ruth slept with Alice that night and Joe slept on the floor downstairs.

2

The next day

"This was my bedroom while you were at the war, Joey" Ruth said. "But Daddy and Mummy and me made it all good for you again so that you could sleep here when you came back." She looked proprietarily around the spare, tidy room.

The rest of the house showed the attentions of Alice and probably the other neighbours, Joe observed dully. The hopeful vase of greenery on the kitchen table did nothing to mask the acrid scent of disinfectant that pervaded the house from top to bottom and added another element to Joe's sense of dislocation.

Clumping back down the stairs, he sat in the kitchen with Ruth on the other side of the table. Alice had left them alone to rediscover the house, but he knew she was hovering somewhere near. Responsibility was weighing densely on his shoulders. Joe thought vaguely that he probably needed to make some decisions, but he was dully unsure of what they were. Instead he addressed the immediate.

"Do you want to sleep here tonight, Ruthie? Instead of at Auntie Alice's?"

"Yeees," doubtfully

"What's the matter? Don't you want to?"

"Whose bed will I sleep in?" The little face crumpled. "I want Mummy."

"Darling Ruthie, I'm so sorry that Mummy and Daddy aren't here any more, but I'm here to look after you now."

Ruth was now crying with deep, tearing sobs.

"I want my Mummy and my Daddy."

Joe walked around the table, lifted her from the chair, cradled her in his arms and rocked her gently. She nestled into him, still sobbing, and the warmth of her little lean body crept into his chest. He held her until she was still again.

They all slept at Alice's again that night.

The visit to the raw new graves at the cemetery had been as terrible as Joe had anticipated and the biting wind that scoured his face as he walked back to Oak Tree Place was almost a comfort. On his return to Alice's house where she and Ruth were waiting he pushed aside the dragging grief and attempted, mainly for Ruth's sake, some normal conversation.

"How is everyone in the Place, then?"

"That would take a long time, Joe." Alice understood his effort and spoke encouragingly.

"Well you can start, can't you?"

"I suppose so." She cocked her head.

"Well then."

She leaned forward, arms crossed on to the table. Joe looked at his aunt, really looked, for the first time since he had come home. She had always been slight but now she looked thin and strained. As he looked at her he remembered the excitement of his uncle suddenly bringing home his beautiful young bride to the Place. How proud and delighted Uncle Johnny had been and how smitten Joe had been by his new aunt! He smiled.

Alice stopped. "What are you smiling about?" she asked, smiling in return.

"I was thinking of Uncle Johnny bringing you back to the Place," he said.

"Oh yes, I was a bit of a surprise, wasn't I?" she said drily.

"I thought you were the most beautiful thing I had ever seen," he said slowly. He was surprised and rather proud of his ability to pay his aunt the compliment, but he embarrassed himself at the same time.

Alice laughed. It was the first time anyone had laughed since Joe came home.

"Ah Joey. What a sweet little ten-year-old you were. You were rather beautiful too!" Joe blushed red.

"How things do change," Alice murmured and for a moment Joe thought she was referring to him. When he realised she wasn't, he didn't know what to say anyway.

"So tell me about the Place," he said quickly, but his thoughts were still with Alice's arrival there. He had adored her immediately, but his parents had been much more restrained, he could remember that. His mother was not inclined to like surprises and she was reserved in welcoming Alice. Even then Joe knew that his mother liked to be in charge of things and there was Uncle Johnny going and getting married without a word to her, or even to Dad, his own brother! Dear Mum. Dear Mum. She'd come round though, bless her. His mother's faults were granted immediate loving indulgence.

Alice and Jessie Barlow were poles apart in every way and for a while it seemed that Alice was determined to flout Jessie's rules of behavior just to annoy her. Joe heard enough of his parents' conversations to know that his mother disapproved of Alice's way of dressing, way of speaking and way of behaviour—the very things that Joe found so entrancing. He loved her vivid clothes, her bright red lipstick. He loved to watch her light a cigarette and delicately pick a shred of tobacco off her tongue with a polished fingernail. He loved to hear her loud delighted laugh, even if his mother did shudder theatrically at the sound.

Alice flitted—there was no other word for it, Joe thought—in and out of the house in Oak Tree Place and treated Joe with a gravity that he found heady. Sometimes she said things to him that he didn't understand and he knew that she knew he didn't understand, but Joe basked in her attention.

He had been in love with her in a childish way. Now she was just another person, a faded version of the butterfly of old. While he was a faded person who'd never even been a butterfly …

"So tell me about the Place," he repeated determinedly.

"Well," Alice began again "let's start with the Oak Tree."

"Carry on!" said Joe with an attempt at heartiness, but his eyes strayed to Ruth at the end of the table playing intently with two clothes-peg dolls who appeared to be muttering to each other with great intensity. "Carry on." He must stop repeating himself.

"We'll start with the Oak Tree" said Alice again.

"Why not?"

"Mrs. Edie Craggs," said Alice in a tone that had echoes of a fanfare.

"Does Mrs. Craggs live at the Oak Tree now?" Joe asked in surprise.

"Yes indeed. She has two rooms upstairs. So she needs to be in the story, doesn't she?"

"If you must."

"Don't be like that Joe." But the censure was mild and delivered with a smile.

"So it's Mrs. Craggs for a start."

"Yes … well. She hasn't changed much as far as I can see, but perhaps you'll see a difference. She's still the same old"—she glanced quickly at Ruth who was absorbed in her game—"battle-axe!" she whispered wickedly. "Charlie's good"—she glossed over Charlie quickly—"and Lily still seems to think that the sun shines out of her mother-in-law. She looks more like her every day."

"Lily owes her job as well as her husband to Edie Craggs so she's probably showing how grateful she is."

"Thirteen years is a long time to carry on being grateful."

"Thirteen years? That long?"

Alice shrugged. "It was two years to the day after Johnny and me."

"Oh well" he deferred "You would remember then. Do Charlie and Lily look any more suited than they used to?"

"No, not at all," said Alice with relish, "and hardly likely to be now I'd say."

There was a small pause in the conversation until Alice said "So that's the Oak Tree."

"And nothing much has changed there."

"No not really. I still do a bit of skivvying there. It's been hard for Charlie recently—but then it's been hard for most. I can fill in when they need me. It makes it easier for Charlie."

"Charlie has it pretty easy anyway, as I remember."

"Joe!" Alice's voice was admonishing "That's not true."

"Well, his mother will look after him just like she always has done."

"Joe" Alice said sharply "That's so far from the truth. You don't know the story—you were too young to know the story."

"Well tell me then" He leaned back in his chair.

Alice drew a line on the tabletop with her finger.

"Mrs. Edie Craggs says she was in the theatre and you'd think from the way she talks that she was some sort of glamorous important creature." Alice's eyes glinted. "What she *was* was a chorus-girl."

Joe smiled slightly at Alice's curled lips.

"And she got herself into trouble and had Charlie."

They both cast glances at Ruth playing intently at the end of the table before they turned to each other again.

"She gave Charlie to her mother to rear while she went back to being a chorus-girl. He was still only a baby when she hooked a husband—just what she was after, of course. He came from a family with money, so he had what she wanted. Lord knows what his family thought. Quite a bit older than her—silly old fool—but he lived for twenty years after they were married, which was quite a surprise, I'm sure. Edie Craggs lived high and respectable and as far as anyone knows she never mentioned Charlie to her husband. Never even went to see Charlie. Ever. Sent a bit of money though," she added grudgingly, "but nothing regular."

"And now she wants to make up for all that."

"Looks like it. When her old man died she took to Charlie like a limpet. He was twenty-two."

"How do you know all these little details?"

"Oh," Alice said airily, "you just hear these things."

"And she bought him the Oak Tree?"

"Not straight way. Charlie has had a few jobs. Done a few things."

Joe thought for a moment.

"So her name really wouldn't be Craggs then?

"Everyone just calls her Mrs. Craggs because she's Charlie's Mum. Her name is something hyphenated, if you don't mind. That'd be a bit rich for the Oak Tree. It suits her to be Mrs. Craggs."

"So there are two Mrs. Craggses at the Oak Tree."

"Mrs. Edie Craggs and Mrs. Lily Craggs. You should have seen Edie's face when she heard someone talk of her as "*Old* Mrs. Craggs"!

Joe laughed as Alice said "But of course Mrs. Lily Craggs is the only real one."

"Oh yes." Joe rolled his eyes. "I remember that Lily is a real one!"

Alice was laughing lightly as well, but she said "No, don't let's be cruel, Joe. It can't be easy for Lily when most people know she was the barmaid who Edie pushed on to Charlie because she was good at running the pub while Charlie wasn't."

"Do you think she minds?"

"Well, she has a husband so she's settled, but who knows with Lily what she's thinking? She's a close one, that. But she does look more and more like her mother-in-law every day though—a real pair of duchesses they are, and they think they're so superior."

Alice was about to say something more when Ruth slipped off her chair and came to lean against her, regarding Joe intently.

"Are you going to be my Daddy now Joe?" she asked with a frown.

"Ducky, I'm your big brother, but I'll be just like a Daddy."

"And I'll be just like a Mummy," said Alice quickly, with a catch in her voice.

"Thanks Alice." Joe looked at his aunt tentatively. "We'll manage, won't we?"

"Of course we will."

Ruth took her peg dolls off to another chair and continued her game.

There was a pause, then Alice said carefully "She should live with me, I think Joe."

"No!" Joe's response was immediate and fierce. "No!"

Alice coloured and pressed her lips together, looking down at the table before continuing.

"It's much more sensible if I have her Joe, I'm sure you can see the sense in it. I can look after a little lass much better than you can. She needs a mother."

"She needs me!" Joe was distraught. "Alice, I love her and I'd die for her! She's all I have and I'm all she has! I know you love her too but she's not your flesh and blood!"

As he said the words, Joe recognised but suppressed that this was a cruel thing to say to a childless widow. Alice's eyes filled with tears and she gulped them back before responding.

"She means the world to me too, Joe. You don't know—*you really don't know*—how much she means to me."

"Oh Alice, I do know, and I understand that you think you'd make a better home for her. But I'm going to do everything I can to be her Mum and her Dad as well as her brother."

"What about when you get a job again and have to go to work every day? What about then, Joe?" asked Alice evenly, her tears brushed away. "What about then? What will you do with her then?" She was warming to her argument.

"I'll manage. I'll find someone to look after her."

This was a brutal response. For all of her short life, Joe knew that Ruth would have regarded her aunt's house as a second home, just as he had always done; it would hardly even have been necessary to ask Alice to care for her if ever the need arose.

Alice's eyes filled with tears again and Joe was remorseful. He was however careful not to concede any advantage.

"Alice, I'm sorry. You can look after her of course. If you want to."

"Of course I want to." Alice was weeping quietly. "How could you think I wouldn't want to? I want her to live with me!"

"That's not what's going to happen, Alice."

"You should think about it."

"No."

"Just think about it"

"No need. She's going to live with me."

"She hardly knows you Joe and you hardly know her! You don't know what to do for her. You've only seen her twice since she was born!"

"I know that I love her and I know that I can look after her."

"You might change your mind ... "

"No, Alice."

"Just—"

"NO!" Joe exploded.

They had been speaking intensely and quietly, but this last outburst made Ruth look up with a frown of anxiety. Both Alice and Joe sat back in their chairs and smiled at her in reassurance. She smiled back uncertainly.

The discussion was ended as far as Joe was concerned. His heart was beating fast after the argument but he drew a deep breath and felt a sense of achievement. Alice remained quiet and withdrawn until Joe and Ruth left, just a little later.

3

Five minutes later

Alice sat at the table for some time. Joe's stubbornness had found her unprepared. Jessie and Ned's deaths left a hole in her life too, and she was sad and she missed them, she really did. But she would never ever tell a soul that her very first thought when they had both died—when they were dying even—was that she would now have Ruth to herself. She hadn't thought to arm herself with convincing arguments to put to Joe because she had not for one moment imagined that they would be necessary.

She shook her head ruefully at her silliness.

Slowly she rose from the table and went to gaze out the front window, leaning forward with her hands on the sill, considering, not seeing.

Living from day to day, week to week, on the sidelines, that was past. There were possibilities now that had never been thinkable while Jessie and Ned had been alive. For a few moments she allowed her mind to skip to those possibilities … Then she shook herself mentally.

Joe would be easy enough to overcome, she was sure. A few weeks of trying to cope should be enough. She smiled thinly.

4

The same evening

They slept in their own house that night. Joe put Ruth to bed in the small back room with the side window and once alone, he curled in the middle of his parents' large soft bed and finally allowed himself to cry desolately and with childish abandon, yearning for the touch of his mother's hand, the comforting protection of his parents' presence. He wept for the loss, he wept for the unfairness, he wept for the emptiness.

He slept deeply from exhaustion and his sleep was blessedly uninterrupted, but the heaviness returned as soon as he opened his eyes the next morning. Ruth was already dressed, Joe observed with some relief, but her eyes were wide and uncertain as she sat at the kitchen table and watched him come down the stairs.

He managed to prepare a creditable breakfast but he could summon up little in the way of conversation. Ruth ate dutifully, then slipped from the table and opened the front door.

"Where are you going?"

Ruth stopped in her tracks and turned a confused and anxious face.

"Outdoors to play?" It was a plea.

"Oh Ruthie, I didn't mean to stop you. I just wanted to know where you were going. I didn't mean to stop you. Of course you can go and play," Joe babbled desperately. Ruth regarded him gravely for a moment, but smiled briefly before going outside.

Joe gazed for some time at the back of the door, then turned woodenly back to the kitchen. How was he supposed to know what Ruth did and didn't do? What was allowed and what not allowed? He felt overwhelmed; everything was just too much trouble. He slumped into a chair and closed his eyes. Mistake. Get up, Joe. What did he need to do? What would his parents have been doing now? What was absolutely necessary to do? He didn't have the faintest idea. He had observed the detail of daily life in his home without ever registering its timetable or its execution.

He pushed up from the table, brushed the crumbs off the breadboard and placed it in its sloped position against the end of the dresser. Heated the kettle, washed the dishes, dried them and put them away. Those were the things he knew. He looked around and couldn't really see anything else that needed attention. His mother scrubbed the step each day, he knew that, but he couldn't bring himself to do that yet. It was a signally female thing to do, tied up with a casual gossip with next-door doing the same thing and a housewifely sloshing of the bucket of water over the cobbles when finished.

Upstairs he thought he should make the beds. He made beds very well these days, tight and secure as he'd been trained. Much good that particular aspect of training had been in the trenches, God help us, but he thought he'd probably make beds the army way for the rest of his life—when he had to make beds, that is. Not now. Downstairs again.

Now what? He picked idly at the vase of greenery on the table, then shuffled to the door and dragged it open.

Alice's endeavour to bring him up to date with the Place's residents had petered out with the Oak Tree, so when Joe came out of the front door at the same time as Mrs. Galvin came out of the door of number three, he was unprepared and vaguely antagonistic. He greeted his neighbour edgily.

Ellen Galvin was around the same age as Alice but had always been more a friend of his mother than his aunt, her quietness and reserve making her seem older than her years. She and her brother had lived in Oak Tree Place with their parents, then alone there after their parents' deaths. Ellen's marriage to the dark, good-looking Irishman had come out of the blue and surprised everyone, then gone on to confound those who waited lasciviously for the evidence of necessity.

She conveyed her condolences with an awkward formality, and nervously chattered on. Joe could not remember actually having had a conversation with her before. Mr. Galvin was at work, she said. Yes, at the brick works. Her brother Cedric who used to live with them had married and gone to live with his wife's parents in Purley. His new father-in-law had a shop. Cedric was going to work there. Lucky old Cedric, thought Joe. He felt churlish and didn't bother to hide it, he was too weary for pretence. Mrs. Galvin looked at him with a sympathy that Joe ignored and said that she was there at all times and that he must call on her whenever he felt the need. Yes. Thank you. They were neighbours, after all and what were neighbours for? Yes. Thank you. Thank you.

Joe turned abruptly and re-entered the house; he had forgotten why he had gone out. He should have been more polite to Mrs. Galvin, he could feel his mother scolding him. No Mum, it was alright. Doesn't matter. Doesn't bloody well matter.

Joe roamed the house again. He steeled himself to open cupboards to examine contents but closed them again without disarrangement. His sense of dislocation was intense. He regarded the tousled bed with its familiar covers and quilt. Should have been aired and made by now, Joe. His mother's rules had been rigid; life had been starched and organised, the house cleaned with fervour and routine that saw saucepans taken from the rack and polished every Friday despite their already immaculate condition, windows cleaned every second Wednesday, the copper kettle cleaned every week and of course the front step daily. Joe felt a decay encroaching already on the orderliness and his depression deepened. Think, Joe, think.

He was actually officially on leave for two more weeks before his demob, so surely, he thought with relief, he didn't really have to do any damned thing. But no, he did have to apply himself to learning about Ruth's life and her daily activities. What did she eat? What did she wear? He would have to apply to Alice for some, if not all, of this information and felt irritated. He frowned and considered the situation. Finally he searched out a pencil and a sheet of paper from a writing pad and walked the few yards to Alice's house with some bravado.

Alice provided the answers to his questions in such detail that it might have been thought that she sought to overwhelm him with the complexity of his undertaking but Joe wrote down every last detail and was pleased. He tacked the paper to the back of the larder door.

That evening the three of them went to the Oak Tree. Ruth scampered into the back parlour with the assurance of a regular visitor, leaving Joe and Alice in the long dim room with only a few other souls. It was cold outside, but the atmosphere in the pub was warm and thick with the smell of recent disinfectant competing with the stale cigarette smoke and hoppy beer perfume. Charlie was behind the bar and as Joe and Alice walked in, both the Mrs. Craggs' had erupted from the parlour and stood in mute anticipation beside him, one on each side.

To Joe's overworked mind, the three grave figures made an almost comical picture. He knew them well. Charlie was a big man whose dark good looks were unbalanced by a sullen disposition that showed in his expression. As a publican his bonhomie was somewhat forced and easily breached, a fact well known to some of the Oak Tree's more ebullient customers. The two women flanking Charlie, mother and wife, differed in age but little else. Both were impregnably coiffed and corseted and each had an air of confident control. If Sam had been with him, Joe would have muttered "skittles" out of the side of his mouth because Sam would have seen, too, that that's what the three figures looked like—upright and bulbous and ready to be knocked over. They would have had a laugh about it. But Sam wasn't with him, it was Alice, and she was walking towards the bar with a smile, holding Joe's arm.

The searing pain of loss suddenly engulfed him again so that he hardly heard the words of condolence from each member of the Craggs family in turn. Charlie put a pint in front of him and he grasped it gratefully, taking a long draught before replacing it on the bar.

He was not all that used to drinking at the Oak Tree. Although he knew the pub well, he had hardly been a regular customer before he joined up and his visits had been almost always with his Dad. The Oak Tree had not been a pub favoured by him and his mates.

But it had been the Oak Tree Joe had seen in his mind when he and Sam fantasised about the pints they would drink when they got back to Blighty. Sam's fantasies ran more to glamorous London hotels overflowing with free drinks for returning heroes and legions of willing women. Sam didn't stint himself where fantasies were concerned. But Joe's life and memories were so closely bound to the Oak Tree that his anticipation could only deliver him there.

He took another long pull on his pint. It wasn't by any means the first he had had over recent weeks, but it felt like it. He felt it travel down his throat and it didn't seem to stop until it reached his toes. Then it did a return journey, spreading out into his chest.

"Joe," said Charlie tentatively "We'd all been planning a Welcome Home for you here at the pub, but of course ... " His voice trailed off.

"We thought ... " Lily began to speak but was overtaken by her mother-in-law.

"*What* we thought was, Joseph, that your friends and neighbours would like the opportunity to greet your return and to express their condolences on the sad loss of your dear parents. *If* it might be convenient for you, Charles, Lily and myself would like to host such a gathering here at the Oak Tree tomorrow evening."

This was more an edict than a question, but there might have been a slight quaver in Mrs. Craggs' voice all the same.

Joe was silent, his eyes cast down. He didn't speak, not sure whether he could.

Finally Alice squeezed his arm hard and he raised his head, reluctance manifest in his silence and his expression. But as the pressure on his arm increased he croaked woodenly that that would be very kind, thank you Mrs. Craggs. He dreaded the occasion.

5

The following evening

It so often happens, Joe reflected the following afternoon, that the things you dread turn out not to be so bad, whereas the things you look forward to eagerly are those that ...

The late afternoon was grey and cold, but a good crowd of people turned up at the Oak Tree. Mrs. Craggs and Lily laid on a spread and the beer flowed readily. Joe's back was thumped and his cheeks kissed and his hand pumped and squeezed until he felt that his body was someone else's.

Alice was watching him carefully and came over to him as he was being embraced by Dora. This embrace was being executed with difficulty as Dora was low down in the old chair and Joe was leaning over her. Her knotted arthritic hands clawed at his back and he was supporting himself on the arms of the chair. He was aware of the ridiculousness of the picture and he was laughing as he tried to extricate himself.

"Thank you Dora," he said finally "Thank you very much."

He was still laughing as he turned to Alice. His face was flushed and his straight blond hair fell across his forehead. Alice leaned up to push it back and he put his arms around her. Alice grimaced and averted her face.

"Whoa Joey, how many pints have you had?" she asked "You smell like the brewery!"

"Don't know. Don't care." He was still holding her, and Alice reached around to unclasp his hands from her back.

"Careful, Joe love, take it a bit slower or you'll not last the evening.

He blinked and smiled with the confident assurance of a nearly-drunk young man.

"Come over here, sit a while." said Alice.

She led him to a settle against the wall and fetched him a plate of sandwiches. People approached, condoled, some cried a little and they all offered help. Joe practised his un-attaching trick and managed it quite well, thanks also to his intake of pints. He retained practically no memory of the names or faces of that night and would afterwards only assume that all his parents' friends had been there, but he felt buoyed by the familiarity of the bodies and the surroundings. He surveyed the room with maudlin affection.

The evening also completed Alice's interrupted account of the Place's residents. Dora had been a fixture of his childhood and he could not think of the Place without her presence. She had lived in number two since Joe was a baby and to Joe she'd always been an old lady. Michael Galvin had conveyed his condolences with gentle formality before retiring to sit by his wife where they looked very much unlike the established married couple that they were. His dark Irish good looks and her pale careful neatness seemed incompatible, but Joe accepted them as part of the Oak Tree Place landscape. They both regarded the assembly with silent gravity, she leaning into his side.

Then Alice introduced him to the newish occupant of number one, Stephen something, a teacher at Beulah Road school. Dent, that was it, Stephen Dent. Seemed a pleasant fellow.

It was a group of four people entering the pub together that completed the roll-call of the Place. Joe rose eagerly, easing through the crowd to greet them, making his way directly towards the figure swinging confidently in on crutches, his left trouser-leg folded up on itself at ankle-height.

"Len."

"Joe."

They regarded each other with broad smiles, then fell to hand-shaking and back-slapping. Joe felt his friend sway awkwardly and steadied him as he stepped back.

"Joe?"

He turned to the slight young woman at Len's side.

"Are you looking after this hero then, Ida?"

"Oh yes," she smiled "he's being well looked after."

"I am, too" said Len, placing his arm round his wife and nodding at the same time towards his parents.

"Mr. Dawson, Mrs. Dawson" said Joe "How are you?"

"How are you, more like," fussed Len's mother, on the brink of fleshy tears, "What a homecoming for you, you poor young man, after all you've been through!"

Strangely, Joe reflected, this was the first time anyone had mentioned the fact that he had just come back from years of what was unimaginable to anyone who hadn't been there. The last few days had centred round the death of his parents. He felt a warmth towards Mrs. Dawson for her understanding. But then, she would, wouldn't she? With Len and all.

"We're next-door neighbours and I haven't even seen you since I came home," said Joe. Then quickly "You are still next door, are you?"

"Yes, yes" said Mr. Dawson, heartily "We're all still there. We've just spent a few days with my sister in Maidenhead. She needed a hand with a few things there after her Walter passed away. Only came home this afternoon to hear the dreadful news. Missed it all. Missed the funeral – sorry Joe."

"That's alright, I missed it all too—and the funeral."

"Oh my poor dear boy," Mrs. Dawson raised her hands in sympathy "how did that happen—where were you?"

Without answering, Joe turned away and spoke to Ida. "Are your Mum and Dad well, Ida?"

"Yes Joe, they are. I'm so very very sorry to hear about your Mum and Dad. They were lovely people. We'll all miss them."

After Joe's murmured reply there was a pause then a general dispersal to bar and table. Joe and Len faced each other.

"How are you, Len?"

"How are *you*, Joe?"

"I hardly know how I am."

"That'll pass, Joe, it will. It'll be alright, you'll see. It'll pass."

"There's such a lot to pass, Len" Joe said bleakly. A pause, then "Sam died too."

"Ah Joe" Len stepped forward to take hold of Joe's arm. "Ah Joe, Joe. So close to the end of the damned thing."

"After."

"What do you mean?"

"He died of flu in London last week. I was with him. He wanted to kick up his heels before he went home. Talked about coming back here with me for a while even. Might have done. Should have done."

Len just kept grunting "Joe, Joe, Joe" in dumb empathy.

"I couldn't get a doctor to come. Couldn't get him to hospital. Then I did and he died."

"Ah Joe, don't ... "

Alice appeared at Joe's elbow. He turned and look at her wildly. She'd been watching him. He felt a rising sense of suffocation.

"I've been telling Len here that the reason I wasn't here when my Mum and Dad died was because I was in London watching my best friend die instead!" he said loudly and with careful articulation.

Alice flinched but Joe went on relentlessly "He died of the flu too. So don't tell me that my Mum and Dad didn't suffer. They ALWAYS say that, all of them, but what do they know? They don't know. I know. I know. Everybody suffers. Everybody suffered. Sam suffered. I saw him suffer and then he died. After all the things he'd done and all he'd suffered already, he had to DIE OF THE BLOODY FUCKING FLU!"

The silence which fell on the room was caused by Joe's raised voice, but most people had not heard his words. Those closer, who had heard them, were shocked but excused him immediately. Sympathy surged like a sticky wave.

The hum of conversation resumed haltingly, and at a lower level.

Joe burst out through the pub door into the biting cold. As he had only to cross the Place to his doorway, the tears had no time to chill on his cheeks. He had forgotten to collect Ruth from the pub's back parlour but when he remembered he couldn't go back because of his bleeding head and he didn't remember how that happened either.

6

18 months later.
August 1920

Joe leaned back against the bar and stretched his shoulders, pint pot in hand. The windows and the door of the pub were wide open to allow in the remnants of the warmth still remaining in the day and the heady perfume of the sun-soaked grass from Oak Tree Field. Joe took his pot, walked out of the pub, down the cobbled passageway and round into the field, leaning against the pub wall and regarding the scene with benign melancholy. The residual sun-warmth from the pub's side wall leached into his body as he drew a deep breath of the sweet air.

The almost secret area that was Oak Tree Field was bounded by the pub's walls, its outbuildings and miscellaneous fences of various ages, materials and states of repair. The grassy enclosure presently provided rest and fodder for the fire engine horses, but it had always been a favoured playground for the local children, Joe among them. Many an esoteric game had been contrived in this small enclosure and the old oak tree in its corner that shared its shade between the pub and the field had been home to many an improvised tree house, rope ladder, and a broken bone or two.

The abandoned smithy on the far side of the tiny field looked picturesque in the soft light, not the tumbledown wreck revealed by the full light of day. Its roof was still surprisingly intact, and the Oak Tree used it as casual storage for empty and half-empty crates, hay for the horses and sundry rubbish, so there was something of a trodden track across the grass to its wide doorless entry. It showed sharply in the slanting evening sunlight. Idly Joe sauntered across the uneven surface to the smithy and looked inside, taking a sip from his ale as he did so.

Comfortable childhood memories were trickling back until Joe frowned as he saw something glinting on the hard earth floor beside a pile of crates and bent to pick it up. It was the hair clasp that Ruth had given Alice for her birthday a few weeks ago. He frowned as he realised that Charlie—or Lily—or Mrs. Craggs—had imposed on Alice's employment and required her to carry goods to or from this storage place.

He strode back into the bar and placed his empty pot on to the counter with a more than usual firmness. Charlie looked up.

"Joe?"

"Charlie. Have you had Alice fetching and carrying heavy things?"

Charlie frowned. "What d'you mean, Joe?"

"She shouldn't be asked to do that, Charlie."

"Do what, Joe?"

"Carry heavy things about. She's a woman, and anybody can see she's not strong."

"Yes. I mean I don't."

"Someone does."

"Who?"

"Someone here."

Charlie's face was a study in innocent bemusement. "Who? When?"

Joe was slightly deflated by Charlie's obvious innocence.

"Look here Charlie, I found Alice's hair clasp in the smithy by the crates. And I don't think," he added with his voice rising "that she should be fetching and carrying those heavy things. She's a woman."

Charlie's face was a study in confusion. He blinked rapidly.

"I never ..." he stammered.

"Well somebody has had her do it."

Charlie and Joe regarded each other. Each appeared to be considering the possible identity of person responsible and neither could decide.

"I'll have a word with Mother ... and Lily" Charlie said. "and I'll make sure that it doesn't happen again. Sorry Joe."

At this moment, Lily made her entrance to the bar. Not a hair out of place, she stood at the other end of the counter regarding her domain with apparent complacency, but her eyes darted everywhere and her hands moved restlessly, making small rearrangements.

Charlie leaned over the counter to Joe with panic in his eyes. "I'll talk to Lily and Mother later Joe. No need for you to mention it."

Joe looked at Charlie. Such a big man but such a weak vessel. So completely under the thumb of the two formidable women in his life.

"Make sure you do, please Charlie." He doubted that he would; Charlie was not one to stir the pot there.

Because this doubt was as good as a certainty, Joe took the clasp to Alice and made her promise to refuse heavy carrying at the Oak Tree, which she admitted, flushing, that Charlie's mother had sometimes required her to do. "And you know what she's like, Joe—you can't refuse Edie Craggs—it's like a Royal command!" she giggled uneasily.

"I thought that what you did was a bit of cleaning," said Joe.

"Well, while I'm around, I suppose ... "

"You mustn't, Alice. You're a woman."

Alice smiled slightly.

"Women can, Joe—and do."

"But you shouldn't, Alice." Joe in fact wondered how anyone could imagine that his aunt, as slight and small as she was, could carry anything much more than a quarter of tea. "It's not right."

"Oooooh" said Alice archly, "and where did you get those ideas, Joe Barlow? Certainly not round here!" Head on side, she continued.

"Joe, you don't have to protect me, but ... I am glad that you care."

"Well you don't have anybody ..." he said lamely.

Alice's eyes glittered but her tone was controlled.

"Joe, I have you and Ruth. You're all I need."

Joe didn't really want to get into yet another Ruth-discussion but he pressed on.

"Are we, Alice? You're a youngish woman and you should marry again. You should have children of your own." This statement was enough to make Joe embarrassed to deliver it.

A forced smile. "As a youngish woman, I'll make my own decisions then, thank you!"

Joe had overreached his capacity for this conversation, but he continued doggedly. "You could get a better job than the Oak Tree."

"Oh could I indeed?" Alice raised her eyebrows "and where would that be, Mr. Barlow?"

Joe was deflated. He didn't know, but he was sure there must be something better around than cleaning at the pub.

"Well I'm going to look out for you. I could find you one, I'm sure."

"Joe, don't worry about me," Alice said briskly. "The Oak Tree suits and you know that I help Flo Keily down the road when she needs me with the laundry. And it's really none of your business anyway," she frowned, a beginning resentment.

"I could ask around anyway."

"Joe *don't*." She was obviously annoyed now. Joe looked confused.

"Joe, the Oak Tree and Flo's really suit me. I can take Ruth with me. Other jobs I couldn't do that."

"Oh Alice, you don't need to think about that—you know I could get somebody else to look after her while I'm at work!" There they were on dangerous ground again.

"And you know I wouldn't let anybody else look after Ruth!" Alice's voice was sharp.

To ease the tension, Joe laughed.

"Ruth is so lucky to have you, Alice. And so am I."

But it was hard to say the words.

7

Five minutes later

Alice bit her lip in agitation and drummed her fist on the table. It wasn't happening as she thought it would.

Damn Joe, damn him, damn him, damn him.

She summoned up the easy scorn she held for a clumsy boy stealing the advantages that were surely hers by right. But this familiar path of thought did not lead to any solution, it was all just a circle. She could see herself walking desolately round this circle forever if she did not find a way to break out of it. She laid her forehead on the table and allowed herself to moan softly; the ache was physical.

If only Joe had died like Johnny … He could have died, couldn't he, and solved all her problems? Something quick and painless, she allowed. Then she and Ruth could have lived—she snorted mirthlessly at the phrase that sprang to her mind. Life was hardly disposed to deliver happily-ever-after, not to her, anyway.

Suddenly she shivered. No, don't think about that—it's dead and gone. *He's* dead and gone. *They're* dead and gone. They must be. No one knows she's here, tucked away in this sleepy suburb— if they'd known she was here she would have been dead and gone herself. She fought the wave of panic that rose like a fierce blush. With huge effort she dragged her breath back and began to breathe slowly again.

Think about Ruth. Soothing.

Patient, just a little bit, that was what she had to be. After all this time, a little longer shouldn't be all that hard to bear. Something had to change some time soon. Had to.

She shook herself angrily. She should be doing something to *make* things change, but she just couldn't think of anything. She wished she was cleverer, wished she could talk to someone about all this, someone who would advise her, give her the solution to all this waiting.

No, speak to no one, Alice, no one. You never know what will get back. Fewer people now knew her secrets, that was one good thing. Just keep wishing for the time being, it's all you can do.

8

A few days later

In the year and a half since his tumultuous return to the Place, Joe had found that it was good to have Len next door. Their shared and exclusive experience was a bond and Joe had found himself rather closer to Len than he had been before the war when, despite their proximity as next-door neighbours, they had not knocked about together much at all.

It was ironic how the term "lucky" could change in degree so much over the last few years. Len was lucky that he had Ida, and both his parents. His disability was not so great when compared to many alternatives; in fact he was getting an improved prosthetic foot fitted soon. He joked that he would rather have a wooden leg and get a job as Long John Silver in the panto at Christmas.

"Me and ten thousand others." added Len.

"How did it happen?" asked Joe. He had never asked before.

"Nothing special," said Len lightly, "one bullet right through and out the other side. It was the infection that did the damage. Then it was a Blighty wound, so I was shipped home to Ingram Road. Oh Joe, it didn't half stink ..." the words were flippant, but Joe fancied that he heard an unspoken plea in Len's account.

"You did your bit. No shame in being shipped home to lose your foot."

"I'm not shamed, Joe. I know I did my bit." Len's voice rose with quick indignation and Joe backtracked.

"'Course you did."

It was Sunday afternoon. Joe and Len were seated with their backs against a small wooden shed, smoking and taking a break from working on their respective fathers' allotments. It had wrenched Joe's heart to cultivate and harvest the vegetables sown by his father, but they had been harvested nevertheless, and it was simply practical for Joe to continue on with the plot; he was actually beginning to enjoy it. He had, with schoolboy reluctance, helped his father on the allotment for years, but wished now that he had taken more notice along the way.

The weather was balmy; Ruth ran and laughed with a new friend nearby and the young men's cigarette smoke curled, joined and diffused. Len looked critically at the vegetable garden beds where he had just sown cabbages and turnips. He squinted down the rows.

"Dad'll say that line's not straight."

"Looks alright to me."

"It'll have to do anyway." He turned to look at Joe "You're lucky living by yourself, Joe, you really are. I know you lost your Mum and Dad and that's terrible, really terrible of course, but ... I wish that Ida and me didn't have to answer to Mum and Dad for everything. It's like still being a youngster. I do get fed up."

Joe said lightly "You try cooking and cleaning and see how you like it!"

"Ida does that," Len said with a puzzled air.

Joe concealed a quiet scornful chuckle. *He* could cook—quite well, he thought. He could clean—hardly up to his mother's standards, but then not many people could do that—and he could look after his little sister. And then he could work at Jackson's and hold his end up there.

A feeling verging on satisfaction crept through Joe's consciousness, rather like the warmth of the sun. But no sooner had he registered the quietly pervading pleasure than his brain snapped into action and killed the feeling stone dead. Single bullet. In its place crowded the loss of his parents, the loss of Sam, the memories of the tunnels, the darkness and the terror ...

He lurched forward to throw away the butt of his cigarette and clasp his arms around his bent knees, fiercely trying to push back the dark wave, the muddy wave, the heavy sour-smelling earth that was on top of him.

"What's wrong, Joe?" Len's voice came from afar, and it echoed. "What's wrong, mate?"

It was broad daylight, it wasn't a dream, but it was. It was happening again. A blinding, waking dream. His eyes were wide open but he saw only darkness and his mouth was tight closed against the invading earth that would surely suffocate him in just another few seconds. Sweating and trembling, he clung to Len's voice. The voice was a hand, reaching, grasping, holding, pulling, pulling, pulling him out of the dark … His mouth flew open despite his grinding teeth and tight lips as he gave in to his desperate need for air but the dark cloying earth did not after all rush in to choke him as he dragged into his lungs instead the miraculously sweet, warm afternoon air. His breath turned to a shudder.

Joe flung himself backwards again against the shed, desperately ashamed that Len had witnessed his weakness. His attempt at nonchalance was transparent and his pallor belied it. His breath was still ragged.

Len said nothing, but shifted uneasily beside him. Finally he said "You all right, mate?"

"I'm alright, yes," said Joe, thankful for the distant note in Len's voice as he regained his composure.

As the moments passed this thankfulness gave way to irritation. He did not want to talk to Len or anyone else about what had just happened, but he felt a rising resentment that Len seemed so embarrassed by what was, after all, a small occurrence in the scheme of things. If it happened to him all the time like it did, chances were that plenty of others suffered the same thing.

But what if they didn't? What if he was the only one? Did that make it better, or worse? Was he peculiar, a marked man, destined to lurch through his life with these dark shrouds descending on him without warning? The familiar questions hammered at his brain and he suppressed a whimper with great effort. He coughed and spat.

"Have you had a job since you came home?" He addressed Len suddenly with an accusing brusqueness. "I mean, has anything come up that you'd like?"

Len sighed, taking up the normal conversation with relief.

"Dad offered me to get me a job at his works, but that was when I first came out of hospital and I didn't feel up to it. Not right then. Now he says it's not on—Potter's is putting people off these days, not taking them on. So I would have been put off anyway, I s'pose."

"What about—where was it that you worked before you joined up?"

"Oh them!" said Len sourly "I went to see them last year and all they would offer me was a junior position. That's not on, Joe— you and me we're over 21 now and we can't be doing a junior's job. I was doing more than that before I joined up. I want a fitting position. I reckon they owe me that."

Joe's recovery was completed.

"Len," he said cautiously "jobs aren't all that easy these days."

"If you mean for men with one leg, I can still do plenty, you know."

"Of course you can, I know that, but one leg, two legs, it's pretty hard. Some of my mates are getting desperate."

"I'll find something by and by."

"'Course you will." Joe was glad to end the topic, but Len went on "Of course Ida works for that dressmaker woman—calls herself a *cost-oom-ee-ay*, ha!—in Beulah Road over the stationers there, just around the corner, five minutes' walk."

This seemed to indicate on Len's part that income was not a desperate problem, nor his home comforts. Joe thought of Ida, and the quiet, complaisant little girl she'd been when they were all at school together. She had adored Len even in those days and Joe could well imagine her being a diligent seamstress.

"She's a good wife, a good wife. I'm a lucky man." Len sighed again and looked off into the summer haze. "You should get married, Joe," he said lazily.

Joe laughed dryly at the abruptness of the suggestion. "All in good time, pal."

But he wondered how any wife would feel about sharing a bed with a madman who perhaps didn't beat his head against walls any more but who choked and sweated and screamed in the night. And even in the day…

The sun went behind a cloud.

9

January 1915.
Selhurst

They'd all enlisted at the same time, after the recruiting drive at the football match at Selhurst in early '15. Him, Peter and Bill. Mates through school and beyond, they'd shared most things and this would be no exception. They'd all been thinking about it before, of course, eager from the first day of the war, but the brass band and the parade did for them that day. Joe still remembered the surge of excitement as they looked at each other and decided, without having to say a word that it was going to be *then*. They grinned and occasionally jostled each other, gauche and awkward, as they waited in line to sign up under the approving gaze of the dispersing crowd. Joe's memory of that day was of three skinny boys in a remote sunlit world of unknowingness that the smell of trodden grass would always recall. He was just 18.

They had thought to do all of it together, but they were split up pretty damned fast after initial training as the Army deployed, with seeming randomness, more and more men to fill the bloody gaping holes in the ranks in France and Belgium. That they had all three survived to the end was a triple miracle, and one that none of them undervalued; scarred as they all were they were at least alive, and physically more or less intact.

They had all survived the same war, the same trenches, the same sucking mud, the same fear, boredom, heat, cold and misery. They talked about it, the experiences of luck, good and bad, that surrounded them, the bravery and the comradeship. Joked about the food and the lice. Sometimes they even talked lightly about the fear, but none of them spoke the truth about the fear. From the comfortable warmth of peacetime in the pub or at the football indeed it hardly seemed possible that such fear could have existed. It was in the solitary dark of sleep that their treacherous minds called up the coppery taste and the clenching bowels that jolted them to sweaty wakefulness.

Joe had heard enough from his friends around and about to know that no one who'd been over there had come back the person they had been before they went. Some did seem to be untroubled, but he just wondered how deep they'd buried it all and whether it would rise, sooner or later. He'd heard a story of a man half-killing his wife in the bed beside him when he was in the grip of a nightmare of recall. He'd seen men completely broken down, shuffling vacantly in the street—shell-shock they were calling it—seen good family men changed to irascible tyrants and a whole lot more taking every opportunity to drink themselves to an all-too-temporary oblivion.

He felt the swell of panic rise in him again waited helplessly, but this time it sucked back like a retreating wave, leaving him limp with relief. All these things that he and others were suffering, yes, yes, yes. But how many of them had nightmares in the daytime? How many of them could not control the tide of terror that rose like – oh God, it rose like that stinking swill of mud and muck that was the reason for it all.

10

November 1916.
Hill 60, south of Ypres, Belgium.

The tunnel had been under construction since before his battalion was assigned to Hill 60. He didn't know its extent or its intent, apart from blowing the enemy to Kingdom Come, and sooner rather than later in everybody's opinion. He heard low snatches of the flat-vowelled accents of the Australian tunnellers as they passed during the nightly shift-changes and pitied them. He couldn't imagine how they sounded so cheery with what they had ahead of them; even the trench seemed preferable, and that was saying something.

He'd never go down a tunnel of any sort ever again if he could help it. He'd walked the Woolwich tunnel as a boy with his Mum and Dad just after it was opened, admiring with them the white-tiled shine and the feat of engineering. Quite unexpectedly, in the middle of the walk, the blood began to pound in his ears, the air was suddenly sucked from his lungs and a heavy pressure like a hundred smothering blankets fell on his body, pressing down on him as his parents strolled and marvelled at the fact that they were actually walking under the Thames. He couldn't stay, had to get out, out from under all that water, heavy, heavy, heavy on top of him. He'd pushed ahead of them, loping unevenly, eyes fixed on the spot in the wavering concentric circles that was the tunnel's end, willing it closer, closer, *please! Quickly,* before all the shiny tiles and the water and mud fell in on him, pinning him down, stopping his breath …

When his parents reached the top of the stairs he was leaning against the red bricks of the domed entrance building admiring the view of Tower Bridge in the distance with apparent composure and only a bit pale, but when his father had casually suggested taking the bus home from this end rather than a return walk through the tunnel, Joe's relief made him weak with dumb gratitude.

He still felt queasy as they waited for the red familiarity of the bus. His mother linked her arm into his, an awkward gesture for a woman not given to physical demonstration and Joe looked down, surprised. "Do you remember Camber Sands, Joe?" she asked.

"Yes, I think so, yes, I do, why?"

"Do you remember the sand castle and the tunnel?"

"No. No. Why?"

"Nothing really. We went to Camber Sands in a chara for the day once when you were just a little one. You loved the waves."

At this point his father joined the conversation.

"You had a bucket and little spade son, do you remember? You played with some bigger lads building a castle with a moat. You dug a tunnel in the sand and all. A deep one, and you wriggled into it."

Joe looked vacantly at his parents, confused and uneasy, but they exchanged a glance and stepped back into the queue of people waiting for the bus that was now making its way towards them.

He remembered the bus-stop conversation for a long time because there had been something stiff and unnatural about it. Now as he thought about tunnels it came to him again, this time as a nostalgic echo of past, better, normal times. He had been young then, of course, only fifteen, and he would not panic like a youngster now, not with his experience. But even railway tunnels still made him uneasy.

◆

The tunnellers came to their shift through the night in ones and twos to avoid the random shots the Germans fired, and it was one of these volleys that had the rangy tunneller catapulted into Joe's support trench, landing almost on top of him. He clambered back and grinned at Joe, his teeth white in the night.

"Sorry, mate!" he said with a short laugh and more than a hint of rum on his breath, "But thanks for the billet!" He slumped back, groping for a cigarette with an automatic movement and offered one to Joe. Others in the trench had, like Joe, been trying to get some sleep; they mostly returned to trying as a flurry of shooting continued.

"Don't mind if I stay for a while, mate?" he asked dryly. "Name's Sam, Sam Curtis, Number 6 Tunnelling Company at your service. I'm a tunneller," he added unnecessarily.

"Joe Barlow," said Joe as they shook hands in a cramped gesture.

"London?"

"More or less," said Joe.

"I'm Australian."

"You don't say?" Joe smiled.

"Ye-es," said Sam, stringing the word out to two syllables, "from Kalgoorlie. About as far from here as you can go before you're on the way back. Bonzer place. Not everybody's cuppa tea, but it suits me. Born there." This last piece of information was offered with pride, just before he added "And it's bloody sight warmer and drier than it is here. That makes it" he grinned again "bloody beaut!"

He shrugged himself into a more comfortable position.

"No need to get there yet. Set out early tonight to duck the bloody bullets, but it didn't work. So I've got some time up me sleeve."

"What's it like, tunneling?"

"What's anything like round here? Bloody hard work, bloody dangerous and bloody uncomfortable. Job to do."

"Where do they go, the tunnels?"

"Hope they go under the bloody Germans!"

"Don't you know?" Joe was horrified at the thought of tunnels being laboriously carved into the unknown.

"Course we bloody do. I was jokin'."

"Oh." Eventually Joe added "Should have bloody known that."

This brought a short burst of laughter and a dig in the ribs.

"No, we know where we are alright. It's knowing where *they* are that's the problem sometimes. They can be right up your bloody arse unless you're listening hard."

Joe shuddered.

"We got one o' theirs a while back. God it was funny. We thought we could hear a windlass near our workings. Them tunneling too, y' know? A bit close, we thought. Listened for a coupla days and it was making all the right noises for a windlass, but o'course we couldn't blow without bloody orders from above and getting them down to listen was always a bloody hard job—they don't like it much. So anyway we got this Major down eventually, all brave and smart, got him lying flat on the ground with the geophones on, and would ya believe it, not a bloody sound. I looked at me mate Jack and winked, then I picked up a handfula dried clay, held it over the Major's head and let a couple a' grains fall on to the geophone. Musta sounded like the charge of the Light Brigade. He was up and off like bloody greased lightning, shouting like buggery that we had to blow. Well that was the last we saw of him down there, so me and Jack went back to the top-level dugout where the charges all get done up and reckoned that we ought to blow them before they blew us. So we did. Only a little one, just enough to blow into their shaft, shake the ground and stop them working it. We shouldn't a' done it without more bloody orders, but we reckoned that the Major's yells were loud enough orders for us. That's what we said when we were hauled over the coals after, anyway." He chuckled at the memory.

As they talked for a while longer in the darkness Joe could not see Sam's face, but he sensed a sort of economy, a spareness of feature. When the Australian eventually heaved himself up and left the trench, he left a Sam-shaped space behind.

Joe hadn't expected to see him again, and it was only his voice that Joe recognised in the little café in the small village behind the lines where he and his pal were dourly stowing away as much of the local red wine as they could during a precious day's leave from the front.

The group of Australians would never have been mistaken for British soldiers. They had a swagger and a physical presence that marked them even before their accents gave them away. And although the Tommy could swear with the best of them, the Australians outdid them effortlessly. Joe watched them for a while with some envy for their exuberance before edging over to re-introduce himself to a delighted Sam, who presented him to his mates, yelling over their noise, as someone who had saved his life on the way to his shift the other night.

Joe laughed at this exaggeration but the noise level made it impossible to explain and he and his pal Clyde were drawn immediately into the boisterous group.

It was the beginning of a day of leave that Joe remembered fondly although some parts would remain a bit blurred. The vitality of the Australian tunnellers seemed limitless and their drinking capacity was impressive. Clyde gave in early and plodded off with some other Tommies and Joe was left feeling like a cabbage that had somehow popped up in a flower bed. But he gladly trailed along as they roamed limits of the small village and loudly concluded that they needed to be somewhere more exciting. He didn't know how or where they suddenly acquired the truck—didn't ask. Despite his growing weariness he was eager enough to climb aboard to be transported anywhere they cared to go, the expedition heady with imagined escape.

He dozed on the journey despite its discomfort and the raucous songs being sung all around him. He had smiled at first because they were mostly songs he knew, songs the Tommies sang. These Aussies weren't as different as he'd thought. Comforting, that, for some reason.

The next village seemed much the same as the one from which they'd come, but there was a fresh round of drinking and a half-hearted effort to find some female company that resulted in failure as the streets in the small village emptied on the approach of the crowd of rowdy young men.

As they bumped back towards the lines, Joe was blearily euphoric with wine and companionship.

After that day, Sam sought Joe out two or three times to have a cigarette and a "bit of a yarn" as he called it. His laconic accounts of his miner's life in Kalgoorlie were as exotic to Joe as the moon and Joe's reciprocated accounts of London seemed to him a pale exchange.

Sam, however, hung on his every word quizzed him avidly for some time before he revealed that he was due for leave soon and had never been to London. He wanted to make the most of it.

Joe grinned, sure that Sam would make the most of it with or without his advices, but he had a sudden idea. He was due for leave soon, with luck. Could Sam hang fire until they could go together? Sam was sure he could, sure that he could exchange his leave with a mate or two—easy for him it seemed in the relaxed framework in which the tunnellers moved. Didn't mind waiting if it meant he'd have a real live guide to the city he'd only ever heard about.

It was nearly three months later that they tumbled off the train and walked up the road to Oak Tree Place, having spent two hectic days and nights in London where coincidentally they bumped into Len on his way back to barracks after a brief period of leave too, and they had had a memorably riotous night. None of this was to be revealed to Joe's parents under any circumstances.

Joe laughingly guided Sam around people on the street as he walked happily unheeding. His enthusiasm and wonder at the perfectly ordinary streets of England was as boundless as it was infectious.

Joe enjoyed showing him off like a trophy. "My friend the Aussie."

The population of Oak Tree Place embraced Sam with warmth. Joe's Mum's native reserve melted in his presence, and she was girlish and motherly at the same time, sparkling in her efforts to accommodate every whim of both "her boys". Joe was somewhat taken aback at this unusual effusiveness; his mother was always loving but quite undemonstrative. However he claimed full expansive ownership of his home life when he saw that Sam was impressed.

It was a time to relish, that leave. They had so many drinks bought for them at the Oak Tree that they reeled back across the Place, and during the day Joe showed Sam his boyhood haunts which took on an exotic gloss as he saw them through Sam's ingenuous eyes. Sam delighted in baby Ruth as much as Joe; they played with her until she slept through exhaustion. An ease grew between the two of them and by the end of the short leave they had reached a level of companionship that was deep and comfortable.

Those few days of comfort and indulgence made the return journey to their respective units all the more dreadful, dread that increased with each mile that brought it closer. On the train to the coast Joe recalled wryly the first journey, when it was all such an adventure, how quickly the feeling of adventure had turned to one of disbelief and horror, then pummelled out to a grim normality in a world ruled by mud, lice, rats and terror, where the sight of dead and putrefying bodies was accepted with a ghastly equanimity.

Oh God, it was so different going back when you knew what was waiting for you.

11

Still August 1920

The purple summer evening lay softly on the Place outside as Joe cleaned his boots and laid out his clothes. Somehow he was never up early enough to do these things in the morning; he had a devil of a time getting Ruth dressed, breakfasted and delivered to Alice as well as looking after himself.

He had eventually completed the dreary task of sorting out and disposing of his parents' few clothes but the furnishings remained in the same places that they had always occupied. The Toby jug, the green glass vase and the old fairing that his grandfather had won for his grandmother while they were courting still stood in their accustomed places on the mantelpiece.

Restless and wakeful, Joe walked outside and down to the road, then back. He didn't care to stir too far from the house in case Ruth called out in her sleep, as she sometimes did.

He climbed the stairs to tuck Ruth in again now that she was asleep; she slept with furious intent and her bedclothes were always in disarray. Fondly he straightened her warm little body under the blankets, smoothed the bed, brushed the tangled dark hair off her face and kissed her gently. He overflowed with love for his little sister.

The consuming love that he felt for Ruth had come as a surprise to Joe. An only child, he'd assumed—when he thought about it—that there was probably something that prevented his parents from having more children. Not that he thought much about it at all except to be quite glad that he actually had a room of his own, a luxury compared to most other boys he knew. Len of course had had the same only-child advantage although his family had moved to the Place when Len was eight or nine and there had been talk, Joe remembered dimly, of another child—or children perhaps—who had died.

Joe had never really questioned his status as an only child; he had plenty of friends but he possessed a quiet independence that was fostered by the secure but undemonstrative nature of his life at home.

It was on his brief leave before embarkation that Joe's mother told him, with an unusual diffidence and a certain amount of embarrassment, that she was to have a baby. Joe was flabbergasted; the thought of a possible sibling may have loitered around his consciousness when he was younger, it was the last thing he expected at this stage of his mother's life. Why, she was—he calculated quickly—thirty nine. That was almost forty! Initial bemusement was tinged with embarrassment.

His mother's unfamiliar air of uncertainty made him come around the table to hug her awkwardly and assure her of his delight at her condition and the prospect of a brother or sister. To further demonstrate his happy acceptance, he attempted to put his hand on her belly in a laughing gesture, but she had hastily pushed him away. Her sense of propriety did not allow for such intimacy.

Over the next few months his mother's condition had become increasingly obvious and the subject of much discussion and pleasant conjecture in the Place and the High Street. Jess Barlow was respected (some more timid souls might have said "feared", Joe knew) in the neighbourhood and there was a lively interest in this late and unexpected blessing. In the end, though, the district was deprived of involvement in Ruth's birth as it had occurred early while Jess was visiting her own mother in Southampton. She had been warned by everyone against taking such a journey so late in her pregnancy but was insistent that her ailing mother needed her.

It was Alice who had stepped into the breach. Soon after her Johnnie went away to the war she'd moved to Colchester to stay with her own mother and she had taken it upon herself to travel to Southampton to care for all three of them: Jess, Jess's mother and tiny Ruth, when she was born. It was hard to imagine how they would have managed without her.

Ruth survived her early birth well and when she came home to the Place at the age of six weeks she was a bonny baby. Joe's father had gone to fetch Jess and Ruth and the homecoming was a splendid affair. People turned out from everywhere and as the trap from the station turned into the Place it was like a Royal visit, it was said.

Joe's first glimpse of his sister was on his first brief home leave and he smiled as he observed that Ruth's presence had changed the house completely—it smelled different, sounded different, felt different. His Mum and Dad were different, engrossed with the baby, softer. His mother still ruled the hearth and managed the household with scouring efficiency, but the joy in the house was almost palpable. Joe approached Ruth's crib cautiously, clumsy, watched her sleeping with awe, marvelled at the delicate tininess of her fingers with their pearly nails and finally stroked her downy head, warm and sweet under his big hand. When she woke and smiled at him—a gummy, delighted conspiratorial smile which bunched her cheeks and sparkled in her eyes, Joe was immediately, permanently, and utterly bewitched.

The unexpected and exquisite pain of this feeling of love sometimes took his breath away. It was little Ruth that he thought of on those terrible nights and days in the stinking, sucking, trenches. Other men had pictures of wives, mothers and sweethearts with which they communed, but Joe had Ruth in his mind at all the dreadful times. It was Ruth he was fighting for. He had been utterly fascinated by her, delighting in her every action and desperately devouring the fresh unblemished spirit of her to take with him to the darkness of the trenches.

Now he was home. In maudlin mood he leant his head against the side window of Ruth's room, heavy of heart and eye, unseeing of the glistening cobbles and the furred brick walls of the passage beside the pub leading into darkness.

As he sighed and turned away, a small movement there made him turn back to see Alice walking quietly through the cobbled passage. It was indeed a night for walking; too soft and gentle to waste indoors. He started to go out to join her but stopped abruptly. His present state of mind was not inclined to conversation and with Alice most conversations were sparring matches anyway, always turning on Ruth and Alice's irrational conviction that she should have her total care.

Joe glared down at the now-empty passage, rising irritation subsuming his melancholy. Alice grated on him with her damned persistence, always trying to show him that she was so much better than him at caring for Ruth. But she wasn't, she wasn't. He had learned so much since he came home and all of it was focused on Ruth, he could provide everything she needed. He straightened her bedclothes proprietorially and padded down the creaking stairs.

What Alice needed was a distraction from her obsession with Ruth. If she had her own child, she would let him and Ruth alone. Why couldn't she do something sensible like that? She was still a good-looking woman, Joe could see that, quite young enough for children of her own and although she did not appear to have any men friends it was surely only because her world was so limited these days. Just Oak Tree Place, the Oak Tree with its menial work—and Ruth. There must be someone out there for Alice. Anyone would do.

◆

Joe's plan for Alice was only formed to the extent that he had tentatively identified a target when he himself was ambushed.

She had been walking down the High Street with a friend when Joe first saw her. He was on his way to the Palace with two of his mates. A new Charlie Chaplin was showing and they were looking forward to a laugh. So it was in a jovial mood that he automatically reached out to catch the hat that had freed itself from its wearer's head and was bowling merrily down the street. In some disarray she caught up with it and, laughing, took it back from Joe with thanks and a flash of the eyes before they were modestly cast down. But the smile remained in her eyes and she seemed quite disposed to linger. Joe touched his cap.

"Joe Barlow."

"Lydia Mason," she replied pertly as she jammed her hat back on her head and attempted to secure it. "Thank you again for saving my chapeau."

Joe knew what a chapeau was. Desperately he searched the rest of his French vocabulary, eager to communicate common ground.

"A pleasure … mademoiselle!" he managed. His knowledge of French shrank to nothing. He had once had at least ten other words. The girl laughed and returned to her friend but cast a backward glance that made Joe's heart leap.

Peter laughed at Joe's expression.

"Too much of a handful for you, pal." he warned. "Her father's the new manager at Anderson's."

"And I'm Joseph Barlow, as good as any man and better than most!" laughed Joe. At that moment he felt that he was; a heady surge of confidence made his blood rush around his body at twice its normal rate; he felt it fizz like sherbet.

Throughout the film he craned to see Lydia in the cinema through the smoky half-light and afterwards he loitered obviously at the entrance, heart pounding, the sight of her emerging from the picture palace making him weak, but Lydia and her friend swept straight past him as he stood foolishly on the street, gazing after them.

Only as the girls were small figures about to pass from view around the corner into Brigstock Road did Lydia turn and laugh at him, provoking and mischievous. It was enough. Joe strode, as quickly as he could manage without actually running, after the vanished figures but came to a confused halt as he found them, paused and giggling, leaning against the fence of Cotford House, half-hidden by the overhanging trees. He tried without success to appear casual, causing the girls to fall into peals of laughter.

Flushed from his charge up the High Street and his own blushes, he stood dumbly, gazing at them with desperate embarrassment.

"*Mister* Joe Barlow, what on earth are you doing following us?" enquired Lydia with elaborate innocence and between giggles.

Joe managed a wobbly smile, hoping that his position might improve if he could just stand his ground. Which, with more speed that he anticipated, it did.

"Would you like to take me and Beryl to the pictures, Joe?" asked Lydia, adding unnecessarily "This is Beryl, by the way."

"Pleased to meet you, Beryl. Yes I would. When?" Joe was too eager to pretend nonchalance.

Ignoring Beryl's nudges, Lydia said boldly "Next Friday night?"

Despite his bemusement at the speed and the very satisfactory turn of the conversation, Joe's thoughts flew to getting rid of Beryl.

Lydia was the arranger. "We'll meet you outside the Palace, then?"

Joe Barlow's mother would not have approved. He saw her face clearly, fixed with determination to observe social proprieties.

"Could I not call for you?" he enquired diffidently, wary that any changes he might suggest would bring the whole arrangement undone.

Beryl shrieked and Lydia smiled with superior wisdom.

"No thank you," she said firmly and the matter was closed.

A time was fixed and Joe was left standing in the street as the two girls tripped away, their avid chatter—and their laughter—floating behind them as they disappeared without a backward glance.

12

September 1920

He confided in Lydia his plan for Alice, but not his reasons. Lydia was full of enthusiasm to get on with the scheme, her eyes sparking at the prospect.

"How will we do it, Joe?" she said excitedly "When will we start?"

"Well" said Joe slowly, "it seems to me that we should first of all clear the field for action."

"Yes?"

"I rather think that he might have a lady friend already. I've seen him once with a girl."

Lydia was crestfallen "Then why do you have him in mind for your auntie, for goodness sake?"

"Look, I didn't know he had a friend when I thought of him and I still think that he and Alice would make a very good couple. We'll just try to find out whether the present field situation is serious."

Lydia laughed with delight. "Oh Joe you are such a clever soldier! Tell me your plan, corporal!"

"Dunno," confessed the corporal with a comical grimace which made Lydia fall back laughing on the grass.

The early autumn afternoon was gentle and mild as they sat on the picnic rug by the bandstand over which Ruth now trailed her gaggle of friends. She was diligently embracing a role assigned to her by the bigger children and was intent. Shouts echoed in the afternoon stillness.

This was the third time Joe had seen Lydia. The second, the arranged meeting at the Palace two weeks before, had been awkward with Beryl constantly imposing her presence between Joe and Lydia in a disagreeably knowing way. To make things worse, Lydia appeared content to allow her these designs and indeed appeared to collude with her. It was not until they were all three walking away from the cinema that Joe was able to walk beside Lydia but for this delight he had to pay by having Beryl on his other arm, and Lydia seemed fractious and bored. Conversation had flagged and just after they passed the railway station Lydia had briskly decided that this was as far as the girls needed escorting. Joe found himself standing alone in the street as the girls again trotted off, disappearing round a bend within a hundred yards or so.

He felt humiliated and foolish, both feelings slowly supplanted by annoyance. Lydia might well be the most beautiful girl he'd ever met, but she was a spoiled and temperamental girl who was out of his class anyway. He was well rid of her.

He had managed to sustain this attitude until another chance meeting that very day had found Lydia and a friend strolling away from the bandstand after the concert. The friend, who remained un-introduced, stood in the background for a few minutes before a resigned retreat.

Joe's previous annoyance with Lydia vanished as he eagerly asked her to join him and Ruth. An initial hesitation, then she accepted prettily and perched on a corner of the shabby rug looking, Joe thought, with a feeling that was a combination of sinking and soaring, absolutely adorable. Not only that, but she chatted and laughed and was such an agreeable companion that Joe was newly beguiled.

Lydia had most of his life's history out of him, and one would never have thought that her circumstances were so different from Joe's, from the interest she showed. Joe found his words tumbling over themselves in his eagerness to share his life with her.

Which is how they came to be discussing his plans to marry his aunt Alice to Stephen Dent, the school teacher who lived alone in the first cottage on Oak Tree Place.

"We'll have to find out," said Lydia.

Joe's head reeled at the sound of the inclusive "we", now used several times.

"But another day, Joe, I have to get back now. It's getting late; Mummy and Daddy will worry."

She hesitated, then added with a sigh "You're a nice man, Joe Barlow, but you don't really want to get mixed up with me."

For once Joe showed some restraint and suppressed the denial that rose vehemently to his throat.

"Why is that, then?" he asked with commendable indifference, and a smile.

"Ah Joe," sighed Lydia. She was disinclined to elaborate.

"Come on, I'll see you home."

"No, no, that's not necessary, Joe. Thank you,"

"Of course it is, it's getting dark soon." Although it rankled with Joe that Lydia could chat so easily with him on the one hand and then reject him so quickly, the obvious disparity in their social positions put him at the disadvantage; he was once again the supplicant. Eventually Lydia agreed that he might escort her then, but only part of the way to her house.

They had barely left the green open expanse of the recreation ground, and dropped off Ruth into Alice's care, when Joe stared in amazement at Stephen Dent in the very life, walking on the other side of the road, and moreover, with a young woman on his arm.

Heartily Joe hailed him and they quickly crossed the road. Joe introduced Lydia.

"How do you do, Lydia," said Stephen. "May I present my sister Joanna? Joanna, this is Joe Barlow, my neighbour in Oak Tree Place—he lives in number six at the end closest to the Oak Tree. We're bookends of sorts," he laughed.

Stephen and his sister may have wondered at Lydia's excessively animated conduct, as she seemed very inclined to giggles during their brief conversation. It appeared that Joanna was living as a companion to an elderly widow up on Beulah Hill. Lydia found that awfully amusing, her laughter gurgling and unrestrained.

Still smiling broadly, she brightly suggested that a picnic on the following Sunday when the band would be playing again might be an excellent idea and would Stephen and his sister consider joining them? She would be delighted to provide the sandwiches and oh, why don't we ask Joe's Aunt Alice to join us too?

Stephen and Joanna agreed that this all seemed an excellent idea.

Joe and Lydia took their leave and proceeded in a dignified manner down the road until they were out of sight of the other couple, then Lydia squealed with delight and performed a little jig. "Am I not the best arranger you have ever known, Joe Barlow?" she asked, swinging on Joe's arm and laughing up at him "Am I not the very best arranger?"

◆

The following Sunday was not the golden autumn day of the week before, but the party had an animated and enjoyable afternoon picnic before the chill in the wind drove them back to crowd into Stephen's little house for a warming cup of tea. Then, at Joe's suggestion, they moved to the Oak Tree to top off a pleasant outing with a drink.

Alice did not want to go with them to the pub, but everyone else was insistent, especially Joe and Lydia, so she consented with some reluctance. Lydia's comic-anxious glance at Joe made him smile at its complicity; it was not just the plan for Alice and Stephen that was progressing well.

Joe fronted the bar.

"Afternoon Joe," said Charlie.

"Afternoon Charlie," said Joe cheerfully, placing the group's order. He leaned on the bar and looked over his shoulder at his friends at the table by the window. "We've been on a picnic at the bandstand, but it got a bit chilly."

"Who?" asked Charlie

"All of us. Me, my friend Lydia, Joanna—that's Stephen's sister, Alice, Stephen and Ruth. Grand time. Grand time" he was watching with approval the fact that Stephen was leaning towards Alice telling her something intently. Alice looked faintly uncomfortable and Joe again became concerned for the grand plan.

"That's Stephen's sister?" asked Charlie with a frown.

"Yes, and a very nice sort of girl she is, too."

"I'm sure."

Charlie's surly tone caused Joe to regard him briefly but without concern. Poor old Charlie might be having a bad day but Joe's day was going very well indeed.

But the carefree feeling of the bandstand and the easy banter of Stephen's kitchen was dwindling into an awkward silence by the time Joe carried the drinks back to the table. Alice drank hers quickly and excused herself, pleading tiredness. Joe looked enquiringly at Lydia but she shrugged, pouting her annoyed incomprehension at Alice's behavior, and said crossly that she was tired too and needed to be home before it was dark.

Lydia sighed theatrically as she and Joe walked away from the Place. She had consented to his accompanying her part of the way to her house, the enormous ivy-covered mansion on Brigstock Road a few hundred yards from the railway station.

Joe felt his previous satisfaction trickling away. "What is it?" he enquired cautiously.

"What a waste of time!"

"What do you mean? I thought it all went rather well."

Lydia snorted. "Oh yes, but what happened at the end of it all, then? Your auntie couldn't wait to leave, could she? Waste of time," she repeated.

At this point Joe could not give a fig for Alice's future.

"I never thought it'd be that easy, you know," he said tentatively. "Not all at once it won't happen quickly, I don't think."

"If I understood what you meant I might be able to comment." Lydia was pointedly condescending.

Joe flushed but did not attempt a reply and they walked in silence until they reached the bend in the road before Lydia's house.

"No further, Joe, thank you" Lydia was dismissive.

Dumbly Joe watched her walk away, her hair bouncing on her back and catching the dying light. He stood woodenly unmoving, but felt his spirit leave his body and run after her, entreating. He ached with wanting her.

If it had not been for the war, Joe may well still have been a virgin, but of course he wasn't. There was that first time when he and Sam and some others had made a project of it, fuelled with wine and egging each other on. That was the first time, but not the last. The last had been in London just before Sam … he pushed aside thoughts of Sam, intent on fostering his thoughts of Lydia, his fantasies of Lydia, his man's need for Lydia, as he made his way back to Oak Tree Place without registering a single step of his journey.

A heavy-eyed Ruth awaited him in the Oak Tree's back parlour. Joe nuzzled her neck as he carried her to their house and she locked her arms around him, her angular little body warm and supple. He lay beside her on the bed and watched her sleep, distracted at last, immeasurably grateful for her presence and for the fact of her.

13

Next day

Joe's perfunctory tap at her door before opening it and coming in with Ruth made Alice jump.

She stood up from her chair hurriedly and forced a smile.

Joe looked at her. "Are you alright, Alice? Not poorly?" he asked with some anxiety, "you look very pale."

"What on earth do you mean? Of course I'm not poorly. No Joe, no. Just overslept. Must have been yesterday's fresh air."

She bustled around, bringing out Ruth's few playthings and putting them on the table. Despite her determination to appear normal, she moved cautiously, crab-like.

Joe remained standing in the doorway. "You don't *look* well," he ventured.

"There's nothing wrong with me that another cup of tea won't fix." Alice said briskly, summoning another smile from the depths of she didn't know where, but anxious to get Joe out of her house uncurious and unworried.

Joe hesitated, but Alice could see that he wanted to be convinced. Yes, Joe, it's easy for you when everything's alright, isn't it? Much easier for your comfortable little life. Well, have it your own way, duckie. I know how to get rid of you.

"It's just women's problems, Joe."

He was gone in a flash. Alice smiled grimly, but with the sound of the door's closing she was able to relax and hobble back to her chair. She looked at Ruth and felt the intense pleasure of her presence soothe her pain.

14

October 1920

It was almost cold enough for a fire and in easier times there may well have been one in the pub's old fireplace. Despite its lack, old Dora sat, hunched, peering into the dark recess as if willing it to light.

Stephen was at the bar and Joe greeted him with warmth, his presence a distraction from his increasing melancholy. The Alice-and-Stephen plot was miles away from his mood tonight and the men drank in companionable silence, if a somewhat morose one on Joe's part.

Joe was startled when Stephen spoke.

"Alice looking after Ruth?" he asked.

"Er, yes," Joe replied. "Going to fetch her in a minute or two," he added.

The plan to matchmake Stephen with Alice had been much more actively embraced by Lydia than by him even when it seemed to have some impetus, but now it was of no interest at all to Joe. But Stephen continued.

"Nice sort of woman, your Alice."

Joe blinked and the grand plan dragged itself slowly and grudgingly back over the edge of his consciousness. Hell. "Nice woman?" What did that mean? Joe was out of his depth, but Stephen continued with a slight shake of his head. "Must be hard to lose your husband in a war. Damned hard. Such a waste."

"Oh yes." This at least was firm ground. "Uncle Johnny died in a prisoner-of-war camp in '16, you know. Poor devil. Captured really early on at Wipers and then as far as Alice has ever been able to find out he died of typhoid while he was penned up by the bloody Bosch. He was one of the very first to volunteer you know. He was a good man."

It occurred to Joe with a blinding suddenness that he had no idea to what extent Alice still mourned his uncle Johnny and he had never spoken to her about him. Stephen had not responded to his account of Uncle Johnny's imprisonment and death, but finally contributed "Walks a lot."

"What?" Joe's mouth hung open at the seeming irrelevance, but Stephen was looking at him evenly.

"Alice walks a lot at night" he expanded.

"Suppose she does," Joe said weakly. To be sure, he saw his aunt from time to time walking past his house in the dark of night, but as he often did the same thing, he thought little of it. Stephen turned away from Joe and looked down into his drink. He drew a breath as if to say something when Charlie walked down behind the bar towards them.

"Same again?" he asked, looking at their almost-empty glasses.

"No thanks Charlie" they said in unison.

Joe pushed himself away from the bar. He had spent far too much time there, but Stephen remained leaning on it and didn't turn to Joe as he addressed him.

"Alice is a bright girl, Joe, but she's too kind, too accommodating."

Both Joe and Charlie initially looked bemused at the comment. Then Joe bridled; Stephen must think that he took advantage of Alice, having her mind Ruth as she did. What did he know, for Heaven's sake? Bloody impudent to assume things he didn't have any idea about. He opened his mouth to ask indignantly what Stephen meant by his remark when he was forestalled by Charlie, who leant across the bar, shoving his face into Stephen's. He had turned red with fury and spat as he said "None of your fucking business, you … *teacher*!"

Joe's immediate thought was that Charlie was making his case for him, but somehow that wasn't how it looked.

Stephen slipped off his stool and walked out with Joe; a muttered "Goodnight" was the only conversation.

15

Later the same month

Joe was not proud of the considerable time he had spent loitering in the vicinity of Lydia's house without a single sight of her, but he excused himself readily. It was not until he despaired of ever catching sight of her by these means that he presented himself at her front door early one evening.

Though he was scrubbed and carefully dressed, the maid who answered the door regarded him doubtfully and would not at first allow him entry. He waited under the elaborate portico, gazing discomfited at the heavy front door until she returned with an indifferent invitation to come inside.

He was directed into a parlour where a fire burning in the grate burnished the three people in the room with what seemed to Joe to be a metallic lustre; indeed they were as motionless as bronzed statues as they fixed their eyes on him. Lydia was the first to move, rising from her chair and walking steadily towards him with a frown on her face. Despite this, Joe felt a rush of pure joy at the sight of her and smiled widely in spite of his awkwardness.

"Joseph." The word was flat. There was no questioning inflection, no lilt of pleasure, only unease and the never-before use of his full name.

"Lydia." Joe's response was not a considered one, it was just all that he could manage.

Lydia introduced him to her parents, again using his full name. It would appear that Lydia had met this young man called Joseph Barlow in the company of some friends at the bandstand one Sunday. No mention was made of pictures at the Palace or the Oak Tree or anything as intimate as a single conversation between them.

With demonstrable effort, Lydia's mother bade him seated, put aside her book, gazing at him silently and without expression. Lydia's father was more accommodating, engaging Joe in a fairly stilted exchange which, however, dwindled after a few minutes. Lydia remained silent but stared coolly at Joe. As the silence lengthened she finally spoke.

"Why are you here, Joe? What do you want?"

Joe was ill at ease, but Lydia's brusqueness needled him and he spoke with firmness.

"I wondered whether you would come to the pictures with me on Friday." A pause. "Please."

The last word had been just a word to fill the silence but it fell into the room like the body of a small dead animal.

It was Lydia's father who moved to ease Joe's embarrassment as he jovially remarked that that sounded like a splendid idea, didn't it, Lydia?

Lydia had not reacted in any way but her mother clucked general disapproval in her husband's direction which strangely seemed to spur Lydia to accept Joe's invitation and arrange that he call for her at five. Though the acceptance and the arrangements had been delivered with almost no animation, Lydia tucked her hand into the crook of his elbow and escorted him to the door with at least some warmth.

"I will expect you on Friday at five then," she said clearly and loudly as she disconcertingly pushed him out of the door and closed it behind him.

Walking back to the Place, Joe had time to rearrange the elements of the meeting more to his satisfaction and by the time he reached there, he was only anticipating the following Friday with pleasurable excitement.

◆

Joe's high spirits and his success in getting Lydia to walk out with him even served to make the conversation with her parents a little less of an endurance test than he had anticipated when he called for her.

Mrs. Mason had fairly obviously decided that effusive acceptance of Joe's social inferiority would provide the best means of undermining him. Although Joe actually appreciated the ploy and grudgingly even sympathised with her motherly apprehensions, the extravagance still made him uneasy and clumsy. Each awkwardness, every fumble, was gobbled up by her predatory gaze and Joe helplessly recalled, in a comical comparison, an aged, now long-dead, family friend who used to eat this way, using a well-practiced tongue to tuck a whole mouthful of food away in his bulging cheeks in order to make some contribution to the conversation of the moment, then tease it out again and continue to chew. He had been fascinated by this as a child and his mother had had to pinch him to stop him staring. He could imagine his social misdemeanours being stored like this by Lydia's mother for future minute examination. No, she wasn't like old Mr. Black at all, she was like some bird of prey … He shook himself.

Lydia was very offhand with her mother, restively dismissing her as being fussy in her outlook and managing to convey that she found her opinions and attitudes both irrelevant and mildly amusing. Joe smiled at Lydia's 18-year-old assertiveness with her mother and kittenish teasing of her father. Joe felt an empathy with Mr. Mason.

Left in the room with him as Lydia went to get her coat and her mother hurried after her, Joe managed a slightly less-stilted conversation with Lydia's quiet father on the subject of his employment, gaining a little confidence as he recounted that Mr. Jackson offered him his old job back after the war without hesitation. Like his father before him, Joe had arranged a job at Jackson's even before he'd finished school and had passed from one to the other without a day's interruption. He liked his work and felt that he was good at what he did. Mr. Mason listened gravely and it seemed with a certain sadness, nodding occasionally during the brief recital. When it ended there was a silence.

Mrs. Mason came back into the room with Lydia and bustled her into her coat, saying as they left that Joe must come to tea. Lydia looked at Joe's confusion with some amusement and assured her mother that he would indeed come to tea one day, when Lydia herself was ready to ask him.

A mediocre film at the Palace had irritated Lydia but had not made an impression of any sort on Joe as he sat contentedly in the cinema with the warmth of Lydia's arm against his own. He tentatively reached for her hand and she did not draw it away. Joe smiled in the dark beside her as he enveloped the small soft creature and carefully and slowly explored its contours and pockets, thumbing the edges of the smooth nails and brushing the lightly-raised veins of the inside of her wrist. As he stroked, Lydia relaxed perceptibly and opened her hand, palm upward, fingers curled, seeming to welcome the touch until the silliness of the film made her squirm and draw away from Joe with a sigh of exasperation and a whispered demand that they leave the cinema.

Leaving before the end of the film was strange; they were the only people in the foyer and almost the only couple walking down the High Street. Although there was a delicious intimacy in this echoing progress, Joe would rather have liked an acquaintance or two to see him with Lydia on his arm.

Although Lydia held his arm and the touch of her hand burned right through to Joe's skin, it was a light and unthinking touch; her attention was engaged more on the High Street shop windows. As she stopped and turned yet again to scrutinise some amazingly unappealing item in a shop window display, Joe played his conversational trump card. To his chagrin, Lydia laughed derisively.

"Really, Joe, really? Stephen thinks that Alice is nice? Oh my goodness, what a recipe for romance!" She wasn't even laughing now.

Joe was piqued. "It's a start, at least," he ventured, but Lydia rolled her eyes and did not respond.

There was no pretence of interest any more. Lydia pulled her coat closer and shivered, increasing the rate of her small steps as they passed the railway station and drew closer to her house. With a degree of desperation, he gabbled on, burbling, babbling, but to no avail. Reaching the gate of her house, Lydia offered her hand to Joe in an act of obvious dismissal. Automatically Joe took the hand, but held on to it like a drowning soul, clasping it in both of his.

"Can I see you again?" he blurted.

"Oh Joe, I don't think so." There was a weariness in Lydia's tone; weariness with an edge of irritation.

Somehow Joe drew back from pleading and hid his expression by turning away abruptly. But helplessly he turned back, revealing all his pain.

"…Think about it?" His voice cracked.

"Oh really, Joe," began Lydia in exasperation, beginning to walk away, then she paused. "Alright then, come to tea one Sunday if you like. Say Sunday week?" The abrupt change of heart was accompanied by a delighted smile. "I'm sure Mummy would like to see you again." She gurgled a laugh and tripped up the path to her door.

"What time?" he called after her breathlessly

16

The same evening

It was with surprise and concern that Joe saw Len sprawled on the bench in front of the Oak Tree, obviously the worse for drink. He stood in front of him and adopted a jolly tone.

"Wotcha Len!"

Len looked up blearily, his head waving with the effort. He was very drunk.

"Joe." He pawed the air in front of him with his hand. "Siddown, ol' pal."

Joe ruefully sat down beside him on the bench. It was cold; not a night for bench-sitting.

"Can I help you indoors?" It was in fact only a matter of a few steps, but Len would obviously need help on any journey, even the shortest.

"Nah."

There was a silence, then he added "They threw me out."

Joe was not surprised that Len had been thrown out of the pub. He was in a state.

"They doan unnerstand." Len patted Joe's sleeve unsteadily and repeated "They doan unnerstand."

Joe understood. He had seen it so often—drink to numb the horror of the memories that wouldn't go away. And poor Len had been wounded as well, which must make it so much harder, he thought. He would have the evidence of his endured horrors limping along with him for the rest of his life.

He regarded his friend with sympathy.

"Let's get you indoors, old man." He attempted to pull Len to his feet, the crutches clattering to the ground.

Len wriggled from his grasp and slumped back on the bench. "They threw me out!"

Joe looked across at the house beside his own to where he needed to guide Len and was surprised to see a tweak of the curtain in the front window. Someone was watching from Len's house. He frowned with incomprehension. Who was it and why didn't they come and help? As he stood staring at the house, puzzled, the door suddenly opened and Ida ran across the cobbles to the bench.

"Sorry, Joe, sorry Joe, sorry Joe" her face was puffed from crying as she knelt in front of Len, looking up into his face, drooped in either shame or drunkenness, Joe could not tell. Ida's tears ran afresh as she gazed up at her husband. Joe was embarrassed, still he felt that he must stay, as Ida would obviously need help to get Len indoors. Len's slurred voice came blurrily from the depths of his greatcoat.

"Threw me out."

"They had to do something, dearest" Ida's voice was pleading through her sobs. "You hit your mother!"

Suddenly Joe realised that Len had been thrown out, not by the pub, but by his own parents. At the same time the enormity of Ida's words and the picture of Len hitting his mother rose to shock him.

"They doan unnerstand!" Len's cry echoed around the Place.

"Hush dear, hush. Please hush" Ida was anxiously scanning the Place for anyone who might have the misfortune to observe the scene. Joe felt his sympathy switch from Len to Ida. Poor little girl.

"Would it be alright to take him indoors now?" he asked hesitantly. He was sure that neither Len, Ida nor Len's parents would have wanted him to see or hear any part of Len's shame. He wished fervently that he had not seen Len on the bench in the first place.

Ida nodded with a quick look towards the house, where nothing stirred. With difficulty Joe hoisted Len and shuffled him across the Place and into the Dawsons' house. Len's parents were nowhere to be seen as Joe and Ida struggled up the stairs with the rubbery figure, finally getting him on to the bed in the small back bedroom, crying and babbling. Ida was still weeping and Joe was wrenched with pity for them both. Fucking fucking fucking war, he thought, in an impotent fury. So many fucking lives ruined and you didn't have to be dead. The living suffered longer.

Suddenly Len began to laugh. The sound was hideous—it bounced off the walls. Ida made to quiet her husband, lying beside him on the bed and taking his face in her hands. Joe yearned to leave, but felt compelled to stay until his friend was more calm. Len's cackling laughter, however, became louder and more discordant and seemed to last for an age, until he finally lapsed into hiccuppy giggles. With his eyes closed, kept repeating that they didn't understand, in a diminishing chant.

As Len now seemed to be on the brink of sleep, or at least a drunken stupor, Joe was making to leave the room when Len said clearly

"Blighty wound. Good job. Bloody hurt but I did it, didden I?."

Though Ida' eyes were swollen with weeping, the look that she darted at Joe was sharp and alert. Joe saw the bleak knowledge there and his stomach lurched.

He understood alright.

Full of disgust and jumbled thoughts, Joe walked to his own door and was surprised to find it wouldn't open. At least, it opened to a tiny gap but something was blocking it.

"Alice!" he hissed through the slit, "Alice, are you there?" He was too surprised at the apparent barricade to be worried at first, but his anxiety stirred when there was no answer. Alice had been sitting in and listening for a sleeping Ruth while he'd been out. But maybe she'd taken Ruth to her own house for some reason. Irritation replaced anxiety as he strode to Alice's door. It was not locked—their doors seldom were—and he pushed inside. No Alice, no Ruth. Back to his own door. Rapped impatiently.

"Alice!" too irritated to be quiet. "Alice, are you there?"

There was a sound of dragging furniture and Alice's face peered round the door. "Oh Joe!" she said.

He pushed inside. The kitchen table had been pulled across the room to be wedged against the door.

"What on earth have you been doing?"

Alice's face was pale in the darkness; the fire had gone out and the lamp too. The room was cold, Alice was shivering.

Again. "What on earth have you been doing? Are you playing at something? Is Ruth alright?"

Alice spoke jerkily. "There was someone outside, Joe. I … was frightened."

"Alice, we live beside a pub. There's always someone outside, you should be used to that."

"They were crouching, creeping, sitting on the bench, waiting."

"Hell's bells woman, that was *Len!*"

"Len?"

"Len."

"I thought it was someone after me."

"Why on earth would someone be after you?"

"I don't know…"

"*Is* someone after you?"

"No, of course not."

"Of course not. Then why the table and the light?"

"I suppose I just got myself into a state."

There was an evasiveness to Alice's replies that grew as she became more aware and less obviously terrified. It was the first time that Joe had seen Alice less than in control. It was confusing.

"Are you sure there's not something else, Alice?"

"No, no, no, nothing. I must be going now that you're back."

She scuttled to the door, unhooked her coat and put it over her arm. Without a word, Joe accompanied her to her own door where she went inside and Joe heard the surprising click of the lock as he turned away.

17

Six months later.
March 1921

He was about to go indoors following a stroll around the Place and up the alley at the side of the pub, aimless and vacant, when Ellen Galvin came out of her door. She stopped him as he passed.

"Joe, please don't forget if ever you need someone to look after Ruth for you … "

"Thank you, Mrs. Galvin" said Joe. "We seem to manage well at the moment, me and Alice between us."

"Ah yes, Alice," said Mrs. Galvin with an air that Joe couldn't quite identify. "It's nice to see her getting on so well with Stephen, isn't it?"

"Who, Alice?" Joe asked stupidly.

"Of course, Alice," smiled Mrs. Galvin, delighted at his surprise. "Did you not know that she visits him quite regularly? Hope for a romance, perhaps."

"Er, yes, perhaps. Yes, yes." Joe needed time to come to terms with this surprising information and backed away.

"Um, thank you for offering to look after Ruth and I would ask you if I ever needed … "

"We can always make room, you know. We'd love to have her stay, dear wee thing," she rattled on "and Joe, if there's ever anything you need advice on, or if you need to talk about anything, Michael and I are always here, you know that, don't you?"

She peered earnestly into Joe's face. This was a side of Mrs. Galvin that was not often seen. He smiled at her.

"Thank you very much, Mrs. Galvin. I will remember that." Not that he ever would. The idea of ever needing to confide in young strait-laced Mrs Galvin and her brooding Irish husband was incongruous. But it was kind of her to offer.

She hesitated briefly before turning to go indoors again. Joe had the impression she would say more if he encouraged her, but the door closed quietly and the moment was gone, to his relief. His mind was not tuned to female chat.

Too restless to stay indoors, he took Ruth and went over to the Oak Tree. Ruth was in the back parlour before Joe could front the bar, intent on the small store of toys which awaited her there; going to the Oak Tree was a treat. Joe leant on the bar and waited for Charlie to serve him, but it was in fact Mrs. Edie Craggs who majestically sailed down behind the bar to ask his pleasure.

"How are you managing, Joe? With little Ruth and everything? Isn't she growing? Dear little soul." In another person this might have sounded bubbling and chatty, but in Mrs. Edith Craggs it was solemn and portentous. Joe responded with equal gravity, trying—and failing—to imagine her as a chorus-girl.

"Joe dear." Mrs. Craggs hesitated, then continued. "Joe dear, I would be more than happy to care for Ruth at any time, you know. I don't know that it's good for her to be in Alice's charge for long periods. She is, you know"—she dropped her voice—"a little common."

Joe was a little stunned to find himself half-defending Alice before tailing off in confusion. How exceptional of Mrs. Craggs to be so vocal; was she normally able to indicate her rejection or acceptance of anyone or anything by a steely gaze and the lift of an eyebrow.

He concluded, "Well, thank you. I am managing well though and I think that Ruthie is happy."

"I'm sure she is, dear. So timely, your return."

"In some ways, yes."

"You did return. So many didn't."

"I know that."

"Of course you do. Of course you do. So many of your friends, and your poor dear uncle, as well."

"Yes, poor Uncle Johnny. Rotten way to go, in a prison camp like that."

"Your aunt should marry again. Have some children of her own instead of doting on little Ruth the way she does."

Joe was surprised by the continuation of Mrs. Craggs' Alice-opinions, but he evasively agreed that she possibly should. He did reflect that Mrs. Craggs had always been quite hostile towards Alice, and together with Joe's mother they had made a pretty daunting pair. Woe betide anyone or anything that was not to their taste or standard; it was obvious that Alice was a permanent target.

So it was mildly curious that Edie Craggs was thinking about Alice's future even if the comment she had just made was delivered with an element of disapproval in it.

Mrs. Craggs, meanwhile, was continuing her theme, slyly (now there was the chorus girl!) suggesting that a romance might be brewing with "someone who lives rather close?"

Joe seemed to be the only one who didn't know. He was wryly amused.

At that moment Dora lurched awkwardly to the bar and set her glass on it with a bang which was not so much peremptory as inadvertent. Her hand was so crippled that it could hardly hold it, and the grip on the stick she clutched in her other hand was no less sure. Joe reached over and put his arm around her.

"What can I get you, Dora?"

"No, Joe, Dora's drinks are free here," said Mrs. Craggs surprisingly.

Dora smiled a smile of amazing sweetness at Edie Craggs and said in a clear but quavering voice that this was true and she was very grateful.

"And if it wasn't for the kindness of this young lady here" she continued warmly, still smiling at the dominating figure behind the bar, "Dora would be in the poorhouse as well as very thirsty."

Joe was still amazed at the free drinks, and his mind took some time to get around to the poorhouse reference.

"What do you mean, Dora?" he asked with a smile.

"Nothing at all" said Mrs. Craggs briskly. "She means nothing at all."

"Indeed I do mean something-at-all" insisted Dora. "You know I do."

"That's enough now Dora. Here's your drink and Joe will help you back to your chair." Mrs. Craggs was firmly dismissive.

Joe thought he might winkle out the additional information from Dora as he guided her back to the chair by the fire, but she was so breathless from this simple exertion that Joe had not the heart to press her. Instead he returned to the bar and the watching Mrs. Craggs.

"It's very kind of you to give Dora free drinks". He began his exploration carefully.

"Not at all. It doesn't amount to very much."

"What did she mean about the poor-house?"

Mrs. Craggs regarded him evenly and then made an obvious decision.

"She pays no rent on her cottage. She has so little money that she couldn't afford to pay anyway."

"That's amazingly kind of you" said Joe. "And Charlie," he added as an afterthought.

"Yes, well. Dora was a good friend to my dear late mother and I couldn't see her suffer."

"Oh." The story that Alice had told Joe of Edie Craggs leaving her infant son in the care of her mother sprang to his mind. Perhaps Dora had been involved … "Oh."

Mrs. Craggs looked at him levelly. Joe was in a welter of re-evaluation of Mrs. Edie Craggs. Perhaps, he thought, his previous impressions had been those of a boy rather than the man that he now was. Perhaps she'd always been a bit more complex than he'd noticed.

He wondered, without giving it a great deal of thought, whether this might apply to other people as well.

18

The same day

Alice was not pleased to be quizzed. Joe thought his enquiries casual enough but Alice was on to him in a flash.

"Not that it's any of your business, Joe, but I ... I borrow books from Stephen sometimes, that's all. He's kind enough to lend them to me. That's all," she said again.

Joe was amazed. He had never seen a book in Alice's house and in his surprise he scanned the room in case he had, over the years, simply ceased to see books that existed. There were none. But on the other hand, there had been that observation from Stephen about Alice's intelligence. Joe looked at his aunt with new eyes.

She bustled around the room avoiding his eye and re-tying the hair ribbon on Ruth's hair with an expertise that Joe had never managed to master. Alice was prickly—again—so he mentally shrugged, took Ruth's hand, and left.

Restive, disinclined to go back to their own house, Joe took the few extra steps and knocked on the door of Stephen's cottage. They entered the small room that comprised the entire lower floor that was identical in size and aspect to his aunt's, but spare and masculine: the main difference, however, was the books; a commodious bookshelf along the wall was crammed to overflowing with them. Although the room was otherwise neat and orderly, piles of books stood by the fireplace and there were several on the table.

Stephen was welcoming, putting aside his reading, pulling out a chair for Joe and finding a picture book for Ruth. Joe's life had so far not comprised many books and his first sight of Stephen's room had overwhelmed him. Incredulously he had asked Stephen if he had read them all?

He suspected that when Stephen laughed and said no, he was only trying to make him feel less awkward. Over the months, as a tentative friendship developed between them, Stephen had gently begun to try introduce Joe to the pleasures of reading and it seemed that he was doing the same for Alice, but in Joe's case it was without too much success. Joe admired Stephen and took every opportunity to talk with him but reading made him bored and restless. For Stephen's sake, though, he did try.

But *talking* to Stephen was another thing and Joe was an eager audience. He was in awe of Stephen's learning and enthralled by his ideas. He reckoned that reading came a poor second to listening and was happily seduced by any proposition that Stephen cared to expound. But sometimes it got a bit beyond him …

Ruth sat on Joe's knee, leaning her dark silky head against his chest. He in turn stroked her hair, kissing the top of her head from time to time.

Listening to Stephen made him feel like a youngster, as it always did, almost as if he was still at school. He *had* been to the war, though. That was something out of the ordinary that he'd done. He might be trying mightily to bury the memories and the terrors, but he had seen and done awful things; he must surely have learned from the experience. Surely it had made him a man?

A flawed version of a man, perhaps, with his night-time and daytime apparitions and his yearning for a clearly unsuitable and unattainable girl, but he was doing man's work and living a man's life and providing for his sister. Still, here he was after those scarring years that he knew had changed him, living in the same house as before, doing the same job as before, his memories assumed by the world to have rolled up neatly like a rug behind him. Stephen's ideas—those that he understood—tickled at the edges of his mind. A puzzling little worm of something stirred in his chest. It was not quite discontent, but a lack of quiet. He wriggled: the feeling was physical.

Stephen was talking politics today. As he moved in his chair, Stephen eyed him appraisingly.

"Bit much for you, old man?"

"Sorry, I think I'm a bit tired. Sorry."

"No need to be sorry, you're good practice for me. When you get that faraway look I know I've gone on too long. The Debating Society should pay you as an editor."

Casually he went on "You should come to a debate one night. Just to listen," he added hastily as Joe's eyes had widened.

"Yes, I will do. One night," said Joe. Stephen was enough for him at the moment. He had had enough of politics for the day, too. Leaning back in his chair, he looked around the room and asked "How long have you lived here then?"

"Came here just before you came back, just after the war, Joe. Couple of years now."

"Where were you then?" Joe was surprised that he had not discussed the war with Stephen before this. True, neither he nor his other war-returned mates talked much about the war, but somehow it was not necessary among old pals. They just knew. He was suddenly interested to hear Stephen's opinions and experiences.

Stephen looked at him consideringly. "Several places. I drove an ambulance."

Joe's surprise showed. "You what?"

"I drove an ambulance."

Joe's eyes were calculating. "You drove an ambulance?"

"That's what I said."

"Were you a … ?"

Stephen was amused. "Yes, I was a conchie. Conscientious objector on grounds of religious belief. Christadelphians do not kill."

"Oh." Joe was mightily embarrassed. Apart from being stunned by the surprising information that Stephen was a CO, he didn't know what a Christadelphian was. He took a stab at it being a religion of some sort, cleared his throat and asked

"What do Christdorphians believe then?"

"Christadelphians" Stephen corrected. "Brothers of God."

"Is it a church?"

"Well, yes, although many ecclesia don't have churches or buildings as such. They meet in their own houses mostly."

"Ecclesia?"

"Just another worth for congregation, I suppose you'd say." Stephen stood up and walked to the fire, standing with his back to it, legs apart, smoking his pipe.

"It's all irrelevant to me now anyway" he said, "I'm a lapsed Christadelphian so I'm not a good authority on the subject."

"Why did you … lapse?"

"Several reasons, Joe. All of them contributed to it."

Until now, Joe had seen Stephen as almost infallible, but here was a new Stephen with problems and a past: most disconcerting. He hesitated, uneasy at the thought of revelations that might be at variance with the Stephen he admired, but his indecision was no match for his curiosity.

"Tell me about it. If you want to."

Stephen looked at Joe thoughtfully for a few seconds, during which Ruth slipped off Joe's lap and curled up on the one easy chair in the cottage. She danced her fingers along the arm, singing quiet little chants for her inevitable make-believe characters.

"Ah Joe, it was a lot of things. My parents joined the Christadelphians when Joanna and I were children. We were obviously taken along and duly absorbed the beliefs; they were all lovely people and very devout."

"What are the beliefs?"

"Nothing too dramatic" said Stephen, laughing at Joe's concerned expression. "Not too different from your beliefs, I would imagine."

"They're not *my* beliefs any longer" said Joe stolidly. "I don't have any beliefs. Not after the war."

"Yes," said Stephen, That was one of the factors that destroyed mine as well."

"Can't believe in a God who'd allow that."

"True. Too true."

There was a pause.

"But what else was there?" Joe asked "you said there were other reasons."

"One main other reason. I had the horrible temerity to fall in love with a girl who was not a Christadelphian."

"Why did that matter?"

"Christadelphians do not approve of their members associating with other denominations, and especially not marrying them."

"You're *married?*" Joe's mind raced, jumping from scene to scene, unable to take in all the possibilities.

"Not any more."

Joe was relieved but put this relief aside for the moment as he delved for detail.

"You've *been* married?"

"Oh yes, I've been married."

"What happened?"

"Louisa was as devout an Anglican as I was a Christadelphian; neither of us wanted to fall in love with the other because we both knew it would cause great difficulties. But you can't always control these things with reason." Stephen smiled with a rueful bitterness as he continued.

"We both worked at the local school. Lou was an orphan and had been brought up in an Anglican orphanage. She was a lost little soul—the orphanage cast her out at age fourteen; she was expected to earn her own living from then on. So she more or less just stayed on at school, going from student to student teacher then teacher. She was so sweet and loving, amazingly content with a life that was very austere and had little of a future to offer. I found her goodness and sweetness irresistible, and she might have seen in me the haven she'd never had in her deprived little life.

"Whatever the reasons—and reasons are all very well but not at all reasonable!—we fell in love and decided to marry. That was when the bad things started.

"My parents refused to meet her. They insisted that if I continued to see her, I should have to leave their house. The brethren from the ecclesia lectured and counselled me daily, threatening me with total exclusion from meetings and the church itself. This was the beginning of my disenchantment. My parents were loving and kind and the decision they made on the basis of religion caused them great pain. I couldn't see the sense in deliberately causing oneself such pain. The more the brethren argued their case, the more I felt repressed and rebellious. Absolutism in any matter is a hard argument to maintain, and I began kick against the restrictions.

"So I left home, married my little Louisa, and proceed to live happily ever after. Until," Stephen closed his eyes "she died in childbirth one year later."

"Stephen." Joe was aghast. "You poor devil." How inadequate. "You poor, poor devil."

"Poor, poor Louisa, Joe. Poor, poor little baby who died too. It was a girl, you know. We were going to call her Phoebe."

There were tears in Joe's eyes, but Stephen just stared bleakly into space. After a few moments he cleared his throat and continued.

"At the time it seemed like a punishment, Joe. So I went back to the brethren and asked for forgiveness, which was readily given. I rejoined the ecclesia and made peace with my parents, which was one good thing to come of the whole disaster. I read and re-read the Bible, tried to make some sense of it all, but mainly I just needed some peace and solace and the sheer familiarity was comforting. I really don't think I was thinking very much at all—I was pretty numb."

"I should think you were, Stephen. Poor devil" Joe said again ineffectually.

"Then of course came the wonderful war." Stephen continued "and all the dilemmas that that situation posed."

"Christadelphians don't go to war?" Joe guessed.

"No. And yes, I did have a moral tussle with that. But having lapsed once and un-lapsed" Stephen smiled "I felt that I should really hold to the convictions of my religion. So I pleaded conscientious objection and was granted exemption. But I volunteered to drive an ambulance or work in munitions or join a medical corps, stretcher bearer, or anything that would help the war effort."

"Without actually fighting."

"Yes. Silly, that discrimination, isn't it? Help the fighters but don't fight."

"You know, you men," Joe felt an almost fatherly warmth "were very much respected by us soldiers."

"A lot of us died."

"Yes I know. There was not much difference between us in terms of risk."

"Oh yes and no. Doesn't matter now anyway." Stephen knocked out his pipe and continued, "what did happen was that my religious beliefs were shattered again. I just found it unbelievable that any God could allow such suffering. It didn't make any sense."

"Yes, by God!" exclaimed Joe, unaware of the irony "That's exactly what happened to me! How could He allow such a terrible thing? It's quite impossible to believe in any God that would!" Joe thumped the table and Stephen smiled again.

"So we're in agreement, it would seem?" he said

"Completely."

"In my case it meant another separation from my parents and I was in any case quite embarrassed to seem so uncertain of my own beliefs, so I moved from north London to south, took this position at Beulah Road school and moved into Oak Tree Place. The rent is modest and the neighbours congenial!"

Joe assumed that "congenial" was a compliment and beamed at Stephen.

"A jolly good thing you did, too." He laughed. "It'll be the making of you, my son!"

Joe scooped Ruth from the chair, and piggy-backed her back to their house, full of compassion for Stephen. He fleetingly reflected that Alice would indeed be very good for him.

19

Eight months later.
November 1921

Ruth's sixth birthday in late November had been a day of excitement for her, a day of special-ness at school and a birthday tea
with Joe, Alice and Ruth's special friend Lillian. She came in from
farewelling her friend and sat by the table, hands in her lap, eyes
vacant.

"What are you thinking about, sweetheart?"

"Nothing."

"What sort of nothing?" Cajoling.

"Just nothing."

"Have you had a nice birthday?"

"Yes."

"Are you sad that it's over?"

"Yes."

"Never mind," said Joe heartily "there'll be another one next
year."

"I might die."

Joe's heart lurched. Before he could frame a reply, Ruth added
with total composure "Or you might die."

Joe searched for a response. Ruth's calmness defied plati-
tudes; he could think of absolutely nothing to say. He tried.

"We won't die!" he said, uselessly.

"Mummy and Daddy did."

"Do you miss Mummy and Daddy a lot?"

"Yes." Then a qualification "Some days a lot. Today a lot."

"You know they're up in Heaven watching over you, don't
you?" Joe had no difficulty in using the mores of belief when it
suited.

"I don't want them to be in Heaven. I want them to be here. I
want to see them."

"Ah Ruthie, so do I!"

It had slipped out in an anguished moan before he realised he'd said it, and Ruth looked up in surprise, then a considering frown. The idea that she was not grieving alone seemed to bewilder her.

Joe took her on his lap and cocooned her in his arms, rocking her gently.

"We all miss Mummy and Daddy, sweetheart, all of us. You and me and Auntie Alice and Mr. and Mrs. Galvin, and Charlie and Mrs. Craggs … "

"Mrs. Craggs?" Ruth sat up straight on his lap.

Joe chuckled at her surprise, pleased at having diverted her, even if it was by mistake.

"I don't think Mrs. Craggs."

"Which Mrs. Craggs don't you think?" Joe was smiling still.

"Charlie's Mum Mrs. Craggs."

"Oh Ruthie, that's not so. She's a very nice lady."

"She's not nice to everyone. She's quite nice to you and she's very nice to me and calls me her dear little girl, but she's not nice to Auntie Alice. She tells Auntie Alice to go away all the time. Once she said that *she'd* look after me properly if Auntie Alice would only leave."

"Goodness. But how do you know that, Ruth?" Joe was gently perplexed.

"I hear her talking when Auntie Alice is cleaning. She doesn't like Auntie Alice. One day she made her cry."

"Goodness gracious, that's not nice, is it?"

"But Charlie came and then he talked really loudly and Mrs. Craggs cried too and she said that Charlie should look somewhere."

"Look somewhere? What do you think she meant?" Joe was intrigued despite himself.

"Somewhere or else. Or elsewhere. Or something like that".

"Goodness." Joe's felt a proprietary indignation that Ruth be exposed to this employer-employee wrangling. It seemed that

Edie Cragg's antipathy to Alice was not confined to an acid comment or two across the bar to him, but it wasn't right that Ruth should be a part of it. Another disquiet about Ruth's wellbeing. He held her tightly again.

He loved her quite desperately. He loved to look at her perfect little body in the bath, losing its baby roundness and taking on the sweet curves of childhood. He loved the way her physical development made her sure-footed and fleet and fluid in her movements, he loved the dimples on her hands and the way her fine dark hair curled in the nape of her neck, so different from his own head of undistinguished dead-straight mousy stuff.

Tucking her into bed, as he did quite soon, was always sublimely delicious, feeling the warmth of her small warm body through her nightgown hugging him tightly before she snuggled down. Tonight as he left her room he absorbed his anxieties into a complacent memory of the pleasant day he'd provided for her.

20

Later that month

He had not seen Len since that night of awful memory and when he did, Joe was embarrassed. Len, however, seemed to have no memory at all of the incident and greeted him in his usual easy manner. Joe felt a quick surge of irritation; the advantages of being drunk!

Len was speaking. Joe sharply picked up the thread of the conversation.

"What did you say?" he asked.

" … and Mum and Dad are leaving Ida and me in the house by ourselves!" Len was finishing a sentence, triumphantly.

"Where are they going?" Joe was bemused

"I just told you—they're going to stay with Dad's sister in Maidenhead for a while. She needs some company, she has such a big house there and of course since Uncle Walter died … "

Joe looked hard at Len. Was he putting on a front or did he not remember the fact that he had hit his mother? Surely he couldn't forget a thing like that?

"Lucky for you," he said.

"Yes, isn't it?" Len was beaming. "At last, a house to ourselves, just me and Ida."

Joe couldn't help himself. "How will you pay the rent?" he asked rudely.

Len looked aggrieved. "Dad's going keep paying it," he said with a shrug.

"Ah," said Joe.

"Well, *they* won't be paying any rent to my Auntie Florrie, she's no need."

"Ah," said Joe again.

"What's it got to do with you anyhow?" asked Len truculently. His face began to flush with what seemed a combination of anger and embarrassment. Joe looked at him speculatively, wondering just how much was real and how much was bluster. How much he might really remember.

Then he looked at Len leaning on his crutches and felt deflated. There Len was, war finished early on, might even have come through it all like Joe and lots of others had done; he'd never know that. How must he feel? The rest of his life … A sudden spurt of sympathy took Joe by surprise but was just as quickly extinguished.

"Nothing to do with me at all, pal," he said with weary indifference.

Mr. & Mrs. Dawson left Oak Tree Place with little fuss. They presented their departure as temporary and necessary for the well-being of Mr. Dawson's sister. They said that they were looking forward to living for a time in the beautiful house in Maidenhead and Mrs. Dawson even became animated at the thought of the nearby river where she could take pleasant strolls. This was Mrs. Dawson, who had never walked without intent in her entire life.

A few neighbours had gathered to farewell the Dawsons and to Joe they all looked ill-at-ease, as if they knew the sham of the situation, although he knew he was projecting his own unease. Joe could see the bleakness in the depths of Len's parents' eyes as they pretended and he felt contempt for Len as the cause. The cause, however, seemed blithely unaware of these undercurrents and waved his parents off with enthusiasm before turning to the house and his wife.

Ida's face was pinched and pale but Joe found himself envious of the sweet and loving smile she bestowed on Len as they went indoors, arms linked.

◆

That Saturday evening he spent half an hour in the biting cold watching Lydia's house. A futile pursuit and one that made him ashamed of himself, especially as he had done it so many times. What he expected to see or what he would have done about anything he *did* see were unexplored options. He kicked the fence savagely and turned back down Brigstock Road.

He had not spoken to Lydia since the trial of tea with her parents at the end of the previous summer, a visit of strangled conversation, terror of doing the wrong thing and no time at all alone with Lydia. An awful two hours. But he had not disgraced himself—to his knowledge—and felt at least morally able to think in terms of seeing Lydia again. But she had dismissed him at the end of the afternoon with no more than a kiss on the cheek and a gentle push out the door. She didn't even walk down the short gravel path to the gate with him. The remnants of his pride would not allow him to try to contact her again, but here he was. His vigil was shaming and he feared that someone would see him. Even feared that Lydia would see him. So why did he do it? Stupid, that's what he was. That's why he did it.

Eyes down, he had to be hailed three times before his own name impinged on his consciousness.

"Joe, Joe, Joe!" Peter and Bill were standing on steps of the clock tower on the island in the middle of the road, laughing at his preoccupation. Another man with them, older than his friends, was smiling. Joe's spirits lifted at the prospect of some good company and he eagerly made his way across the road to greet his old pals and be introduced to their companion.

"Joe, this is Martin Addison. Martin, Joe Barlow," said Peter. Martin and Joe shook hands and then Martin rubbed his together.

"Let's get into the pub before we freeze," he said, to a general murmur of agreement.

The four men made their way across the road to the Prince of Wales. This was familiar territory to them, or at least to three of them, as it had always been their favoured haunt; a young man's paradise, this—a gymnasium on the first floor and plenty of beer downstairs.

They took their drinks and sat down. Joe was mildly curious about Martin and why he was in company with his mates—he must be about ten years their senior. He looked covertly at him. A bit of a dandy, actually; much better dressed than most of the other customers in the bar and sporting a splendidly luxuriant moustache. Of this Joe was envious, having abandoned his attempts to grow one when the result was almost invisible. Peter and Bill were hanging on Martin's words and there was an air of suppressed excitement about them.

Almost immediately it all gushed out from Peter, with interjections from Bill.

"Martin's been in America," he said, pausing for Joe to be impressed.

"He's made a lot of money."

"He's got land over there and owns two hotels and a skating rink."

Joe looked again at Martin; such substance required respect. A little in awe, he asked where Martin lived.

"Well," he said. There was a faint twang to his accent that was intriguing and attractive. His smile crinkled his eyes and his tanned face looked rugged and healthy compared to the fresh pinkness which Joe so detested in himself.

"Well," Martin repeated, "guess I don't live anywheres at the moment. Sort of travelling round enjoying the scenery and seeing old friends."

The thought of the money that that sort of lifestyle required was breathtaking. They thirsted for detail and Martin was quite pleased to provide it. He told them of his emigration and the vast opportunities which America afforded to a young man. He had initially worked as a kitchen hand, he said, then had the good fortune to be introduced to a man who offered him a job delivering new cars to customers all over the country.

"It was a great life," he said with enthusiasm. "Driving these cars is quite an experience, I can tell you. They really travel, and what with the good roads and wide open spaces, they could've asked *me* to pay *them*!" He laughed.

"I made good money, but that's not how I made my lot. The opportunities for investment in America are so many that making a fortune is the easiest thing in the world."

He laughed at the three young men's wide-eyed attention and continued: "Now that the war is over the whole country's growing at a faster rate than ever. Opportunities everywhere—everywheres." 'Everywheres', and 'OK' and 'swell' were part of Martin's exotic vocabulary, duly and admiringly absorbed by his trio of listeners.

The scene Martin painted was engaging. Joe pictured himself driving a brand-new car for miles and miles into a rosy sunset. From the somewhat glazed expression on his mates' faces it would seem that their thoughts were similar.

Hang on. Nothing was that easy. If it was that easy everybody would be going to America. Joe willed his mind back to his present surroundings, eased back in his seat, took a deep pull on his pint and placed the glass back on the table.

Peter and Bill, however, were eager for more details, which Martin willingly provided. It did seem as if he'd done well, fallen on his feet with a few lucky breaks but he was anxious to be modestly deprecating about his own abilities. Things just seemed to happen to him and to his advantage.

He insisted on buying the next round of drinks and the three friends regarded each other as he went to the bar, each smiling broadly.

"Sounds too good to be true," said Peter.

"If it does, it probably is," said Joe, quite pleased with his own profundity.

"They don't call America the land of opportunity for nothing," said Bill. "I like the sound of it, don't you?"

They all had to sheepishly agree that they did.

"But," said Joe "we thought that way about the war, if you remember."

The two others cried him down. This was nothing like the war!

There was a small silence as they all let their own thoughts wander.

Martin came back with the refills and the conversation resumed, but it always kept returning to Martin and to his experiences, which he remained happy to relate. He was a good raconteur and his images were lively. As with their joint decision to join up, Joe could feel the mounting excitement of another venture about to be launched.

He was imagining how excited Ruth would be at the prospect of such an adventure, when suddenly Bill began to cough. The cough became a spasm as he leant forward on the table, racked and helpless. Joe and Peter looked at each other and, as one, lifted Bill under his arms and helped him outside the pub, out of the close smokiness into the cold night air.

"Be back," said Joe over his shoulder to Martin. "Just an attack. Won't be long." Martin nodded and seemed satisfied to wait their return.

Joe and Peter were used to poor old Bill's coughing. It usually happened in the pub where the atmosphere was most heavy with smoke, but it could be triggered by other things as well—wind, exercise, anything, nothing. Another lasting gift from the bloody war. They waited till Bill was in control again, wiping his eyes and taking deeper breaths. They regarded him not with pity but with empathy. His affliction was also theirs; they suffered it together.

Bill and Peter had turned to make their way back into the pub when Joe, fresh from Martin's tales of smart cars, stopped to look appreciatively at a shiny dark green Napier coupe as it came towards him down Brigstock Road and slowed to turn into the High Street. The passenger side was close to him and the passenger's head was thrown back in carefree laughter before it turned slightly and Lydia's eyes met Joe's. There was a long moment before the car turned into the High Street, and Joe had time to watch Lydia's laughter change to disdain as her gaze flicked lightly over him and she turned with an exaggerated flounce towards the indistinct figure of the driver.

When Peter came out to look for him, Joe was almost out of sight, plodding slowly up the road towards Oak Tree Place.

21

Seven months later.
June 1922

More than six months later Joe could reflect that the one good thing about that night was that it had saved him money. If he had stayed in the pub with his friends he, too, may have been seduced by Martin's stories and passed over good money to him, never to be seen again.

Maybe. He liked to think that he might have been more suspicious and a little less easy to dupe. Perhaps. But whatever he may or may not have done, the fact remained that Peter and Bill were stripped of most of their meagre savings by a confidence trickster who was already known to the police in other areas of London. He had apparently been on the last leg of his south London trawl, and was to disappear almost immediately afterwards. He had used many names and no one knew his real one.

"They say he'd never even been to America, apparently" said Bill ruefully. "Born and bred in Ipswich, they think. Or Margate."

"He had a good accent, have to give him that," said Peter.

"How would you know?" asked Bill, but without rancor. "Learned it all from Zane Gray, I bet."

This was familiar ground. Joe was with his two friends, this time in the Oak Tree, where they were in the process of re-living the anguish of not only losing their money, but having been tricked so readily.

"I'd like to meet him somewhere on a dark night," said Bill.

"If you'd ever recognise him again," said Peter. "I'll bet he's lost the whiskers and that tan'd be long gone – wherever it came from in the first place. And there'll be a new name."

They all nodded sagely and a small silence fell.

"Thing is, though," said Bill, "I do still want to go to America. I always have. I mean, the fact that our friend Martin Addison-so-called—he spat the name contemptuously—was a liar and a con man doesn't change the fact that it *is* the land of opportunity, does it?"

"'Course not," said Peter, "but we've not the means to get there, have we?"

Bill and Peter sighed in unison, reminding Joe of a music-hall act.

Martin Addison had told a plausible story about his close friendship with the captain of a passenger liner who could be bribed into taking people—selected people, only bona fide guaranteed-by-Martin good eggs—to fill vacant steerage berths to America for a fraction of the normal fare. That night in the pub they'd eagerly agreed to pay him the necessary and had handed it over next day. They'd been coming to see Joe to include him in the wonderful deal when the police had started to make enquiries at the pub and Martin Addison took to his heels. He had left them with brochures showing the details of the liner in question, the sailing date, the name of the captain and the name of another contact for when they arrived in New York. Of these only the name of the liner and the sailing date were genuine.

Peter and Bill did, however, consider themselves fortunate that Martin Addison had been rumbled and that they had been spared the embarrassment of turning up at the wharf requesting their spurious passage from an equally spurious ship's captain. Many other duped souls, mostly young returned solders, who had not seen the newspaper accounts of the scam and its progenitor, did so.

Peter and Bill did go to the local police to report themselves as duped but did not have to reveal their gullibility to the world, nor had they sold their belongings and said their farewells. They cringed with horror at the thought; at least they were spared this acute indignity, but they still yearned for something more than life was affording them at the moment.

22

Two months later.
August 1922

The summer of 1922 was almost over and Joe yearned, too. He had not seen or heard anything of Lydia since the brief glimpse that night outside the Prince of Wales and mostly he could convince himself that he was well out of the situation. He had almost recovered his pride, but there had been the occasional maudlin walk past her house and a razor-sharp inspection of any vehicle in the driveway. On one occasion his stomach had flipped as he spied the shiny dark green Napier, reminding him again of his inadequacy.

His life was constituted of his work and Ruth. He went to the football or the pub or the pictures with his pals, but not much else was on the horizon but more of the same. His life was a bog that he struggled through each day and the nights were still torn with dreams of suffocation. Without Ruth it would have been insupportable.

And here he was with his mates again in the Oak Tree. They fell to discussing the film they'd seen the previous evening and the conversation trailed off. Joe was just about to drain his glass and leave when he saw something amazing.

Lily Craggs had been sitting behind the bar in her usual position of Queen-of-all-she-surveyed, occasionally moving herself to graciously serve a customer or to adjust some item on the bar or behind it. She moved with stately deliberation, turned her head carefully as if it carried a crown, smiling a vestigial smile that rarely changed and never reached her eyes.

She had been sitting serenely for a minute or two when Charlie, from the other end of the bar, approached her quietly. Joe's vantage point gave him an angled view so that he saw Charlie's large blunt hand quite clearly as it rested on Lily's arm. Joe was about to turn away from this small gesture of married intimacy when he saw Charlie's hand envelop Lily's arm and squeeze and twist. Lily started and cringed slightly, but maintained her composure as Charlie passed on down the bar towards Joe and his friends.

Joe was stunned, hardly able to believe that he had witnessed such casual cruelty. He stared at Charlie who was oblivious of his scrutiny as he served another customer. Joe felt his three pints sloshing uneasily in his stomach. He turned and left the pub, making only cursory farewells to his friends who were surprised at his abruptness.

He walked straight to Alice's house to collect Ruth, and was so shocked at what he had seen that he had to tell Alice about it.

"I can't believe it!" he concluded. "I just can't believe it! Why would Charlie do a thing like that? Poor old Lily. Poor thing."

Alice was quiet. She turned away as she finally spoke.

"You might have imagined it."

"Not likely, Alice. I know what I saw."

"Well, different people have different ways."

"A bit too different in my book. Nobody does that sort of thing without rhyme or reason. Or without being sick in the head. And Charlie doesn't even have the excuse of being in the war to make him that way. It's plain disgusting, that's what it is."

"None of your business, Joe."

"At least you're right about that." Alice's disinclination to match his outrage made him surly. "I don't know how you can think it's alright though. It's just not."

"Joe, you've still got a lot of living and learning to do." Alice spoke sharply.

Joe was indignant. He collected a sleeping Ruth and carried her back to their house with only a reluctantly muttered "Goodnight Alice and thank you."

The Alice Campaign, which is what Lydia had dubbed it, had lost its spice when Lydia was no longer driving it, although Joe wished avidly at times like this that he could remove the presence of Alice from his life somehow. She was always there, trying to make him feel as if he knew nothing, always fussing about Ruth, still acting as if she just knew he could not cope.

Sometimes—like now—Joe seethed, and sometimes, he grudged, it was a convenience. He did want it both ways.

The small cruelty that Joe had witnessed in the Oak Tree changed how he felt about the pub. He was troubled by the memory and found himself dwelling on it more than he would have liked. He was perceptive enough to realise that what he had seen bore the hallmark of habit. Lily's reaction was pain and slight shock, but certainly not surprise or outrage. Joe was sickened at the thought and could not bring himself to indulge in the heavy banter Charlie offered across the bar. He looked at him with new eyes, seeing in his mind Charlie's bulky frame inflicting more on poor Lily than the casual twist that he had seen, limited as that had been by the fact that it was delivered in public.

Shocked though Joe was, he did not consider taking any action. A half-hearted and anyway unsuccessful plot to manipulate Stephen and Alice was one thing, and family into the bargain, but Charlie had been a fixture at the Oak Tree since Joe could remember, a large adult person when he was a small boy. Lily, despite her barmaid background, had always been remote and, although now revealed as a good deal more vulnerable than one ever would have imagined, difficult to consider in need of help.

Joe was tired of other people's business anyway; he had enough to do being quietly miserable on his own account. But his mind's constant reprising of the scene in the bar meant that the Oak Tree was not the same any more.

23

Three months later.
November 1922

It was a most amazing night.

Joe was moping, the encroaching winter chill serving to make him edgy and irritable. Ruth was in bed, reading did not appeal and a huge discontent clouded his mind.

He raked up the fire and sat moodily in front of it, not bothering to light the lamp, throwing himself into the chair, slumping heavily, limbs awry, his thoughts scattered but regularly returning to Lydia and his inability to drive her from his mind. With a sigh, he surrendered himself to the memory of her, weakly acknowledging that this was a self-indulgence that would only make him more unhappy.

The quiet knock on the door was so unexpected that at first he didn't react. The knocking did not cease but became a soft, relentless tattoo and when he opened the door the figure from the dark outside threw itself upon him with such force that he at first thought he was being attacked. Before he could respond, however, he realised that he was holding Lydia.

Moreover, Lydia was holding him. Not holding him but possessing him—she was covering his face with kisses, pressing herself against him, using her hands and arms to press his body closer and closer to her own.

At the same time she was babbling "Joe, oh Joe, oh Joe, my darling boy!"

Joe's body denied any incomprehension and responded with a blazing surge of desire. This was the stuff of Joe's dreams, his aching waking dreams, his wily sleeping dreams, his every other thought. If it were not for the fact that the door was still open and the cold air from outside was sweeping over their embraces, he may have been able to pass the whole thing off as a dream.

A particularly potent dream, though, that smelled of violets and trailed the cold from outside.

He kicked the door shut and pushed Lydia back against it, securing her arms with his hands and looking into her face while at the same time making sure that the contact between their bodies remained.

His voice was no more than a whisper. "Lydia." He tried again. "Lydia."

"Oh Joey darling, Joe darling, I'm so sorry to have been so very mean to you. I'm sorry, really I am. So sorry! Please say you'll forgive me?"

This was so close to the words Joe had long desired to hear that he felt light-headed. His answer was never in doubt.

"Of course I do," he croaked. This was, however, not the time for conversation. He took the opportunity kiss her, marvelling as her mouth responded under his and her body writhed against him. Entwined, their bodies moved stumblingly into the room and bumped against the armchair by the fire. Lydia threw herself into the chair and, uttering little whimpers of frustration, began to tear at her clothes, shedding them in a frenzy of torn button loops and lumped layers. She had to stand to rid herself of her skirt and petticoats, which she did with a little more style, beginning to slow in her actions and looking up at Joe with an unreadable expression.

For a moment Joe stood, stunned at the spectacle of the pale and lovely body that was being revealed to him. His own body was reacting violently and enthusiastically.

He watched his beautiful girl making herself completely and utterly naked in the firelight. It must be a dream. Nothing that was happening made any sense, but it was such a lovely insensibility that he didn't want to make any sense of it. Not yet. Not yet. Let it last, please let it last.

Lydia turned around with her arms held wide from her body, turned once, turned twice, displaying like a bird. Her hair hung half-free, swinging over her white shoulders and curling over her breasts where the nipples burned bright. She spoke.

"Love me, Joe. Please." She stopped twirling and came towards him, pressing her naked body against the roughness of his clothes. Joe's arms instinctively surrounded her, but Lydia stepped back and began to unfasten his buttons …

His penis snapped out of his trousers like a flag in a high wind and Lydia half-knelt, passing her breasts over it lightly, the nipples tickling softly. Joe's knees buckled and Lydia laughed quietly. There was an audible hiccup at the end of the laughter. He pulled her up roughly and lifted her to carry her up the stairs in a fever of haste, but Lydia pushed herself free and lay down on the rug in front of the fire.

"Here, Joe," she said. She reached out her arms to him, lustrous in the diminishing firelight, beautiful beyond belief and dreams. He lay beside her attempting to stroke and caress, but Lydia moved impatiently and he was suddenly on his knees over her, plunging wildly, all restraint shattered.

It did not take long. He moved off her body, slick with sweat in spite of the cooling room. Lydia did not move, but she exhaled a shuddering sigh that was almost a moan.

Joe was filled with love and tenderness. He cradled her body, stroked her hair and blinked away tears. Eventually the hard floor and the gritty rug began to impinge on Joe's consciousness and he moved to rise.

Lydia stood too and put her clothes on again while Joe watched, now warily silent. She dressed slowly, the wanton passion of the previous hour receding behind each successive layer of clothing. Eventually she had replaced all her clothes apart from her coat and hat, the latter still being wedged behind the door stop where it had fallen. Fully clothed, she smoothed her skirts with a familiar gesture and sat down. Joe likewise had dressed, albeit with a little less care, and they regarded each other now from the distance between the two chairs. Joe smiled uncertainly;

Lydia looked grave and he was instantly apprehensive. She drew a breath and spoke first.

"Would you like to marry me, Joe?"

Joe's wariness exploded with delighted laughter. He asked jokingly "Do you want me to make an honest woman of you?"

"Yes." This reply was delivered soberly and Joe immediately stumbled to her side, kneeling compassionately in front of the armchair, unconsciously adopting the position of the classical suitor. He took her hands in his and gazed intently into her eyes.

"Lydia, please marry me. I love you dearly and I want to make you happy. I want to live with you for the rest of my life and I love you dearly. I love you very much." The statement sounded like music to him, so he said again, "I love you, Lydia."

"I love you too, Joe. And yes, I will marry you. When?"

Joe rocked back on his heels. "As soon as you like, my darling girl. What will your parents say about it? I should speak to your father, shouldn't I?" He was as eager as a puppy.

"It's alright, dearest girl. Everything's alright. I'm here. I love you."

Suddenly Lydia began to cry. Joe was immediately guilty, immediately taking upon himself the responsibility for her sadness and totally understanding that she must regret her passionate actions. He could barely believe them himself. He pulled her out of the chair, sat down in it again and tugged her into his lap.

"Everything's alright. Don't cry. There's nothing to cry for."

Lydia began to cry harder, her initial sobs now interspersed with little wailing cries. Joe was distraught. He patted and stroked and muttered comforting words. Eventually the cries diminished to sobs once more and Lydia pushed herself away from Joe, finding her handkerchief and blowing her nose with firmness. This was encouraging to Joe and more like the Lydia he knew.

"I have to tell you something, Joe." Her tone was solemn and Joe felt a small stirring of alarm. He didn't speak.

Lydia continued, leaning her head against his chest so that he couldn't see her face, but holding firmly on to his hands with hers.

"I want to tell you about Mummy and Daddy."

This was an unexpected line of conversation and Joe relaxed. Lydia's parents were of little interest in his present state of mind, but he was prepared to listen to anything Lydia might want to say. She drew a breath.

"I know that Mummy had brothers and sisters but she never talks about them, or her parents. They lived somewhere in the East End and I don't think they had much money, but Mummy left her home when she was very young. She worked in service and lived in the houses she worked in, and the last one was Daddy's family. She was very beautiful when she was young and Daddy fell in love with her."

Lydia paused to raise her head and look into Joe's face.

"Daddy told me all this, Mummy never spoke about it. Daddy and Mummy were married and I was born—a pause here—six months later."

This relaying of this information brought on another bout of sobbing, and while Joe would offer any sympathy that Lydia required, this was not exactly something that he himself would have been too worried about—especially not after all these years. But he made an understanding murmur.

However, Lydia's sobs did not seem to be connected with her birth, as she cleared her throat and said firmly "Not that that matters to me, of course." Joe grunted in agreement.

"I must tell you all this because I want you to know, Joey darling. I want you to know *everything*. Please don't stop me."

Joe had no intention of stopping anything that was happening that night. He had his beautiful Lydia in his arms, had just made love to his wonderful Lydia and his lovely Lydia was speaking to him in a way she never had before. There was no artifice, no condescension. He was in Heaven.

"Daddy's family didn't want him to marry Mummy, but he did. They threw him out of the house and the family business—I don't know what the business was and anyway it failed a couple of years after that—probably because he wasn't there to save it." She added this aside with a loyal little raising of the chin.

"Daddy never seemed to be doing the right thing as far as Mummy was concerned. You'd think that it was her who'd married beneath her station, not poor Daddy. Her was always trying to please her, but never could. She wanted everything her way and when she got it she wanted more. She never let up. Poor, poor Daddy. Oh I hate her! It wasn't his fault, he was just trying to please her."

"What wasn't his fault?"

It came with a wail and fresh sobs. "Daddy's in jail!"

Joe started up in his chair. He would never, ever, have imagined that Lydia's father …

"Why?" he asked "How? When?" and then again "Why?"

Lydia revised her statement. "He was charged this afternoon and he says he'll probably spend the night in jail and be let out tomorrow. But he'll have to go to court and be tried and probably go to jail again for a long time!" All of this was delivered with sobs and a panic which rose with each word.

Joe repeated his questions, at the same time wondering at the strangeness of Lydia's actions in coming to him on the night of her father's arrest. He put this thought aside and tried to make sense of Lydia's explanation.

It would seem that Mr. Mason had embezzled money. Something about a scheme for subsidising the training of returned soldiers at Anderson's and he had appropriated funds. Accountants called in to Andersons' were looking at other questionable practices. He had confessed this to his wife and daughter this very afternoon before he went to the Police Station, where it seemed he was held at this moment.

Joe felt a strong surge of sympathy for Mr. Mason. He had been kind and polite to Joe, if remote, at their few meetings. How terrible it must have been to pretend all the time to be the successful businessman he knew that he wasn't, and he must surely have known that he would be found out sooner or later. Poor man to be driven to such acts. Joe's thoughts moved on jaggedly.

"What about your mother? Shouldn't you be with her?" he ventured diffidently, not wishing to seem to criticise, and especially as Lydia's *not* being with her mother this night had benefited him in ways he wouldn't want to relinquish.

"I will never have anything to do with her again," said Lydia, enunciating each word with deliberate separation. Then she added dolefully "She's gone, anyway."

"Gone? Where?"

As he spoke, a tendril of flexible ice reached up Joe's spine, curling smoothly and spreading as it reached his chest. He stopped stroking Lydia's arm, but she didn't seem to notice as she was intent on telling her story.

"I don't know. She just packed and went. I wouldn't go with her. I couldn't stand it. I hate her. She's always tried to run my life as well as Daddy's. Well she won't any more. Do you know that she actually hit poor Daddy today when he was telling us about it all before he went to the police? She was hitting and hitting, and screaming, and he just stood there … and now she won't even be there when—if—he comes home tomorrow. I had to stay, to be there when he comes home. If he comes home," she added with that rising panic in her voice again.

Joe's voice was dull. "So you're alone."

"Yes."

"You didn't need to … come here tonight," he said. "I would have looked after you if you had asked me. I would have done anything I could to help. I would marry you under any circumstances. You didn't need to … do that."

"Oh Joey!" cried Lydia in horror. "You don't think … ? Oh Joey darling boy, I really love you and I really want to marry you. I always have done, it's just that Mummy and Daddy … "

"Then why did you wait till tonight?" Joe tried to be remote.

"I suppose it was all the other emotional sorts of things that were happening to me, Joey. I just suddenly realised that I should … should … do what I really wanted to do."

Joe hadn't recognised that he was holding his breath until he let it out. The ice in his chest thawed, warmed and evaporated. They kissed again, long and slow and intoxicating, but Lydia then pulled herself out of the chair and rearranged her clothes.

"I must go home, Joe."

"Stay."

"No. I must go."

"Why?"

A slight irritation. "My parents may not be there, but the housekeeper might just wonder where I am." Again the hint of tears. Joe was remorseful.

"I must just ask Alice to listen out for Ruth while I take you home."

"No!" Lydia was horrified. "She mustn't know that I've been here with you! What would she think?" A pause. "What would she think of me?"

Joe considered. He wanted to see every situation from Lydia's point of view, even if he would personally like to shout her presence from the rooftops.

Lydia said briskly, "I can walk home by myself, Joe. I came here by myself after all."

Joe demurred and they finally agreed that he would walk half-way with her and then sprint back to Ruth

When he arrived back in the Place, breathless, Ruth had not stirred but his excursion and his visitor had not gone unnoticed.

24

The next day

More distress was in store for Lydia. Her father, broken and shamed, took his own life.

Typically, it would seem, he did it in a way that would cause least trouble for his family. He walked straight from his overnight stay in the cells to the railway station just up the road from the big, expensive house that he could never afford, buying a ticket to Brighton. Self-effacing to the last, no one remembered seeing him as he made his way further on to Beachy Head and jumped to his death, as dozens had done before him for their own dozens of sad reasons.

Lydia was inconsolable and a little demented. Still in the Brigstock Road house but without staff or company, she wept and often railed and beat her fists against the walls. Her mother had returned briefly to the house to entreat Lydia to come with her to the rooms she'd taken across London, far from Brigstock Road and the terrible embarrassment and shame of it all. Lydia was adamant that she would not go with her, despite her mother's insistence that the bailiffs would surely be at the house within days. She had finally retreated, at least temporarily, walking slowly up the hill to the railway station, dark-veiled against the possibility of recognition.

Joe was seriously worried about Lydia's state of mind but was at a loss to know what to do about her.

He could understand and totally sympathise with her sense of loss and displacement, but he was unable to divert her.

Nevertheless the wedding had been hastily set at the Register Office for early in the New Year, and this time was fast approaching. Joe was concerned. In her quieter moments Lydia was adamant that the wedding go ahead, despite Joe's suggestion that they delay it for a little. At other times she seemed unaware of the arrangement at all. Plainly this could not go on, and Joe enlisted help from Alice.

In former times Joe might have left Ruth in the care of the Craggses at the Oak Tree while he and Alice ventured down to Brigstock Road, but his perception of the Oak Tree and its previous cosy familiarity had been sullied and he was disinclined to entrust his sister to anyone there. So he asked a delighted Mrs. Galvin to have Ruth for the hour or so they expected to be away. He smiled a little as he left her in such eager hands.

That smile was long gone as they approached Lydia's house and Joe was now unsure that he had been wise to involve Alice. As soon as they set out along the road to the clock tower, Alice had started to press him on Lydia and his forthcoming marriage.

"Joe, you don't know her all that well" she'd ventured.

"Well enough to know I want to marry her. And she wants to marry me," he added, defensive in spite of himself.

"Ah," said Alice.

Joe knew he should not have risen, but he did. "What do you mean: *Ah!*"

"Joey love, think about it."

Joe knew what Alice meant, knew very well what she meant, had thought about nothing else for the last week or more since … but he was about to get what he had yearned for for so long and would not admit even to himself, let alone Alice, the niggling puzzlement and anxiety.

"I have thought about it and I know what I'm doing."

A few minutes passed, their joint footsteps echoing off the footpath.

"What about Ruth?"

"What about her?"

"Will Lydia be able to manage a youngster?"

"Of course she will. She's very fond of Ruth."

"So I shan't be needed to look after her any more then."

Joe had in the last week frequently imagined the life that he and Lydia and Ruth would lead—joyful and loving, all three of them. No thought of Alice had intruded.

"I expect not, Alice. Not," he added perfunctorily "that I'm not grateful for all you've done for Ruth and me since I came back."

"Well," said Alice carefully, turning her head away from Joe, "I'm always there if you need me."

The previously immaculate house already looked frayed at the edges. No staff to tend the gardens or the household. Plainly the house would be surrendered too, whether to foreclosure or some other call on it, Joe didn't know, but it was surely time Lydia was out of it.

It took diligent and continued ringing to get Lydia to answer the door, and that was only after she had eventually inspected the callers from an upstairs window. She opened the door with seeming reluctance and welcomed them thinly, although offering her cheek for Joe's kiss. She was dressed in some nondescript garment and her hair was carelessly twisted up. Joe ached with love for her and desire to ease her obvious pain.

He sat on a chair by her side, catching her listless hand in his and covering it with his other, impotently willing her back to the Lydia of old. It was Alice, capable Alice, who took things in hand.

"Lydia, my dear," she began. Lydia looked woodenly at her.

"Lydia," Alice began again in tone tinged with exasperation, "come home with us. Please come home with us. Leave this house with its sad memories and start again with Joe and all of us in Oak Tree Place. He is so worried about you."

Lydia did seem to have understood what Alice was saying. Her eyes wandered around the room as if she was seeing it for the first—or the last—time.

Alice continued, dogged. "You can stay with me until you and Joe are married. I would like to have you stay and would really like to help you get you ready for your wedding." Brightly she prodded: "What are you going to wear?"

Lydia smiled. It was the first smile Joe had seen since the death of her father, and he was moved to his all-too-easy tears.

Lydia looked at him. "Don't you start," she said.

Their cautious laughter scuttled around the room like a mouse. But it was a beginning.

Alice went upstairs with Lydia to pack some clothes. Joe wandered around the room, inspecting without touching the various elements of the ruined family. He was filled with revulsion for what the objects represented; willful demands on the one hand and weak submission on the other. With his poor little Lydia caught in the middle.

Joe hit his forehead with his fist. On the other hand. On the other hand! It must be true that his Lydia was entitled to some of the spoils of this horrible mess that was so affecting her? As far as he knew, no one had come near the house since the arrest or the funeral; if they had, Lydia had not admitted them, he was sure. It was obvious that this could not be the case for too much longer.

He searched for a suitable receptacle and found a large carpetbag in the depths of a linen cupboard. Feeling decidedly guilty, he proceeded to wrap some of the smaller drawing room items in napkins and towels and place them in the bag. As he proceeded he began to feel less constrained, beginning to evaluate his choices with more discernment—easily moved, easily sold if the need should arise. He worked quickly and soon the bag was so full that it was beginning to be too heavy to move for any distance.

He went out the kitchen door and peered into the dusk. The summerhouse, where he had famously taken tea in anguished tension with Lydia and her parents, was bleached pale by the dark afternoon as he carried the heavy bag towards it. The summerhouse seats had hinged tops for storage of summer-useful items and Joe managed to stuff the bag into one of them. This would do until he came back tomorrow with a handcart which he knew he could borrow from Charlie. He slipped back into the house where Lydia and Alice were descending the stairs with difficulty and two large suitcases. Alice looked bemused.

Joe hurried forward to help as Alice said "There's a big trunk still upstairs, Joe." She rolled her eyes.

Joe pointedly ignored this ironic gesture, but it was plain that all this luggage could not be moved tonight. Actually, thought Joe, it suited all the better. He could bring the handcart to collect all of Lydia's things as well as the carpetbag and he would take care to oversee the operation. He'd tell Lydia about his burglary on her behalf when she was in a calmer state.

Alice had been able to direct Lydia to pack a small valise with toiletries and a few clothes. They locked the door of the big, full, empty house behind them and walked back to the Place, arm in arm, Joe carrying the valise.

Lydia shivered in the cold. Alice and Joe squeezed up to her from either side.

"I feel better," she said wanly.

"Good!" said Alice and Joe in unison, one with exasperated briskness, the other with loving concern.

25

Later that month

A week later Alice watched Joe and Lydia from her window as they walked from the Place arm in arm, Joe luminous with love and pride.

In a matter of days they'd be married. She'd initially and instinctively tried to talk sense to Joe and Stephen had tried in a diffident way but Joe was adamant that the wedding would take place. It was as if he feared postponement would mean abandonment. Alice thought this was probably true, as Lydia's present state of mind was so at variance with her previous attitude to Joe that it beggared belief. Alice was willing to wager that she didn't know half of it either.

Accommodating Lydia was quite easy, even a little boring. She hardly spoke, ate little and did not respond to any of the conversational gambits that Alice tried. She slept on the old chaise downstairs and at every opportunity was indoors at Joe's house.

Alice was in two minds about how things were going. On the one hand if Joe and Lydia married she was sure that she would be needed in Ruth's life more than ever as she couldn't see Lydia handling mothering at all; she hardly acknowledged Ruth and definitely did not make any effort to engage her. Too tied up with her own affairs, of course. Laughable really.

Alice frowned. On the other hand, if she redoubled her efforts to talk Joe out of marrying Lydia, and always supposing she could, then things would stay as they were. Was that a better thing? She hadn't been making much progress with winkling Ruth away from Joe. None at all in fact.

So, so, so … let them marry? The marriage seemed absurdly wrong to everyone except Joe, but how did it fit with what *Alice* wanted? Weighing up the possible outcomes was making her head ache.

Alice had seen Lydia's arrival on that tumultuous night that had begun this present nonsense, had seen her leaving so much later and of course the family's scandal was the talk of the neighbourhood. But if she'd had to put a word to Lydia's present actions, she'd choose "unnecessary". Puzzling.

Still, wasn't the important thing that she could not see a married Lydia vying with her for care of Ruth? Of course it was, so let it happen.

Alice could not see the marriage lasting more than a few months anyway, so yes, let it happen. When Lydia came to her senses she'd be off to greener pastures and Alice could regroup then.

But it was still a puzzle why she was here in the first place. A puzzle but not really a threat.

26

The next month.
December 1922

Charlie was coming out of the Oak Tree with a covered dish when the brewery wagon arrived.

He hailed Joe, who was cleaning the downstairs window of his house, a rare day off work because of a bereavement in Mr. Jackson's family.

"Joe, Joe, take this for me, will you? I need to see to this delivery."

"What is it?" Joe's new-found revulsion for Charlie made him curt.

"It's some soup for Dora, Lily made it for her. Can you take it to her, please?"

Joe took his time climbing down from the chair on which he'd been standing. He wiped his hands on his trousers and took the bowl from an impatient Charlie.

"Thanks Joe." Charlie smiled uncertainly, obviously puzzled by Joe's antipathy.

Joe didn't speak, but strode the four cottage-fronts to Dora's, bowl in hand. He knocked to no reply, so carefully pushed open the unlocked door.

It had been years since he'd been in Dora's house but the smell was the same. Even in his childhood Dora had seemed immeasurably old and the smell of her house, a dark mushroomy odour, had emphasised her ancient status.

The cottage was second in the row, and although the outside looked crisp by virtue of the whitewash that was sloshed on the whole row with regularity, the inside was dark because of the drawn curtains.

Dora sat asleep in the one armchair in the place, in front of a dead fire. She was rugged up and looked peaceful, but Joe, who

"]

briefly inspected the covered bowl ,thought that he should wake her to take advantage of the hot dish. This he did without difficulty, Dora snapping from sleep to wakefulness at his first touch. She was pathetically glad to see him, patting his hand and arm with her knotted hands, smiling up at him.

Joe carefully passed the bowl to her but she almost dropped it, so he stayed to awkwardly feed the soup to her in her comfortable chair, chatting stiffly at first about the Place and then more avidly about the subject uppermost in his mind, his imminent wedding. Dora smiled and nodded and clucked and cackled with enjoyment at the fact of his presence and the news she was hearing. The soup seemed to do her good; her eyes sparkled, belying their heavy wrinkled lids.

"Your Mum and Dad should see you wed." she said.

Joe wondered if Dora remembered that his parents were dead but her next words confirmed that she did.

"It's a shame, Joe, a shame, that they can't be with you."

Joe agreed with a slow nod.

"I never wed," she said forlornly, gazing into the dead fire. Then she looked up with a twinkle. "Too late, do you think?"

Joe chuckled. "Never!"

Dora coughed as she laughed. When she had recovered herself her air had become serious.

"My friend Mary took all the time I had," she said.

Joe was intrigued. "Who was Mary?"

"Mary was my friend. In the beginning Mary was my friend. Her Mum and Dad took me in, you know, when my own Mum and Dad just went off one day and left me."

"They just left you?"

"Never saw them again, ever. Moonlight flit, it was, in broad daylight while I was playing with Mary and out of the way. I used to wonder whether they just forgot me."

"That's awful, Dora. How old were you?"

"Thirteen. Same age as Mary."

Thirteen. Old enough to know the truth of abandonment, poor thing, thought Joe. Old enough to feel the pain of rejection, old enough indeed to feel the embarrassment of having been thrust on another family without warning.

"They treated me well," said Dora, unconsciously addressing Joe's thoughts. "I worked for them, of course, but they treated me well. I was grateful to them."

"And Mary was your friend. What sort of things did you do together?" asked Joe with a smile. "Dancing? Parties? Picnics?"

"Oh my, no," said Dora with an air of alarm, as if she was being found out at some forbidden activity, "Mary did of course, but not me. Not me, not me."

"Not at all, not ever?" asked Joe with growing sympathy.

"Once," said Dora with a serene smile of remembrance, drawing the word out as if to suck its sweetness.

"Only once?" said Joe incredulously.

"It was lovely," said Dora, ignoring his question.

It came bubbling out, the thin old lips quivering with the excitement of the memory, the eyes alight. They had allowed her to attend a dance. Joe found it hard to understand where or how this happened, but Dora had worn one of Mary's dresses and had been accompanied by a young man who worked for someone who worked for someone else. The dress was blue. She danced the polka. She wore flowers in her hair.

Dora's excitement in the recounting of a treasured memory obviously tired her and her speech became slower, her eyes more ruminative than sparkling. She coughed.

"I'd better go," said Joe.

"Oh, don't leave yet, love," said Dora pleadingly. Joe eased back into his chair reluctantly but with a reassuring smile at the anxious old face.

"Alright, Dora love," he said, "but you'd better not tire yourself too much with talking."

"I like to talk. Never get a chance though, Joe. No one to talk to."

This was such a sad statement. Joe immediately felt the guilt of youth that he didn't take the time to visit her occasionally. Encouragingly, he said "Go on, then, Dora, tell me more about your growing up. What sort of things did you do?"

"The Craggses were not well off, you know, dear. They took me in out of the goodness of their hearts and looked after me. I was happy to do what I could for them because if it wasn't for them the Lord knows where I would have been."

"The Craggses?" asked Joe. "Was it Edie's family that took you in?"

"Yes. Edie is Mary's daughter. My friend Mary's daughter."

So, thought Joe. That explains a little more of the responsibility that Edie Craggs feels for Dora. She was more than a friend to Edie's mother—she must have been like family.

"Edie doesn't know it all," said Dora with seeming irrelevance.

"What all?" asked Joe

Dora's eyelids had been drooping but she snapped awake again, tucking her chin into her chest and looking at Joe with a considering frown.

"Joe Barlow, I've lived here in Oak Tree Place for more years than I can count. I could tell you more about the people who've lived here and who still live here than anyone else could ever know." This was delivered with a gleam of triumph. Joe was all at sea, Dora's train of thought—if there was one—eluding him completely. He spoke placatingly.

"I'm certain you could tell me lots, Dora. Are you sure you wouldn't rather rest now, though?"

"No. I want to tell you some things about growing up in the Craggs' house. You might not think that it has anything to do with you but I want to tell you just the same."

"Go ahead, Dora, go ahead. I want to listen to anything you'd like to tell me."

At this stage Joe was sure that there would be little story and lots of tangents.

Dora drew what was, for her, a deep breath. It took considerable effort but seemed to give her strength because when she spoke her voice was strong.

"Mr. and Mrs. Craggs were lovely people. Very kind. They only had one child and that was Mary. They thought the world of her. I was friends with Mary at school and when my Mum and Dad left me I was playing at Mary's house. That night I stayed there and then after a while when my Mum and Dad didn't come back, the Craggses just kept me with them. It was a comfort to me then to be living with my friend who I loved. Oh I did love her then. She was a beautiful girl—long fair curls and her Mum always tied a big ribbon bow on top. Big blue eyes—she could melt anyone with a look. Her clothes never seemed to get dirty, her shoes never scuffed and her hair always *bounced* and shone … " Dora smiled as she continued.

"Mary was a very pretty girl but she was never what you would call a *kind* person, Joe. Not like her Mum and Dad. It was a real surprise to me to see how she worked on them to get what she wanted. And she did, all the time. She'd cry, or scream, or sulk and always got her own way. It was a shame to see her Mum and Dad so sad when she did these things so I always tried to help. I began to look after Mary so that she didn't worry her parents. I became her sort of pretend maid. She liked that; Mr. and Mrs. Craggs could never have afforded even a part-time maid, so Mary was pleased to have me by her. I didn't mind if it kept her Mum and Dad from being worried by her tantrums; they were truly lovely people and they didn't deserve to be sad."

Joe said "You loved them a lot, didn't you?"

Dora looked surprised. "Oh, I don't know. I don't know that I ever thought about love very much. I just wanted to do things for them."

"I think that's love," said Joe firmly. Dora smiled briefly.

"That Mary was a one, you know. Her Mum and Dad had spoiled her, that's the truth, but as time went by it was more than just being spoiled. Little by little it got worse. She had tantrums when she didn't like things, dreadful tantrums. Then she began to have tantrums for no reason at all. But worse than those were the cruel bits. She hit me, she scratched me, she twisted my arms, just for the fun of it. She liked doing it."

Joe's mind flew to the scene at the Oak Tree where Charlie had twisted the skin on his wife's arm. Charlie was this Mary's grandson. He shifted in his chair.

Dora was in full flight. "I think now that it would have been better if Mary'd been locked away somewhere. But of course that's easy to say now. *Then* it was a case of hide it and keep it hidden. I kept it hidden as best I could, and her Mum and Dad liked it that way."

"Locked up? Was it that bad?" asked Joe.

"Oh yes, it was that bad," said Dora, "and it got worse. She'd throw things and break things and make her hands and arms bleed from beating on the walls. Sometimes her head, too, she'd beat it against the wall. She'd imagine awful things and scream and shout. Then suddenly she'd be as nice as nice could be. Until the next time. And you'd never know when that would come."

"Poor Dora. It must have been hard on you."

"I didn't think that while it was happening, I just did what I could. Then," Dora went on quickly, as if ridding herself of the memories by recounting them, "then, well, it happened, didn't it?"

"What happened?"

"It got so that Mary didn't go out any more. She stayed in her room most of the time, and when she came down it was just to eat or cause trouble. One day she ... she shedushed the butcher's boy!"

The combination of the quaint mispronunciation and the thought of a small aproned boy on a large bike being pounced upon by this mad Mary was too much for Joe and he couldn't help laughing.

Dora looked at him vacantly, still in the world she was recounting. With difficulty, Joe brought his expression back to normal, but his body still heaved with suppressed mirth. Dora continued.

"He wasn't a very nice lad, that butcher's boy. His family was a bad lot. But two or three times—or more p'raps—when he delivered the meat, her parents couldn't stop her, Mary would laugh and take him upstairs to her bedroom. Of course he was only too willing, too willing—thought it was a great lark." Dora shook her head with reproof. "A bad lot," she said again.

"Anyhow," she said, "Mary's Mum soon put a stop to those deliveries, I can tell you. But the damage was done by that time."

"What damage was that?" asked Joe, guessing the answer.

"Of course she'd fallen for a baby," said Dora scornfully.

"What happened?"

"Well, it was easy to hide it," said Dora. "Mary didn't go out at all so there was no one to see her getting big. Her Mum and Dad were really upset, of course, but they just had to get on with it. I looked after her as best I could and the baby was born quite easily in the end with just her Mum and me to help. When you're only fifteen it's easier, you know." Dora looked up at Joe, who nodded as if he had always known this fact.

Before Joe could ask any questions, Dora continued.

"It was a shock, you know, but birthing Edith changed Mary completely. Such a surprise, and such a blessed relief. Her Mum and Dad were so happy when days, then weeks, went by with Mary as good a mother and as nice a person as you could wish for." Dora smiled with tender memory.

"Little Edith was a lovely baby and a dear sweet child." A pause. "It was a lovely time."

Dora drew breath again.

"Of course we had to move house. That was easier than explaining the baby all around the place. So we moved and Mary was passed off as a widow-woman. Easily done."

Joe remembered that Stephen had moved from north to south London to escape his past as well. A fresh start. As Dora said, easily done. He noted that Dora had used the word 'we' to include herself in the Craggs family. Surely she had earned that.

"So the story has a happy ending?" Joe asked mildly.

"Oh I think you could say that. In the end," said Dora. Surprisingly she added bitterly "When Mary died it was a happy ending."

Joe was taken aback. "But I thought she got well?"

"We weren't to be that lucky," said Dora acidly. "It didn't last, this good bit. Didn't last. For the rest of her life there were good bits followed by bad bits followed by good bits followed by worse bits. You just never knew … "

"And Edie?"

"Poor Edith. We all tried our hardest to keep the worst from her. She never really knew how bad her mother was. We sent her away to Mrs. Craggs' sister sometimes, sometimes we just kept Mary locked in her room and then of course when the good times came she would be the best and most loving mother in the world to the poor wee mite."

"But Edie was well looked after."

"Oh yes, she was loved as much as any little girl could be. As I said, we hid the worst from her. But we couldn't hide it all the time, or every time, so Edie started living more at her aunt's than at home. It was for the best, but oh, we missed her little face!"

Joe thought of Ruth, how we would miss her if they were parted. It didn't bear thinking about. But the grim scene that Dora had painted—three adults dealing with, and attempting to hide, the apparent madness of another person in the house—was indeed depressing. How terrible it must have been for them.

"Then when Edie grew up," continued Dora "she went out to work as a dancer and—you probably know all about this— had Charlie, then actually handed him to her mother to look after! I'll never forget the day she came. Mary was having one of her good times and it was just like a happy family, even though poor Mr. and Mrs. Craggs were shocked that Edie was acting so like her mother."

"So like her mother?" said Joe in horror. "Was Edie mad too?"

He hadn't meant it to come out like that. It was just that Edith Craggs had never seemed anything but controlled and capable;

the thought of madness lurking somewhere there was as frightening as it was incongruous.

"No, no, no dear," said Dora, patting his arm. "Edie was never anything like what her mother was. Just the baby with no father, that's what I meant." She chuckled. "Edie's nobody's fool."

Joe was reassured. A bastard child was nothing at all, compared with his initial thought.

"So you had another baby to look after," he smiled.

"Yes," said Dora pursing her lips. "But this poor little one didn't get away like his mother did. When Edie got married she came to see us before, to explain that she couldn't take the risk of visiting very often because her Clarence didn't know about Charlie. And she didn't. Visit, that is. Hardly at all. Poor Charlie."

Joe thought here were a lot of poor people in this story and that he was sitting with not the least of them. He regarded Dora with compassion as she went on: "Mary was all over Charlie one minute, and locking him in the wardrobe the next. Hit him so hard that his ears bled more than once. Black eyes, a broken finger … we had a hard job keeping an eye on her all the time. By this time we couldn't even send him away to Mrs. Craggs' sister because she'd passed away. Then Mr. Craggs died too and Mrs. Craggs was poorly most of the time. We just had to manage."

"Sounds as if it was you who had to 'just manage'" said Joe. Dora shrugged and continued.

"Of course Charlie was away out of that house just as soon as he could be, although he did come back to see us sometimes. He was a lovely lad, Charlie."

"But," Dora added darkly, "there are some things that leave marks on people. You can't see the marks, but they're there."

This would have been a cryptic remark had it not been for what Joe had seen Charlie do to his wife behind the bar in the Oak Tree. He concentrated hard. It was difficult to see Charlie as a small frightened child when that cruel twist of skin kept rising into his mind's eye.

Dora was now really exhausted. Her eyelids fluttered and she allowed Joe to tuck her into her chair. As he made to leave, her gnarled old hand shot out and clutched his sleeve.

"Charlie's a dear boy, I can't help loving him. But you need to watch him, Joe." Before Joe could frame a reply, she added "It's not his fault. And there are things he doesn't even know, or you, but then that's for the best. But I do. I know it all. Not just ... all of it. All of them. All of you. Your Mum and Dad and Alice and Ruth. Everybody. I've lived such a long time, you see ... "

These last words were delivered in a slowing voice which slurred to a mutter before sleep finally overcame her.

Joe took the soup bowl back to the Oak Tree and left it on the bar without a word.

27

Still December 1922

It was unseasonable weather to be sitting on the bench outside the Oak Tree, which was not yet open for afternoon trade, so Joe took note of the two men sitting there. Not from round these parts, he was sure, there was something about them that was discordant. As he opened his front door one of them hailed him from across the Place.

"Hey! Excuse me?"

Joe turned and retraced his steps, being met half-way by the two men.

"You live there?"

Joe said yes automatically before he reacted to the bluntness.

"Long?"

Joe frowned. "Why do you ask?"

"We're looking for an old friend who we think moved down this way some years ago."

"Oh, from where?

"Essex."

These men were going to be sparing with their facts, Joe thought warily.

"Name?" He could be as terse as they.

"Green. Sweet Violet Green," the younger of the two men leered.

"No, sorry," said Joe with relief. Somehow he didn't think that a reunion between these two men and their friend Violet would be an altogether happy occasion.

Five foot two, blue eyes, bottle blond, thin, great legs, chip off her front tooth..."

"Nah, sorry," Joe managed. The chip off Alice's front tooth was one of her endearing features.

"You'd know most people round here, would you?"

"Oh yes, nearly everybody. I've lived here all my life." Reticent became voluble. "I know everyone who comes to the pub, everyone in the shops, everyone who lives up and down the road and in the streets around here. Everyone", he finished a little breathlessly.

Both men looked at him consideringly.

"Why don't you try the pond area up on the London Road?" he said. "It's bigger and busier than this little pocket. You might find someone there who knows your—who was it?—Violet Green."

"Thanks" said the younger of the men, "but I think we'll just hang about until the pub opens and ask around before we go on."

Joe gulped, nodded and walked unsteadily to his house.

For a moment he stood still, thinking. Then he threw on his coat and made off towards Beulah Road where school was just out. Stephen and Ruth, as they sometimes did, were walking together up the road, chatting companionably.

They were both surprised to see him, and even more surprised when he took Stephen's arm and turned him back from his route.

"Must talk to you!" his sweaty urgency was intense.

"Whoa, fella, whoa," said Stephen, "What's the matter?"

Without answering, Joe took Ruth's arm, practically dragging her into a nearby house and knocking sharply on the door.

"Flo—Mrs. Keily, can you please look after Ruth for an hour or so until I come back? It's something quite important that's come up."

Flo Keily looked surprised and very interested. "Yes of course, but what is it? Can I help?"

"Yes, by looking after Ruth. Thank you." Joe turned and hurried back to a bemused Stephen, standing on the footpath.

"Look, this is what's happening. Two ugly-looking characters are in Oak Tree Place and they're looking for Alice. They called her Violet Green but described her—her chipped tooth ..." Joe gulped and went on.

"I told them I'd never seen such a person and didn't know any Violet Greens, but they're going to stay until the pub opens and if they ask again some one's sure to tell them."

"How can you be sure they shouldn't be told?" Stephen was always so reasonable.

"A feeling. If Alice is using a false name, at least we should give her the opportunity to explain why. There must be a reason and I just don't like the look of these men."

"Right," said Stephen, accepting. "So what now?"

"I think you should go and talk to the men—they'll still probably be sitting outside the Oak Tree. Somehow tell them enough lies to get them to leave before the pub opens."

"What if I tell them that I knew a Violet Green with a chipped tooth and that she emigrated to America? Or something like that?"

"Canny!"

"Well, something like that. I'd better hurry before the pub opens."

"Go!"

Joe watched as Stephen covered the last few yards to the top of the little hill and turned into Oak Tree Place.

It was almost half an hour before Joe saw, from his lurking vantage point down Sandfield Road, the two men leave Oak Tree Place and make off down the road. He felt as if he'd been holding his breath the whole time. He left it another few minutes before galloping back to the Place, to find Stephen in the Oak Tree, placidly nursing a pint with a smug smile on his face.

"I enjoyed that!" he said. "Didn't know I had it in me to tell so many lies at once!"

"What did you say?"

"Well," said Stephen expansively, "I sauntered up and said 'Hello, you're not from round here, are you?' And then I boasted that I had lived in this area for just about ever and knew everybody."

"That's what I said!" Joe chuckled. "A pair of country bumpkins we are, know everybody, everybody's business and never travelled more than a mile in our lives!"

"Hey, this is my story!" Stephen was enjoying himself.

"They asked me about Violet, of course and I thought I'd better not recognise the name, but I did recognise the description. I said 'Oh my, yes, she used to be a neighbour of mine!' I just said neighbour, not next-door neighbour, note the finesse, my lad! A bit vague I was."

"And?"

"And—I said that I thought she'd married a widower from Devon and gone to live there."

"You could have made it Cornwall!"

"I told you, it's all about finesse!"

"Do you think they'll keep looking around here?"

"Well, if they try looking where I told them I used to live, they'll not find a lot, I can tell you. Sent them up to Beverstone Road—long enough road to keep them occupied for a while if they do follow it up, and I've never been there in my life. I hope Alice never has."

Their mutual chuckles wound down.

"Hadn't we better go and see Alice?" Stephen said.

"We certainly should. Should be interesting, don't you think?

Joe was eager for the confrontation. Alice expressed pleasure as she opened her door to them but as they entered they brought such an obvious air of portent that she was frowning as she put the kettle on for some tea.

"What is it?" she said. It was obviously something.

Joe blurted importantly "We've just seen off a couple of ruffians who were looking for you."

The bald statement had immediate effect. Alice whimpered and clutched the back of a chair. Stephen reached out to support her and helped her sit down. He pulled his chair towards hers, taking her hand between his.

"Don't worry, love. They've gone. We sent them away."

"H … h … how did you d … do that?" Alice was shivering.

"We lied to them."

"Yes, we lied to them to lead them up the garden path. And away from you," Joe added. "Who are they, Alice?"

Alice didn't answer. She still shivered and her eyes were glazed.

"Make some tea, Joe" ordered Stephen, not taking his eyes off Alice.

There was a silence broken only by the gurgle of the water into the teapot, rattle of crockery, the soft clunk of the cups and saucers on the table.

When Alice had taken the first sips of her tea, her hands still shaking, Stephen prompted softly: "Can you tell us about it?"

"I don't think I can."

"Of course you can, Alice" Joe was indignant. "We just risked a lot for your sake. The least you can do is tell us why we did."

"Joe, if Alice doesn't want to talk about it," Stephen was speaking softly, "we shouldn't try to make her do it. And," he added, "we didn't risk anything and you know it."

"No I don't know it." Joe was pugnacious. "They looked like a rough and ready pair and I reckon we've got a right to know why they wanted Alice. What if they come back? How would we get away with our lies if they found us out? Who are they anyway? We've got a right to know that. Unless," he leaned forward "unless, unless, you want us to tell them where you are, Alice, so you can deal with them yourself?"

For the first time Alice showed a spurt of emotion other than fear and distraction. "Shut up Joe."

"Yes, Joe, let's calm down here. Alice," Stephen said cajolingly, "perhaps it would help you to talk about it. But only if you want to."

"I don't want to. I don't want to. I can't!" Alice began to sob. Her tea had slopped into her saucer. Stephen stood and replaced it with another from the dresser.

"Thank you." Dully. A further protracted silence.

"Oh, this is getting us nowhere," said Joe wearily. "Alice, you need to at least tell us something about whatever it is that's going on. Otherwise we can't help you if these men—or some others, perhaps, turn up again."

Alice didn't speak but she appeared to be considering.

"I can't tell you something without telling it all and I don't really want you to know. I am too ashamed."

Stephen stroked her hand. "Alice, love, we're both grown men and we've seen and heard lots of things. I don't think you could shock us or make us think that you are shameful."

Joe knew that Alice was going to tell them. He sat down.

"When I tell you about it all I will be putting my life in your hands, do you know that? I have to you promise that you won't tell a soul, ever, ever, ever, ever."

"Of course." Their reply was in unison.

"No, that's not good enough," Alice said distractedly, "you have to swear properly, seriously. And, and—I haven't got a bible." She looked around the room as if expecting one to materialise.

"We don't need a bible, Alice," said Stephen soothingly. "How about we just promise, on our honour?"

Alice frowned and bit her lip but then consented. Stephen and Joe solemnly swore on their respective honours not to divulge to anyone what Alice was about to tell them.

She began her story which sounded as if it was going to be more of a confession. Surprisingly, it went right back to her childhood. Joe had a vague idea that she came from Colchester but apparently she was born in Croydon. So close!

"It's very bad, what I'm going to tell you. It's very bad about me and I've never told anyone the *whole* thing, not even my Johnnie. If I'm going to tell you, I want to get it all out at once, so please don't interrupt. It's going to be hard enough to tell you in the first place. When I'm finished you might not want to say anything to me anyway.

"My Dad was long gone by the time I was able to wonder about him, and Mum said good riddance to anyone who asked about him. There were other men, lots of them, and I got used to a string of Dads, some good, some bad. But I sort of got stuck with Fred when my Mum died when I was 14. Or he got stuck with me. He wasn't a bad sort, really, he didn't hit me or anything but he drank too much and hadn't had a job for years. I moved with him to Bermondsey where his son lived and there was where it all started to go dreadful." Alice broke off here and looked piteously at Stephen and Joe. "It's so awful," she said.

"Go on, just go on." Stephen was holding her hand again, but she shook it free and clasped both hands in front of her with precision. She took a breath.

"Sid was Fred's son. He had, umm, a couple of houses in the area and we had a room in one of them. It's hard, you know, in one room with a Dad who's not your Dad … But we never tried anything, you know—he wasn't a bad sort, really. I got a job in the pub on the corner, cleaning, washing, and that. But Sid said I didn't earn enough to pay the rent on the room."

Joe could see what was coming, and from the look on Stephen's face, he could too. Alice looked at them and surprisingly smiled drily.

"Oh yes, you can see what's coming, can't you? But if you think that's the point of the story, the bad part, you can think again. This is nothing."

Neither Joe nor Stephen said a word. Alice continued.

"Yes, well, there you are. Yes, I worked for Sid in one of his houses and earned the rent. All my takings went to him and he doled out enough for me to get by, but not to get away. For a while I didn't care too much—after the first few times I sort of got used to it a bit." Here Alice paused to consider the impact she was having on her listeners. Again the dry smile.

"But when Fred died—this would have been about three years after we went to Bermondsey—I decided that I'd really had enough of the life and I thought I'd try to get a real job and some money of my own. But of course this was not what Sid wanted, not at all, so he started to bash me about a bit to teach me who was boss.

"Two or three times I ran away, maybe four. Once with one of the other girls. But I always underrated what a big net of low people Sid was involved with. I'd be going on nicely p'raps for a week or even two, once I even had a job and a room, but I was never far enough away from him or his rotten mates. They always found me and tipped Sid off. He'd come and get me and there'd be another bit of rough-house to teach me a lesson. Trouble was, of course, that to get further away like I needed to do, I needed money in the first place, that I didn't have. I walked to Waterloo once and tried hopping on a train without a ticket to see how far I could get but I got tossed off even before the train started!"

Alice was warming to her story. She was assuming a bit of a swagger, a bravado and a sly pleasure in shocking. Not that he and Stephen were shocked, of course. Take more than that to shock him, anyway. But Alice was well away.

"To get out of Sid's clutches I needed money, but he wouldn't let me earn any—well, of course I was *earning* it alright, but he was pocketing it. So I began my own little secret business. I started to pinch money out of the pockets and wallets of the men I was fucking."

Joe had never ever heard this word on a woman's lips and from his expression, neither had Stephen. Joe couldn't help his indrawn breath while Stephen recovered his momentary unbalance and managed to look slightly bored, as if he heard the word every day and what's more, from women.

Their joint discomfiture obscured the admission that Alice had made. She repeated:

"I stole money from wallets and pockets ... "

She may have been going to say it again, or she may not, but both Stephen and Joe prevented it. Joe began to cough and Stephen pushed back his chair to get a drink of water.

"I stole money ... "

"How did you manage that?" Joe really didn't want to know, but any diversion would do. Funny though, the brutal language had caused Alice to become another person, one he didn't know. Her story suddenly became reality, from the voice of a stranger. She was sharper, glossier.

"Not everyone was just in and out, you know." She leered slightly. "Lots of men have a bit of a doze, you know, especially if they've been drinking and I would go through their pockets if I got the chance. A few bob here, a few bob there, I began to see my way out. I had to be careful to hide the money, but I managed to keep it safe.

"I had been on the game long enough to have a few regulars", she continued. "One of them was a man called Arthur Wallace who was a big man around town. Sid said I should be proud of myself to have hooked him as a regular. Huh! That was supposed to be praise—what a joke! Especially as Arthur drank like a fish and nearly every visit he was so drunk he couldn't even manage to get it up."

Joe blushed deep red. To hear a woman speaking in this way was almost painful. Alice's determination to shock was an outstanding success.

"Well, we managed, of course," said Alice complacently, "and he always left a happy man. After a lovely little snooze. He was my best source.

Until ... "

Alice's demeanour changed. She drew in on herself, her continuing account holding no hint of the swagger of the previous few minutes.

"Until ... Oh God. Oh God. One night Arthur woke up and found me with his wallet in my hands. He leapt right off the bed and tried to strangle me he was so furious, bashing my head against the wall and shaking me like a dog shakes a rat and then he threw me on the bed and got his hands round my neck. He was a big man and I knew he was going to throttle me —he would've done it without turning a hair. But I managed to grab the big iron knob off the bed-end—I knew it came off because that was where I stashed my money—and hit him on the side of the head. That didn't stop him so I hit him again—and again, and I think again. He sort of fell backwards and sagged a bit and there was this *terrible* sound when his head or his neck or something hit the sharp edge of the hollow pipe where I'd taken the knob off. He sort of just hung there, with blood going everywhere. He was looking at me. He was looking at me sort of calm and a bit surprised and then his eyes rolled back into his head and I knew he was dead. Knew I'd killed him."

Alice waited. Neither Joe nor Stephen said a word as the clock on the sideboard ticked more loudly than it had ever done before.

Finally it was Stephen who said "And then?"

"I ran" said Alice simply.

"I ran. All I could think of was getting away, and of course— of *course*—I was terrified. Of the police, of Arthur's sons and all those people, of Sid. Of anybody who saw me with blood all over me. I'd only managed to grab a coat as I ran to cover me up. And I had no other clothes on. And no shoes. If it had been winter I probably would have frozen to death and I think I would have thought that a good thing at the time except that it would have taken too long and they would have found me before I died and they would have killed me ... " Alice tried to giggle but it turned into a strangled hiccup.

Neither Joe nor Stephen were close to giggling.

"So I kept running, didn't I?" Alice was speaking faster and faster as she told her story, as if she'd been slashed open and it was all gushing out.

"I tried to keep to the back streets so as not to be seen, but the back streets frightened me—I imagined every time I saw someone that it was one of Arthur's sons, but every time I went on to a bigger road there were too many people to see me looking so strange in my coat and no shoes and they'd be able to remember that if the police or anyone asked them. So I was terrified whatever I did and wherever I went. I was terrified and exhausted and cold and trying to think of what I could possibly do. I found a pile of rubbish in a laneway outside a bottle yard and crawled into it, just to give me time to think. Then I got too frightened to come out again anyway, and just stayed there because I couldn't think of anything else to do. I just started to think that so many people must be looking for me by now that someone was sure to find me and that would be that. Either the police or Arthur's two sons or Sid. Sid would give me up in the blink of an eye and probably to Arthur's boys who would do dreadful things to me. I just knew that I was going to die, one way or another."

Alice paused here momentarily as she relived the events she was disclosing. Joe could see the memory in her eyes. She looked up and surprisingly she smiled slightly.

"First and last time it's ever happened to me, but then I found a knight in shining armour. Or rather, he found me, sort of."

This statement was so removed from the context of the grisly story she'd been recounting that both Stephen and Joe had some trouble adjusting.

"I stayed in that rubbish pile and shivered and cried for hours, but I gradually realised that no one had caught me yet, and if I did something, actually did something, then at least I might …

"Anyway, it was still dark when I crawled out. I knew that in daylight I'd stick out like a sore thumb in any crowd, so if I was going to get away, I had to move in the night time. As I wriggled out, I made out the shape of a man walking towards me down the lane. I panicked. It was too late to crawl back under the rubbish, so as it was dark, I just huddled down against it as close as I could, tucked my head in and hoped that in the dark I would look like part of the pile.

"The man stopped by the pile and I thought that was it, I was finished. Then there was a bit of a pause and next thing I knew, I was being pissed on. I'd really managed to look like part of the rubbish!

"I often wonder what would have happened to me if I'd managed to keep still, but it was such a surprise to feel it on the back of my coat that I sort of moved and the man noticed. He often said later that he was sure he didn't piss for days from the shock.

"Anyway, he caught hold of my coat and pulled me up and turned me round and I think—I know—he was pretty astonished to find I was young and blonde—I was blonde then—and *not* the worse for drink. And practically naked, of course.

"I was all over the place, but he was just apologetic for what he'd done. He was really embarrassed, trying to wipe the back of my coat clean to make amends. I just stood there and I must say that the feeling of his hands and being looked after, even if it was just wiping piss off my coat, made me feel wobbly. I started to cry again.

"Look, he was nobody's fool and knew that there was something pretty wrong going on there, but he was, as I say, my knight in shining armour and he didn't even ask. Not then. He buttoned up my coat, put his arm around me really tight and walked me out of the laneway and across a couple more streets to a little place that did rooms and he knocked and knocked until the woman came and he got a room. She didn't want to let us in, but he must have given her money or something because next thing I knew we were in this little room and I was safe and off the street and nobody knew where I was. But I couldn't stop crying.

"J … he was so gentle. He took off my coat and told me to get into the bed, but I didn't want to because I was covered in blood. It had all dried by then, but I was scared I'd get on the sheets. So in the end I stood in the wash bowl on the floor and he washed me down. Just like a mother would do to a baby. And he never touched me. I mean, he touched me, but he never *touched* me. I scrubbed my hands and fingernails till they were sore and finally did get into the bed. He climbed in beside me and I thought I was going to have to perform then, but he didn't ask and suddenly I was as tired as I could ever remember being and fell asleep just like that. I'm going to make another cup of tea."

Both Joe and Stephen looked up in surprise at the diversion. Joe could see from Stephen's face that he had been as engrossed as him in the unfolding story.

"I'll get it" they almost spoke in unison.

"No, let me stop talking for a few moments and get another pot. My throat's really dry."

"Not surprised, Alice. I've never heard you talk so long before."

"I've never told this story before, Joe."

"That's not surprising either."

"You can see why I swore you both to keep quiet, can't you? I've put my life in your hands by telling you."

"Oh Alice, your life is safe with us!" Stephen looked so earnestly at Alice that Joe felt excluded.

Alice just smiled slightly. Settled in her chair again with the fresh tea, she took up her tale.

"Yes, well. Next morning I hardly knew where I was when I woke up. My knight in shining armour was already awake, but he was laying on his side there just looking at me. Well, I felt that I owed him such a lot and I didn't have much else to thank him with, so I reached out and felt for him. Look, you don't have to know those bits, just be told that I had to work pretty hard there. But he was very grateful for my efforts in the end."

Joe wondered if there could be any more casual details of this sort—he felt he'd had more than a good dose of them at this stage.

"In fact." Alice had not paused, "he was ridiculously grateful. He cried even. Seems that, although he was a grown man, it was the first time he'd ever managed to do it. With a woman."

Alice looked at them mockingly, enjoying their discomfiture.

"So by the time we got all that out of the way," she continued "it was the middle of the morning and I was no better off then I'd been last night really, with no clothes and nowhere to go. I was washed clean of the blood, though, that *was* an improvement.

"Of course I wasn't going to tell my knight the truth about the predicament I was in, so I told him a cock-and-bull story about my mother's boyfriend bullying and beating me and putting me up to his pals from time to time for their use as they pleased and then last night him coming into my bed while I was asleep, and that I hit him (that was the blood) but he tried to throttle me (that was the bruises on my neck) and I managed to escape and he'd now be looking for me and my mother was a terrible drunkard so she never knew what was going on and this boyfriend of hers had lots of friends who were thugs and crooks and they'd be looking for me too and if I had some money and some clothes I would be well away from there.

"It was," Alice continued, "a very convincing story."

"Just missing some of the facts," said Stephen agreeably.

"Yes. Well I thought that I might push my luck and get some money as a result of this sad tale, but my knight had other ideas. He thought I was wonderful and wanted to help to save me. And he had a plan then that I didn't know about. He went out and bought knickers and clothes and shoes for me. This was the first time in my life that I had had new clothes from the skin out and even if they weren't what I would have chosen, they fitted well enough and I felt like a human again when I put them on. And so much better.

"J … he decided that we both had better get out of London. If that's what it took I was pleased enough for him to come with me and really it made it a bit easier on me to be one of a couple and not a lone woman. So we took a train to Brighton. We spent a week in Brighton in a boarding house by the seaside and it was one of the happiest weeks of my life. I managed to put Bermondsey out of my mind for most of the time and strangely enough it seemed that J … my knight actually adored me. Very heady stuff, to be adored, you know. Makes you look at life in a different way."

"Look," said Joe abruptly, "why don't you stop all this 'knight' nonsense and call the man by his name—that we've guessed by now, I think. It was my Uncle Johnnie, wasn't it?"

Alice looked a little crestfallen.

"I was going to tell you," she said.

"Well, I've saved you the trouble." Joe was pleased with himself. "Did you ever tell him the truth about your meeting?"

"No."

"Why not?"

"It never seemed the right time and anyway … things changed. Let me go on.

"Go on then."

"We got married, of course. In the beginning I'd told Johnnie that my name was Alice. That was the name of one of the other girls who worked for Sid and she was my friend. She was pretty sick you could tell and then she just sort of disappeared one time and never came back so I thought, because I knew all about her, that I'd pinch her name. I didn't want him being able to tie me up with anything that might be in the newspapers about Violet Green, so I became Alice Barnes to him and then I became Alice Barlow when I married him. I was a bit worried about coming to Oak Tree Place, you know. It's only eight or nine or so miles from Bermondsey, but once I saw what a sleepy little place it was, so different from Bermondsey, I felt that no one from there would ever think of looking for me here."

"It took them a while," said Joe. "Do you have any idea why they might suddenly have thought of looking for you here?"

"Yes." Alice was quiet. "Yes, I think I know. I caught the bus back from the High Street one day last week when I had a lot of shopping to carry and a bus coming in the other direction was stopped at the clock tower as our bus went past slowly. I saw a man looking straight at me and I knew, I just knew, that something would come of that look."

"I hope," said Stephen, "that Joe and I were clever enough to make them think that whoever was on that bus was mistaken about you."

"But no, we might've done the opposite," Joe interjected "because we more or less confirmed that Alice *had* lived in the area! Even if you said she'd moved to Dorset."

"Devon," said Stephen abstractedly.

"Not as clever as we thought!"

"Oh dear."

Stephen's soft exclamation was so mild and so different from the substance and language of Alice's (or was that Violet's?) story that it sounded strange, but reassuringly normal. But nothing here was normal, or ever could be again. How could he look at Alice with the same eyes?

28

Still December 1922

They had left. Looking at her differently from when they came in. Then they'd been intrigued and questioning, now they were stunned and disbelieving.

Alice felt light, empty but strangely triumphant. They'd never thought she was so … interesting. Just the same old Alice, they'd thought. Well, they didn't any more.

But *she'd* never thought she'd ever tell anyone about all that stuff; she'd never even told Johnnie. But that had been a good thing, considering.

Who was it that said about confession being good for the soul? She didn't know about a soul, but the emptiness she felt wasn't unpleasant, it was sort of restful. Restful with a bit of an edge to it though.

Arthur's sons. Sure to be them looking for her, and Stephen and Joe had messed up tricking them away. They'd probably be back.

The feeling of lightness curdled into the old panic. This was closer than they'd ever been. When she came to the Place with Johnnie she was as nervous as a kitten, sure they'd find her. Over the years the feeling just got commonplace and she began to be able to forget it sometimes for days at a time. Oh, she still examined every face that passed her window, but it was cursory and just an old habit. She'd almost—almost—forgotten the reason.

Oh God, just as well she dawdled through the shopping. She could have so easily marched back into the Place to be confronted by the two of them sitting outside the pub. Her heart thumped loudly in her chest and the vestiges of her feeling of lightness and difference evaporated.

She'd better stay indoors and watch the window carefully.

29

Six weeks later, mid-February 1923

Oak Tree Place became different. No longer the placid site of Joe's upbringing, not even the wrenching scene of his homecoming, but a place where strangers might lurk or be anticipated with dread.

Joe was wary and vigilant. He did not wish Alice so ill as to have her discovered, but care of his own family was his priority and the boyish irritation he had felt for Alice was now edged with hostility that this new situation was of her making.

Joe and Stephen had discussed the likelihood of a return of the two men, who Alice was sure were Arthur's sons. They talked of the advisability of warning other residents of the Place, but Alice begged them not to as it would just draw attention to her plight, even if they told a plausible lie about the reason. So it was just the three of them, watching, waiting, careful all the time. It was damned tiring, thought Joe.

He never came out of his door now without a quick glance up and down the Place. He thought of locking his door but the explanations required for that would be too difficult. He made do with closing it very firmly behind him.

If it was damned tiring for him, he allowed that it must be very damned tiring for Alice, at home in the Place for most of the day while he and Stephen were away at their work. But it was her problem, he thought righteously.

Then his watchfulness sometimes wavered as he had other things on his mind and they were much more pleasant things.

Just six weeks after their wedding Lydia told him he was going to be a father as well as a husband. Joe was ecstatic. Ecstatic at the thought of fatherhood and ecstatic that this was something that would bind Lydia to him even more than marriage.

"Are you pleased, Joe?" Lydia looked at him fixedly.

"My darling girl, I have never been so pleased about anything in my life. It's all I could ask for, you and Ruth and a baby."

He paused for a moment.

"I just wish my Mum and Dad could be here, that's all."

"I do too," said Lydia. Joe didn't know whether she was referring to her own parents, or to his.

Lydia's mother had sent a tumult of letters to her daughter in the weeks before the wedding, and she had come twice to Alice's house to speak to her daughter. Each contact and communication had been upsetting for Lydia, but she remained adamant in her decision to marry Joe and stay in Oak Tree Place. Mrs. Mason had treated Joe with chilly contempt and viewed the Place with pained distaste. The letters had of course entreated Lydia to come to her and not to go on with her sudden and foolish plans to marry him. That would've been what he expected.

On one occasion Lydia did in fact visit her mother, an undertaking that made Joe anxious because he thought it would give Mrs. Mason time, space and surroundings to persuade Lydia to abandon him. But Lydia walked determinedly to the railway station early in the morning and came home in the late afternoon pale and drained. She was very quiet in the succeeding days and disinclined to talk. But she didn't leave.

She was composed and seemed to be accepting of her severely reduced circumstances. Their wedding was a quiet affair but the day was filled with friends and loving kindness. All the friends were Joe's.

Joe's happiness on his wedding day was filtered through a fine screen of anxiety for his new wife. He felt a huge sense of responsibility, much more than when he had taken on the job of caring for Ruth. Poor darling girl, trustingly putting herself into his hands for the rest of her life. Joe's heart was bursting with love, pride and a determination to make everything right for her again. He would improve his lot and be worthy of her. He would build such a life for his beautiful wife that she would never regret marrying him.

Lydia had looked pale but very beautiful at the wedding and if she seemed subdued, this was completely understandable. She had been through such a lot, and marriage was a solemn undertaking.

Joe felt a surge of such protective love that his eyes pricked with tears. His two darling girls, Lydia and Ruth.

And now there was to be another. He had a feeling of certainty that this baby would be a girl. His household would be full of his women. Joe bathed in complacent bliss.

Alice's reaction to the news was rather too knowing and canny for his liking, but he blithely ignored this and marched on to tell Stephen, who congratulated him warmly. He told Ida and Len and avoided the yearning in Ida's eyes. He told Dora who clucked delightedly, he told Ellen Galvin who said she'd start knitting immediately, and finally, because his joy overcame his aversion, he went to the Oak Tree and told the Mrs. Craggses, old and young, and Charlie.

"When is the baby due, dear?" asked the elder Mrs. Craggs.

"September," said Joe baldly.

This was the earliest date that a baby could be born to him and Lydia if it had been conceived in wedlock, which, as Lydia explained to him, it hadn't. This baby was the result of the first night she had come to him.

Joe thought it entirely appropriate that their child should be the outcome of that night, but he understood Lydia's reserve on the subject and her reckoning that they could explain away an early baby when the time came. Joe was sure they could; in truth he didn't care a scrap.

◆

Joe was glad when he had finished the cradle he was making at work because he didn't like to tax Lydia with his absence from home. She was in fact not coping very well with expecting and tended to a listlessness that was disquieting. Several times he had come home from his work to find her red-eyed from obvious weeping, which distressed Joe mightily. When he asked her what was wrong, no answer was ever forthcoming.

Joe understood that these were difficult times and redoubled his efforts to make life happy and easy for her. She did not protest when he insisted on performing those menial household tasks which were now her responsibility, although of course Joe felt himself an expert. This often extended to cooking, of which lamentably but understandably Lydia had no experience and did not seem all that inclined to learn. Joe cheerfully took it on, and more often than not found himself preparing shopping lists for Lydia so that essential items would not be forgotten.

It was only when she was late in delivering the shopping to their house one day that Joe became aware that these lists were being passed on to Alice.

"I don't like being seen in this state," said Lydia irritably when Joe tentatively suggested that Alice should not be burdened this way. "I feel foolish and fat and ugly."

Joe perhaps should not have laughed, but the proposition was so ridiculous that he thought that she must have been joking. He certainly should not have laughed.

"It's alright for you, Joe Barlow. You men. It's alright for you. What do you know? You just cause all the trouble then sit back and let us suffer. What do you care? You don't know how it feels—you'll never know how it feels. Everybody looking at you, everybody wondering about you … "

Lydia dissolved into tears.

Joe glanced uneasily towards Ruth, who was sitting at the table. To his surprise, she exchanged with him a look of complicity that was so adult, so commiserating, that it took him aback. He found himself pacifying Lydia almost absently as he allowed the realisation to unfold that his baby sister was no longer a baby. He smiled.

"What's there to smile about, Joe? Don't you dare laugh at me!" squeaked Lydia through her tears. Joe pulled her close so that she couldn't see his face and felt a surge of tenderness. He reached out his arm towards Ruth, who willingly allowed herself to be enfolded.

"Well I don't know how I'm going to manage with only two arms when the baby comes," he said laughing.

"I'll hold the little baby, Joe" said Ruth.

30

Two months later.
April 1923

Joe began to allow himself to feel a cautious optimism that his day-nightmares might be leaving him.

He prodded the optimism only lightly so that he didn't tempt their return but it had been some weeks now without a visit from the black horror during the day. The nights were a different kettle of fish. The dreams were still as vivid and terrible and he dragged himself into wakefulness still flailing and gasping. The propinquity of the marriage bed, so blissful on the one hand, was also cause of anxiety.

Before their marriage he had diffidently suggested to Lydia that he might be prone to bad dreams. He had said nothing about the day-time tides of panic. Lydia had seemed unimpressed, saying that she herself had bad dreams sometimes and didn't everyone? Joe supposed so.

It was only two nights after their wedding that Lydia was made to realise that what she had thought of as bad dreams were pale things. Joe erupted from his black sucking suffocation into the silvery moonlight of their bedroom with ragged gasps of thankfulness to see Lydia drawn back into a corner of the bed with the covers clutched under her chin, eyes wide and frightened.

Sweating and still panting, Joe reached out a shaky hand to Lydia, saying hoarsely that he'd just had a nightmare.

"I can see that, Joe," she said tightly as she ignored his hand and shrugged back under the covers. "Are you alright now?" An afterthought.

Joe turned on his back and gazed at the cracks in the ceiling. He didn't answer until his trembling stopped some minutes later.

"Lydia?" It was plain that she was not asleep but she took time to reply.

"Yes?"

"I did tell you that I could have nightmares sometimes."

"Yes."

"I'm sorry that I frightened you."

"That's alright." It was plain that it was not.

"I've had the nightmares since the war."

"Oh."

"I think a lot of us soldiers have them."

Lydia turned on her back, too. "Why?" Then she added petulantly "You *frightened* me, Joe."

"I'm sorry, sweetheart, but it's not something I can control. I would if I could"

"Why do you have them, Joe—do you know?"

"Oh yes, I know." He was heavily ironic.

Lydia leaned on an elbow and looked at Joe, then flopped back down into the bed and said "Well go on then, tell me."

"Another time, love. Not now."

"But I'm awake now and I'll not get back to sleep easily. Tell me why you have such bad dreams. Tell me so I can go back to sleep."

The moon had been overtaken by cloud and the room was dark, but not as dark as Joe knew dark could be. Again he demurred and Lydia gave up asking, already drooping again despite her protestations. Within five minutes her breathing indicated that she was sleeping.

As was usual after his nightmares, sleep was not remotely within Joe's reach. He knitted his fingers behind his head and looked at the pale outline of the window. He wondered if he would ever tell anyone the nightmare story. He doubted it. He'd never want anyone to know how it really had been, so he had no option but to keep it to himself. The stories that his mates sometimes volunteered—usually after a few pints—couldn't come close to the one he held close to his chest.

Better not to think about telling anyone, really. Better not.

Not even Sam, of course. He could talk about anything with Sam, except *that*, because of the shame. Joe curled up with the anguish that overtook him every time he thought of Sam, and tears pricked his eyes.

He straightened himself again and lay on his back. Oh Sam, Sam. If it wasn't for Sam …

◆

He was resting—to use the word loosely—behind the lines on that day. He had finished cleaning his gear and was sitting against the wheel of a cart, snatching a moment of relative peace in the twilight. He must have dozed momentarily because he didn't hear the initial buzz of activity.

It was not until the CSM was barking at Sergeant Trenerry right beside the cart to get 30 men together at the double and report to the timber depot that he scrambled to his feet inwardly cursing that he'd been found at the wrong time and in the wrong place. The sergeant yelled "You! Timber duty! Now!" and he groaned but trotted the few hundred yards to the stock of timbers used for shoring up the tunnels. More disgruntled soldiers joined him, grumbling that this was sappers' work, where the bloody hell were they?

"They've all gone forward with timbers already, private!" said the sergeant, appearing suddenly. "This is an emergency. There's been an accident underground and more bodies are needed to get timbers to the tunnel, even puny bodies like yours, so get to it and load that bloody cart!"

Joe began to hurl the timbers on to the cart with immediate frenzied thoughts of Sam. Was he underground? Was he in the dark horror of a collapsed tunnel, gasping for breath, choking? Joe tried vainly to remember when he had last seen Sam and what his shifts were. Couldn't think. Just get the timbers to the tunnel.

Before the cart was fully loaded, Joe was dragging at the harness of the mule, urging it forward over the deeply rutted ground. A hundred yards or so from the tunnel location, the cart was unloaded again and the timbers manhandled towards the tunnel mouth. Joe stumbled and cursed as he part-carried, part-dragged the crudely pre-cut setts towards the strangely small and inconspicuous tunnel entrance. Men teemed in and out, sandbags were dragged out and thrown aside. Joe stood in the middle of the melee, gasping for breath.

"Don't stand about, you men, get those setts down to the men at the level!" The authority in the voice from just inside the tunnel entrance was unmistakable, even if the rank was indistinguishable. The men in Joe's work party stumbled forward with their loads, some curious, most blindly obedient. Joe lurched forward with them but risked a question to the officer as he passed.

"Who's down there?"

"None of your bloody business, private. Move on!"

"Sam Curtis?" he blurted.

The officer had been turning away, but he looked back sharply.

"I said none of your bloody business!"

It was enough. It had to be that Sam was down there. Sam, strong and fearless, was even now being pressed down into the earth, unable to breathe, unable to move. Joe hitched the timber and blundered into the descent.

Immediately it was dark. Noises were absorbed as if with blotting paper, foreign smells pervaded, stale air made him breathless, a humid damp made him sweat. He could not see ahead, there were too many men in front. Too many men behind.

He was blind and deaf and it was just pressure and shuffling bodies. Down they staggered. Each step down increased the pressure in his head, pinched his nostrils, swelled his throat. He began to gasp, began to suffocate. The walls were caving in on him, coming closer with every step down that he took. He couldn't see them but he could feel them, dark murderous crumbling monsters, reaching out like waves on a beach, a little bit further with each drumbeat in his head.

Closer, closer. The steps were interminable and he stumbled now on each one. The sett being carried behind him jabbed into his back and he fell into the man in front of him. The blood was now

pounding in Joe's ears so loudly that he didn't hear the oath of pro-
test. He began to whimper. He knew he was going to die.

"What's the matter, mate?"

The man behind him had bent to make the query sympatheti-
cally but the voice in his ear boomed like an explosion.

He dropped the timbers he was carrying, put his head down
and butted and punched his way back up the stepped incline to the
mouth of the tunnel. The cries and curses that followed him up were
just a wave of sound and the buffeting he received from timbers and
bodies was unfelt.

He erupted from the tunnel and ran like a drunkard, dragging
air into his lungs. The sour smell of the trenches was like perfume.
He dragged at the neck of his tunic to allow the cool night air on to
his skin.

The shame came immediately. As his breathing calmed, he was
consumed with it. Sam was going to die and he was doing nothing
to help.

◆

Joe stared at the ceiling, the shame still bright and palpable. He
turned his head to look at Lydia, sleeping soundly, hands curled
under her chin. What sort of man had she entrusted herself to? A
gibbering coward. A coward who didn't have the courage to help
his best friend.

◆

With returning calm, the guilt increased. His exit from the tun-
nel had gone relatively unnoticed in the seething activity and he
cowered behind an empty cart at a distance but just within sight
of the tunnel entrance, watching and ashamed. But he knew he
couldn't go down there again.

Sam, Sam, Sam. The thought of what he might be suffering was
enough to start his heart pounding again.

He began to cry like a baby, anxiety and shame combined in
the helpless tears. He sobbed feebly. He'd managed his fears in
the trenches under fire, he'd managed his fears of gas, of snipers,

of bombs, without panicking and bloody crying, but he could not go under the ground. What the hell was the matter with him? Hundreds of men no better or worse than him did it every day. He was just a coward through and through. Sam, Sam, Sam.

The cart he was sheltering behind was unloaded and empty. Self-preservation gradually impinged on his misery as he began to consider how best to cover his cowardice. He emerged cautiously from behind the cart and with a quick look around, he began to lead the tired horse back towards the timber depot, passing other carts hauled by horses and mules and some by soldiers. He passed the cart he'd helped to load such a short time ago, skewed in the soft ground where they'd abandoned it in favour of manpower. Such a short time ago.

Sam, Sam, Sam.

The horse's soft breath was soothing; a strange bucolic note in nightmare-land. Joe rubbed his face against the animal's neck and thought of the fire-engine horses in Oak Tree Field. He gratefully let his mind wander and his steps stutter as the horse plodded on and led the way with measured progress. The moon emerged and turned the scene into a mirror of its own landscape. Soldiers passed him in ones, twos, groups, looming and waning like spectres. His mind played tricks; he saw the ghost of Sam in the distance, striding towards him through the mud, hand raised in greeting. He blinked and squeezed his eyes shut at the pain of the apparition.

It was just a stray shell, single and unexpected. At the last possible moment the whine broke through Joe's preoccupation and he made to throw himself into an abandoned communications trench beside the boggy track he'd been treading. He leapt over the banked-up mud that the track had created, tried to take cover, tried to cleave to the soil, but it was too late; he was still mid-air as the explosion split his eardrums. There was an instant in which he felt grateful for the redemptive pain but he was not aware of the rag-doll tangle of his limbs and the hurling of his body a good ten yards along the trench, which collapsed behind him like an enclosing blanket.

Collapsed behind him, over him, beyond him. Bits of cart, bits of horse, bits of nameless crud thudded down into the mud.

Then it was quiet for an instant, before the shouting and the running.

"Casualties?" shouted a voice.

"Horse, for one," replied another.

"Someone in charge of it?"

"Must have been. No sign."

"Poor bastard."

"Yeah."

Another voice. "Casualties over here!"

Retreating footsteps.

Joe heard none of this, nor did he hear the approaching footsteps, urgent but slipping and stumbling in the mud and detritus.

"Joe? Joe? Joe!"

"No one here, mate."

"I bloody saw him. I saw him. He dived into the trench. I saw him."

"A goner, mate."

"Give us a bloody hand, will you? Fucking DIG!"

Joe was deaf to all of this, but consciousness returned. At first it was as slow as the breaking dawn, but as he became aware of his position, it returned with a rush of panic unlike anything he had ever experienced. He was curled into an untidy ball and unable to move, his head tucked into his chest and his spine resisting the inexorable downward pressure of whatever the hell it was on top of him. He remembered the shell's explosion, remembered his headlong flight and he knew just where he was and what was likely to be on top of him. And how much of it. Briefly he thought of the justice of his fate, but the thought was fleeting as the panic took over. He wriggled, but this caused incredible pain to his back, where something resting on it had allowed a little pocket of air to be contained under his body. But nothing was static—he could feel mud dribbling in at the sides of his sanctuary and the weight on his back was intense; he knew he could not hold it up for long. He screamed.

Told himself that screaming was to show rescuers that he was there, but in fact he was screaming in sheer terror, the terror of a realised nightmare. He stopped pretending and screamed and screamed and screamed. He knew he was going to die and he would never be found and his body would rot here in this fucking foreign mud.

He stopped eventually, after he didn't know how long. Sobbed for a while, then screamed again, his throat raw. The air under his belly was hot and heavy, his knees slipped out from under him with an enormous shift of the mud above, and he held himself only on his forearms. He was finally silent as he waited for the strength to leave his numbing arms and then it would all collapse around him, if he didn't suffocate first. He was not calm, his mind was clear and he was terrified. Past screaming, he whimpered softly, like an animal. He couldn't feel lower body, his arms ached unbearably and he began to slip.

The weight on his back increased suddenly and unbearably. As his arms gave way and his head was propelled into the mud, the breath was pushed out of his body with a last despairing grunt.

The pressure on his back increased, then lifted. He still could not hear anything—would not again for weeks—but he could feel a lightening, feel activity. Then there was a blast of air that he sucked into his flabby lungs as he felt hands on his body, twisting, pulling, extracting him from the tomb. He heard himself, inside his head, mewling like a kitten. With difficulty he stopped and tried to get up on his hands and knees. It hurt like hell, but miraculously everything worked. One leg, two, both arms. Hands were pulling at him now, there were faces, there was a face …

"Sam."

◆

Joe turned on his side, stretched his legs and tried vainly to sleep again.

31

*The following month.
May, 1923*

Lydia would only stroll at night on Joe's arm, and had only begun to do so at all now that the weather had become a little warmer with the approach of summer. Tonight, though, there was a definite chill and Lydia shivered. Joe drew her closer but she pulled away.

"What is it, sweetheart? What's wrong?" Joe stopped walking and looked down at her anxiously.

Lydia pulled her arm from his angrily and stamped her foot.

"For pity's sake stop asking me what's wrong!" she almost hissed. "Can't you *imagine* what's wrong? Can't you *imagine* how I feel? You just keep asking and asking and clucking around like an old hen and never try to *think* about me and how I feel! I'm cold and I'm fed up!"

Joe was stung but unable to think of a response that was defensive as well as placating. He stood dumbly as Lydia continued her assault, her voice rising shrilly.

"I am big and fat and ugly and living in a little horrid house and I have to look after your precious sister and clean and cook and do awful things that I wasn't brought up to do and I have to cope with being this way and my mother is a selfish beast, my father's shamed and dead and it's all too unfair and horrible!" Early in this diatribe Lydia had started to sob and the last words were almost lost in a wail.

Joe was still dumb. Strangely the part of Lydia's word-torrent that resonated in his head was that she objected to Ruth. Unable to frame any sort of retort, he took her unresisting hand and placed it through his arm. He turned for home and they did not speak again on the way until almost at the Place, when Lydia said with weary resignation "I'm sorry Joe."

There had been other small outbursts, but this one was not so easy to deny or to recover from. Lydia seemed tiredly disinclined to do so and Joe was for the first time unable to dismiss it all as a symptom of her condition, even though he wanted to believe that was the cause. The words hung in the air between them.

Joe examined the facts for the hundredth time as he walked to Jackson's in the early chill of the following morning. She really wasn't being reasonable, he thought. Everyone had worked so hard to make her welcome, to save her trouble and to ease the discomfort of her pregnancy, mind and body. It was hardly fair to turn on him when her situation was of her own choosing—she could have gone with her mother, or something …

But it was her choice to come to him. She had chosen him and he had been glad, so glad, that she had done so. He was still glad. The thought of his previous depression and yearning was still close enough to remind him that his present situation was infinitely more pleasing to him. It was how he wanted his life to be. It was. And he was still determined to make it better, for Lydia and for Ruth and the baby.

The hurt of Lydia's mention of Ruth still discomfited him, however, so one decision he did make was to ask Alice to take more of the responsibility for Ruth before school as well as after. The concern that had been uppermost in mind so recently, the anxiety about Alice's pursuers, had diminished as his own domestic concerns bloomed to occupy his mind.

It seemed to be an ideal solution, really, until the baby came. Things would be different then, of course.

Alice seemed delighted. Her eyes narrowed briefly as Joe explained the situation, or at least his Lydia-extenuating version of it.

"Of course, Joe," she said coolly, "Lydia needs her rest and I can cope with Ruth far better than she can in her condition. She's sometimes a handful," she added proprietorially as she straightened Ruth's hair ribbon.

So it began again, Ruth to Alice in the early morning light, collected from Alice in the dusk.

But Lydia's listlessness and lack of interest in any of her surroundings only increased. She often remained in her bed for most of the day, and Joe knew that she cried often. She insisted that she was uncomfortable at night, so Joe slept on the floor beside the bed. He was wild with anxiety as Lydia remained sad and more and more distant.

Except for the day that, walking home from work, he saw the dark green Napier coming up the road towards him. He stopped as it drove past, the driver muffled in cap, goggles, scarf and leather coat. Joe paused and watched it disappear down the High Street.

When he opened the door Lydia looked grim and was again tearful and listless, sighing audibly as she moved the pots on the stove. Joe put an arm around her and guided her gently to a seat on the sofa, feeling pulsing surge of the baby as it moved. Lydia pulled away sharply.

"Good day?" he asked.

"No."

"Did anyone come to see you?"

"What do you mean?"

He couldn't help himself. "In a green motor car, perhaps?"

"What do you mean?"

I thought I saw a green Napier coming out of Oak Tree Place as I was coming up the road," he lied.

"Nonsense" Lydia flared. "What *are* you talking about?" He face was flushed but she brimmed with righteousness. "No motor car of any description has been *in* Oak Tree Place today to my knowledge."

She couldn't resist adding "As if a car like that would have any business here!"

She'd gone a bit too far and Joe saw her check herself quickly.

"But did you have any visitors?" Joe pushed, knowing he shouldn't.

It was welling up out of Lydia anyway. "Yes I did. An old friend of the family came to call. Came to call! How grotesque! I was so ashamed to receive him in a place like this. I was so ashamed! And he didn't bring his motor car into Oak Tree Place, Mister, so there. He left it somewhere half-civilised and walked here. You did not see a green Napier coming into or out of this wretched Place, so you're lying, aren't you?"

He was silent. Lydia hissed. "He left. I could see the disgust on his face. I was so ashamed!" she repeated.

"You chose to be here," Joe finally managed weakly.

"Yes. Yes. Yes I did." The fight was gone and the statement was delivered in measured descending beats, as if in capitulation to a ghastly fate. She sat heavily.

Joe was dumb. He ached for the words to mend the situation but found none. The green Napier zoomed in his brain.

32

Two months later.
July 1923

The windows of the Oak Tree were open; the July twilight wafted in a gentle summer breeze. Steven was speaking and Joe and Len were listening.

"… North End Hall earlier this year, really interesting. Do you fancy Canada at all?"

"Do you?" asked Len.

"I don't know really," said Stephen, "but I am thinking about different things. Sick to death of the nasty aftermath of the teachers' strike and the attitude of the Council with all its puffed-up characters. They didn't give a fig for the teachers or the children."

"So you're really thinking about emigrating?"

"Might do. Yes, really might. This chap Andrews made Canada sound quite attractive."

"Pretty cold. I'd choose somewhere warmer if I were you"

"He said the cold in Canada is dry and healthy and there's more room between houses and wide streets for air circulation so less illness, too."

"Still cold," said Len.

"Lots of work. Good money if you're prepared to work for it."

"So you'd give up teaching?" asked Joe.

"Might do. Want to be able to consider everything. Open to offers!" he laughed.

"I don't know why you don't just make the best of what you have here!' Len said irritably.

Stephen looked at him in surprise and then realisation. He was diverting in his response. "I only have my poor sad self to care for, not a lovely wife like you have, Len. You wouldn't want to subject Ida to a frontier life!"

"She'd go if I wanted to," said Len ungraciously.

Joe was stung on Ida's behalf. "Well it's not something that she'll have to face, is it, Len?"

"Look, if I wanted to emigrate I could and I would, even with my foot. I'd manage all right. I just happen to think I have a duty to stay here and support the country I fought for."

To Joe's knowledge Len had not done a day's work since his return from France. His disability also made it next to impossible for him to be considered a suitable immigrant to any country. And he'd shot himself in the bloody foot! Joe felt the familiar exasperation rise but smothered a sharp response and turned again to Stephen.

"Well, good luck with your investigations, then, mate. Let's know how you're thinking, eh?"

The small figure of Ruth burst through the door of the pub.

"Joe, come quickly, please. Lydia wants you." There was panic in her voice.

Joe was halfway to the door before he realised he still had his glass in hand. He turned and ran back to the bar. Turned again. Once out of the door, he ran towards his house, Ruth scuttling behind him.

Lydia was pacing backwards and forwards, breathing deeply; as Joe came through the door she turned from the other side of the room, hissing wordlessly through clenched teeth.

"What's wrong, dearest? What is it?"

"If I knew what was wrong I'd do something about it!" Lydia flared.

"I'll call the doctor."

"*NO!* It will pass, it will pass."

"What is it that you're feeling? Where's the pain? Is it the baby?"

"Of course it's not the baby, it's not due for weeks!"

"Perhaps it's early?"

"NO!"

Lydia's pacing became more manic, the room was too small for her. Joe pursued her and held her as tightly as her belly would allow, catching her hands in his. "Darling, I must do something for you. The doctor … shall I call Alice?"

"NO!"

Joe caught sight of Ruth's pale face as she almost cowered in the corner of the room.

"Ruthie love, go and fetch Auntie Alice, will you please?"

"NO! NO! NO! It's not coming yet. It's not coming!"

"No, sweetheart, of course it's not. Let's just get you to bed and you'll feel better."

"I need to walk. It's not the baby, it's not."

"Let me support you, darling. We'll walk if that's what you want."

Ruth had left the door wide open and Alice came running in. She took in the situation and in what seemed like an instant had Lydia pointed upstairs, Ruth next door and Joe making tea.

"What is it?" Joe had managed to ask.

"What on earth do you think it is, you silly man?" she answered scathingly.

Lydia was still saying "No, no no, no" as she lurched upstairs with Alice's arm around her.

"Oh yes it is, dear," said Alice.

The midwife lived less than five minutes away at a brisk walk, Joe covered the distance in two. It took just another minute for her to collect her things and trot after Joe to the Place. Joe was instructed to stay downstairs as the midwife creaked up them.

For Joe it was an anguished hour later that Alice appeared to ask calmly for two more cups of tea and a glass of water.

"What's happening?" His hand shook as he poured the water from the waiting kettle on to the tea leaves. "Tell me please what's happening. Is Lydia going to be alright? Is it the baby coming early? Is Lydia alright? Do you need the doctor?"

"Calm down, Joe. Yes, Lydia's going to be alright, I'm sure. It's the baby coming, that's all."

"But it's so early!"

Alice gave him a sideways look and Joe remembered inadequately that the baby was always going to be six weeks earlier than they'd told everyone. But this—his mind couldn't do the sums—was too early, surely?

"I'm sure it's going to be alright, Joe." Alice took the tray up the stairs with annoying calmness.

33

Some hours later

It was a boy. Joe was summoned up the stairs by Alice as the midwife packed away her daunting tools of trade. They both looked proprietarily at the swaddled baby as Joe leaned over the cradle full of joy and wonder.

Lydia leaned back on her pillows. She looked incredibly beautiful to Joe, her hair damp and curling, face pale and eyes dark with exhaustion. He kissed her carefully on her forehead and squeezed her hand. She responded with a wan smile.

The baby was beautiful, of course. Perfect in every detail, plump and bonny. His eyes were opening and shutting slowly as he began to take in his new world. They were dark and blue. His hair was vestigial as it curled in damp small spirals on his perfectly-formed little head, but it shone in the light from the lamp and looked like gold. Joe's big hand cupped over it.

"You are so brave and clever, sweetheart. He's beautiful."

"Yes, he is."

"A boy."

"Yes?"

"I thought he'd be a girl."

"Well he's not."

"It's not that I wanted—"

"I should think not."

"Just thought it would be—"

"Well he's *not*, he's a boy and he's going to be called Henry."

"Henry?"

"Henry Ronald—Ronald for my father."

"And Henry for ?" It was not a name that Joe would have thought of. It seemed far too big for such a small baby.

"I just like it." Firmly.

Joe privately thought he'd call his son Harry and was more than content.

The morning, when it dawned, was bright and fair, entirely suited to Joe's euphoria. He hung over the cradle waiting for Henry-Harry to wake, delighting in his body as he was lifted and changed and watching with awe as Lydia fed him from the bottle, her engorged breasts covered with cabbage leaves to soothe the anticipated swelling. The faint odor of decomposition was at odds with the perfume of baby-powder and milk. With the baby sleeping again, she leaned back into her pillows and closed her eyes. Joe crept out of the room.

Ruth had been allowed the day off school after the disruptions of the previous night, and she was sitting at the kitchen table, swinging her legs and waiting for him.

"I'm the baby's auntie, aren't I Joe?"

"Yes, sweetheart, you are."

"Do you think he'll call me Auntie Ruth?"

"Better wait and see when he learns to talk."

"I'm going to be a really kind auntie. I'm going to buy him sweets and toys."

"I'm sure he'll like that."

"When can he eat sweets?"

"Not for a while yet, love. He just drinks milk for quite a long time yet."

"He's got no teeth of course."

"No, not yet."

Ruth continued to swing her legs and gaze at the window.

"You said he wouldn't be born till September and it's only July still."

"Yes, he's a bit early."

"Is he properly cooked?"

Joe laughed. "I think the word you want is "developed", Miss. And yes, he seems to be properly developed. Fully developed. Very well developed. A fine specimen of a baby indeed."

Joe sat at the table opposite Ruth, who was content to continue her thoughtful gaze towards the window. He wondered how the early arrival was being viewed by the Place's occupants. The robust chubbiness of his new son would put paid to any stories Lydia might try to spin about a premature baby. He grinned. Too bad. It had been last November that he and Lydia made this baby, so by his rough estimate the baby was in fact a bit early, but to hell with that and what anybody thought, anyway. He would just continue to smile as he was at the moment. He wished fervently that his parents were there to see their grandson and share his joy, but he managed to also grin at the thought of how his mother would have been embarrassed at the early birth. Her sums would have been sharply accurate and such obvious evidence of premarital misbehaviour would have been anathema to Jessie Barlow. Joe wondered how she would have handled the gossip. She'd always been such a model of morality and merciless in denigrating those who deviated from her standards. She might have been glad to have been spared the gross indignity of such a deviation occurring in her own family. Ah no, of course she'd rather have seen her grandson. How she would have loved him.

When not hanging over the cradle in crooning adoration, Joe was loath to leave the house in case Lydia needed something. He only went to the pub that evening to "wet the baby's head"—as Charlie put it—after Mrs. Galvin insisted that she'd love to sit with the new mother and baby and had no interest in going to the pub with the rest of the Place's population. Ruth also stayed indoors, delighted with the joint novelty of the new baby and the presence of Mrs. Galvin, who made excellent cocoa, it seemed, with froth on top.

There was no reason for Joe to stop smiling, so he didn't even try. Smiled till his face ached.

34

One year later.
July 1924

Harry walked on his first birthday. Walked from the leg of the table to the easy chair where he collapsed into Joe's arms with gurgles of delight and achievement. The next day he walked some more and in next to no time he was only needing a finger to hold as he made his rocking way across the cobbles of the Place.

Harry and Ruth now shared the small bedroom overlooking the passageway to Bensham Road. Joe waited till they were both asleep before he broached the subject yet again with Lydia.

"Lyddie love, can you perhaps think about it a bit more?"

"I have thought about it. I just don't want to go!"

"Will you just look at the booklets?"

"I am not interested in looking at any stupid booklets."

"It would be a lovely fresh start for us all. So good for Ruth and Harry. We could own our own *farm* – just think about how they'd love that."

"I … would … not … love … it."

Into the silence Lydia added:

"What do you know about farming anyway? Nothing!"

Eagerly Joe countered "They'll teach me. I'll go to a farm here and learn about dairying before we go. And out there there's all sorts of help. The government's set it all up and they must know what they're doing."

"Pish."

Another silence.

"I don't know how you can ask me to do such a thing, Joe. I wasn't brought up to live in a horrible far-away country and be a farmer's wife and do all sorts of horrible things with animals and dirt and no help. Even though it's true I don't have any help here," Lydia added savagely.

"I try to help. And you do send out the washing," Joe said wanly as the old argument reared its head again and distracted them from the discussion he was hoping for.

"*Everybody* sends out their *washing*!" Lydia said imperiously.

"Not here they don't."

"Of course not," said Lydia "round *here* is where they take it in!"

A marriage going on for two years old should surely have settled down a bit more than theirs had, thought Joe. He looked at his wife across the table as she read the newspaper, riffling through it to find the coy chat of the fashion page and reading with deliberate exclusion.

Joe had to cast his mind back a long way to remember the laughing Lydia who'd been so carefree and vivacious. The light had left her, he thought. Oh, there were moments. In the dark of the night in the self-contained world of their bed Lydia was often amazingly passionate, sometimes leaving Joe in her wake as she hurled herself into lovemaking so ardent that the children stirred.

But these nights were alien. After such lovemaking Joe would dare to hope that the passion might leach into the following day, but Lydia was nearly always cooler than ever. No trace of the previous night's abandon ever remained.

Joe worked hard, worked any overtime going in order to bring home as much money as he could but overtime was non-existent at the moment. His slight savings were not significant enough to provide anything like the needs that Lydia professed. Occasionally, though, Joe would come home to a house that had been scrubbed clean, but these giddy bouts of activity were always at a point where the house had grown steadily grubbier and so untidy that the undertaking was more or less imperative.

Lydia had not been brought up to live the way she was living. She'd never cleaned or cooked or had to think about money, so it wasn't her fault; Joe understood her discontent. She was his wife and the mother of his son and he loved them both helplessly.

The house may have been a muddle, but Lydia tended Harry with great care. He was fed, bathed and changed with meticulous attention to detail and timetable. He was taken out for his daily dose of fresh air, come rain or shine, in the big perambulator that lived under the stairs. Lydia liked to sit in her chair and pensively watch him, playing on the rug. Joe and Ruth took the more active part, rolling round on the floor or tossing him high in the air, watching out to see that he didn't crawl into trouble, prodding and tickling him to make him laugh his high-pitched chuckle while Lydia looked on with a smile.

Ruth adored her little nephew and would play endlessly with him. Sometimes it was she who took him for his daily outing, tall enough now to push the pram and as proud as any mother.

She had grown so much this last year or so. Joe thought how pleased his mother would have been with her daughter. How she would have doted on Harry, too. His thoughts meandered.

He shifted, restless. He couldn't see any change in his fortunes in this country, and no change meant a permanently-unhappy Lydia. Surely she could see that? Neither of them had any ties in England—none to speak of anyway, he thought, dismissing Lydia's mother as she had already done. Alice was his only relation but she was only a relation by marriage. No ties, then—fresh start!

It had all started with Stephen's accounts of Canada and then of Australia. As soon as Stephen had mentioned Australia, all of Sam's stories and his love and enthusiasm for his country flooded back to Joe and he was immediately interested. A couple of months ago Stephen had been to a lecture delivered by the Agent-General for Western Australia. Western Australia! That was where Sam had lived. What had he called it? "Bloody beaut." Memories of Sam's tales, his laugh, his curiosity, his delight in new things ... Joe wanted to know everything and Stephen was full of it.

"They need people out there, Joe, and they're prepared to give away farms to get Englishmen to settle. Amazing, isn't it? To think you can get a real farm for absolutely nothing, in a new country without the divisions of this one. But all the same not too different—he said it was just moving from one room to another in the great house of the British Empire! Oh yes, a bit bombastic I know, but still … A man can become anything he wants out there."

Stephen had all the notes, brochures and booklets. It was a project called Group Settlement that attracted him. The British and West Australian governments were jointly promoting a scheme that was to open up the lush south-west of Western Australia to dairying. At present it was more or less totally unsettled, except for some timber concerns. It was surely enticing and Stephen knew all the details.

"It's wonderful Joe. Fares out there subsidised, land free— over 100 acres, can you imagine? House built for you, stock and tools provided. Just have to pay back for these things, and for the first five years it's interest-only, then interest and principal for the next 25 years, and you can just pay that from the farm production."

Stephen was out of breath. Joe had never seen him so enthusiastic.

"And schools, Joe! Where there are eight or more children in the area schools will be built and teachers employed to teach them."

"Do you fancy teaching out there?"

"I've had enough of teaching. I want to be landed gentry!" Stephen laughed.

"You've not had anything to do with farming though," ventured Joe.

"And that's another thing! They'll teach you to farm! Unbelievable. A course on a dairy farm here before you go, then experienced men directing the Group on what to do and how to do it. Foolproof if you're halfway intelligent, I'd think!"

"Is Kalgoorlie anywhere near?" asked Joe.

Stephen looked confused. "Ummm, I don't really know Joe. Why?"

They'd been talking at the Oak Tree, leaning against the bar, and Len and Michael Galvin had wandered over to join them, attracted by Stephen's animation.

"Are you going?" Len asked Stephen.

"I think so. I really think so. If they'll have me."

"Why wouldn't they?"

"Well, there's a medical examination and I do rather think as well that they prefer families to single men."

"'Course they'll have you. You're fit and whole, aren't you?" said Michael. Stephen and Joe both glanced quickly at Len, who had flushed. Michael immediately realised his gaffe and apologised.

"No need," said Len with sharp dismissiveness. "I'll bet I could get accepted if I wanted to."

A small embarrassed silence ensued.

"Yes, well."

"Better be going."

"Yes."

And that was the beginning of it, the current of change that ran through the Place, initiated by Stephen and his firm intention to apply for a place in the Group Settlement Scheme. Michael Galvin was interested and had made enquiries. Len sulked whenever the subject was mentioned—which was often—and Joe was trying vainly to persuade Lydia to see the huge benefits of such an adventure. Joe reflected that if they all went, there'd only be Alice and Dora left in Oak Tree Place. But Len couldn't go, not with his missing foot, and it didn't look as if Joe and his family were going either.

He tried again as Lydia folded up the paper with a sigh.

"Lydia … "

"Joe, I'm tired I'm going to bed."

Joe was not tired and his fervid imagination would not let go of the idea of a new start in a bountiful new country where everything would be different and better. Restless, he crossed the Place and went into the Oak Tree, hoping that one of the Place's other potential emigrants would be there to discuss the project.

None were, but the elder Mrs. Craggs presided over the bar and Joe was so brimming with excitement that he chose to assume Lydia's eventual compliance and regaled her with all of the plans, the possibilities and the new beginnings that beckoned.

Surprisingly, Mrs. Craggs paled and grasped the edge of the bar. "Ruth?" she whispered "You'd take Ruth?"

"Of course," said Joe throwing out his arm expansively, "and Harry and … Lydia."

"Lydia has consented to emigrate to Australia and live on a farm?" Mrs Craggs was incredulous and Joe bridled, despite the conflict that still loomed in that area.

"Well, yes," he said stiffly and defensively.

"Oh my conscience, what is she thinking? What are *you* thinking, Joe? How can you even *consider* taking young children to the other side of the world to an uncivilised country like Australia? Oh mercy, don't do it!"

Mrs. Craggs was becoming pink-faced in her vehemence. Joe looked at her with amazement; Edie Craggs' composure seldom slipped and whatever had caused this bee in her bonnet was a mystery to him. His volubility of the previous few minutes dwindled to nothing and an awkward silence fell.

Behind the bar Mrs. Craggs still stood woodenly, her face still pale and her eyes showed … what was it? Fear? Distress? Panic? Joe knew that Edie Craggs was fond of Ruth and had over the years showed this by an indulgence that had never extended to other children in the neighbourhood but this amount of emotion was foreign and embarrassing so when the lady in question turned, still obviously upset, and left the bar, Joe was relieved. He finished his beer and left too.

35

Three months later.
October 1924

Joe thought that Ellen Galvin might have had something to do with Lydia's change of mind, but all the same it was sudden.

The Galvin's emigration application as going ahead, and Ellen was overwhelmed with excitement. The details and the final approval had yet to be received, but they'd been as good as told that they'd be accepted. Suddenly her lifelong reserve seemed to crumble and everything she said and did was towards their eventual departure; no other topic was open to her. She was uncharacteristically chatting with Edie Craggs whom she'd stopped outside her house as she was passing to go shopping.

" … clothes for warm weather because we won't need coats and things, not in Australia," she was saying authoritatively. Mrs. Craggs looked bemused but she was not about to concede her well-established superiority.

"Yes, my dear, I'm sure. But do you have quinine for the malaria? You should make sure of that. And snake-bite treatment. Sharpe's in the High Street could order that in for you, I'd imagine." Edie Craggs raised her voice slightly as she saw Joe nearby. "And if" she continued "you might be blessed with children out in that desolate country, make sure you have fever treatments and splints for broken bones that you'd have to manage yourself because there are no doctors there, or hospitals, or even schools."

Edie's voice was uncharacteristically shrill by the end of her utterance and she glared at Joe as she delivered it. Ellen, looking amazed and confused by her vehemence, backed into her house.

Joe was still puzzled by Edie Craggs' obvious concern for Ruth but felt he should reassure her about the comfort and amenities that awaited Group Settlers. He was walking towards her when they were approached by a middle-aged man uncomfortably dressed in a tight suit that mocked the respectability that it begged as it plainly showed its wearer to be unused to wearing it.

Mrs. Craggs chose at first to ignore him with a whisk of her grand manner, but then turned and allowed him to speak to her. He was unctuously asking about a family member he was seeking who was said to be living in the district. The man produced a crumpled and blurry photograph and said that his cousin's name was Gerry Moroney. They both informed the man the regretfully they knew nothing of a Gerry Moroney and did not recognise the photograph. The fact that the photograph was a fairly good likeness of Michael Galvin did not seem to occur to either of them as the man shambled off down the road. Mrs. Craggs, her anger at Joe distracted, murmured "Let sleeping dogs lie, mmm?"

"But should I tell Michael?" Joe looked for guidance. "He might really be a relation or something. Or someone with news of his family perhaps."

"He's looking for Gerry Moroney, and we don't know any Gerry Moroney, do we? Best not to get involved with Irishness, Joe, it's deep dark well that one. As I say, let sleeping dogs lie."

Joe was finding himself more and more surprised by Edie Craggs. He would have thought that she'd be on the warpath at the thought of someone with an assumed name living in her son's property. Hell, he thought, nothing stays the same, even here. You could write a book.

Ruth came out of Alice's and hugged him hello, holding his hand as they walked to their house.

As he opened the door his stomach flipped with anxiety. He never knew how he'd find Lydia. It might have been one of her manic cleaning days and she'd be exhausted but more probably these days she'd be tight-lipped and churlish. More and more this was becoming the norm; she seemed to be slipping into a permanently dark mood from which he could not entice her, no matter how hard he tried.

But today there was an entirely different atmosphere. Lydia was coming down the stairs fastening her apron as she came.

There was no sign of a meal and Harry was playing with saucepans in the corner, dressed in the sailor suit that was his Sunday best. Lydia was breathless.

It was fairly obvious, but Joe asked. "Have you been out?"

The tone of the question was far from accusatory, but Lydia flared at him.

"Yes I have. I took Henry to visit my mother."

Joe was surprised. Lydia had seemed to have severed all connections with her mother since before Harry was born.

"You didn't tell me you were going to see her."

"I decided this morning."

"Is she well?"

"Very well thank you."

"What did she think of Harry?" He added "Is it the first time she's seen him?"

"She thinks he's beautiful of course. But she's not too keen on babies. Not very interested."

"How could she not be interested in her own grandson?" Joe was incredulous. "And such a handsome one as well" he said to Harry as he squatted on the floor to pat his coppery curls. "She doesn't deserve you."

Harry stuffed his small hand deep into the pocket of his sailor suit and triumphantly produced a slightly chewed railway ticket which he pressed on to Joe. It appeared that he wanted to Joe to eat it, but he laughingly pulled away and took the ticket from his hand.

"Oh I see, me boy, you've been travelling today, have you? Now where have you been?" He squinted at the blurred ticket.

Lydia descended on him like a hurricane, snatching the ticket from his hand.

"Horrid, Harry, horrid" she said. "Mustn't chew things like that!"

"He gave it to me to chew!" Joe laughed. "I thought your mother lived in Belsize Park?"

"She does."

"Was that your ticket?"

"I don't know."

"You wouldn't let Harry pick up a ticket off the ground, would you?"

"Of course not."

"Then *your* ticket was to Cheltenham."

"Mummy was visiting friends."

"Why did you go all that way when you could have visited Belsize Park much more easily at some other time? Especially as you say she wasn't really interested in Harry?"

"Mummy's friends wanted to see him."

"Oh, I see. Who are they?"

Joe was trying to maintain an easy jocularity but his smile was strained and his eyes were sharp. Lydia was flustered, but Joe knew she was more practiced at dissembling than he was at detecting it.

"Mr.—Colonel—and Mrs. Johnstone, they're old friends. They, they, she used to work for them," Lydia added with a burst of what seemed to Joe to be inspiration.

Joe frowned. It was entirely plausible, of course, but he felt somehow …

"Anyway Joe, you'll be pleased to know that I have been considering this farm in Australia and if you can show me that it's safe for Harry and comfortable for me, then I will think about it. Just don't expect me to do farm work, that's all!"

Trivial matters like travel to Cheltenham were dismissed in an instant.

Lydia was tired and didn't want to discuss it any more that night. A scratchy supper was eaten in almost total silence. Joe didn't want to upset Lydia and have her change her mind, but his heart was soaring with excitement. This would be the real beginning of their lives together. The four of them.

36

The next day

Joe was surprised at Alice's reaction. Full of excitement he'd told her the morning after Lydia had finally and definitely consented to go. This consent may have been grudging and not given in the happy anticipatory manner that Joe might have wished, but it was consent. He was so sure that it was the best thing for all of them that he took what was offered and was happy.

But Alice paled and reached to the door jamb for support, her breath failing her.

"Lydia has said she'll go?" she gasped.

"Yes, last evening. I am sure it's going to be the very best thing for all of us."

"I never thought she'd go."

"Nor did I!"

"Is she sure?"

"Yes, she is now. I finally persuaded her." This was said with some pride in the knowledge that the boot was usually on the other foot.

"You can't take Ruth!"

"'Course we can. She'll love living on a farm."

"No, you can't. It's the other side of the world! What about me?"

"I know you'll miss her, Alice, I know. You've been such a help and such a comfort to us all for years and years. Now you'll have some time for yourself."

"I don't want—" Alice was plainly agitated. "What will she do without me? She's always had me to look after her."

The familiar irritation with Alice's possessiveness began to rise. Joe was far too preoccupied with his plans to be concerned with Alice. She was just being unreasonable and really, she wasn't the sort of person that Ruth should be exposed to as any sort of example, was she? Ruth was his sister and his responsibility.

"Leave her here with me while you get settled down there, Joe."

Certainly not. "Not necessary, Alice, we can all go together. There are houses ready for us, and school for Ruth, and a whole new life!" the last words had an upward lilt that Joe couldn't help.

"Oh Joe, no." Alice moaned and slumped against the door.

Oh for goodness' sake. "'Fraid so, Alice." Joe chose not to see her distress and strode manfully and happily off to work.

37

A few minutes later

This couldn't happen. She could not lose her. She could not lose her.

Wildly her mind raced. What to do, what to do?

She would tell Joe the truth about it all, everything, persuade him to leave Ruth with her when he went gallivanting off to the other side of the world with Miss Hoity-Toity-Useless and their son. They should be enough for him. Why did he have to take Ruth?

But she knew he would. He'd said he'd make a home for Ruth and he had—not as well as she would have done, but he'd managed and although she knew that her love for Ruth was greater than his—or anybody's—he did love her, she was forced to admit. And forced to admit that there'd be no question of him leaving Ruth behind.

She was surprised that Lydia had said she'd go. Really surprised. Totally amazed, in fact. That little self-centred madam was not cut out for anything like farm life, even if it was nice and warm and full of good things like they said. She wouldn't look after Ruth any more than she did now. Her thoughts looped around again to Ruth and the desolation of her impending loss.

If she told Joe everything, that would be another secret for him to keep on top of the Arthur one. Jessie had made it clear to her that she'd go to jail sure as eggs if it ever came out what they'd done, but Jessie didn't know about Arthur, didn't know that she was wanted for a crime a hundred times more serious than the one they shared. She wondered if Joe would be able to keep this secret, especially when the spilling of it would surely lead to her being, one way or another, put out of the way for good, and then she wouldn't bother him any more and Ruth would be his forever.

Or else perhaps she could persuade Joe to take her with them. There was a thought. But even as she formed it she knew it wouldn't work; her relationship with Joe was not a warm one these days and Lydia didn't like her either. Not that Lydia liked anyone in the Place of course. No, they'd not be keen on having her as part of the family in this emigration nonsense.

No, she was either going to lose Ruth forever or she was going to hang. They were the alternatives. No, here was a third—Arthur's sons might still find her and they wouldn't bother handing her over to the police. They'd enjoy themselves instead.

She seldom allowed her thoughts to go this far but now her heart raced and her breath stopped in her throat. She sat down awkwardly.

But it had been nearly two years now since the one-and-only sighting of the men she automatically thought of as Arthur's sons, and in that time neither Joe nor Stephen had even spoken to her about what she'd told them. They had ignored it as if she'd never poured it all out.

So they'd go off to Australia and forget about her and her troubles, and she was going to be left here in this little cottage all by herself until she was as old as Dora, and then she'd die. Die here and never see Ruth again, never see her grow up, never see her happily married, never see her children. Never get to tell her …

She ached for the touch of her, needed badly to hold her. Quickly she pulled on her coat and half-walked, half-ran, out of the Place, down to Beulah Road and the school. She went straight to Ruth's classroom and knocked. Thirty pairs of eyes scanned her from serried rows as the teacher opened the door with a pleasant smile, raising her eyebrows in question.

"Ruth" gasped Alice, breathless from both emotion and her unaccustomed running. "Ruth."

Anxiety showed on the teacher's face. "What's the matter, Mrs. Barlow, what's happened?"

"Her brother. Australia. I have to take her."

"Take her to *Australia*?" Wide-eyed alarm.

"Yes, no. Joe. Please can I have Ruth?"

By this time Ruth herself had come the teacher's side and was regarding her aunt with concern.

"What's the matter, Auntie Alice? Is everyone alright?"

"Come with me, Ruth dear, come with me."

The teacher put her hand on Ruth's shoulder. "Mrs. Barlow, is there anything we can do? You are most upset. Can we make you a cup of tea in the staff room? Ruth can go with you and make it for you. Just have a cup of tea and I'll join you in a few minutes at the end of the lesson."

Anything to get Ruth. "Yes. Yes thank you. Yes."

Alice contained herself with difficulty and managed to even smile reassuringly at the teacher and shake her head seemingly at her own silliness as she turned to follow Ruth down the corridor towards the staff room but when the bell rang for playtime they were not there.

38

That afternoon

It was not until Joe came home from work that Alice and Ruth's absence was noticed, and even then it was only grumbled about by Lydia who said she could have done with some help with the boy, but she hadn't seen Ruth since she left for school that morning.

Of course she was at Alice's then. But she wasn't; Alice's house was empty.

Still there was no need to worry. At this time of year it was entirely possible that they'd gone for a walk, or to visit one of Alice's friends, or even on a mercy mission to Flo Keily if she'd been overcome with lots of washing suddenly.

Only as the dusk deepened to dark did the disquiet begin to grow to anxiety. Joe knocked on Stephen's door and went in.

"Sorry to bother you, old man, but I wondered if you'd seen Ruth at school today and whether she was alright. And have you seen Alice at all?"

"No and no, Joe, sorry. What's the matter?"

"They're both not home and we're a bit worried."

No one had seen either of them. Ellen Galvin had seen Alice going out into the road, but that was early this morning and she'd assumed she was going shopping. "Not," she added thoughtfully "that she had her basket, now I remember."

Stephen volunteered to walk to the house of Miss Fanning, Ruth's teacher. He revealed later that he had only a vague idea of where she lived and it took a good hour of enquiring to find her. But it was then that the news of Alice's strange behaviour and Ruth's removal from school became known. Miss Fanning had wondered, she said, whether she should send a note home but as Alice was as much Ruth's family as anyone was, she had not.

Joe paled as he remembered Alice's distress of that morning when he'd told her about Australia. Surely she wouldn't ... surely she couldn't think of *kidnapping* Ruth? What a dramatic word. How absurd. But where were they?

The men of Oak Tree Place were mobilised. Joe, Stephen, Michael, Len and Charlie fanned out through the streets, knocking, asking, explaining, searching. The party grew larger as more men, and several women, joined it. The night drew in, but a full moon lit the streets and gardens as they ranged the streets, the alleys and the parks.

Joe and Stephen met at the end of an unproductive street. Joe was on the way to panic and Stephen tried to calm him.

"Joe, if they're together, and it does seem that they must be, Alice will take good care of Ruth, you know that."

"I try to tell myself that, but I'm not sure any more."

"Now that's nonsense and you know it. But why would Alice take Ruth out of school and be off with her?" Stephen was as puzzled as the rest of the searchers.

"I think it must have something to do with us going to Australia," said Joe. "She was upset when I told her this morning. But I took no notice at the time."

"Oh. Can you think of anywhere she might take her?"

"We've checked everywhere and everybody I can think of." Joe's voice cracked. "What if she's taken her away—really away, like on the train to somewhere? How could we find her then?"

"I'll check at the railway station. You go back to the Place to see if something's happened there. Look Joe, she might even be back there by now, wondering at all the fuss."

Joe grunted and loped off as Stephen walked quickly towards the station.

The Place was deserted, but Joe checked Alice's house nevertheless. It was strange to go into Alice's without her being there. Joe gazed around the room, seeking a clue to where she might be, where she might have taken Ruth. He turned the few newspapers on the table. Everything looked the same.

Lydia was standing in their doorway with a wakeful Harry at her side. She didn't have to say anything. Once again Joe searched the yard behind the Oak Tree. If Ruth had been hiding by herself that would be an obvious place. But Ruth had no reason to hide and anyway, it seemed pretty certain that she was with Alice. But he searched there all the same. Every outhouse, every cranny. The places he remembered he'd hidden himself in far-off games of hide and seek.

He was still there when he heard voices from the Place. He hurtled out of the field and down the passageway to see a tide of twenty or so men and women rolling in from the road, bearing in their midst like two pieces of flotsam, Alice and Ruth.

Stephen had Ruth in one arm and his other shepherded Alice protectively. The babble of the voices transmuted into a murmur of satisfaction as Joe drew Ruth to him and hugged her wordlessly. From this embrace he glared up at Alice.

"What the hell did you think you were doing, you stupid woman!"

Stephen stepped in. "Enough for the moment, Joe. We'll straighten it all out tomorrow. Why don't you take Ruth indoors?"

Joe stood, still glowering in Alice's direction. He did manage a few words of thanks to the assembled searchers, now voluble with relieved anxiety. Many of them elected to have a drink at the Oak Tree before returning to their homes; Charlie propped open the pub door and then returned to where Alice and Stephen were standing, Stephen's arm still supporting Alice who was teary and shivering.

"Come and have a drink, Alice. Make you feel better." Charlie's natural surliness made the invitation sound more aggressive than concerned.

"No, Charlie, no. Not now." Alice's voice was low.

"It will do you good."

"Not just now, Charlie." Stephen was assertive. "I think Alice needs some peace and quiet."

"And you'd know best, of course."

"Only common sense, old man."

Charlie clenched his fists and seemed likely to throw a punch.

"Hey, Charlie, no need for that," said one of the men of the search party who lingered, "Stephen will see to Alice. You just come and get us a drink, eh?"

The man cast a comical eyebrow-raised look over his shoulder as he led Charlie towards the Oak Tree.

"What's wrong with *him*?" Joe asked irritably.

"Nothing to worry about, Joe," said Stephen. "Not worth the trouble. Just take Ruth and get her into bed. I think she's exhausted."

"I want to talk to you tomorrow," Joe said to Alice, digging the air with his forefinger. "I want to know what you thought you were doing."

"Yes, Joe, yes," said Stephen. "time enough tomorrow."

Stephen had not removed his arm from supporting Alice. In truth it seemed that she would collapse if it were not there. She stumbled as he helped her into her house.

Ruth in her nightgown was fed bread and cheese and was chocolate-moustached with a cup of cocoa before Lydia and Joe, sitting opposite her at the table, asked her a direct question.

"What happened, love? What happened today with Auntie Alice?"

Ruth was beginning to droop, but full of the day's strangeness and anxious to tell.

"I was at school and Auntie Alice came. Miss Fanning said to take her to the staff room and make her a cup of tea, but she didn't want to and she said we'd go on an adventure instead."

Ruth wriggled in her chair and sat up straighter, the better to tell her story. "We went on the bus to Croydon and had cakes. Then we fed the ducks in the park. Then Auntie Alice said we'd go on the train, so we went to the station and she bought the tickets. I didn't know where we were going but I thought that you wouldn't know where I was and I asked Auntie Alice if she'd told you." She looked anxiously at Joe, then flicked a glance at Lydia too.

"What did she say?" asked Joe gently.

"She said that she'd tell you in well time."

"In good time?'

"Yes."

A pause.

"Joe, Auntie Alice wasn't like usual. When she held my hand I could feel her shaking. When we were sitting on the seat at the station it was starting to get dark and I said was it time to go home and she started to cry. She tried to pretend that she wasn't, but she was.

"The train came and we didn't get on it. We just kept sitting on the seat. Then Auntie Alice stood up and said we'd go for another walk but I was tired and I didn't want to. I said I wanted to go home."

Joe's muscles tensed with anger.

"So she sat down again and asked me who I'd rather live with. Her or you."

"She *what?*" exploded Joe. Ruth cringed and Lydia put her hand on his arm. He attempted to hide his fury.

"That's not anything that any of us have to decide, sweetheart," he said with a smile that tested his face muscles. "You are my dear little sister, we all love you and there is not the slightest possibility of you ever living with Auntie Alice. She shouldn't have asked you. She shouldn't have asked you because where you live is nothing to do with her."

"Joe," said Lydia quietly, "let it be."

Ruth was tiring fast and Joe's diatribe passed her by to a large extent as she tried to keep her eyes open.

"But Joe," she said plaintively, "I told Auntie Alice that I lived with you but that I loved her too. Then she cried again and I didn't know what to do. It's awful when grown-ups cry, so I said I wanted to go home. And we were just coming out of the station when Mr. Dent found us and brought us back."

There was a lowering of voice and body as the story reached its end. Joe picked her up and took her upstairs. She was asleep in an instant but Joe sat a long time beside her bed, watching.

39

The next day

Joe was prepared to take the day off work the next day, but Lydia persuaded him to go and to let things settle for a while. A night's fragmented sleep had done nothing to calm his outrage with Alice, and he glared at her front door in case she was watching from behind the curtains as he strode across the Place and out into the road.

But time, and a day amid the familiar fragrance of glues and shaved timber did have a soothing effect and by the time he came home that night he was prepared to be calm in listening to Alice's explanation. Calm but not sympathetic; he thought of Alice's actions with anger still.

Ruth was indoors with Lydia and Harry. If Joe had been expecting a sombre little family, he was mistaken. Harry threw himself at Joe with his usual enthusiasm and Lydia kissed him on the cheek. Ruth was seated at the table and grinned widely at him.

"I've had lots of treats today, Joe," she said. "Mrs. Galvin brought me a pink lollipop, Mrs. Craggs sent me some sherbet and Dora gave me some of her humbugs. Lydia wouldn't let me eat them all, though. So I've got lots left for tomorrow, and I *can* eat my supper, really I can."

Joe slumped into the chair beside Ruth and laughed with relief.

"Adventures seem to suit her." he said over her head to Lydia.

"Hardly, Joe." Lydia spoke with superior knowledge. "It's been a trying day."

"I'm sure it has. Thank you for coping so well."

Lydia did not reply, but she smiled as she turned back to the stove. Joe kept looking at her until Ruth pulled at his arm.

"Joe, is Auntie Alice alright?"

"I'm sure she is, duckie. Don't you worry about Auntie Alice."

"She wasn't alright yesterday. I told you she wasn't like usual. And when we were coming back to the Place Mr. Dent had to help her all the way. She couldn't even walk properly."

"Tell you what, I'll go and see her and make sure she's alright, how about that? I'll go after supper."

"Can you go before we have supper?"

Lydia looked over her shoulder with a nod. Joe stood and went to the door; Ruth didn't ask to come with him but willed him on with her eyes.

Overcome with a strained formality, Joe paused after he knocked on Alice's door. The strangeness increased when Stephen opened it. He stood back for Joe to enter, welcoming him as if the house were his own and smiling warmly. Alice sat at the table, pale still but much more herself than she had been the night before. She smiled too, uncertainly.

"Ruth wanted to know whether you were alright, so I've come to ask," said Joe brusquely.

"Yes, thank you Joe. Joe, I'm sorry," she burst out. "I didn't know what I was doing yesterday when you told me you were going to take Ruth away. I couldn't bear to lose her."

"Yes, well, that's hardly the point, is it?" Joe said forcefully. "You frightened her and put a lot of people to a lot of trouble. Just because you say you didn't know what you were doing. And that's no fit state to have a youngster in your charge, is it? Not knowing what you were doing?

"If anything had happened to her on that *adventure* as you chose to call it, I would have killed you, you know. With my own hands. Easily. Without a second thought." Joe glowered at her.

"Hang on, Joe." Stephen laid a placating hand on his arm, "sit down for a moment."

Ungraciously Joe sank into one of the old ladder-backed chairs at the table, still glaring at Alice across it.

"You'll just have to face it, Alice. We're going to Australia if they'll have us, and that's an end to it."

"Is Lydia really going?" Alice's scepticism was obvious.

"Yes, she's thought about it and she wants to go. It's going to be a whole new start," Joe reiterated. Despite the indignation and anger he'd brought to the door, the prospect of the future in store made his heart leap. He returned to castigating Alice a little less viciously.

"So you'd better just get used to it, you see. And I won't allow you to have Ruth in your care by yourself again after yesterday's performance."

Surprisingly this deprivation did not seem to desolate Alice as it should have done. She lowered her eyes and nodded.

Then amazingly, she and Stephen exchanged glances and smiled.

Before Joe had time to be outraged, Stephen said quietly "Joe, we have something to tell you."

Joe's gaze swiveled between the two faces, Stephen's showing high amusement and Alice's smiling and nervous.

"We're going to be married!" Stephen said.

"You're what?"

"We're going to be married!"

"Oh," was all Joe could manage for a moment. Then he said weakly "Well, you do know how to ring the changes, don't you? I come in here to give you a good jawing out, and I have to end up congratulating you. Sorry, too much for the old nut. I'm flummoxed."

He continued to look at them. Stephen had gone to Alice's side of the table and placed his hands on her shoulders. Alice smiled but looked down on the table and would not meet Joe's eyes as she sat erect in her chair.

"Well," Joe finally managed, "There you are then. I suppose we can let yesterday's business slide now that this surprise has been sprung on us. Does anyone else know?"

"We wanted to tell you first, Joe" Alice said.

Suddenly Joe realised that this was the long-forgotten plan that he and Lydia had devised—Stephen and Alice were actually about to get married, after all this time but with, Joe acknowledged, no help whatsoever from either him or Lydia.

"Have to tell Lydia and Ruth," he said, hurriedly rising from his chair.

"Congratulations to you both, all the best, best of luck and all that … " He was out of the door.

The anxiety with which Lydia and Ruth were awaiting his return was diffused in an instant as he waved aside their enquiries and announced the news. Yesterday's concerns were dismissed. Lydia professed to be not too surprised, deflating Joe somewhat as he attempted to revive memories of the uncomplicated days of their first meetings and juvenile plotting. But still, it was a long time since the conversation in the Barlow house had been so animated.

Ruth was elated at the thought of a wedding, wanting details that Joe couldn't supply, but he assured her that she could ask Alice and Stephen tomorrow herself.

Lydia put Harry to bed and came down the stairs saying reflectively "So is Stephen still going to Australia?"

Joe hadn't thought about Australia till then. He suddenly remembered Alice's smile. He had not registered the faint triumph until now but he knew without having to ask that yes, Stephen was still going to Australia, and now of course Alice would be going with him. With them.

40

Two days later

The initial surprise that the news of Alice and Stephen's engagement brought was quickly overtaken with the pleasant prospect of a wedding. Few of the previous night's search party wanted to dwell on the strange affair of that night, and those who chose to ponder the events drew varied conclusions but were unable to verify any of them and mostly abandoned them to the general relief that the outcome was so happy. The air became festive as people gathered in the Oak Tree for the celebration of Alice and Stephen's surprise engagement.

Alice had removed her wedding ring and her hand was bare. Stephen stood proudly behind his fiancée as they received congratulations.

"Thank you, thank you. Yes, a surprise to you but not to us, eh Alice?"

"No, no, not at all."

Laughter.

Joe and Lydia stood together, looking on. Lydia said "You realise that marrying Stephen means that now Alice won't lose touch with Ruth when we all go to Australia?"

"Mmm, yes, I had realised that. Unless they separate everyone, of course, but they do try to keep families and friends together, they say."

"Oh, then dear Alice will get what she wants, won't she?"

"Yes," said Joe speculatively. He looked hard at Alice and Stephen, laughing together, Stephen's arm around Alice's waist as they chatted to another couple. As if sensing his gaze, Alice turned and her eyes met Joe's. He saw again the small smile that held the glint of victory. Joe registered the smile, but suddenly saw it fade and quiver as Alice's eyes caught sight of something or someone behind Joe. Joe turned to see Charlie coming in to help his wife and his mother behind the bar. That was all. He looked back at Alice but she was speaking to Stephen and her back was turned to the bar.

41

The next month.
November 1924

Stephen's application to Australia House was cheerfully altered to include his wife-to-be, at the same time as Joe and Lydia made their own application. They paused in front of a large map of Australia on the way out.

"Bottom left-hand corner," said Joe. "Or perhaps in a bit from there, or up a bit more! That's the area we're going to. It would be good to be close to the sea, wouldn't it?" It was hard to keep his voice from cracking with excitement.

"Where's Kalgoorlie?" he wondered, scanning the map from top to bottom.

"There," said Stephen, pointing.

"Not too far from where we'll be then, from the looks of it."

Stephen laughed. "Look at the map of the British Isles in that little inset," he said. "That's on the same scale as this map of Australia."

"Never." Lydia and Alice were similarly sceptical.

"You could fit twenty Englands into Australia!"

"About sixty, actually," said Stephen.

"Never!"

They walked down the Strand and had tea and cakes at Lyons Corner House. Joe could never remember being this happy. Hand in hand with Lydia, Stephen and Alice hand in hand beside them. The gritty London pavement was a road to a wonderful future and his feet hardly seemed to touch it. He couldn't stop talking.

"When do you think we'll be going, Stephen?"

"They said 'some months' didn't they?"

"We need to have medical examinations too. Michael and Ellen have already had theirs. Said it was hardly worth the bath and the journey it was so casual."

"Michael's a big strong boy, just what they want out there. They're not about to turn him down."

"I wonder how Ellen will cope?" mused Alice. "She does like everything settled and in its place."

"I wonder how she copes with her big wild Irishman then?" Stephen laughed.

"She adores him," Lydia said decisively. Joe looked at her in surprise. This was the first opinion on a neighbour or the Place itself that he'd heard from Lydia that wasn't scornful or dismissive.

He was exhilarated. Tried to trace the starting point of this feeling. It was the day that Lydia had visited her mother and her friends in Cheltenham and suddenly decided that she would after all go to Australia. The possibility of a new start for all of them. Something must have happened in Cheltenham that day but he didn't give a fig except to be glad about the outcome. Lovely Cheltenham. Lovely mother, who had to be sad to lose her daughter, but she'd brought it on herself … .Mother thus parcelled and dealt with, he wanted to shout his joy to the world. Instead he just kept talking, couldn't help himself.

He wondered about Peter and Bill. How he wished that they hadn't sold up everything they owned to finally scrape the fare to America and left over a year ago now. They could have come to Australia too—what a grand time they could have had. He had only heard from them once since they left and that minimal communication had not included an address. He resolved to leave a forwarding address with Mrs. Arland and with Bill's parents. Just in case. You never knew. Resolves came easily. Everything was possible.

He was only beginning to wind down once he was indoors an hour or so later as he and Lydia sat across the table from each other and Lydia broached her suggestion. She spoke softly.

"Joe?"

Joe looked up, smiling.

"Joey, I've been thinking. What if ... what if you go to Australia before Harry and me, and get things all ready for us. It's bound to take some organising, I'd think. And," she went on before Joe could frame a reply, "the baby really needs to have things organised and clean and healthy and everything. He's too little to cope with country things."

Joe's heart plummeted.

Lydia hurriedly went on. "It would be better and easier for you, too, Joe, if you don't have to worry about us at first, while you're getting settled. And getting things ready for us," she added.

Joe still hadn't spoken.

"Don't you think it a good idea, Joe?"

"Oh Lydia, no!" Joe could not help the anguish in his response. "I wanted this to be something we'd do *together*, our family. Our new start in a new place, new experiences, all *together*," he said again.

With difficulty he continued. "things people do *together* really tie them together, Lyddie darling. I mean, like the war, for instance. What me and my mates went through together means that we all understand each other so much better and how we are and what we do." He was out of breath, aware of the clumsiness of his speech, but anxious that Lydia should understand.

"So this is like the war, is it?" Lydia was smiling, a bit strained.

"No, that's not what I'm trying to say. I wish I could explain it better."

"Look, Joey, I do understand, really I do. But I'm just worried about Harry, that's all. I should think," she said, "that you would be too?"

"Of course I'm concerned, but I'm not *worried* about Harry and Ruth. Those chaps at Australia House, and all those booklets and pictures—and it's the *government* arranging it all, after all. They know what they're doing, they know that children are going out there with their parents, so they'll have all that side under control. You know what they said about schooling and everything."

"It's Harry that I worry about. Ruth is so much older and quite able to look after herself, as you well know. I should think that she could go with you perfectly well. She could help you a lot in the house."

"She's not even eight years old!"

"But she's very capable, and old for her years."

"I'd thought that you were suggesting that both she and Harry stayed behind with you while I went."

"No-o-o," said Lydia slowly, I just meant Harry and I to stay here. "I don't think I could cope with the two of them, without help."

The old ground. Joe's euphoria of the day was evaporating quickly, but he strove to hang on to it. Lydia's next statement put paid to his efforts and it was put more strongly.

"Joe, I am going to Australia to please you, because it's what you want to do. I am happy to do it, but it's what *you* want and it is not my choice. So I do think that my wishes could be considered a little bit more."

The joyful equality of the hand-in-hand walk down the Strand shifted and Joe was back to being the supplicant.

"Oh Lydia, please don't spoil it all. Please be happy about it. Please. It will be so good. You won't regret it, I promise you."

Lydia was silent for a moment, then pressed her advantage.

"Will you think about what I want, then, Joe?"

"You mean you and Harry, and me and Ruth … "

"Yes."

Joe spoke slowly. "They may not let us."

"Well, will you ask, then? I'm sure they'll see the sense of it."

"I can't see them allowing an eight-year-old girl to go out there without some sort of female to see to her."

"You'll have Alice," Lydia said.

It was actually Lydia who made the return journey to Australia House to make the necessary enquiry as she decided that Joe should not take too much more time off work; Joe wondered if she doubted his ability to make her case.

As Joe opened the door that evening, It was plain that the interview had not gone well. The children were subdued and Lydia almost crashed the dishes on to the table. Joe steeled himself for another round of argument and counter-argument and was surprised when Lydia collapsed into the chair and said "Well, you've won, then, you'll be pleased to hear."

Careful to betray no emotion other than interest, he said "Oh, what did they say, then?"

"We have to all go together," she said flatly.

"Oh."

A silence, then Lydia burst out "They said that just as short a time ago as last month, they would have let us do what I *so sensibly* wanted, but they were not going to allow that any more for some stupid reason so we all have to go together or not at all."

"Oh. Why did they change their ideas?"

"They … didn't tell me."

"Did you ask?" Joe ineptly tried to turn the conversation to chatty normality. He failed.

"No. So you've won. You get your way again."

Joe considered that there was nothing he could say that wouldn't aggravate the situation, so he kept quiet. Lydia was muttering into the saucepan she was stirring, a picture of unhappiness.

He turned his attention from the table to see Ruth clutching Harry to her with tears welling in her eyes. He turned back to Lydia and said with unaccustomed anger "Stop it this instant, Lydia, stop it. Look what you're doing to the children. Ruthie darling," he said as he squatted down beside her, "it's alright, it's alright." He was not sure whether it was their tense exchange or Lydia's reference to Ruth and separation that was causing her alarm, or both.

"Are we still going, Joe?" Ruth whispered, without relinquishing her hold on Harry. "All of us?"

"All of us together, sweetheart," said Joe soothingly.

"Yes don't worry, Ruth, we're all off to Australia." Lydia's tone was theatrically weary.

Joe looked at her with exasperation as he lifted Ruth and Harry on to his lap. A couplet that his father had been apt to quote flicked into his mind:

> 'Convince a woman against her will,
> She's of the same opinion still.'

Lydia was used to getting her own way and didn't enjoy being bested. Irritated, Joe thought that she'd better learn. They were, all of them, off to Australia. It would all come right in the end. Everything would be better in Australia, on their very own farm.

42

Still November 1924

The applications for the free farms in Australia had come so thick and fast that the promised dairy-farm educational courses had only been available to the first few potential emigrants before being abolished as too time-consuming. The day for departure was fast approaching; they'd hear any day now.

Joe was by himself at the bar in the Oak Tree. Lydia, now that she was leaving the country, had for some reason rekindled her friendship with Beryl. Beryl of the fussy flounce, Joe called her privately. Joe didn't know how the revival of the contact came about, but Lydia had so few—actually no—friends from her past that Joe was happy for her. Rather more for her than for himself, he thought. Beryl still found him as socially inferior as she always had and made no effort to hide her disdain. Joe wondered, from his secure vantage point as Lydia's husband, just how she justified her social superiority because she seemed to him just the slightest bit common and his mother would certainly have thought so. When she came to visit there was no possibility of him staying in the house.

Full of his own thoughts and plans, Joe was imagining how it might have been if Sam had still been alive. How amazed he would have been at the news that Joe was coming to his country. They would have met up, of course. What times they would have had! How Sam would have loved to see Ruth again, so grown, to meet Lydia and Harry. He might have been married himself by now, a nice country lass it would have been, Joe thought. That nice country lass who'd had to marry someone else because she'd never been able to meet Sam. Ah, Sam. It still hurt to think of him.

"Joe?" He started.

Ida was standing beside him at the bar. Joe looked round for Len, but he wasn't there.

"Hello, Ida. Would you like a drink?"

"No thank you, Joe. Joe, I just wanted to tell you something."

Ida plucked Joe's sleeve and they went to sit on a seat near the wall with a table in front of them.

"Joe, we're coming to Australia too."

"Ida! Wonderful! Er, er, *how*?"

"You do know, don't you Joe, that Len's been longing to go with you all from the first day that Stephen started talking about it."

"Umm, no. Yes. I suppose so."

"He really suffers with his foot, Joe. Not so much painfully," she said quickly, "just the fact of it." She looked long and keenly at Joe before she added "And how it happened."

"Yes, Ida," he said with enough false heartiness to avoid acknowledging that he understood what she was saying, "I'm sure."

Ida sighed. "He does, Joe, he does. He feels … " she didn't finish.

Joe was much more interested to know how Len had managed it. Ida told him briefly. They applied, she said, just like everyone else, knowing that the medical examination was going to be Len's downfall. But they'd only actually applied and seen any hope of success after they'd heard how cursory the medical examination had been for Ellen and Michael Galvin. Len had been insistent that they had nothing to lose by trying to pull it off – and everything to gain.

He'd lied on the application form of course. Left quite a few things out and fudged his war service record. He walked very well, everyone said so, on his prosthetic foot. Hardly the trace of a limp. He wore nice thick socks to the medical examination and said that as long as he could keep them on, he'd be as good as gold. He could and he was. Ida said they'd laughed all the way down the Strand.

They'd not told anyone that they'd applied, of course. But now that they'd been accepted they were cautiously telling their family and friends and trusting them not to blab about it in case it got back to the emigration people. Ida was telling Joe first because she didn't want him to be surprised and to show by any means that he didn't think Len was capable of farming in Australia. Ida said that Joe's opinion meant the world to Len.

"Does it?" Joe asked in genuine surprise.

"Yes it does, Joe. He admires you very much."

This was news to Joe. "Mmmm."

"And if we go to Australia it will mean a whole fresh start and a new life."

Everyone was saying the same thing. Joe looked affectionately at Ida.

"How do you think you'll like being a farmer's wife, then?"

"I'll love it. As long as I'm Len's wife, that's all I want, Joe."

"Oh Ida, Len's a lucky fellow, really he is. He doesn't deserve you."

"Oh no, Joe, I'm the lucky one."

"I won't have it," Joe laughed. "Not for a minute."

Len came through the door of the pub. Joe thought he did walk rather well, not that he'd ever thought to notice it much before. He eagerly made his way across to them.

"Didn't realise you'd come over here already," he said to Ida. "Do you have a drink? Can I get you one, Joe?"

Joe had rarely seen Len so animated. He was smiling broadly as he came back from the bar with their drinks, sitting just a trifle heavily across from his wife.

"I can see that she's told you," he said. "What do you think? Good eh?"

"Capital."

"Now we can all go together."

"Did you ask?"

"Yes, and they said they really liked friends, neighbours and family to go together, so they were really happy to put our application in with yours and the others. We'll all go out on the same ship and to the same place. Same *group*." The word rang with the assurance of the newly-learned.

So it was going to happen after all, Joe thought. Who'd ever have imagined that the whole population of Oak Tree Place would leave, apart from Dora, of course, and move holus-bolus to the other side of the world? How very strange. Charlie would have a lot of empty houses. Instinctively he looked across at Charlie polishing glasses behind the bar. To Joe, big dark Charlie always managed to look menacing, even to an innocent glass, and he was polishing this one with grinding intensity. Joe kept watching him. He was obviously lost in thought as the same glass received the longest and hardest polish ever. Until it broke. Joe blinked and Charlie started, his reverie shattered. He glowered, swore and wound the cloth around his bleeding hand, stumping out to the back room.

Almost immediately his wife popped from the same door and took up her position at the bar. A bit like a Swiss weather-clock, thought Joe—thunderstorm goes in the door, pleasant and sunny comes out. But 'pleasant and sunny' looked rather strained, and Joe thought that he really would be glad to leave all this behind. His eyes moved back to Len as he spoke again.

"Glad to leave all this behind."

Joe smiled at the mirroring of his own thoughts.

"Different for you Joe," Len said defensively.

"No, I was just smiling because I was thinking the same thing."

"But it is different for you, you know. You have a job here with some sort of future if you wanted it."

"Not really," said Joe. "Not at all in fact. Things are very tight at Jackson's. Put off a man last week."

"Didn't know that," Len said grudgingly, "but I haven't had a job since I came back, and it's really getting me down."

"It will be such a good thing for us all, won't it Joe?" Ida said brightly, leaning across the table to touch her husband's hand.

"Yes, yes, *yes*," said Joe. "I can't wait to go. Ruth is really excited. She's told all her friends at school."

"And Lydia?"

"Yes, of course," Joe said blandly.

"If we go soon, we'll miss the worst of winter here and it will be summer over there!" Ida liked the idea.

"It will be funny to have the seasons turned around."

"Yes, but it will be quite warm all the time, surely. No snow, no sleet … "

"No fog, no hail … "

"No worries, no troubles … "

They were all laughing as Charlie re-entered the bar and took up his place behind it, a small bandage around his palm. His wife disappeared again and Charlie continued to glower.

43

That night

Later that night—or actually early the next morning—there was a commotion in the dark quiet of Oak Tree Place. For Joe it began with the wakening of Harry, then other more foreign sounds—scuffling noises, a couple of thuds and several grunts brought him and most of the other residents to their windows.

They were amazed by the sight of Stephen on his back on the cobbles with Charlie astride him, beating him fiercely. Stephen was getting the worst of it until Alice appeared with her large frying pan raised above her head, the darkness and her billowing nightgown giving her the blurry appearance of something not quite human.

The sound of the frying pan on Charlie's head was dull and solid and it did make him release Stephen, but only to turn on Alice, her nightgown suddenly airless and flimsy as she was thrown to the ground.

The fight so far had happened in silence apart from the sound of blows, so Charlie's cry echoed clearly around the Place.

"By God, I'll do for you too!"

Joe ran down the stairs and out the door as Michael came out of his house. They both ran to Charlie and dragged him off a cowering Alice. Stephen was scrambling to his feet. There was blood.

Charlie jerked and writhed in the grip of his two captors, who held him with difficulty.

"Come on Charlie," said Joe, "what's going on here? Calm down, man."

"Whore!" Charlie spat at Alice.

Stephen stepped aggressively but groggily towards Charlie again, fists raised.

"Stop it, for goodness' sake!" It was unclear who Alice was addressing as she deliberately turned her back to Charlie, pushing a now-unresisting Stephen towards her door.

"Whore!" cried Charlie again, this time with tears in his voice.

Lights flickered in The Oak Tree and the front door opened. Edie Craggs was across the Place in a few hurried steps and had her arms around Charlie. "Come on my love, come on, come on indoors, come, come."

Charlie shook her off, at the same time releasing himself from Michael and Joe. He stood still, shaking his head and spraying blood. Then appallingly, he started to sob. Into a horrible silence he threw his head back and bayed with animal anguish, then leaned forward with his hands on his knees, dripping tears and blood. Edie Craggs stepped forward again, crying herself now in maternal empathy, but Charlie ignored her and shambled across to the pub where his wife was framed in the doorway. She had made no move towards Charlie but leant against the door with tears coursing down her cheeks too.

He brushed by her. The two Mrs. Craggs' went into the pub behind him and closed the door.

It was freezing in the Place. With the antagonists gone, the remaining souls attempted to make a shivering assessment of what had happened, but quickly abandoned their efforts in favour of warm beds. Time enough to work it out.

Joe and Len lingered for a moment.

"Always wondered about them, Joe."

"Who?"

"Charlie and Alice. Thought there was something funny there. Have you ever seen Alice out late at night? I have."

"She has trouble sleeping."

"She headed round to the back of the pub pretty often."

"Oh." Joe did not like this line of discussion. It offended him that Len could talk so salaciously about his aunt. She was *his* aunt, after all, and family.

"Well that's none of our business, anyway." He said firmly and turned to go indoors.

But Lydia was waiting for him, bright with excitement.

"What do you think, Joe? Is it a scandal? What a lark!"

"I'm sure there's an explanation," he said stiffly.

"Oh, I'm sure there is. I can't wait to hear it!"

"Lydia, I don't want to talk it and you shouldn't either. It's none of our business." He was repeating himself. He didn't want to talk about it *or* think about it. He went up the stairs leaving Lydia to follow.

44

The following morning

There was an unnatural quiet in the Place the next morning. Apart from turning-out time at the Oak Tree and the odd raised voice of an over-indulged customer, the Place was naturally quiet anyway, but today it sat uneasily.

Joe felt strangely as though he was revealing himself to some secret observer as he came out his door and as he walked across the cobbles the events of the night replayed themselves with sickening clarity. He heard again the thick ugly sound of flesh thudding against flesh …

He turned gratefully towards the distraction of Michael closing his own door behind him and joining him as they walked down the road together towards their respective employments. There was a long silence during which their boots clunked on the frosty footpath, then Michael said "A bit of bother last night, eh Joe?"

"I suppose. None of my business."

Michael considered this statement for a while before he said "No." Then

"Charlie was in a bit of a state."

Joe really didn't want to talk about it. If he didn't think about it and didn't talk about it then he wouldn't remember it. *And* it was nothing to do with him. Nothing at all. But damn Charlie. What the hell was he doing?

Len's insinuations from last night welled up in his mind, despite his resolution. It made sense. A sort of sense in that it was of course possible, but …

Michael spoke again, prodding Joe for comment.

"Alice was pretty handy with that frying pan!"

"Mmmm."

"D'ye think Charlie was hurt a lot?"

"Doubt it."

"I heard him at Alice's door, y'know."

No response.

"Scratchin' at it he was and calling her name sort o' soft."

"Mmmm."

"The shindig started when Stephen opened the door!" Michael chuckled, "Didn't expect to find him there to be sure, though I can't imagine why he took him on like that! But then, perhaps I can … "

"Stop it, Michael."

"Ah, I mean no harm, Joe. A bit of a laugh."

"It's not a bit of a laugh at all," Joe said huffily, "you seem to treat everything as a bit of a laugh."

"Is that true now?" said Michael with a sudden steel in his voice that caused Joe to look at him with surprise.

"I suppose I do laugh, Joe. But I don't know what's waiting for me round the very next corner, so I laugh when I can."

"What's likely to be waiting for you round the next corner then?" Joe's thoughts flew suddenly to the enquiring man. The man looking for one Gerry Moroney who looked an awful lot like Michael Galvin.

"Ah, nothing at all. Forget it." Just as suddenly as Michael had become serious, he was speaking lightly again.

Partly because he was irritated by Michael's intrusion into his aunt's affairs, Joe slyly asked "Do you know a Gerry Moroney?"

Michael stumbled and his face paled to a milky waxiness. He was almost without breath to ask, but hoarsely demanded to know what Joe was talking about.

Contrite because of its obvious effect on Michael, he said quickly "Oh, just someone was asking after a man by that name the other day."

"What man?"

A seedy-looking fellow—small, unimportant."

"What did he say?"

"He was just looking for a relation. A cousin I think he said."

"He asked you?"

"Yes, me and Mrs. Craggs. In the Place, the other day."

"What did you say?"

"Well," Joe considered briefly, "I didn't know any Gerry Moroney and neither did Mrs. Craggs, so we told him so."

"And he left?"

"Trudged off into the sunset", said Joe cheerfully, regretting his impulse to bring the subject up.

Michael was unusually silent and seemed tense until their paths diverged. Joe turned into the alleyway that led to Jackson's off the High Street and Michael continued on to the brick works.

That evening Joe discovered, as others in the Place had done at various times during the day, that Charlie had left. No one had seen him go, but most people were happy to accommodate the two Mrs. Craggs' straight-faced explanation that Charlie had gone away for a while to visit a friend.

Dora had been heard to ask worriedly how he was, but Edie Craggs told her briskly and dismissively that he was well, and Dora unhappily retired to her favourite chair. There was relief among the other residents of the Place at Charlie's absence as not many of them could have easily faced him behind the bar after the happenings of the night before. Couldn't imagine Charlie himself coping with that, either.

The two Mrs. Craggs adopted a remote hauteur that conveyed that, as far as they were concerned, nothing at all had happened in the Place the previous night. No one was foolish enough to broach the subject with either of them, although it was the only topic of conversation, in and out of the pub.

There were those who said they always suspected it, those who said they always knew it of course and those who were totally surprised, but no one doubted it now. Covert glances were cast at Stephen to see how he was taking it.

Apart from some sticking plaster and a certain stiffness of movement, surprisingly well. Alice was confined to bed for two full days and was bruised and shaky on her re-appearance, but in the interim Stephen had stayed in her house and cared for her. The two days had given the gossip time to subside a little, but Alice was still looked at askance when she reappeared, and Stephen was regarded with interest.

Charlie was still away.

45

A few days later

Joe was embarrassed and reluctant to speak to Alice and it was to his chagrin that he was caught dodging indoors as she came out of her door. Gruffly he asked how she was feeling.

"A few aches and pains, Joe," she said. She looked at him with a smile, seeing his awkwardness clearly. There was slight female contempt in the smile.

"Charlie had some fancy about me, I think, Joe, and he'd been knocking back the pints the other night, apparently."

Joe didn't really mean to defend Charlie, but he knew (didn't everyone?) that there was more to it than Alice pretended, and he was stung to reply.

"It looked more serious than a passing fancy. At least as far as Charlie was concerned." Alice's expression hardened and he realised that he'd put himself right into something he badly wanted to ignore. Before Alice could reply, he said hurriedly "Look Alice, it's none of my business."

"Yes, Joe, you're right. But I did rather think you'd be more sympathetic to me than to Charlie. But it seems not?"

Joe flailed. "Of course you have my sympathy, Alice. I'm sorry that you were hurt and I'm sorry that there was such a fuss and I'm sorry that Stephen was hurt. Is that enough for you?" This last question was delivered with a rising rudeness and Alice flinched.

"Oh, Joe, you're such a *boy*," she said as she turned on her heel.

Joe retreated into his house, angry with himself but more angry with Alice for making him so.

46

The same day

Alice gently touched the bruise on her forearm, admiring the colours it was taking on. This wasn't the only one, but it was the most obvious. She stretched her hand out in front of her, tilting her head to see it better.

She was used to it, of course, the odd bruise. But this lot was different—a dozen purpling badges of difference that were helping to change her life. And it was nothing, the bruises and the blood and the pain. Things were working out very well indeed. She thought warmly of Stephen, hard at work at school like the good man that he was. How fascinating it was and how novel and delightful to have a kind, strong man looking after her. How unexpectedly it was all working out for the good.

Poor Charlie. Must have been a shock to him after all these years. He must have thought it was something that would go on forever—or for as long as he'd wanted. There would have been no way in the world that she could have ended it peacefully, so his own carrying-on had done it for her. All going on nicely, it was. Really nicely.

On the other side of the world things would be so different. So remote from this country where, Stephen told her, if you went any further you'd be on your way back! They must surely have different laws out there. They wouldn't care about a long-ago crime in another country, surely. The whole place was full of the families of convicts anyway. Just her type, she thought with a silent giggle. Perhaps even if she got found out they wouldn't worry about it down there. Her heart rose giddily at the thought.

Oh Jessie! You were so determined to keep me quiet; if only you'd known how that lovely brother-in-law of yours who you protected so carefully found me in the first place and brought me back to Oak Tree Place. You thought you knew everything and yet you really knew nothing. Not even the things that were under your nose. So sure of yourself …

She stretched like a contented cat, immediately winced at a sharp pain, and laughed. Everything was going so well!

Stephen was a sweet man and Lord, she was in such a state that night that she told him all about Charlie and his habits, and Ruth and Jessie and just about everything else as well. It had been strange to let it all go like that, at last, babbling on as if there was no tomorrow. But now he was the keeper of her secrets, and she just knew they were as safe as safe could be with him. What's more he didn't appear to give a fig about her complicated life. He didn't judge her.

Strange, this trust she felt—she couldn't think of any other person she'd ever known that made her feel so safe. No, that wasn't true. Johnnie at first had been like that. At first. Her stomach knotted suddenly at the thought of a trust that had soured. But surely Stephen wasn't like that? Was he? How the hell would she know—she was such a rotten judge of people. Her previous content was being nibbled at the edges.

Oh Lord but she was sick of secrets. Sick of being frightened, sick of being careful, sick of being a nobody. Yes, yes, to get away to the other side of the world, by whatever means, that was the answer. Charlie, just stay away until we leave.

47

Two months later.
January 1925

Alice and Stephen were married at short notice at the Register Office in North End just as Joe and Lydia had been, but this wedding was a little more festive. As the happy couple came back to Oak Tree Place with their small wedding party, Alice uncommonly demure in pale blue and Stephen beaming, a significant crowd of well-wishers turned out to congratulate them.

The fact that Charlie had returned and was once again behind the bar at the Oak Tree was a little disconcerting, but although no apology for, or acknowledgement of, his actions had been forthcoming he was docile and at least civil to his customers, who until this happy event had not included Stephen and Alice, and who in any case were still keeping clear of the bar. It seemed that Charlie was going to ignore the events and the ugliness of that night, just as his wife and his mother continued to do. All rolled and tied up like a stored rug.

It might have been an uneasy armistice but it was however gladly observed by the celebrating crowd as it would have been unthinkable to gather anywhere else. If one ignored Charlie, who made this easy by keeping to the background anyway, it was a wonderful occasion, and the happy couple was regarded with proprietary pride by the entire neighbourhood. So appropriate—the widow and the widower—so right for each other, such a good-looking couple, so happy and about to emigrate to start their new life in a new country! Goodwill shone brightly.

It was after the speeches had been made, the toasts drunk and the level of celebration was at its highest that Charlie came out from behind the bar and made his way across to where Stephen and Alice were standing, arm in arm, laughing with Joe and

Lydia. Alice was still laughing as she seemed to sense Charlie's presence, and turned to him.

Joe watched as her laughter was replaced by something that looked almost like fear and she flinched away from Charlie's hand, which had been outstretched to gain her attention. Instantly, though, she recovered herself, backed into Stephen's side and regarded Charlie with bland equanimity. She waited for him to speak.

"Just wanted," Charlie cleared his throat because his voice had cracked, "just wanted to congratulate you both. All the best."

Stephen stepped forward with a smile, putting his arm around Alice at the same time.

"Thanks Charlie. That means a lot to us both."

At least half of the room had been aware of this overture and its implications, and the lifting of any vestige of previous constraint resulted in an increase in the hubbub as the celebrations were resumed with even more enthusiasm. Re-crossing the room to his spot behind the bar, one or two men were brave enough to give him a pat on the back.

Once more insulated by its bulk, Charlie moved slowly down the bar and ostentatiously put his arm around his wife, who was at the time pulling a pint. This action, at the same time highly unusual and highly awkward, resulted in an embarrassed turning away of anyone who'd been watching as Charlie finally and clumsily withdrew his arm but kept his gaze on Stephen and Alice.

Lily Craggs kept her eyes down as she finished drawing the pint, but she blushed and there was a tiny movement of her head which may have been a shake but it was too small to tell.

Joe watched and cringed for Charlie and for Lily. But even if it was as artificial as it looked, it papered over the cracks and everyone could pretend that things were back to the normal. Except that nothing was normal any more. Stephen and Alice were married and there was to be a new tenant in her house as soon as she completed her packing-up, Len and Ida were living in high anxiety that their duping of the powers at Australia House would be found out while Ellen Galvin was so unnaturally chatty that everyone was trying to dodge her. Strangely, Michael seemed distracted and a little nervous, but he may have been prey to his wife's garrulousness and simply bemused.

Joe was in a fever of excitement and happiness. Lydia was throwing herself fully into their emigration and had bought clothes for them all that were suitable for this new life. She had not bought any for herself as she said she had far too many clothes anyway and what she had would suit perfectly well. Joe was enchanted and impressed by this newly-frugal commonsense and tried to help the preparations when he could. Cupboards to be cleared, excesses sold or given away. A real paring-down of belongings that Joe felt was only right for the new life. All new. Just a couple of things from the mantelpiece to make the new house cosy.

Alice stopped him one evening as he crossed the Place from work. Marriage had given her a sheen, Joe thought. Though not much more than a couple of weeks separated her from her previous single state and its frail determination to grapple with life's privations, Alice seemed to now brim with quiet achievement. It suited her, but it confused him.

She beckoned him inside. On the table was the carpetbag that he'd filled with bric-a-brac from Lydia's house in Brigstock Road on the night she'd finally left it.

"Oh rats, Alice, I'd completely forgotten about that!"

They regarded the handsome bag, unopened on the table, both remembering that visit. A faint whiff of the house seemed to float from it.

"Seems so long ago," said Joe.

Alice looked up. "Not so long, Joe. It's just that so much has happened, so much has changed."

Then briskly, "What do you want to do with it? Sell it now? You can hardly take it with you. Does Lydia know about it?"

Of course she didn't. It had preyed on Joe's mind as he'd closed the door of the Brigstock Road house behind him and trundled it, with Lydia's belongings, back to Oak Tree Place. His cheek in stealing from her house would perhaps make her think he was crafty or taking advantage. She didn't know him well really and she'd probably think the worst. By the time he'd completed his journey he'd decided to ask Alice to keep the bag in her house; time enough, he'd thought, to tell Lydia about it when it was suitable, or necessary. But the time hadn't come early on, and then he'd simply forgotten.

"Lord, Alice, I'm not much of a burglar, am I, to forget the swag?" In avoiding her question he answered it.

"Are you going to tell her?"

Joe bridled. "Of course I shall. I always intended to but I just forgot."

"Better make it soon, then. Do you want to take it now?"

Joe's mind raced. It was impossible for him to predict how Lydia would see his act now or even the fact that he'd kept it from her for so long. Would it threaten the new ease that had grown between them?

Alice was looking at him quizzically and with a certain sympathy.

The sympathy needled him. "Of course," he said, picking up the bag, "I'm sure Lydia will be pleased. She can keep the things or sell them for pin money."

Alice couldn't help herself. "*Pin money!* Oh Joe where did you get such an old-fashioned expression? My goodness, I haven't heard it in years!" she laughed. "And certainly never round here. You are giving yourself airs, young man!"

Joe was smarting from the ridicule as he pushed open his door with the carpetbag in his hand. Lydia looked up from her book with a frown.

"What's that?" As she looked at the bag she said "Where did you get it?"

"Let me tell you," said Joe.

Surprisingly, Lydia heard him out without interruption and Joe's relief grew as she quietly opened the bag and began to take out the swaddled items inside. She smoothed out the varied wrappings, placing them to one side of the bag, each revealed ornament to the other. When she had emptied the bag she put it under the table and regarded the collection speculatively.

Joe didn't realise he'd been holding his breath until he let it out.

"What will you do with it all?"

"Sell it, of course. I don't want any reminder of that life, thank you."

She continued to look at the covered table and said "Except for this little carriage clock. I'm glad you took this, Joe, Daddy gave it to me for my sixteenth birthday. I'll keep this."

"Ah sweetheart, I'm glad I can give you something with a nice memory."

Absently she said "You do, Joe, you do."

His heart sang.

48

Later in January, 1925

It was cold and rainy and altogether a most miserable January morning when the anticipated sailing information reached them. Four fat envelopes of tickets, travel documents, luggage labels and information flopped on to four doormats and were eagerly torn open, their contents spread on four kitchen tables to be exclaimed over and scanned avidly.

It was only three weeks off, and indeed the bureaucracy had got it right; they were all going together. The ship was called the *Diogenes*.

"I was sure they would tangle up all the red tape and separate us!" said Len delightedly.

They had all gathered in Joe and Lydia's house to discuss the looming journey. Not that there was much to discuss—all they had to do was what they were told from now on, it seemed.

"Present here, at such-and-such a time with such-and-such a document in your right hand, making sure your shoes are shined!" laughed Joe.

"Just like the army!" said Len.

"Lord, hope not!"

The last few details took on a different tone now that there was an end date for them. Joe's resignation from Jackson's had precipitated old Mr. Jackson's decision to close the carpentry business once and for all, leaving his other two workmates without employment. They assured Joe that it was going to happen anyway and that they had good chances of getting other jobs, but he retained the feeling that things were collapsing behind him and propelling him forward like the breath from a blast.

Not an altogether unpleasant feeling, to be buoyed along by events that, while you may have initiated them, were now moving along of their own accord and carrying you with them. Small annoyances in his life, like the gap in the frame of the bedroom window that let in a sliver of cold air, like the secret irritation he had with the accent of his co-worker Yorkshire Bob, like the creak in the fourth stair that he should have seen to, like … But he'd also be leaving his parents' graves and he thought of them becoming choked with weeds and unloved. He baulked at the thought of asking anyone else to care for them and finally decided that after all, he'd be back some time. Not for a while, perhaps, but of course he'd be back at some time. His mind began to drift to the scene of his return, alight with the success that his new life would bring him, striding across the Place to the Oak Tree, pushing open the door, seeing all his friends turn in surprise from the bar. He laughed out loud. First things first, Joe.

Neighbours and some of the regulars at the Oak Tree had come up with the idea of hiring a charabanc to transport the emigrants and as many others as possible to farewell them, to Tilbury on the day of the departure, making it an easier journey for the travellers and providing a jolly day out for those who accompanied them. Excitement ran high.

◆

The day of the leaving was bitter cold, with a puny sunlight only just piercing the early morning gloom. Light glowed from all the houses in the Place, and from the Oak Tree.

With a jaunty parp of its horn, the charabanc entered the Place and people erupted from everywhere, noisy and exuberant. There was a high-spirited discussion about whether to ride with the chara covered, or with its passengers exposed to the weather. "We always have the hood down when we go on trips!" "But that's in the summer, love, not in February!"

The driver ruled that the vagaries of the weather made it essential to ride covered, and the flimsy fabric remained in place. The day-trippers jostled for the best seats, children clung to claimed window-seats like limpets.

The doors of the emigrants' houses were open so that the light from inside spilled in yellow rectangles on to the cobbles. Suitcases and bundles were swung out of the doors to form four bulky piles, and finally the muffled figures themselves emerged, dawdling and hesitant at this last stage. A small silence fell. The scene was all at once leached of life and became a tableau to Joe's eyes. A tableau of his life so far, his birth, his youth, his parents, his marriage ...

The silence was a short one. Scrambling figures erupted to stow the luggage, neighbours who were not making the trip to Tilbury clustered, kissed, clasped and some cried. Len's parents sat stolidly in the chara looking bemused as Ida and Len climbed in beside them.

No one from the Oak Tree had chosen to accompany the travellers and as Joe turned to look for Ruth he smiled crookedly as he saw her being clasped strongly to the ample bosom of Edith Craggs. He walked across the Place, acknowledging to himself once more that this was the last time he'd do so, shook hands with Charlie and kissed each of the Mrs. Craggs on the cheek. Edie Craggs was weeping, but Charlie and Lily were dry-eyed and unemotional. It was only the second time he'd seen Edie Craggs cry, and it would be the last.

As the charabanc pulled out into the road, Joe turned to look at the Place for the last time. It was as if a skin was being pulled off him as he was drawn away and he felt raw and exposed. As the Place was cut from view he turned back, catching Stephen's eye as he did so. Stephen smiled and winked and Joe's spirits lifted.

Lydia trilled beside him. "Isn't this so exciting, Joe? What fun!" She turned to adjust the shawl she'd swaddled Harry in as he struggled to see what was going on and Joe took him on to his knee so that he could see the passing scene. Ruth on his other side played peek-a-boo games with him. Joe swallowed the lump in his throat and hoped fervently that the future would be kind to his family. He would have said a prayer except that he had given all that up. He just hoped.

Ruth was tugging at his sleeve. "Joe, Mrs. Craggs gave me a present. Can I open it?" She was thrusting forward a small box covered with blue sueded fabric and tied with a scrap of ribbon.

"'Course you can. Let's see what's in there, eh?"

Ruth carefully untied the ribbon and clicked open the sprung lid of the box.

"Goodness!" said Joe, and Ruth sat in silent awe at the sight of a string of lustrous creamy pearls nested in the satin interior. The jeweled clasp glinted in the morning light.

"Goodness gracious!" Joe expanded.

Joe had no experience of jewellery but there could be no doubt that this was an expensive and significant present.

"My, my. You're a lucky girl, aren't you?"

His mind was working overtime. Why would Edith Craggs give such an obviously expensive gift to a small girl who was not even related to her? True, he'd seen a soft side to her with Dora and everything, but still …

"Oh Joe," Ruth breathed finally. "Can I keep it?"

"Of course you can, sweetheart. Mrs. Craggs gave them to you, didn't she? They're pearls, did you know that? They're lovely. But we'll have to be very careful with them, won't we? Look after them and keep them safe."

"Oh yes. Can I try the necklace on now though, before we put it away?"

Joe smiled and handed Harry back to Lydia who was gazing out the other side of the charabanc. As he helped Ruth extricate the pearls and fixed the clasp at the back of her neck, Lydia leaned forward in surprise.

"A present from Mrs. Craggs," Joe explained.

"Well, there's a lucky girl then," Lydia leaned past Joe to finger the pearls. "A very lucky girl."

Joe looked at Ruth, flushed and excited, with the pearl necklace draped over her little collar bones. It looked incongruous—too long, too big and too adult for her childish frame.

"It looks beautiful, sweetheart. Just like you."

49

Later that day

It had been a momentary upset when Joe and his fellow emigrants had found that men were to be segregated from their womenfolk and children on the voyage. They'd discussed it over kitchen tables, indignant at first, then rationalising, then accepting.

"I suppose it does allow them to fit more people in," conceded Len.

Joe had been concerned at the thought of Lydia having to cope with two children in a confined and strange environment, but she shrugged off any thought of difficulty. She'd be perfectly fine, she said. Perfectly fine. No need to worry on her account at all. She actually giggled and seemed to be looking forward to it.

Alice, Ellen and Ida, all said they'd be there, too, so there would be more than enough help to go around. And it was just in the sleeping cabins, after all. They'd all meet up during the day.

At the top of the gangway the bustle and confusion with visitors and passengers was such that the separation was accomplished without anyone realising that it had happened. With Len, Stephen and Michael, Joe was briskly directed through high-stepped doorways and down seemingly dozens of flights of echoing metal stairs, through labyrinthine narrow corridors to the cabin they were to share. A quick count of the bunks revealed that they would in turn share it with four other men, but they were the first.

"Are top bunks better than bottom ones?" Len wondered.

"Depends on whether you're going to be seasick," grinned Stephen.

They claimed ownership of their chosen bunks by planting cabin baggage on them and then, after studying the map on the back of the cabin door to try to establish where they were on the ship and giving up the process, made their way by trial and error up to the main deck again.

The ship had looked overwhelmingly large when they first approached it, then pathetically small as they considered what it had to contend with to get them to Australia. Then on board it again seemed huge. It had a monumental feel and a huge solidity. The deck timbers were smooth and buttery and every painted surface was thick with layers of protection. The uniforms of the officers and stewards were crisp, official and reassuring. The smells were foreign—water and food and paint and a particular fustiness in the corridors and cabins that never saw sunlight. So many new sensations.

Joe leaned on the rail, looking down on the upturned faces of his old friends and neighbours as they sought to find him and the others along the decks. The gangplank was being raised. The sound of the chains was chillingly final, but so exciting. Joe pushed away from the rail and went to find Lydia and the children.

Three long hoots from the ship's siren signaled its departure, making most of the passengers on the rails jump and then relax and smile. Or weep harder. The gap between the ship and the dock widened without any apparent effort on the ship's part and the slick dark water pushed the waving handkerchiefs and hats further and further away.

Joe wove his way through the crowd looking for his friends and finally saw Alice. There was something in her actions and attitude that made him increase his pace and when he put his hand on her shoulder the face she turned to him was anxious and confused. She was holding Ruth by the hand.

"Joe," she said breathlessly, "Joe, I've been looking for you. I can't find Lydia since we were taken down to our cabin. She asked me to look after Ruth and I haven't been able to find her since. I'm so glad to see you—I just didn't know where to look."

"Probably looking around, or she might have got lost in that web of corridors down there." Stephen had joined them and was speaking reassuringly.

The passengers had stopped waving and were moving away from the rails as the docks diminished and the people on them became anonymous. Some had been crying, but the bulk of them turned towards the ship with lively enthusiasm. They flowed from the deck like ants disturbed on an anthill, streaming into the ship's orifices and disappearing.

It seemed a good idea for one of them to stay in the deck lounge, which Alice did with Ruth, while the rest of their party combed the ship for Lydia and Harry. Almost an hour later they were all assembled again after a vain expedition.

"There must be lots of places we don't know about where she could be," said Ida.

"We should speak to somebody on the ship—one of the officers, or someone." Joe was trying to seem only mildly concerned.

"Yes, good idea. I think it's the Purser you'd need to see. You go and find his office in that central bit down there and we'll keep looking for a while longer."

Partly anxious, partly angry and a little embarrassed, Joe explained the situation to the harassed Purser, who advised him to wait for a little longer as he was sure that Lydia would be found. "Can't be far away on a ship, after all," he smiled with dismissive superiority. "She'll turn up in a little while."

Joe turned to leave, but turned back. "Her name's Lydia Barlow, if she should happen to come to your office," he said, "and our little boy's called Harry."

"Right," he said. Then "Oh, wait on. Your name's Barlow?"

"Yes."

"Joseph Barlow?"

"Yes."

"Well, there's a letter for you here already. I was just about to put it on the mail rack."

Joe took the proffered envelope, small and overstuffed, and looked it. It had not been through the post as it only bore his name on the front, in Lydia's distinctive handwriting.

The hand that held the envelope made ineffectual passes at his inside pocket as he stumbled up the stairs on to a mostly deserted deck.

50

Minutes later

Joe's teeth were chattering and his whole body shaking when Stephen found him clinging to the ship's rail with one hand. The other hand held a bundle of pound notes that he was allowing to peel off and be sucked away by the icy wind.

"Oi, oi, oi, Joe boy, that's not the way we treat good money, my lad!"

Stephen leant across and retrieved the remaining notes then gently pried Joe's other hand off the rail. It was cold and clawed. Stephen massaged both of Joe's hands in his as Joe gazed vacantly at the indistinct horizon.

"What is it, Joe lad?" he said gently. "What is it?"

The moan that escaped Joe's icy lips was animal in its intensity. He seemed incapable of speech.

"Tell me, Joe, tell me. What is it? What is it?"

After a time Joe's eyes swiveled and met Stephen's. "Everybody repeats themselves," he said carefully. "Everybody repeats themselves. I've noticed it before."

"Yes, well. S'pose we do. Come on down to the cabin and get warm. Then we can have another look for that wife of yours."

"No need."

"What do you mean?"

"No need."

"Where is she, Joe?"

"Gone."

"Gone *where*?"

Suddenly Joe leapt up from the bench where they'd been huddled and stumbled to the rail again. He grabbed the top rail with both hands and leant back as if preparing to leap over. But before Stephen could grab him he sagged into an awkward sitting position, hanging by his arms, pulling at the rail as if to break it free. He was yelling, not now with anguish, but with anger.

"Bitch, bitch, *bitch*, liar, *liar*, bitch!"

"Come on Joe, come on. What the hell's happened?"

Joe allowed himself to be led back to the bench, but his fists were clenched and he had a couple of punches at the wall before he sat down again. As he flicked his hands in pain from the punches, he fished a letter from his pocket and thrust it at Stephen.

"No sense in trying to hide it. Everyone will need to know."

He slumped forward with his head in his hands as Stephen unfolded the pages and began to read.

51

The letter

Dear Joe,

I'm sorry. I really am. I think I once told you not to get mixed up with me, but you didn't have a chance, did you? You will be mighty upset by the time you come to read this, and after you've read it you will be angry with me and you have every right to be.

Let me start at the beginning with the really bad things. It's going to take some time for me to write and for you to read, I warn you.

I am staying in England and will not come to Australia (I don't know how you could ever have thought that I would) and Harry is not your son.

There, I've said it. Written it actually of course. I am such a coward. It's because I am a coward that I let it all happen in the first place. I will explain now because there will never be another chance to do it and you should know it all so that you don't blame yourself, well not for absolutely everything.

I've told you how my Mother ignored her background. She brought me up to believe that my future was that of a gentlewoman, married of course to a title or at worst, to money. I must say that I agreed with her and I was happy to set out on the path to find myself a husband who filled our requirements. I always assumed that this husband would also be handsome, kind and indulgent, of course. Rather like you, Joe, but with money, background and position, I suppose.

When I met you I thought you were a nice lad, Joe. A nice good-looking lad from a totally totally unsuitable social background but someone who I could tease and amuse myself with. That makes me sound a bit mean. At the time I suppose I didn't think much about it. Sorry.

Then I met Henry. I met him at a charity gathering that Mummy had dragged me to. I can't remember the worthy cause, but one of the speakers was Henry's father and Henry was there with the same bad grace that I was showing, I'm afraid. You don't want to know the details, I'm sure, except that I need to tell you that Henry's father is the second son of Earl Burnside and Mummy quickly established that his brother, the heir to the title, was childless, unmarried and in poor health and that Henry was his father's elder son as well. I hope you can follow that?

I didn't learn this till after that first meeting though. At the time both Henry and I were bored and we got into conversation of course. In next to no time we'd both fled the gathering and were off in his motor car.

That was the beginning. The middle was wonderful and the end was some months later and I was having a baby and suddenly Henry didn't want to have anything to do with me. You see Joe, it was poetic justice that Henry should have been toying with me just as I had toyed with you.

The day that Henry rejected me and chose to deny knowledge of our baby was the same day that Daddy was arrested and Mummy had disappeared and there I was with no-one, no-one to turn to and I turned to you. I knew I could rely on you to be kind, but I could not be absolutely sure what you would think about me carrying someone else's child. This anxiety was probably unfounded as I think you would have taken me on under any circumstances, wouldn't you, poor lamb? But at that time I couldn't be sure about that so I managed it so that you would think that Harry was yours. Poor Joe, you were so trusting that you never really did the sums, did you? Everyone else just assumed that we'd 'done it' long before I came to the Place, but you, you are such an innocent!

Marrying you meant that I was solving my problems just for a time and I thought that I could work something out after a while. At the time I couldn't see any circumstance other than being married to you that could solve my problems—you were a nice boy who I liked a lot, and I thought you would provide me with a bolt-hole at that very time and as I said, I thought I would be able to work something else out given time. That's what I aimed for—and of course achieved.

But I was really at my wits' end at the time with no money and nowhere to go and I could not remotely imagine myself in a home for unwed mothers (could you?). I had no money of my own, silly girl that I'd been, and I felt such anger at Mummy causing it all, and she'd left the house that day anyway and I didn't know where she'd gone or if she was coming back. I knew that I would be turned out of the house soon sure as eggs and I had no one, no one. If I'd had money or known where to go or what to do I might have tried to do something about the baby—not having him, that is, but in the end I'm quite glad that I didn't, of course. But goodness I was desperate.

But I couldn't go on with your life, Joe. The horrid little house, the hard work, the poverty, the boredom, the little narrow people— everything. I was not brought up to live like that. I hadn't imagined that it would be so bad.

And to be truthful Joe, you didn't help. I don't mean you didn't help, of course, but when you did the housework that I couldn't be bothered with, you were like a puppy trying to earn a pat, and Joe (sorry, couldn't help it!) I just felt scorn for you. And those nightmares that wake you up with your thrashing around, they're horrid, Joe. Looking after Ruth wasn't easy, either. She dislikes me so— always looking at me with those judging eyes, quiet as a mouse but always watching. It will be a good thing to have Harry away from her—she'll be really happy to have you to herself again, too.

So you see it's altogether a good thing that I'm doing here, Joe. I finally decided and now I'm certain. I'm going to tell you because I doubt that you'll want to tattle to anyone about it—anyone who matters, that is. Not out there in the wilderness.

Henry did visit Oak Tree Place just before Harry was born, in his car as you so cleverly espied, Joe. I had been writing to him, you see, and he came to ask me to stop. I was fat and unattractive and clumsy and there I was in that horrid little house. Henry could hardly hide his distaste and I don't think I've ever been so embarrassed.

After Harry was born I did take him to see Henry in a fairly desperate attempt to have him acknowledge both of us (in Cheltenham, as you might have guessed by now) and it was a fair disaster, I have to say. Turned away at the door, I was, like a poor wronged heroine in a stage melodrama; not even seeing Harry would soften him. He told me he was engaged to someone else, obviously someone more suitable that I had been. He also pointed out that I was indeed married to someone else, and whose son might it have been anyway? This was so ridiculous that I slapped his face—those golden curls you so wonder at in Harry are straight from the family tree of the Burnsides, and I guarantee they'll turn redder as he gets older. I was so angry, Joe. To make matters worse, I then had to get on the train and come back to Oak Tree Place. Ugh. But, having been rejected out of hand by Henry, I felt my options shrinking again so I agreed, in one mad moment, to go to Australia with you, mainly to stop you pestering me about it while I thought of a way out. I regretted the decision immediately—I would never have actually gone to such a place—and was racking my brains trying to find an escape, when I read in the newspaper that my precious Henry had been badly injured in a riding accident. I was wicked enough to hope he was in pain, and when he died I was sorry I'd wished that, but it was too late to take it back of course.

But I let some weeks go by and then I went to Cheltenham again and this time with no Henry to turn me away, I managed to see his father. Poor man, he was obviously still very upset and was rather vague but terribly polite. I told him nearly everything, except— except that I was married to you, Joe. I said I'd been briefly married, which I'd had to do for my own protection (and that's true!) but that you'd died (sorry!) and since then I said that I'd managed more or less on my own, with only my Mother to turn to. Mummy would have been surprised to be elevated to this helpful position, but as she'll not be called on to confirm it, she'll never know!

I really quite warmed to my story as I told it, and of course with dear little Harry there as a blindingly obvious result of Henry's dilly-dallying with me, he was very emotional. Poor man. Very sweet and not all that old, either.

I thought that I could persuade Henry's father (Lord Burnside if you don't mind!) to give me some money, actually. Some sort of allowance that would continue after Lord B's death preferably, but oh silly me, I hadn't seen the best option, and that only occurred to me right in the middle of our meeting, when he introduced me to his other son, Marcus (Lord Curthoys). Oh I do love a title!

So I changed my direction, clever little minx that I am. Said that Mummy and I were not getting on well and that she was not kind to Harry. Asked (heart in mouth!) if I could perhaps, on a strictly temporary basis, perhaps stay at the house or in some cottage in the grounds until I could find work and support my chee-ild. No actress could have done better.

So I shall make my presence—and Harry's—part of the land-scape and I know I can overcome any complications that present themselves, I know I can.

Lord B and his son are both so sweet and actually Marcus is really much nicer than Henry ever was. I told him that I needed some time to complete the charity work I'd been doing (oh I am so praiseworthy!) which gave me time to get you off on your travels. What a lark!

So, as I said, I came back to the Place that day and continued to pretend to you (you can see that I am pretty good at pretending, Joe!) that I would go with you to that dreadful country you are so keen about. Oh dear, how you could have thought that I would ever dream of such a move I do not know, but then, dear Joe, you were always so easy to convince.

I had thought it would be easy to have you go on ahead, and to write this letter to you once you'd arrived. But that particular plan was one I couldn't manage (I didn't tell you that the man at Australia House said they'd stopped allowing families to split up because several wives had been abandoned by their menfolk! Oh Lordie, if only he'd known what I was going to do!!). So I have been reduced to this last-minute cat-and-mouse game which I am going to find a great test of my cunning. My visit to Australia House was disappointing but knowing that you men are separated from the women and children on the voyage I'm sure it won't be too difficult to get off the ship again before it sails in the confusion around the gangways with visitors and passengers and things and I'm sure I can get off without you knowing. The fact that you are reading this means that I have succeeded. Over the past week Beryl has smuggled my clothes and belongings away from Oak Tree Place and will have them sent to Cheltenham. I could not take the risk of you still being in England Joe—I needed you to be out of the country and out of touch with the civilised world so that you cannot cause any sort of fuss or, even by accident, contradict anything I've said (or anything I might find it useful to say in the future!) I need to be very careful as well as clever.

Please don't be too angry, Joe. It is for the best for all of us. I could not have gone on for much longer as things were, and you will be in your precious Australia with your precious sister and life will be just dandy. I suppose you will miss Harry for a while, but as he's not your son really, I'm sure this will pass.

I am sorry Joe, but really it's going to work out for the best for all of us in the end. I will always be thankful to you. Just so that you don't think too badly of me I am enclosing the money that you paid toward my passage to your new life. Actually it's a share of the spoils from your burglary! Thanks to that I have enough to be going on with and I have <u>expectations</u>!

With affection

Lydia

52

AUSTRALIA March, 1925

Ruth felt the perspiration that popped out on her forehead being dried up by the sun as if it had never existed. Where the sun didn't reach, under her arms and trickling down her front, it felt sticky and uncomfortable. They both found it too hot to hold hands, and Joe had squeezed hers briefly twice in their private sign language to show he was letting go. Swinging her sweaty hand caused a brief cooling of its palm.

They walked slowly down the street to the big white Town Hall, so white that it hurt your eyes to look at it. It had a tower with a flag. They went into a shop whose verandah awning carved a spadeful of shade from the solid sunshine and Ruth seriously chose the sweets that her two pennies would buy before they ambled crookedly to the seashore. They had not exchanged a word since they left the migrant hostel.

The footpath still rolled mildly under their feet after the weeks on the boat, and Ruth felt slightly off-balance. They sat on the fine white sand and watched the waves break gently on the shore. It was cooler here, but the sun was fierce and still without a word they moved back to the stringy grass under the shade of a young pine tree. Joe lay down and closed his eyes.

Sucking hard on a sweet, Ruth considered things. Being nine years old was a good age for considering things. She knew that the grown-ups had all talked a great deal about Joe and her, mainly Joe of course and his predicament. That had been Uncle Stephen's word, but Ruth knew what it meant. Joe had not taken part in the grown-ups' discussions; he had not taken part in anything much since they all got on the boat and Lydia ran away with Harry. Everyone seemed surprised at the time, but Ruth had not been surprised. It *had* surprised her that Lydia had been so happy about moving to Australia, when she'd not been happy about anything else—ever—that Ruth could remember. Lydia's absence from her life was not unpleasant, but Harry … her eyes filled with tears and her arms curved with longing for his little body. What would he do without her? She'd cared for him since babyhood, much more than anyone knew, and it was Ruth that he cried for, reached for, laughed for … What would he do with only Lydia to look after him? He would think Ruth had aban—aband—left him on purpose. He wouldn't know that it was Lydia who'd done it. "Bloody Lydia" she muttered.

Joe's eyes flew open. "What did you say?"

"Uh, nothing."

"Did you swear?"

"I only said 'bloody Lydia'" said Ruth truculently.

There was a silence until Joe sighed hugely.

"Can't scold you for that one, chicken," he said wearily.

"What are we going to do, Joe?"

"Well, you're going to stop using bad language, for a start," said Joe, rolling over and propping himself against the knobbly tree trunk.

"Alright."

"Then, I don't really know. It's not something that you should have to worry about."

"But I do, Joe, and I'm a big girl now, old enough to help and for you to talk to."

"Ah sweetheart." Joe reached out to gather her to his side.

The afternoon breeze sprang up and ruffled the pine needles they were sitting on, raising a resinous perfume. A certain invigoration came with the breeze and seemed to prick Joe out of his lethargy as it lifted the lock of hair that habitually fell over his forehead.

"What are we going to do? I don't really know, love. We could go back to England—I've just about enough money for that, I think."

"Do you want to go back, Joe?"

"Do you?"

Ruth frowned. "I'd have to give back the book that all the girls and boys in my class gave to me when they thought I was going to go to Australia forever. And the necklace that Mrs. Craggs gave me."

Joe breathed a laugh. "Yes," he said, "there is that."

"What would happen if we stayed?" Ruth was still frowning. "What would happen if we go with Auntie Alice and all the others? Would they let you go to the farm without a wife?"

"You were with me when we saw the men from the government. You heard what they said."

"But I didn't really understand it all, Joe."

She had understood quite a bit, though. Holding tightly to Joe's hand although he hardly seemed to know she was there, she stared hard at the men questioning her brother. Joe had been bold and almost rude, she thought, as he explained that his wife had had what he called "last-minute second thoughts" about coming with him and decided that she wanted him to have everything prepared for her before she came to live on the farm. They did have a small son, he explained, and his wife had been anxious about him.

The men had been sharp-eyed and knowing. One of them laughed and told Joe that this had happened before and he knew all about it.

"What do you want to do, son?" he'd asked. "Go on with it and pretend she's coming, or pay back what you owe and scuttle back home?" He had a wide wet mouth and when he was speaking the corners of his lips stuck together and never completely separated. Ruth was watching this in fascination and missed a couple of exchanges.

"…let you know." Joe was saying. They'd trailed along with the others to the migrant hostel which Uncle Stephen said was like the army and Auntie Alice had nearly cried. It was strange to be off the ship and the streets of Fremantle were hot and still. But the breeze had come yesterday afternoon as well, which did make things better, even if everyone was still a bit touchy and tired with the strangeness of it all.

"They said," Joe said "that I could take you to Margaret River with me, and we could still have the farm, but that it would be a lot more difficult without a wife but with a little sister."

"I could help!" Ruth said indignantly.

"Yes, my love, those men don't know you, that's a fact."

"So will we go?" Ruth's eyes lit up and she sat forward.

"I don't know."

"Oh Joe, let's go. You don't want to go back to everything in England, do you? I don't. Except … " she stopped.

"Except what?"

"I wish we had Harry."

Joe seemed to shrink in on himself and he had to cough a couple of times before he said "Yes."

"When we have the farm nice with lots of cows and enough money, maybe Lydia would let him come and visit? "

"Yes, that would be good, wouldn't it?" Joe coughed again.

"Then we'll go to the farms with the others?"

Joe sighed. "We'll go, then."

Ruth leapt up and did a little jig, the breeze pressing her dress to her body and lifting her hair.

"Let's tell everyone!"

53

A few days later

The Fremantle Immigrant Hostel was a hideous institutional building converted from some other use that Joe suspected had an army connection.

It was hot, couples and families were split again and the fleas and flies were rampant. They were told that they'd be off in a day or so; Joe fervently hoped so. It came as a surprise to be told that this awful accommodation was part of their entitlement for only three days and if they stayed longer they'd have to pay. Hell, pay for this? He'd find somewhere else if it came to that.

Len and Michael had quickly realised that this modest town at least had lots of pubs and had just walked a short straight line back to the hostel where Joe was idly playing with Ruth. They were laughing.

"Joe, boyo, you've got to come and taste the beer!" Michael swayed slightly.

"Joe, you've got to! It's completely different and God it's refreshing!" Len was straighter, but he was blinking slowly.

Joe was eager and quickly delivered Ruth to Alice. They collected Stephen and walked across the road to an ornate and solid building that announced on its façade that it was the Freemasons' Hotel.

"You don't have to be one of those, do you?" asked Joe, looking up.

"Hope not," said Michael "or I'll be excommunicated!"

This seemed inordinately funny to them all and they were laughing as they entered the relative cool of the front bar.

Their laughter masked the diffidence with which they tried to plumb the conventions of Australian hotel life. Memories of the Oak Tree faded in the sunlight and the strong beer, which Joe did find to be refreshing, if a bit light in flavor. And cold. Quite acceptable, actually.

Stephen and Joe had a bit of catching up to do on Len and Michael, but they didn't try too hard.

Len said "You know, if we weren't so locked in to this farming lark, Michael and I were thinking that those goldfields wouldn't be a bad place to try your luck."

"Are they still getting gold from those mines in Kalgoorlie?" Stephen asked.

Joe started at the sound of Sam's birthplace being mentioned.

"Oh yes," said Michael, "there was this gold miner in one of the pubs we were in earlier. We were listening to him talk to a couple of men at the bar. Made a big pile of money, he had, and he's going to sell his mine. He says there's still plenty of gold left in it but he's had enough and wants to spend his money and enjoy himself."

"Do you think you'd make a miner?" Joe asked, stopping himself with difficulty from thinking of mines and tunnels and holes of any sort. "It's a damned hard life and even harder if you're not used to it."

"Oh, and I suppose that we're used to all this farming stuff we've let ourselves in for?" Len's truculence was never far from the surface.

"At least it's above the ground," said Joe.

"Yes, there's that." Michael nodded owlishly.

"Hey!" he said suddenly, "there's the gold mine man just come in. The very man! Hey! Hey! Sorry I don't know your name," he said apologetically to the tall spare well-dressed man who'd just entered the bar with a jaunty step.

The man turned with a smile. "Dick Wilson" he said, reaching out his hand to shake those of the assembled four in turn.

Joe couldn't believe his eyes. He was looking at an older, more weathered, still moustached, still flashing-smiled and white-teethed, Martin Addison, last seen in the pub by the clock tower half a world away.

Joe wasn't able to hide his instinctive amazement until he realised that Martin Addison-cum-Dick Wilson was looking at him with a small quizzical frown. He recovered himself with difficulty and assumed what he hoped was a normal demeanour.

"So where are you gents from? Not local, by the sound of you, me boyo? Martin was expansive and his accent still had the attractive American twang.

"London." Len was eager to have Martin-Dick tell them all about his gold mine, but Dick-Martin's attitude had changed when he realised that they were not all Irishmen and his eyes swiveled back to Joe with an entirely different expression, wary and calculating.

It was obvious that he didn't recall ever seeing Joe before. That was not all that surprising as it was Peter and Bill who'd been duped by him, with Joe making a late entry and early exit from the scene. This man would have to be careful of quite a lot of people, though, Joe thought, considering what they'd heard about his London-wide confidence tricks. Joe remembered the disappointment and inadequacy felt by his pals and he felt his anger rise. England had got too hot for him, had it? Trying fresh fields and new faces, the bastard. He forced himself to seem interested and leaned forward to hear all that he had to say.

But Dick-Martin was thinking better of offering his spiel to the four at the bar. He was eager to leave, despite having just arrived.

"Look boys, I've got to be somewhere right now, but I'll shout you all a drink and we'll catch up some other time, eh?"

The language was unfamiliar but the intention was clear enough and they accepted their additional drinks with pleasure as Dick again expressed his disappointment at not being able to stay.

"I'll be here again tomorrow around this time," he said as he backed out, "so we can have a proper drink together then."

The three others were surprised when Joe left his drink on the bar and sidled to the door after Dick Wilson.

"Come back and finish your drink, you idiot!" called Len, laughing. "What the hell are you doing?"

"Shut up!" hissed Joe, peering around the corner of the entrance at the retreating figure. "Damn!" he said and slid out the door.

Dick Wilson was walking a good deal faster than most other people on a street that was still somnolent with excess sunshine. There were not enough people around to cover Joe's presence as a follower and Joe cursed again, although Dick Wilson had not cast a backward glance since leaving the pub. He had spun around the corner of the pub and made his way past a terrace of tiny stone cottages, but then disappeared around another corner. A burly man was just going into one of the cottages when Joe hailed him, his desperation making him cast off his usual diffidence.

"Hey, please, can you tell me if there's a police station anywhere close?"

The man looked at him in surprise.

"Yes, why?"

"I need to tell them about a man so they can catch him—he's just up there, just gone around the corner but if I follow him he'll see me so I need to tell the police so they can look for him and find him."

The man looked quickly up the street and back at Joe.

"You're sure?" he said

"Very sure. He tricked two of my friends back home and took their money and now he's trying to sell a gold mine out here." The words tumbled out.

"Oho!" said the man, "let's go then!"

He started to run up the street. Joe was momentarily confused that he was not being told the location of the police station, but he quickly realised that his new friend was intent on chasing and catching Dick Wilson, and what's more, with some enthusiasm. Joe put his head down and ran after him.

Dick Wilson had in fact disappeared as they rounded the corner but Joe's companion seemed to have a pretty good idea of where he might have gone and didn't let up his pace.

Sure enough, around the next corner Dick Wilson was still hurrying up the street. They increased their pace until their pounding footsteps made Dick Wilson aware of their pursuit. He took off like a rabbit, but his mistake was to look back at his pursuers and he stumbled and fell. Joe's friend was on to him in a flash and had him by his collar.

"Oho me beauty! What have we got here?"

If there ever had been any doubt about his guilt, Dick-Martin's frantic struggling removed it. Pushing him ahead like a trophy, his captor paraded him back to the police station, which had in fact been quite close. It seemed that Joe's friend was in fact a warder at the big limestone prison on the top of the hill, so his authority was unquestioned and Joe's story readily accepted. Due checks would be undertaken and statements required.

Funny though. The sight of Martin Addison's face as he was caught, his wide and terrified eyes that even at that moment clearly saw his future, did not fill Joe with the triumph that he might have anticipated. The fine flashing teeth now looked macabre in the cheesy pallor of his face, a face with all its cocky assurance stripped away and now slack with shock and terror. Joe had had to look away.

When Joe walked back to the hostel in the cooling evening, he found that he didn't want to talk about what had happened to Dick Wilson, or his part in it. He felt a bit sick actually and just wanted to get away to the waiting farm in the wide, clear country.

54

One week later

Alice wished herself back on the boat, fervently wished it. Looking back it had been a blissful holiday, even with the cramped conditions and even with the bit of seasickness she'd experienced—now that was saying something, wishing herself back to seasickness!

She sat high on the cart, the accumulated belongings of the eight of them all in a jumble underneath her or sticking into her. She had a protective arm around Ruth. The men walked alongside and Ellen and Ida were up beside the driver. The light was just fading, but the trees and the tangle of undergrowth were dark with menace already. A foreign and disturbing smell, something like cough sweets, drifted on the cooling air. It was hard to see the sky, the trees were so tall and close.

Stephen had made a joking enquiry of the cart driver as to whether he really knew where they were going. Although the man—he said his name was Bob—laughed and said that yes, he knew alright, Alice could understand the question. They had been riding, or driving, or walking, for something like two hours now, and apart from a short distance from the railway station on a rutted track that Bob had called the road, they seemed to be going through exactly the same piece of land, over and over again. It was like a bad dream, a bad dream that had started the minute they got off the boat, come to that. The hostel in Fremantle had been a shock with its huge dormitories and penal atmosphere; the heat had been horrible and the fleas unbearable. She was still scratching. Fremantle was coarse, hot, foreign and unattractive, and the train journey to their wonderful new farm had been nothing short of agony. No real food, no sleep, scenery that was bleached, monotonous and endless, and then their arrival at the Margaret River station and the unloading and reloading on this wretched jolting cart that was taking them, she was perfectly sure, somewhere that she was not going to like.

She absently pulled Ruth tighter and reminded herself why she was here. She lifted her head and sought out Stephen in the rapidly diminishing light. There he was, striding along dependably, although when he turned his head momentarily she could see that he was frowning. "Even you," she thought.

Alice drowsed a little, and when she was jolted awake by a particularly precarious lurch of the cart, it was pitch dark. A small lantern had been lit and swung on the front of the cart, tipping wildly and shedding little light apart from a small puddle that lit up the driver's face with each swing. She was about to close her eyes again when the driver gave a shout.

"Here we are!"

The men pushed to the front of the cart and the women sat up, peering into the darkness, where suddenly they all saw a swinging light and in less than a minute they emerged from the endless forest into a partial clearing where other lights were converging on the party and a voice rang out in the darkness.

"Welcome to Group 19."

The relief at their ultimate arrival pierced the anxiety that had been keeping the party wound up like clockwork and let the exhaustion sweep in. Stumbling, they groped towards the small welcoming party; Alice could barely contain her tears of relief and weariness as a slim young woman with a small child on her hip reached out to shake her hand.

"You'll be tired," she said. "Come and have a cup of tea. I'm Phyllis. That's my hubby Johnny over there and this is little Johnny. You can't see anyone properly right now and you're dog-tired so we'll leave all the introductions to the morning. Come on, follow me. We've put you all together in the one humpy for tonight and we've made up beds for you. The men here will unload the cart and just leave your things in a pile till the morning, too. A cuppa and a good sleep is what you all need."

In a docile group they shuffled towards the outline of a flat-roofed corrugated-iron shed. Holding her lamp high, Phyllis drew aside a hessian curtain that seemed to serve as a door and ushered them inside. Two other women were lighting lamps and a third lifted a tray of enamel mugs of steaming tea from the bare earth that formed the floor. Ten beds that seemed to be made of more hessian strung between sturdy forked sticks were covered with a variety of blankets.

Alice understood that this accommodation was temporary and everything would be better in the morning but was so tired that the primitive beds actually looked inviting. Bare earth would have looked inviting. Hold on, it almost *was* bare earth! She almost laughed. Actually, she must have laughed, because all four of the Group 19 women were looking at her, not without sympathy.

Phyllis seemed to be the spokeswoman. "This is Val, this is Mary and that's Annie," she said, waving her hand. We thought you'd be hungry as well if your trip down here was anything like ours. As you're from Pommy-land we thought we'd welcome you with a good Australian damper to go with your cuppa."

Val—or perhaps Mary, or Annie—smilingly produced a tin tray of what looked like a large cut-up scone, drizzled with something dark and sticky. Each of them could have eaten a horse, so the warm damper, and their first taste of Australian golden syrup, went down, as Len said "a treat".

It was surprising the difference that even a modest meal could make, thought Alice. Only removing the top layer of clothes, they all fell into the beds. Two beds left over, she noticed. They were expecting Joe's wife and child. Could have saved themselves the trouble. It had taken rather more time and patience than she had anticipated and she couldn't claim any personal credit for Lydia's daylight flit, but what was certain now was that Lydia was no longer a threat. Without her having to do anything at all in the end except wait for the inevitable, she thought, as she tried to focus on the lighter patch in the wall that was the doorway in case she needed to get up in the night. She fell asleep trying.

It was the creaking of the expanding corrugated iron in the morning sun that woke Alice. As she opened her eyes she first saw the regular ripples of the iron roof above her, then the sunlight bleeding in through the gaps between the roof and the walls, which were made of the same material. The hessian doorway that she had sought to discern last night was golden in the morning light and moved gently in the breeze.

She twisted her neck to look around and saw Ruth sitting up with her arms around her knees. They smiled at each other, and Alice signalled to her to follow her outside. By the time they had extricated themselves from their beds and shrugged into their clothes, everyone else was awake, too.

They trickled out of the doorway, tentative but expectant and found themselves standing outside one of several identical shacks, dotted through the trees but within reach and sight of each other. Smoke from a couple of fires already twisted into the sky. Their belongings lay in a pile where they had been unloaded the previous night. The sun shone and the sky was clear and blue.

The smell that pervaded the air was the same cough-lozenge background with an overlay of dust and heat. Clean and dusty at the same time. Then a puff of smoke over-ran it all and Phyllis hurried towards them accompanied by a tall, thin rail of a man whose strides matched two of those that Phyllis took. She was slightly out of breath as they came up to the waiting group.

Phyllis was proprietorial.

"This is our foreman, er, people," she said, plainly unable to decide how to address them as a group. "Mr. Harris. Mr. Alec Harris. He's the expert gentleman who tells us all what to do, apparently." This attempt at archness evoked no response from the assembly or from the foreman, who in fact frowned slightly.

Alec Harris had a dog-eared piece of paper in his hand that he lifted and read from.

"I'll just check you off before anything else," he said.

"Stephen Dent, Alice Dent?"

"Present!" said Stephen with schoolroom alacrity that he then tried to disguise with a laugh. No reaction from the foreman.

"Len Dawson, Ida Dawson?"

"Here, both of us," said Len.

"Michael Galvin, Ellen Galvin?"

"Yes sir, here sir." Michael's tone was just short of mocking and Alec Harris gave him a quick glance from under his battered hat.

"Joseph Barlow, Lydia Barlow, Ruth and Henry Barlow?"

There was no immediate answer and the foreman looked up with a frown, his gaze obviously seeking the small child listed. His eyes lit on Ruth, who tugged Joe's arm.

"I'm Joe Barlow," he said eventually and with difficulty, "and this is my sister Ruth. My wife and son are not here."

"Where are they?"

"They couldn't come. Yet. At the last minute."

"So it's just you and your sister?"

"Yes."

"Well, it's your funeral," shrugged the man, "but it won't be easy. There is a school now, for the little lass, it's not far, and there are other kiddies. "But," he repeated "it won't be easy for you."

Alec Harris strode towards the outer perimeter of the partly-cleared area that was dotted with the strange corrugated-iron sheds and swiftly allocated one to each of the four families. The foreman referred to the sheds as "humpies" and the brutal name suited them. No one spoke as they regarded the rickety buildings. Just a gap for the door, no windows, dirt floor and a campfire outside for cooking. Cooking stoves were coming, they were told, but in the meantime … The humpies were temporary, of course, until the farms were cleared a bit and the real houses built.

"How long?' ventured Len.

"As long as it takes, mate," returned the foreman with a shrug, "but the sooner you start the sooner you'll be finished. Stow your stuff, have a bit of breakfast and then come over to my hut," he pointed, "and we'll have a yarn about things. The others'll be there too. You lot are the last to arrive."

The men wordlessly returned to the pile of belongings to sort them and stow them in their humpies, the women and Ruth trailing behind to carry the smaller items. The sense of unreality was intense as the heat of the day increased and crackled in the trees. No one spoke.

Ida had made a fire that was licking a coat of soot on to the sides of a bright new kettle. A small pile of provisions they'd been encouraged to order in Fremantle had been duly delivered and although the bread was stale and the butter almost liquid, passable toast was made. The tea was black.

"I'll just pop over to the pub and borrow a bit of milk," said Alice with what might have been an ironic twist to her mouth, or suppressed tears. They stood and chewed and gulped and blew at their tea. No one seemed able to start a conversation and they avoided each other's eyes until finally Len said "Well, whose bloody stupid idea was this, then?" and they all erupted into lunatic peals of laughter, prolonging it until their eyes watered and they staggered against each other.

"Go on over to that foreman's hut and find out what's going on, Lennie," said Ida, still laughing. "We'll get organised back here."

Len looked at his wife with mild surprise at her assertiveness but trailed through the trees with the other men towards the foreman's hut. The laughter of seconds before died suddenly and was absorbed by the trees.

Alice tried to turn her attention to some necessary tasks. There was doubtless plenty to do but the strangeness of everything around her and whatever it was that she actually had to do unnerved her and she found herself staring vacantly at the ground. There was no ritual, no comfort, nothing familiar, the heat was sapping, the flies a constant irritation and the feeling of hollowness was overwhelming. Alice looked up as the four Australian women from the previous night, with half a dozen others whose accents in time revealed a mixture of English and Scottish origins, made their way over to the newcomers and, with the benefit of ten days previous occupation of the site, proceeded to give advice, and also to chat.

It was almost a wry comfort to learn that the other settlers were just as dumbfounded at the conditions they found themselves in. The glowing advertisements and the hearty reassuring interviews were the same all over. So it was not just them that had been hoodwinked, thought Alice. Not just them that felt silly.

Phyllis and her husband and baby son had come from Victoria on the other side of the country where Johnny had been a farm worker. Annie, Val and Mary and their husbands were also Australians with various rural backgrounds who had been lured by the possibility of actually owning their own farms. There were to have been twenty families in the Group, with the remainder made up of English and Scottish families—Phyllis confided in a respectful tone that there was actually a bank clerk amongst them. The hopefulness was universal then. They were all hoping for something more, or perhaps even just something different. It was certainly giving them that. There were in fact only nineteen families making up the Group at that time—Phyllis laughed that one of the wives had taken one look at the humpies and it had apparently been the last straw to an impending hysteria.

"She fainted," Phyllis laughed. "Just collapsed in a heap like wet washing. Then when she came to she just started to wail and carry on, really loud. She was laying there screaming like a stuck pig, kicking her heels into the ground while her poor husband fussed around and tried to calm her. But she wouldn't calm down and in the end they both went back on the cart with the bloke who brought 'em here with the others."

"Just as well," said Annie stolidly, "If you don't want to be here, it's better not to be here. It's not gonna be easy." Her appearance and demeanour seemed suited to the struggle ahead, Alice thought. She resembled a bulldog and Alice languidly consigned her to people she wouldn't get on with.

For her own part, Alice could not find the strength to look as if she wanted to be there; it was beyond her acting ability. It was impossible to enthuse about anything—the ghastly humpies, the dust, the flies, the horrible towering trees and the sheer remoteness even from the little civilisation they'd seen in the last week …

Everything she was learning was adding to the list of horribles. Where were the cosy farms and green meadows of the brochures? Asking again didn't make the answer any more comfortable or palatable. Phyllis, baby on her hip, told them baldly that it would be at least a year—in her opinion, and her Johnny's—before a single house could possibly be built. "Look around," she said, gesturing widely with her free arm at the impenetrable forest, "*that's* got to be cleared first just to make space for a house, let alone for paddocks."

"A whole year in these tin huts?" asked Ellen incredulously.

"Cooking on a fire outside?" Ida's tussle with this morning's cooking fire was still evident on her hands and face.

"Oh, they say that they'll be bringing cooking stoves soon that'll be inside," said Phyllis with authority, "but they don't know when."

By virtue of her background, nationality, and natural assurance, Phyllis dominated the discussion but Alice wondered how long it would be before the slight comfort they were deriving from her confidence began to rasp into irritation. Wouldn't really like her for a next-door neighbour. The heat was increasing and the flies clustered around her eyes and mouth; one of the English women handed her a switch of leaves to slap around her head and Alice thought about having to do this for the rest of her life. The tall trees that surrounded the humpies were a formidable enclosure. Some of them sprawled over the randomly-sited humpies but they only provided a sort of half-hearted shade except deeper into the surrounding forest where they clustered together and their upper branches were entangled. But the prospect of cool shade was not enough to entice anyone into their depths; the new arrivals were rigid with apprehension of what other things they might find there.

"Snakes?" said Phyllis dismissively. "Of course there are. But they're more scared of you than you are of them."

"How do you know?" asked Alice rudely.

"Look," said Phyllis patronisingly as Alice's not-quite-irrational dislike of the woman grew, "all you have to do is make a noise when you're walking through the bush, stamp your feet sort of thing. They'll wriggle off when they feel the vibrations. Look where you're walking and don't do anything silly like jump over a log without checking the other side."

Alice thought that jumping over a log was just about the last thing she'd be likely to do in this place—catch her even venturing into that ghostly forest of hideous trees. That'd be the day. What on earth was she doing here? Why on earth hadn't she fought harder to stay safely at home and keep Ruth there too? She'd panicked, that's what she'd done, and not stopped to think of consequences. And now here she was, stranded, depressed and uncomfortable.

Automatically she looked round for Ruth and noted listlessly that she was playing tentatively with two boys of about her own age and a younger girl. She was too tired and hot to register any pleasure that Ruth had found some playmates. Only yesterday—or was it the day before?—she'd been concerned that Ruth had only adult company. That was when she had nothing better to think about.

The conversation with the other women was just going around in circles as each strove to outdo the other with tales of duplicity and dashed expectations. She wandered back to the humpy that would apparently now be home to Stephen and her for a year at least. She walked inside and the heat was solid; the walls and roof seemed to radiate it inwards. There was no window, but there was no breeze anyway. The dirt floor was only beginning to compact with the imprints of occupancy and it puffed grey and gritty as she trod towards the pile of belongings at one end.

The kindness of the other Group members in constructing the beds that they'd all slept on thoughtlessly the previous night had not occurred to any of them at the time, but now, faced with the enormity of their situation, the time and trouble involved in creating the only pieces of furniture they now owned, irritated Alice suddenly. Primitive they were, just hessian stretched between small forked logs. They looked so sad and poor.

There was nothing to do! Sweep the floor, Alice? Ha. Clean the windows,? Ha ha. Do the washing Alice, ha ha *ha!* A trip to the fly-buzzing latrine where she was forced to squat above a pit behind more hessian was almost the last straw and tears were pricking her eyes as she walked back to the humpy. How could she exist here? She wondered only vaguely about Ellen and Ida, too preoccupied with her own heat and misery to care too much about anyone else. She'd have to get out, no doubt about it. Have to. Could not possibly stay her in this hot, smelly, fly-blown *horrible* place. She'd have to convince Joe to let her take Ruth with her, Ruth couldn't possibly stay either.

Feverishly she began to think about packing her clothes and possessions and wondered how she could contact the man who'd brought them here yesterday. She'd ask that foreman. If the woman who'd gone hysterical could get out, then she could too. If she'd known what she knew now, she'd have turned on the hysterics yesterday too. She was intent on stuffing clothes into a little bag when Stephen pushed aside the hessian door-flap.

"Whew," he said "Hot in here. What are you doing, love, unpacking?"

Alice stopped, her back still turned to Stephen.

"Where would I unpack *to*?" she asked shakily.

Usually Stephen was perceptive to atmosphere, but he seemed stupidly buoyant. "We had a good talk with Mr. Harris," he said, squatting beside Alice. "It's interesting how they're planning to do things here, and the others have already started. We're latecomers of course. We—"

"I said, where would I unpack *to*?" said Alice grimly.

Stephen stopped. "We've got to put together some furniture of course, and we did ship one of my bookshelves and your dresser, so that's a start—when they arrive."

"I don't want to stay here." Even as she spoke, Alice knew with dread that she was in fact going to stay. She was going to be persuaded into staying and she was going to give in because in reality she had no option but to stay. Little money, not enough to get back home, not enough to find her way around this dreadful country. She'd burned all her bridges.

The tears she'd been holding in check threatened to overcome her and she covered her face with her hands, still squatting on the floor in front of her suitcase. Stephen put his arms around her waist and attempted to bring her to her feet but she resisted sharply. He lost his grip and was suddenly on his back on the dirt floor. Alice screamed "You see, you see? There's not even a bloody chair to sit on!"

The makeshift beds that they'd slept on the previous night had been shifted that morning into their respective humpies, and Alice now threw herself on to one of the two now remaining. Slight as she was, her action was precipitate enough to cause the bed to collapse and she tumbled with it. Stephen was still on the ground leaning on one elbow, red in the face with suppressed laughter. At this point she could have given in, should have given in, would have given in perhaps, but for the frustration that screamed for release.

How long had this been building, this pressure to explode? How many years of pretence and concealment, yearning and aching, fear and dread? All come to this … this … *place!*

She picked up one of the sturdy sticks from the collapsed bed and began to strike out. Even in her red-eyed frenzy she did not try to hit Stephen, but lashed out at their cases, their bundles, the hut walls, the beds, smashing into them with demented fury, as Stephen watched from his position on the floor. When she hit the walls the sound was deafening and the walls themselves seemed to hit back as the stick rebounded from the corrugated surface, until, finally spent, she dropped her arms and stood dishevelled, breathing hard.

Stephen's amusement had dropped away and he scrambled up from the floor. "Finished?" he asked dryly, taking the stick from her unresisting hand.

"Finished." Alice managed to convey a double meaning.

"Alice my love, you'll feel better when we get settled in a bit more."

"Settled in? Settled in? No one can *settle in* to this excuse for a building. Look at it! *Look at it!* It's not fit for animals!" Trickles of perspiration ran down her face and she rubbed them away impatiently.

"Well? Well? You can't pretend that this is what you thought we were coming to?"

"I know it's not what we were expecting…"

"Bloody lies we were told."

"Bloody lies we were told." Stephen affirmed.

"So what can we do?" Alice's anger was spent but her belligerence remained.

"I don't think there's much we can do, love. If I thought there was something, I'd do it. I think the problem lies in the optimistic stuff we were all fed back home when it comes to the lies."

Alice sat disconsolately on the only good bed as Stephen continued. "The scheme still looks good, even if the beginnings aren't what we'd like, or what we all expected."

"Lies."

"True. But we have to get over all that. And we can, you know. Mr. Harris was saying—"

"He probably tells lies too," said Alice, pushing aside the hessian curtain with a sweep of her arm as she walked out of the door.

She instantly regretted leaving the humpy. It had seemed stiflingly hot in there, but the heat that struck her as she walked outside was bright and metallic and took her breath away. Having made her comment and her exit, she couldn't go straight back into the humpy and she looked around with something like panic for a refuge. She couldn't remember which of the humpies had been allocated to Joe and Ruth, or even to the others.

None of the figures moving slowly around the camp area were familiar and the nightmare feeling swept over her again.

Alec Harris seemed to materialise out of the glare.

"Mrs. Dent, isn't it?" he said. "Not a good idea to be out in this sun without a hat, my girl. You don't want to catch the sun. Or get burned, not that nice English skin, you don't."

Alice looked at him blankly; he could have been speaking a foreign language.

He repeated himself slowly. "If you stay out in this hot sun too long you will get sunstroke and you'll get sunburned as well where you're not well covered. Do you have a hat?"

Of course Alice had a hat.

"Well you'd better put it on and take care to wear it all the time when you're outside, young lady."

He patted her paternally on the arm and walked on.

Slowly Alice turned and went back into the humpy. There was no refuge anywhere.

55

Two months later.
May 1925

A routine of sorts prevailed in the humpy village. Amazingly, the hideous hot weather had abated and it was now pleasant—well, less *un*pleasant, Alice demurred—to walk around out of doors, and the humpies became less stifling. Most of the settlers had taken it upon themselves to cut windows in the rippling walls, pushing out the corrugated iron with a stick to hold it and this ventilation caught the early morning breeze to make the rickety huts less stuffy and claustrophobic. Rudimentary furniture had been constructed by the men from the ubiquitous kerosene boxes and the kerosene tins themselves cut, bent and hammered into buckets, scoops, pans and more.

Initial foreign feelings had been smoothed by everyday repetition of endless chores into something that was nearly comfortable. No, thought Alice, not at all *comfortable*, just less unknown. The dirt floors were still dirty, if more compacted now, the humpies still doorless and ugly beyond belief, the flies and ants still marauded, the forest still loomed dark and baleful and the birds screeched in awful discord. The work that the men were doing was progressing so slowly that Alice's despair increased by the day. Stephen, as with all the other men, even those with farming backgrounds, had suffered badly from back strain and blisters on his hands for the first weeks of unaccustomed toil, pouring kerosene on to his hands to harden them each night.

Alice grimaced as she realised that she now said 'kerosene' for 'paraffin' without even thinking about it. She did not, however say 'kero' like the Australians and was sure she never would.

But be it paraffin, kerosene or even kero it did the job and Stephen's hands developed callouses that scratched when he held Alice at night when she cried.

Stephen was tender and sympathetic and more than a little guilty at her continuing distress. Len had said the other day that he blamed Stephen for having the emigration idea in the first place. This was true, Alice thought mutinously, and Stephen knew it, but Len had been joking. He was beginning to actually settle in, she could tell, and as for bloody Ida, she was thriving, little Miss Happy Drudge. Alice was scornful of the time and trouble that Ida spent in trying to make their humpy comfortable; the paper frill along the edge of the kerosene-box dresser made her snort with derision.

But Ida and Ellen had even mastered breadmaking in the new ovens they now had, while Alice couldn't raise the enthusiasm to do more than boil a kettle and make desultory use of the frying pan. She let the fire go out frequently from sheer boredom at keeping it going. However, she made breakfast for Stephen and wearily packed the apple and billy of cold tea which he'd take out to whatever location he was working on to consume on his 10 o'clock break. 'Smoko' they called it here and it did indeed include time for a pipe but Alice fastidiously refrained from using the term, determined not to allow this ghastly country into her life or her vocabulary.

Stephen had mentioned appreciatively that Mrs. Sugden had come out to where her husband had been working with Stephen with hot tea and a fresh cake the other day, but Alice wasn't about to take that hint. No thank you.

The only thing that was positive in her life was Ruth and in truth she was the only thing that kept her functioning to even a halfway level of normal. If it wasn't for Ruth she would hardly stir. Ruth was the reason she was here. Alice sat at the rough table and treacherously allowed herself to think of the life she'd left behind, the life she'd be leading now if she wasn't so irresistibly and helplessly tied to Ruth. It was a Monday morning; she'd be helping Flo Keily with the washing perhaps, sharing a cup of tea in her steamy wash-house and having a gossip. Or she'd be cleaning the pub bar, polishing the pump handles, cleaning the fireplace, seeing Charlie … God how she'd love to see Charlie, she thought with a sudden urgent rush of desire that made her tingle. Charlie with his knowing eye and his heavy hands, hands that knew what she needed, hands she missed. Oh God how she missed them.

Comparing Stephen's hands to Charlie's was like comparing water and gin. Stephen was careful, respectful of her body. Even knowing where that body had been in its life, he still treated her as if she were fragile and innocent. So gentle. At first it was sheer bliss to feel so protected and soothed, but *that* had worn off. Stephen was just too gentle, too accommodating, too understanding.

Oh yes, she was never satisfied, was she? Way back from Sid and his casual use of her, Johnnie with his problems, Charlie with his occasional slap around and now Stephen who she knew she should appreciate more but was not damned well going to, that was a good selection, wasn't it? A good variety. Funny to think that it was Charlie that she was missing so. She'd not thought that would happen, seemed at the time an opportunity to get away. Now she'd give anything to get back. She'd take Ruth when she went of course, she'd have to do that. Couldn't leave her here, could she?

She imagined walking back into Oak Tree Place holding Ruth by the hand, imagined the look on Charlie's face, imagined with glee the shock on the faces of Edie and Lily.

She'd have to find a way to do it. She hugged herself in half-pleasure, half-frustration. She wasn't good at finding solutions, wasn't good at actions she supposed either. Most things in her life had just happened to her and she'd just coped. Sometimes hadn't even coped, just escaped like she had from Arthur's sons. A lot of 'justs' in that summary. Some luck and no planning, that was her. And the luck was a combination of good and bad.

At least here she felt safe from the repercussions of what had happened to Arthur. She reckoned that not even they would find her here. But she'd even sacrifice that safety to go back to civilisation. She'd find a way, somehow.

Charlie, Charlie, I wish you knew how I was thinking. I shouldn't have treated you so badly and now I want you so much so that's my punishment for making you suffer so.

Her thoughts made her body tingle pleasantly and she stretched sensuously. The present impinged rudely as the hessian door billowed in a sudden breeze and more dust flew into the humpy. She regarded this without expression and let her thoughts droop back into everyday depression. She had too much time to think, that was the trouble.

Ruth walked to school each week day in the company of six other children from the Group. The school was only two miles distant and one of the children was the son of the foreman Mr. Harris whose age of nine and cocky knowledge of the bush meant that he was seen as a suitable custodian for the small schoolgoers initially. That they now nearly all felt equipped to make the journey without supervision was not something that Archie Harris was prepared to acknowledge and he collected and herded his small charges with a determination that did not allow for dissent. If Alice had been inclined to see a lighter side, she might have been amused at the sight of the little flock being driven with such purpose. She could only see Ruth disappearing into the dark and dangerous forest each morning and ignored the pleasure and satisfaction that Ruth herself was obviously deriving from the journey and from school itself as she joyfully erupted again each afternoon from that same dark and dangerous forest, full of the days' happenings.

It made Alice ache with love to see how Ruth tried to be a helpmate to Joe. Ida had (officiously, Alice thought) taken her under her wing and taught her some of the dreadful things that she wanted to learn, like how to make bread and keep the fire going in the stove and light it again when it went out despite all efforts. In spite of Alice declaring that this was well above and beyond the capabilities of a child of nine, Ruth had in fact learned to make creditable bread and showed signs of becoming more or less proficient at other cooking, give or take a fairly regular disaster like the flaming frying pan and the charred scones that Joe made a joke of by throwing them at the crows to see which was the blackest black.

Ruth was so determined, Alice thought with wonder. To see her small hands kneading the bread dough or to see her cutting potatoes with a huge knife and frowning concentration made Alice yearn to take her in her arms and cocoon and protect her. Ruth in her turn was still as affectionate as she'd been all her life, but Alice frequently thought with panic that these times and actions must be finite.

The proximity of the humpies to each other made it easy for women to help each other out with shared batches of bread or scones and Alice could see that Joe and Ruth were seen as a special case by many of them and they certainly did not want for donations of food and other help. Ruth was seen as a poor little scrap of a lassie with a poor wronged big brother and the maternal feelings of most of the Group's women were raised by their plight, details of which had quickly done the rounds of the camp. This would have been by courtesy of Ellen, Alice felt sure. Bloody Ellen hadn't stopped talking since they all decided to emigrate.

This charity suited Alice in that she didn't have to worry herself about cooking for them—she had hard time raising the energy to prepare dinner and tea for Stephen. The men were usually home for their dinner at around midday and back to work again, equipped with an afternoon smoko, by 1 o'clock.

Alice reflected that the houses of Oak Tree Place had not been splendid, but this routine would not have seemed the problem there that it posed here in these primitive humpies with their grit and stuffiness and ugly make-do furniture. She felt put-upon, no doubt about that. She resented everything she had to do just to survive here. Water came from the creek, dragged up in kerosene tins with cloth-wrapped wire handles that still cut into her hand. This duty was necessary if she ran out during the day before Stephen had had a chance to bring up more when he came home from his work. She'd only had to do it once actually, when the brimming tin had been tipped over sort of by accident when she was kicking the dresser in fury and frustration and it had overturned. She couldn't think of how to explain it to Stephen, so pushed the wretched dresser upright again and fetched more water. She'd explained the puddle by saying she'd overdone the sprinkling of water on the floor to lay the dust.

She'd only been an average sort of cook at home, and of course there it had only been herself to cook for so it didn't matter if she only ate bread and jam if she felt like it.

But now she had to think about Stephen and his workman's day and workman's appetite. Cooking was so different here—if you ran out of anything, you couldn't just take off your pinny and dash down to the shop for the sugar, or the flour, or the eggs. Every blasted thing you did was a huge task. All provisions had to be thought about and ordered and if you forgot something you were in trouble, keeping meat for more than a day in the summer was impossible even in the rickety contraption known as a Coolgardie safe with its dripping water and its wet cloths which she couldn't be bothered mastering anyway and come to think of it, butter was always just a runny liquid, except for first thing in the morning when the overnight chill had made it firm. Water had to be carried and conserved, the lavatory was beyond description and that had to be filled in and shifted with alarming regularity too, firewood had to be collected incessantly and washing was done in the creek. Not that washing achieved anything of course; clothes were dirty again immediately and the weekly bath was really just a waste too. Dirt was everywhere. Dirt and depression.

She knew she wasn't the only one who felt this way. "Misery breeds misery" Jessie used to say bracingly as she dared the possibility of succumbing to such a negative emotion, but Alice had noticed the languid demeanour and vacant gaze of at least two of the other English women that suggested that they too felt a deep unhappiness with their situation. Even so, Alice knew that her own wretchedness was deeper and more significant than theirs and she felt no companionship of feeling.

The attempt at suicide by one of these women, even as half-hearted as it was, shocked the Group. Little Mrs. Collins, native of Leeds, never been as far from home as London before this, was so confused and unhappy that she plunged into the forest to deliberately lose herself and, as she sobbed later, to starve or be bitten by a poisonous snake or killed by a wild animal. In the event she thrashed in circles for hours and when Mr. Harris and the men set out to find her she was in fact only a couple of hundred yards from the camp. Her husband was angry and embarrassed and Alice didn't think that his wife would be much happier or any more resigned to her situation after he had taken her back to the humpy and given her the promised 'talking to'.

Alice idly considered befriending her; they could perhaps compare miseries. But there were enough comforters, she thought as she watched Ida and Ellen join the well-wishers as they surrounded the poor woman the next morning. Enough to send her off into the bush again.

Alice wondered whether she'd ever feel like doing what Mrs. Collins had tried to do. She was surely sad, discontented and generally fed-up but she reflected that, even if her feelings reached their deepest level of depression, she couldn't ever abandon Ruth. Ruth would eventually learn the truth, and she was the only one who could tell her.

56

Four months later.
September 1925

In the winter, walking to school had been hard. Even with her mackintosh and rubber boots. The rubber boots had kept Ruth's feet dry at first but they rubbed blisters on to her heels and ankles so she'd taken them off in the end. It was easy enough to rinse most of the mud off her feet when she got to school, and again when she got home. Her feet got cold though.

It seemed as if it had rained every day that winter. There was mud everywhere and the men's work had got very slow, Joe said, because of the mud and with everything being so wet. The humpy stayed fairly dry, but lots of times Joe had had to re-dig the gutter channel around the outside of the walls so that the water didn't come through inside and just flowed away down the hill to the creek instead. It actually did come in a few times, but it didn't matter all that much as there wasn't much to get wet. It had been cold, too—everyone said that they didn't expect it to be so cold in Australia and some people had even left their coats and mack-intoshes back in England, but that was silly because her teacher Miss Fox at home had helped her and the rest of the class look up the part of Australia she was coming to and found out all about the animals and the weather and she knew it was going to be nice and warm in summer and wet and quite cold in winter, but not so cold as at home. So she and Joe had brought their coats.

It hadn't been *that* cold anyway and over the last few weeks it had been warmer, and very nice really. The walk to school was much easier and more fun, even if Archie bossed them about a bit; she was nearly the same age as Archie and he didn't boss her that much. In fact he taught her quite a lot of useful stuff like how to make a whistle from a gum leaf and how to tell north from the sun. He had promised to show her the Southern Cross in the sky at night, but they hadn't got round to that yet because it was so often cloudy or raining or the tops of the trees were in the way. She told Archie that she'd seen it on the boat on the way out, anyway, but he didn't believe her and said it couldn't have been the real Australian one.

School was really good. Miss Anderson was a very good teacher and very pretty with curly brown hair and a lovely smile. She was from Perth but had been sent down to the Group school by the government and she stayed at the farm that belonged to Mr. & Mrs. Padman a mile or two down the track. It was the opposite direction from Group 19 otherwise Ruth could have walked part of the way home with her, but other children got to do that. There were twenty children at the school and they went from Grade 1 to Grade 5, with everyone in the same room, of course, as there was only one. The school room smelled lovely, of fresh cut new wood just like Mr. Jackson's where Joe used to work back at home and Ruth loved to stand and breathe in the smell if the room happened to be empty sometimes. When the children were all inside the smell got different—it smelled of ink and clothes and lunches. There were windows down the sides, a fireplace in the corner for winter and the tops of the windows opened to let in fresh air. It was brand-new. The desks were not delivered yet and they had to sit on long forms and take turns to use the two tables for writing and drawing. There was a blackboard, however, and some books for reading and learning geography. At first there was no chalk but Miss Anderson managed to buy some. Miss Anderson sometimes took them all on walks in the bush. She was Australian and she knew a lot about wildflowers and plants and birds and animals, even though she was born in the city. She just found it very interesting, she said.

It was Spring now and Miss Anderson said that it was the very best time for wildflowers, They'd seen lots, and picked them to press and dry to make a collection. Some of them were so little and shy that they seemed to hide, while others were really colourful and bright. Miss Anderson said that there were hundreds and hundreds of different wildflowers in Western Australia and lots that haven't even been discovered yet! Ruth asked her how she knew they were there if they hadn't been discovered and Miss Anderson said something about probably.

Joe said that Ruth would talk about Miss Anderson in her sleep if she could.

The other children in the school were from two other Groups that were nearby. First of all they were going to have a school on each Group but they said that was a waste of sauces when Groups that were close together could share. Ruth was not sure what kind of sauce because they hadn't had any yet. Six children in the school were from Group 19, eight from another Group and six from another; Ruth wasn't sure of their Group numbers. Being in one room was fun but sometimes it was hard to concentrate when you accidentally listened to bits and pieces of other lessons. When Miss Anderson read stories everyone listened all together and that was lovely.

So Ruth loved school, and even though she knew that the grown-ups had a pretty hard time with so much work to do, the Group camp was fun too. She tried to look after Joe because bloody Lydia tricked him when she didn't come with them. Ruth thought that that was dreadfully unkind and horrid but she was not really surprised when she thought about it and she couldn't imagine Lydia in a humpy but a little mean part of her would have liked to have seen that. But what Lydia did made Joe very unhappy and he still thought about her, Ruth could tell. She knew as well that they both thought about little Harry and missed him very, very, very, very much. Ruth hoped he was not missing them too much because she couldn't bear the thought of him being unhappy. How she'd love to cuddle him again and dress him and play with him give him his tea like she used to do. She glowered and hoped that bloody Lydia was looking after him. She wondered when they might see him again. Bloody Lydia. She said that once to Joe back in Fremantle sitting under that tree by the beach, and he let her, but she wasn't allowed to say it really. If she knew a worse word, though, she'd use it because bloody Lydia deserved it.

Ruth was learning about the Group. Archie's Dad Mr. Harris was the foreman, he told the men what to do and helped people. Joe told her that the men were working together to clear every block of about 5 acres of trees (that'd be like from Beulah Road to Northwood Road and over to Osborne Road, Joe thought) and then people would come and build houses for everybody, which will a be good thing, to have proper houses instead of the humpies. Then when everybody moved from the camp to the houses, they'd all finish clearing the trees on their own blocks, make some fences, grow some grass, get some cows (Joe promised some chickens too) to eat the grass and give them milk, some to use and some to sell—and there they are, happy farmers. Ruth drew a picture at school of what their farm will look like and Miss Anderson pinned it up on the wall with some others. The cows were a bit too big for the field, but the house looked good.

It was funny that Mr. Dent—Ruth kept forgetting to call him Uncle Stephen, it sounded not polite—was going to be a farmer when he'd always been a teacher; she kept thinking he should be teaching at their school, like he used to teach at Beulah Road. Auntie Alice was different in Australia from how she used to be in England. She was sort of nervous but maybe she was scared of the bush. Quite a lot of the ladies were, Ruth knew, but goodness it was silly to be scared because there's nothing there to hurt you. Perhaps a snake if you didn't take care, Archie says, but we've never seen one yet. And there are certainly no lions or tigers or things that will eat you. The kangaroos are beautiful and very shy, they thud and crash off through the bush like bouncing balls when they see you. Ruth saw a mother kangaroo with a little joey in her pouch the other day—he was peeping out and was so beautiful. She yearned to pat one.

If it wasn't the bush and the animals that Auntie Alice was nervous about, Ruth didn't know what else it could be. She thought Mr.—Uncle Stephen was probably the nicest man anyone could think of being married to (except Joe) and Auntie Alice was lucky that he asked her. She didn't like the humpy, and probably all the other ladies feel a bit like that too, but it's not forever, and lovely new houses will be coming soon. Ruth sniffed a deep breath in sweet anticipation—just think, they'll smell like the school! Lovely. She will have a bedroom of her own, too, with a wooden floor!

Auntie Alice had scared her a couple of times. Once was back at home when she came to the school that time and said she was taking her out for the day. It was very strange and unusual. Ruth didn't like it at all and was very very glad when Uncle Stephen— he was Mr. Dent then—found them. Ruth rode on his shoulders, she remembered, and Auntie Alice and Uncle Stephen talked quietly to each other all the way home so she couldn't hear. She still didn't know why all that happened but the next day Auntie Alice and Uncle Stephen said they were getting married, so maybe that was when they decided.

The second time was just the other day. Joe and the men were still out working and Auntie Alice had come to their humpy to help Ruth get their tea ready. She really didn't need help and was a bit annoyed that Auntie Alice was there because she really liked to do things by herself and she knew she could. She said that Auntie Alice should be home getting Uncle Stephen's tea and Auntie Alice let out a funny sort of hissing sound. Ruth didn't like it when grown-ups, especially Auntie Alice, did things that they didn't usually do, like that hissing sound, but she ignored it and hoped that ignoring it would make it float out of the door. Auntie Alice didn't make the sound again but Ruth was careful not to look at her because she knew that she was crying and she didn't know what to do when grown-ups cried.

57

***Three months later.
December 1925***

It had been almost a year since they came on to the Group. They'd seen all the seasons now and Ruth thought that Spring was close to the best, but Autumn was the best. Summer and winter were not the best. In order of bestness, it was Autumn, Spring, Summer and Winter. Autumn was best because the hot weather of summer started to get a bit cool and you felt more comfortable and there were less flies. It was a pity that this was followed by wet winter with its mud and rain, but then it turned into Spring with the wildflowers and some warm sun to dry everything out again. Good, not-so-good, good, not-so-good, that's how it went.

Five families had left their Group and six families had come in, so the Group still had twenty families. Ruth thought it was lucky for the last families to come in as a lot of hard work had been done on the locations in that past year, but they were nice people and they couldn't help that.

Joe said that they were ready to ballot for the blocks. It was an exciting time and everyone went to watch as Mr. Harris and all the men stood around a table with a big pot on it. Mr. Harris drew numbers and called out names and everyone got a block of their own. Mr. Harris made sure that Uncle Stephen and Auntie Alice were next-door to Joe and Ruth because Auntie Alice had especially asked him. But it was a bit different from being next-door at home with only a wall between the houses.

When Joe took her out to see their new home-block it was quite exciting but it really didn't look any different from all the other bush except that they were lucky that the stream that ran through the camp was also somewhere on their block and they'd find it sooner or later. They walked on to Auntie Alice and Uncle Stephen's block and it was a long, long walk. Joe said it was a mile or so, but Ruth thought it was longer than the walk to school but perhaps that was because she was used to the school walk now. The narrow track that the men had made while doing the clearing was easy to follow to Uncle Stephen's though and Ruth felt she could find her way there quite easily by herself if she wanted.

The houses were still coming and no one knew when they'd be there. So some of the men, including Joe, took down the humpies they'd been living in on the home camp block and put them up again on their own blocks! Everyone was so pleased to leave the home camp that the humpies even seemed more comfortable there.

Auntie Ellen and Uncle Michael: she still had to roll the names around her mouth before she could say them, just like Auntie Ida and Uncle Len, but they had said that they were as good as related and that they were honourable aunts and uncles. They also said that they should stick together as much as they all could in this new place and Ruth didn't have many real relations so they'd be glad to fill the space. Ruth thought that was very nice. Anyway, Auntie Ellen and Uncle Michael's block was just down the track a bit more and Auntie Ida and Uncle Len had a block that shared a back boundary with hers and Joe's. So they were all still neighbours, but Ruth had to smile at the difference from Oak Tree Place. They'd not been able to walk to Auntie Ida's through their block because the trees and undergrowth were so thick. They just knew they were there because of the map of the blocks.

She was looking forward to Christmas. The Oak Tree Place people were all going to spend Christmas Day together at Auntie Ida's and share the cooking and the food. But before that there was the big party at the school where all the parents from the three Groups were going to get together and have a dance and the children would get presents and Father Christmas was going to come and they'd all sing carols. Ruth hoped that the little children wouldn't realise that Father Christmas was Mr. Slattery dressed up. She shouldn't even know that herself, but she'd accidentally come in to Auntie Ellen's humpy to find her and some of the other ladies giggling as they draped red material over Mr. Slattery and anyone could see that this was to make his Father Christmas clothes. Especially as Mrs. Slattery was sitting at the table making a white beard out of cotton wool.

Ruth missed Archie. Mr. Harris and Archie had left in the middle of winter; Mr. Harris was going to another new Group to help the men start it up. Mr. Bannister had come instead and he didn't have any children. He was different from Mr. Harris and Ruth didn't like him very much although she never said anything. He certainly didn't like children, she thought. He never even looked at them, but he did look at the men and more especially their wives. Ruth had watched him one day as he kept looking at Auntie Alice walking back to her humpy. Auntie Alice had a really silly smile on her face and was walking very slowly in a way that made Ruth feel uncomfortable. He wasn't even nice looking, sort of smooth and shiny and a bit fat and the men said that he wasn't a patch on Mr. Harris who had done a lot of farming things and was a much nicer man anyway. But they had to do what Mr. Bannister told them to, at least until the Group work was finished and they all had their own farms and houses. But they often argued with him and tried to change his mind about things he told them to do. Joe said they all seemed to know more about the work they were supposed to be doing than he did and they wondered what he'd done before he was made foreman of the Group. When they asked him he just told them that he'd done enough.

Perhaps he wouldn't be at the Christmas party. Ruth hoped he wouldn't, but it really didn't matter. The party would be good anyway and she was nursing a lovely Christmas secret that no one but her knew about.

But before school broke up for the long Christmas holidays (much longer than Christmas holidays at home, but that was because everything was back-to-front in Australia), Miss Anderson had the idea of a going on a picnic to the beach. All the children thought that was a really good idea, but she needed some grown-ups to help with things and everyone who heard about it thought it was a good idea too, so that all of a sudden everyone was coming, babies and young children not at school and just about all the grown-ups as well. So it was not going to be on a school day now, but on a Sunday, three weeks before Christmas and it was going to be very exciting.

58

A week later

Joe was in charge of the Group horse, the original working animal on the Group in the initial clearing stage. Poor thing had been worked hard, eagerly sought-after for the power it could lend to the puny efforts of the men of the various working parties.

The children had named Group 19's horse George and George was well tended and fed as befitted his position as important contributor to clearing and carting. He may have been surprised to have been harnessed to the cart this morning, as he was not usually worked on a Sunday, and even more surprised to find himself led through the bush pulling the Group cart loaded with chattering women and children and various baskets, rugs and bundles.

Joe and George were following two other Group carts from where snatches of song could be heard wafting back through the trees as the three carts progressed slowly, the men of the Groups walking beside. They were being led by Miss Anderson herself, who had apparently made herself familiar with the route they had to take. Joe was impressed by her ability as there was little or no track that he could see, although by the time his third cart came along there was quite a bit of smashed undergrowth and evidence of passing.

He passed George's lead rope to Stephen and made his way forward till he came to the indomitable Miss Anderson, and noticed that the trees were thinning and the growth more spare and bushy. They had all lived for so long in the shadow of the giant trees around the camp and in their labouring that this thinning was quite heady. Joe felt like taking deep breaths. When he said this to Miss Anderson, she told him to wait until they got to the beach, and then he'd really feel like taking deep breaths.

"How do you know the way?" asked Joe "I can't see a track at all."

"I was shown the way by Mr. Padman when I first went to board with them," she said, "and I've walked this way a lot of times since them. And," she said with sly sideways smile "there are blazes on the trees!"

Joe laughed. "I didn't see them."

"I shouldn't have told you."

Now Joe began to see traces of a track. They'd been walking for nearly two hours but the energy of the Groupers didn't fade. None of them had been to the beach despite its relative closeness and they were all stimulated by the anticipation and the release from routine.

A long uphill slog brought them to a crest where they all paused. Though still half a mile away, the sea glittered and beckoned. Deepest blue on the horizon where it seemed to blend into the sky, closer to the shore huge ragged patches of brightest aquamarine mixed with the blue and shimmered with light. Waves built and broke on slick black rocks, sending booming showers of white spray into the air. The feeling of space and freedom was heady.

"I see what you meant about saving those deep breaths," said Joe.

"Beautiful, isn't it?" Miss Anderson was smiling and lifting her face to the wind. "I come here as often as I can because I just love it."

"You come alone?"

"Often I do. But sometimes with Mrs. Padman—she loves it here—sometimes with a friend."

Unloading the carts and allocating bundles, the party's pause was almost momentary as everyone was so eager to get to the beach. The plunging, sandy downhill journey seemed to be over in a minute.

Joe walked on to the most beautiful beach he'd ever seen. A crescent of fine sand stretched between two rocky headlands, dazzling white in the harsh midday light. A small valley reached crookedly inland from the middle of the beach, clothed with low grayish vegetation and slashed by a sandy creek bed. On closer inspection it could be seen that there was a trickle of water in the creek bed but it lacked the energy to reach the sea. The waves that broke on the shore, however, swirled up the creek and sucked it across the beach with a triumphant hiss. The children were captivated.

Nominally in charge of the party by virtue of her position, experience and organisation of the picnic, Miss Anderson directed the erection of stick-and-blanket shelters from the sun for the adults and began to herd the children into games.

Suprisingly soon she flopped down beside Joe, Stephen and Alice under the shelter of their flapping blanket.

"D'you mind?" she said as she wriggled, laughing, into a comfortable position in the sand. "No hope of forcing them into anything organised at the moment. I've just set limits on where they can go and left them to it."

Joe peered out from the shelter. The children were shrieking with delight as the waves glissaded up the beach into the creek bed, standing ankle-deep as the retreating water coursed by their legs. He stood up and wandered over to them, the fine sand collapsing under his feet and invading his boots. He bent and removed them, curling his white toes into the whiter sand with sensual pleasure. Leaving his boots and socks in a pile and rolling up his trousers, he made his way past where Ruth was splashing delightedly with the other children, stepped over the tiny fissure that was the end of the diminishing creek bed, and trudged along the beach to where it came to an end in a rocky outcrop that stretched out into the water. He eyed the sparse vegetation and began to climb the incline slowly, catching hold of the gnomish little plants for handhold. The climb was not great but he was sweating when he reached the crest. The wind was stronger on the exposed headland as he shaded his eyes and gazed up and down the coast.

His sense of inadequacy was immediate. As far as he could see each way, the shoreline scalloped in headland after headland, presumably with beaches in between like this one, until the end was lost in a blue haze on the horizon. The universal grey-green vegetation grew down to the water and the effect was of a quilt thrown over an unmade bed of considerable disarray. He could hear the boom of the waves breaking on the rocks off the shore and felt more significantly than he had done so far, the distance he was from home. Oh, the space. The monumental space of this place. The untrodden, uninhabited square miles of it.

He was suddenly clutched from behind. Ruth giggled with delight.

"I climbed up after you!" she said triumphantly. "Isn't it lovely here? I wish we lived closer so we could come here all the time. I'd come here every day if I could. Can we come here again Joe? Can we? Please? Will you bring me?"

Joe smiled and took her hand. "When we can, when we can," he said.

They began to walk beyond the high point of the headland and suddenly the wind was gone and the sound of the waves was deadened as they plunged into a thicket of scrawny trees growing on the leeward side. Unlike the low scrubby bushes they'd traveled through for the last part of the journey here, and those that clothed the slopes behind the beach, these stunted trees, gnarled and sculpted by time, wind and salt spray, were free of undergrowth. Their twisted spindly trunks stood stark and clear, their bunchy foliage making a dense canopy above the bare sandy soil. After the noise of the sea and the buffeting of the wind, the silence and stillness were strange.

"Oh Joe," breathed Ruth, "isn't this lovely? A little bit spooky but in a nice spooky way." She began to run between the tree trunks, dodging and swinging as she looped around.

"I—love—this—place!"

Suddenly she disappeared. Bending almost double, Joe lurched through the tree trunks calling her name. She had only been a few yards away from him.

"I tricked you, didn't I?"

It was fairly obvious that the trick had been inadvertent, but Joe was so pleased to find her unharmed but lying at the bottom of a shallow depression that he was happy to agree. He helped her out of what seemed to be another dry creek bed and dusted her down.

"Come on, let's get back. I feel like some food, don't you?

The breeze dropped as they slithered down the slope and skirted the waves gliding up the shore, their footprints washing out behind them in the wet sand.

"They're not called umbrella trees for nothing!" said the knowledgeable Miss Anderson when Joe mentioned the spooky trees. They grow up and down the coast. Beautiful things, aren't they?

Joe had not thought them beautiful but didn't venture this opinion.

"They are very ancient species," she went on. "Like a lot of the vegetation in Australia. Being an island and a pretty old one means that we have a lot of unique flora as well as the fauna you've all seen."

Stephen was looking at Miss Anderson with amusement.

"You wouldn't be a teacher, by any chance, would you?" he said teasingly.

Miss Anderson grinned ruefully. "Can't seem to help it," she said.

"I know how you feel, I do it myself. Always seem to think I'm at the blackboard with a pointer."

"You're a teacher?"

"Was a teacher. Now I'm told that I'm a rich landowner."

"I can't seem to help it," repeated Miss Anderson, "because I just find the information so fascinating myself that I feel sure that everyone else will find it fascinating too!" She grimaced. "I've been told that's not always the case!"

"Oh, I find almost all information fascinating too," Stephen enthused. "Anything new is fascinating."

Alice intervened with heavy playfulness.

"That's about a hundred times that the word "fascinating" has been used!" she said.

"Oops, thank you, my lexicologist" said Stephen.

Alice coloured. Joe hadn't known what the damned word meant either, but Stephen and Miss Anderson obviously had. Joe realised that Stephen was showing off and was vaguely irritated.

It did seem that Miss Anderson indeed couldn't help herself as she discoursed at some length about the local plants, animals and their habits, and the land they were farming. She was a city girl, but obviously a country one at heart, and had learned much from the farming family with whom she boarded.

Joe's attention wandered as he gazed out to sea, watching with hypnotic fascination the waves breaking on the offshore rocks. Every wave broke differently but he felt like cheering when a particularly big one sent the spray hurtling high into the air. He found he was anticipating these and he smiled at his childishness, turning back to the conversation. Miss Anderson was laughing, but earnest.

"It's true," she was saying. "Mr. Padman has lost a cow down one of them. They find them all over the place on this coast, the caves. It's limestone, you know, and water and underground streams can wear it away quite easily. Over a few thousand years, that is!"

To Joe a cave was a hollowing-out in a vertical hillside and it took some explaining—again by Miss Anderson—to make him understand that sometimes vast caverns lurked under the soil along this coast, often with just a small hole in the ground to mark them. Men actually tied ropes around themselves and were let down into these discovered caves to explore them—with a candle for light. Joe's stomach lurched at the thought.

"Mostly, though," continued Miss Anderson, "the farmers just put a bit of a fence or something around the entrance hole so they don't lose any more animals and leave it at that. But some of the explored ones are absolutely huge, with lakes inside them even. One or two are open for visitors to be shown around, didn't you know?"

Not on your life, thought Joe. Never.

"Are there likely to be any of these man-traps on our Group land?" asked Stephen.

Miss Anderson was not quite sure. She didn't think so, but she'd ask Mr. Padman. His lost cow had strayed from his land, though, which was much closer to the coast than any of the Group 19 farms.

"What happened to the cow?"

"Oh, they got it out with ropes and a pulley and a good deal of help, apparently. It wasn't a deep cave at all. But the cow had two broken legs and so they killed it."

"A lesson to us all," said Stephen, mock-serious. "If you do fall into one of these caves, don't break a leg!"

Joe thought that this was another thing to watch out for. Snakes and now treacherous holes in the ground. He hadn't seen any snakes yet, perhaps it would be the same with cave holes. He bloody well hoped so.

The journey home was long and tiring, but the sprits of the Groupers were high with relaxation and novelty. Sunburned and weary, salt-crusted and replete, only a few women attempted to sing on the way home; most preferred to drowse. If some were already dreading a return to the heat and drudgery of the humpies, at least today had provided a bit of a change.

59

The next day

Len had really done well so far, thought Joe, but it was yesterday's hike that proved a bit too much for his foot. He'd sat on the beach with his shoes and socks on when practically everyone else had shed their shoes and paddled around at the edge of the sea. Then suddenly he'd rolled up his pants and removed his false foot and hopped down to the shore. Or tried to hop, which was impossible in the sand; Joe had hurried up the beach to lend him a shoulder when he saw what was happening. One by one the other families turned in amazement at the sight and Ida, who'd been helping the women clear up the remains of the picnic, ran to his side in the water, but he waved her away, leaning on Joe. She backed off a little, but stayed on the wet sand, her eyes on Len.

"Well, you've done it now, pal," Joe said.

"Damned right I have. Let them all see, I don't care. Bloody foot was driving me mad after the walk here and I'm not going to pass up the chance to get it into some cold water, so what the hell anyway."

Joe looked down at the stump of Len's leg. It was red and swollen.

"Is it normally like that?" he asked.

"More or less. Today it's a bit more than more. Actually it hurts like hell."

The other men at the edge of the sea were gathering round.

"Bloody hell man, how long have you been like that?"

"How have you managed?"

"How did you get them to let you come out here?"

"I lost my foot in '16, and I'm managing well, thanks."

"And they let you come out here?" the man persisted. "What about your medical?"

"Ah well," said Len as sagely as he could manage while leaning on to Joe and twisting to get his stump into the water, "they didn't ask to see me feet."

The assembled men laughed. They fell to discussing their own medical examinations and most agreed they'd been pretty hit-and-miss but a couple of them said that they'd been through really exacting ones and Len was lucky to get away with it.

"Does your foreman know?" one of the men from the other Groups asked.

"Not so far. But I've got a feeling the time is coming," said Len.

Len's limp had been almost invisible up till now; Joe often watched him walk across the uneven ground of the home camp and was impressed by his balance and confidence. But this morning as they gathered at the foreman's hut it was obvious that he was in pain, and most of the other men were looking carefully at the ground, unwilling to seem complicit. Joe and Stephen stood beside Len, with Michael close.

Bill Bannister looked at the assembled men and seemed to sense the tension. He frowned "What's up then?" he asked.

The men shuffled and muttered.

"Right then," he said. As he allocated the jobs to various working parties, Bill Bannister kept darting looks around the men.

"Alright, I've got some contracts here. Eleven acres on Location 1938 at three quid an acre with the use of the horse and tackle every other day. Barlow and Dent?"

The abandonment of sustenance payment of ten shillings a day and the imposition of contract work had been viewed with suspicion by most of the settlers, but it seemed to be working out alright, although the suspicion remained. Anything proposed by the Government was unlikely to be to the Groupers' advantage.

Some more contracts were allocated.

"Then another eight acres at three quid. Location 1940. Who's up for that? Smith, Dawson and Hubbard?"

Cec Smith shuffled and kicked the dust.

"What's up?" demanded the foreman. "Come on, something's up, spit it out."

"Rather not work with Dawson." The Yorkshireman's eyes were downcast.

"So that's the trouble! You're not a bloody namby-pamby schoolboy now, Smith, you'll do as you're bloody well told and like it. I don't give a damn about your precious little girly tiffs or your wants. Just take the bloody contract and get on with the bloody job, will ya?" Bannister's face was becoming red.

Joe waved his hand. "I'll work with Dawson and Hubbard. Cec can work with Dent."

Bannister's face became even more red. "No you bloody well won't!" he said loudly, "No you bloody well won't! You'll do as I bloody say!"

Some of the men were turning away from the embarrassing sight of the foreman losing his temper yet again. At this stage, Joe knew, they all had a good grasp of what they had to do and could easily arrange themselves for working parties. The foreman's liaison duties between the Groupers and officialdom was perhaps still valid, but Bannister's advice on rural matters was insignificant and according to Australian farmer-turned-Grouper John Turner, sometimes questionable. They all hoped for his transfer to some other, preferably distant, Group.

But they had to deal with him until that pleasant day arrived. Joe caught up with Cec Smith as the men divided into work parties and collected chains, axes and sniggers.

"I'll change with you," he said, "just go down the track a bit. But for Christ's sake, man, don't spill the beans to bloody Bannister. Let him find out if he must, but keep it secret for as long as you can."

"Doesn't pull his weight," said Smith truculently.

"Oh hell, give him some leeway. You saw that stump yesterday. He deserves a bit of support."

"Shouldn't be here." Smith was determined to maintain his stand.

"Quite a lot of us shouldn't be here." Joe was trying to be placatory while his own anger rose. This little rabbit of a man. Stephen joined them with Michael and some of the other men.

"Come on Cec, give him some rope."

"We're all in this together, Cec."

"Don't let Bannister know, for pity's sake. He'll crucify him and he doesn't deserve that. He's a bloody war hero."

Cec Smith knew when he was beaten but had a last word.

"Well I'm not working with him. Joe can do it. I'm coming with you, Dent."

That was one more day they'd bought for Len, Joe thought.

Jack Hubbard was a nuggety little Yorkshireman whose voice reminded Joe of Yorkshire Bob at home at Jackson's whose accent had so irritated him. Jack, however, was a pleasant, genuine and open soul whose accent Joe found not in the least irritating, and he was a hard worker.

He and Joe insisted that Len take it easy that day. They were working on Len's block, still clearing, as were the men on other blocks. This initial cleared acreage would qualify them for the erection of a house and the issue of farm implements and animals to allow them to become real farmers. Progress was slow and the work hard although it was becoming more natural to them than it had been during the initial weeks, full as they'd been with shock and pain.

But by now the work ritual was established. Taking on the trees as a working pair, they grubbed round them with a mattock, cutting the roots with a grubbing axe until they were beginning to totter. When five or six trees were in this state they ran a wire up the trunk as far as they could and pulled them down one after the other. They then lopped and chopped the felled trees into lengths with the cutting axe.

Impossibly large trees, of which there were many, were ring-barked, the thin layer of bark that supplied nutrients to the tree's branches circled with a shallow cut that effectively and immediately starved the tree. When the tree was dead and had released in death its tenacious root-hold, it was an easier business by far to pull it down – or leave it standing to become, undemanding of its environment, a bleached and ghostly sentinel.

The days when they had the use of George were keenly anticipated, but this was not one of them and smoko was a time to relish.

"How's the foot, Len?"

"What foot?" but he laughed. "Better than yesterday, not as good as it'll be tomorrow."

"I reckon you just pulled that show-off stunt to get a ride home on the cart yesterday, cadger!"

"Shut up, Joe."

"Do you think they'd send you home if they found out?"

"Dunno. Don't expect it's something they've come across too often. Might have to have a meeting or an inquiry or a trial or something. Rather not put them to that trouble though."

This last was delivered lazily as Len squirmed in an attempt to make himself comfortable, his leg elevated on a log, the stump still raw and shiny.

"After this morning, I reckon we've got a good chance to keep this foot of yours a secret after all, mate. That's if we can keep bloody Cec Smith quiet."

"Oh, we'll keep him quiet all right," said Jack.

"Oh?"

"He's from a village close to where we used to live. Didn't know him, but I've heard the word that he might have skipped out on some debts he owed around the place. A word to the wise should keep him quiet."

Joe and Len laughed.

That should do it.

60

Christmas Eve, 1925

Christmas Eve was a Wednesday and Ruth was dancing with excitement.

They were all going on the Group cart again, just like the picnic at the beach, but this time only as far as the school, which Ruth now thought was not very far at all, though she had felt it was a long way when she first started walking it nearly a year ago.

Mr. Bannister had tried to tell the men that they had to do some work before they went, but Joe said they howled him down and said blow it, they were all going to have two days off, today and tomorrow, so there. Joe was laughing when he told her, and she liked the idea of Mr. Bannister being told off by the men. She thought he might be angry though, but Joe said he wasn't.

He was coming to the party. Bother.

The dress that used to be her best one was getting a bit small for her now she was ten. Auntie Ida had had a look at it and said that there was nothing to let out, but she let down the hem a bit. Ruth didn't mind; it was a bit tight when she waved her arms around, that was all. She felt pretty and excited. Auntie Alice had put her hair in rags last night which made it a bit uncomfortable to sleep, but she had lots of curls today, curls that felt lovely when she turned her head fast and they bounced around. It was a really special day.

Tomorrow she'd give her lovely secret presents to her Oak Tree family, but today she'd get one herself from Father Christmas-Mr. Slattery.

The day wasn't too hot, which was good because everyone would have been uncomfortable in their best clothes if it had been hot. As the cart bumped along the track and the dust flew up in clouds behind them (and sometimes on them!) Ruth sang along with the ladies; she knew all the words of the songs they sang.

When they got to the school, it was decorated with branches and crepe paper chains and it looked lovely. Miss Anderson hadn't done it all by herself, some of the ladies had helped. The table had a red crepe paper cloth on it and the food was laid out with a net over it to keep off the flies. As soon as everyone was there they had tea so that the sandwiches didn't get dried out and the sausage rolls were still a bit warm.

Then it was Father Christmas time and all the children got a present. Mr. Slattery gave her a wink from inside his cotton-wool beard and she felt really grown-up to be in on the secret of his identity.

She was too grown-up to be getting presents from Father Christmas.

This realisation, after all her excited anticipation, was sudden and confusing. Vaguely cross, she went and sat on one of the logs in the playground and stared at her present. She should be delighted with a game of snakes and ladders and she was, really. Really she was.

She was the only one to get a game of snakes and ladders. Some of the other children got the same present as each other and she finally worked it out. All the girls of the same age got the same thing, and all the boys of the same age got the same thing. They were all wrapped up in the same sort of paper so they must have come from that Boans shop in Perth. It also meant that she was the only ten-year-old girl in the three Groups if she was the only one with snakes and ladders. On the one hand this made her feel special and on the other hand it made her feel a bit lonely.

Joe walked towards her with a questioning look.

"What are you doing sitting here all by yourself, sweetheart? Do you like your present?

"Yes, I do. We'll have lots of good games with it."

"I'm sure we will. Something to do in the evening, eh?"

Ruth looked up at her big brother and the funny feeling she'd been having about being grown-up or not grown-up dissolved. Joe was surprised at the ferocity of her hug as she paused briefly before running helter-skelter across the playground to join the other children.

•

Her excitement was fully restored next day as they made their way to Len and Ida's for Christmas dinner. She'd tried to carry the basket with the surprise presents in, carefully covered with a tea-towel so that Joe couldn't see, but after a little while it was just too heavy so Joe was carrying it, teasing her by pretending to look under the tea towel and pretend-complaining about the weight of the basket.

"What's in it?" asked Joe plaintively. "It weighs a ton. Is it baby elephants?"

"They'd be wriggling!"

"Not if they were asleep. You might have bought them so that they could grow up and work for us."

"An elephant would be good, wouldn't it?" Ruth's eyes sparkled. "Really strong. They could pull down lots of trees really fast."

"But they'd need buns."

Ruth rolled her eyes.

They had to walk nearly all the way back to the home camp and then take another track to Auntie Ida and Uncle Len's. The fact that their block was right behind Joe and Ruth's didn't mean that it was close to get to; the forest was still dense and unknown between them. But that wouldn't be forever—soon there'd be a path and she could go and see them sometimes. She really liked Auntie Ida, and recently she liked Uncle Len more than she had before. She wasn't sure whether she had changed or Uncle Len had, or if it had just happened, but then she was sure it was Uncle Len when she thought about it.

Auntie Ida had really gone to a lot of trouble for the Oak Tree Place Groupers. Their shifted humpy was decorated just like the school, with lovely green branches and paper chains and streamers. It smelled so good with the scent of the leaves and the lovely smell from the cooking stove in the corner.

When Auntie Alice, Uncle Stephen, Auntie Ellen and Uncle Michael joined them, it was a bit crowded in the humpy and rather stuffy. Auntie Alice looked very pink, but they'd had to walk even further than Joe and her to get here, so she was probably hot. She had brought really easy things, Ruth thought with critical assessment, the potatoes and the custard for the pudding. Auntie Ellen had made the pudding and it was bubbling away in a saucepan heating up.

Ruth tried not to be a nuisance, but she had to suggest several times that they have presents now before anyone took any notice of her. This was probably because the grown-ups were not giving each other presents, but everyone had brought something for her. It was good to be the one young person amongst them—lots of presents!

She opened each of the four presents in turn and tried not to show off doing it just because everybody was watching her. She thanked everyone prettily (Joe was proud of how well she did it, she knew that) and gave them all a kiss, but when they began to talk again with each other she was forced to call out.

"Wait! Presents are not over yet!"

The adults dutifully became silent and attention turned to her. She carried the basket inside and removed the tea towel with a flourish, revealing four rusting jam tins filled with the grey sandy soil that they trod every day. The silence grew.

"You might not think," said Ruth importantly, "that these look like good presents." The adults looked gravely interested.

"But they are!" she couldn't contain her glee. "Do you know what they are? Can you guess? I'll bet you can't!" She danced and bent over, hugging herself and giggling with excitement.

"Do you know, Joe?" asked Alice.

"No, it's been a secret from me, too. Didn't know a thing about all this 'till this morning when she made me carry the basket here. Total secret"

"It's a nice tin of dirt to put on when we feel too clean," suggested Uncle Stephen.

"Nooooo!"

"Dirt jam?" said Uncle Len.

"Nooooo!"

"Well I give up." Everyone said they gave up. Taking a deep breath, Ruth made the announcement.

"It's oak trees."

Silence.

"Or they will be oak trees when they grow. There are acorns in the dirt and if you look I think you can see them just beginning to grow, see?"

"Where on earth did you get acorns?" Joe was incredulous.

"Mrs. Craggs gave them to me before we left and I kept them hidden. They are from the oak tree."

She didn't have to say which oak tree. Everyone beamed at her and she felt very clever and grown-up.

61

Three months later.
March 1926

Progress was so slow. The houses were coming, they were told, but they'd been told that many times before. The clearing was progressing at snail's pace, and three more families had left, just walked away from all they'd done so far.

Three more families had come to fill the spaces. Joe was inclined to agree with Ruth that those families were lucky ducks because they'd had a lot of their work done for them. But there was still so much to do.

The home paddocks had been more or less cleared for all the locations and once the houses were built they'd be dandy. Oh yes, dandy alright, if dandy was everything else they had to do then— clear twenty times more than they had so far, fence it and make it into pasture. Thinking of what lay ahead as one huge task was depressing. Stephen said you had to think of what you could do in a week, or a month, do it and then you could feel pleased with yourself. Then on to the next week, or the next month.

Joe thought sourly that Stephen was full of such advice.

Since late last year the men of the Group had worked on contract, the system that was viewed with suspicion when it was introduced. Anything that Bill Bannister directed was unlikely to appeal to the men but it did seem to be working out alright in spite of their misgivings. Sustenance payments were suspended now that they'd been allocated their own blocks, but if you were a good and willing worker, working on contract could earn you more than you'd been getting. Joe had just finished a contract with Jack Hubbard and even though progress was slow, he earned more than susso in a week.

He had managed to get only a rough idea of the area and limits of his block but it was hard not to feel a bit proud of having such a big parcel of land that was more or less his own. He'd actually taken days to find the survey pegs and the whole damned place still looked the same with the same huge trees and the same work ahead.

Enough. It had become a way of life, a way of waking up and getting on with things, a way of working till you dropped, eating like a horse and sleeping dreamlessly. That was the best part; his nightmares still came but they were less often. While he still woke sweaty and terrified when he did have them, he could get back to sleep much more readily. Exhaustion had advantages. And he hadn't had a daytime nightmare since he came to Margaret River.

Joe was smoking, sitting on a felled log in the insubstantial shade offered by the surrounding eucalypts, a carpet of their dry shed leaves under his feet. He wondered if he'd ever get used to evergreen trees. He wouldn't like to be a park-keeper in a eucalypt park. Instead of raking up piles of leaves in the autumn, he'd be raking leaves from those confounded trees all year round and just more in summer as they quietly got rid of their unwanted leaves and grew new ones. Harsh names they had, too, not gentle like birch or beech but jarrah, karri, marri …

Harry. He had to forget, he had no claim anyway, it was useless to pine, but the pain and the loss remained raw. For over a year Harry *had* been his son and the fact that Lydia had told him that he wasn't didn't change anything. He felt what he felt. It was love and he couldn't change it.

Lydia, well that was another thing. The stupidity of his obsession with her now rankled and embarrassed; blind love had reshaped itself into clear-eyed contempt. Which was not at all a bad thing and perhaps this contempt would in time fade to indifference. But he wasn't mooning around any more; in fact the image of Lydia had on occasions added some strength to his chopping arm, but then to be honest it was more himself that he wanted to blister, for his stupidity. He did wonder though, how she was faring. The promised divorce papers had never eventuated and he would have enjoyed thinking that perhaps all her clever plans had gone astray if it were not for the fact that this might mean that Harry was suffering in some way. Oh Harry, dear wee Harry. Rationally he knew that Harry was almost three, not all that much younger than Ruth had been when he came home from the war, but in his mind he remained the tottering little baby, reaching out his arms and chuckling ...

At least he still had Ruth.

Exploration of their block had found the stream that ran through the home camp, across their block, and Stephen and Alice's next door (funny how readily one can adapt to "next door" being nearly a mile away) and eventually to the sea at the beach where they'd had their picnic. There was a little more water here in its upper reaches than there'd been at the beach end; it was not a torrent but the winter rains would bring a swelling. Such a good thing to have a block with a stream.

On the Sunday of their eventual finding of the stream they had made their way down its sandy bed, surprisingly easy progress when compared with wading through the bush and undergrowth. The stream was shaded by trees, the stream bed wide and shallow. The water was cold and a clear brown, like tea, coloured by the vegetation that drooped and fell into it even further upstream. Ruth hopped on stones, splashed in remnant pools, sang in a high piping voice and was sure that every turn they rounded, they were going to come to the beach. She bubbled with plans for future picnics at a beach now made accessible.

But it was late afternoon and they hadn't reached the beach, forced to turn back by the fading light. Next time, Joe promised.

"And then we'll have a picnic? We could get Auntie Alice and Uncle Stephen to come with us because the stream goes through their block too and they could just join in with us. Oh Joe, we're so *lucky*! I can't wait to go to the beach again."

There was huge excitement when the materials for the houses were delivered to each block and the workmen arrived too to build them. Joe and Ruth had long decided on the best place for theirs and carefully directed the two young Englishmen builders to the spot.

"Right-oh, then we'll make start," said the tall one, whose name was Fred. He was from Liverpool and could talk a blue streak.

Douglas, from Tunbridge Wells, was younger and less chatty but very friendly. They were both young and were both taking some time to see a bit of the world.

"Not much of the world to see around here," said Joe

"Oh, we thought we'd take a look around to see if taking up some land round here might be a good idea," said Fred.

"What do you think then?"

"Look, I don't mind a bit of hard work but clearing all this sort of thing," he waved his hammer at the surrounding forest, "well, it's a bit too much for the blood."

"It's not that bad," said Joe defensively.

"Well, all praise to you and your chums for sticking with it, that's all I can say. We think we'll move on after this contract and look for something more congenial."

This was, to Joe's knowledge, the second time in his life that he'd heard the word "congenial". He really must find out what it meant.

It took amazingly little time to erect the sturdy four-roomed house with a verandah and two steps at the front and a verandah at the back. The wood was jarrah, dark and dense and as hard as nails. The interior was unlined and the roof was made of corrugated iron from the disassembled humpy, which itself had been built without the use of nails so that the iron could be re-used for this very purpose.

The cooking stove was installed, their sparse furniture shifted in and the workmen left. The silence fell like a soft blanket.

Joe watched Ruth stand in each of the four small rooms and inhale deeply.

"Oh Joe, I do love that smell!"

"Yes, love, I like it too."

"It reminds me of Jacksons. Do you miss Jacksons? Do you miss Oak Tree Place?" Ruth was quizzical.

"Not really," he lied. Sometimes he'd give an arm to be back with a pint at the Oak Tree. "Do you?"

"Sometimes," Ruth said thoughtfully. "Not as much now as I did at the very beginning of being here. I think," she said owlishly wise, "that having Auntie Alice here made it better—easier. And the other aunties and uncles."

"Yes, it wasn't all strangers to get used to, was it?"

"Some of the strangers are nice though."

"Oh yes, 'course." He spoke vacantly and he walked around the house, inspecting the workmanship with a critical eye.

The meal they ate that evening had a specialness to it that owed nothing to the scotch collops and the rice pudding. Joe felt an ownership of the sounds of the bush that night.

62

Six months later.
September 1926

It was a good one, this winter, thought Ruth. Now that they were in the house it was much more comfortable and the rain water ran right under the house and down the hill instead of creeping inside as it had so often done in the humpy. It was warmer, too, with their lovely fireplace and even if the wind did come through some of the very small cracks between the boards of the house, Joe soon stopped them up and they were cosy again.

Now it was almost spring again and getting warmer. The wildflowers were all coming out and summer was on its way. The creek had got really big—more like a real river than the tiny trickle that had been there when they first moved onto the block.

One of the new families had moved into the house that Mr. & Mrs. Barr had abandoned on the block next door. Ruth had never got to know Mrs. Barr but she did know that she'd been very unhappy to be in Australia at all, and that finally Mr. Barr had "bowed to the inevitable" as Auntie Ida said, and taken her away. Auntie Ida also said that Mr. & Mrs. Barr didn't have enough money for a fare back to England, so she didn't know what they were going to do. Try to get a job in Perth or Fremantle, probably.

Ruth thought about the three hot days that they'd spent in Fremantle and although the heat was hard to remember exactly on a pleasant September morning on Group 19, the memory was clear enough for her to feel to great pity for the Barrs.

But the exciting thing was that the new family that had moved in, fresh from England had three children, and one of them was ten years old. His name was Robin and his birthday was in October so he was just one month older than Ruth. Ruth found it interesting to see how pale the people just arrived from England were, compared to the Group Settlers, but they were probably all that pale themselves to begin with. Robin's mother, Mrs. Edgar, didn't seem to be worried about all the sudden changes she was having to handle, and was already setting about getting a garden going at their house, something that Ruth and Joe had been going to do at their place, but hadn't yet. The other two Edgar children were Betty and little Iris, both too young to go to school. Iris was three, the same age as Harry, so Ruth studied her hard and tried to imagine Harry doing the same sort of things. But Iris was a bit of a cry-baby and Ruth knew that was something Harry would never be.

Robin was really good to have so close. There were so many games they played and made up, but their most favourite was tracking. They devised a range of signs—a pointing-arrow made of sticks, a bent sapling, a marked tree, knotted grass and carefully-placed stones showing the way to their hiding place and sometimes it took the looker ages to find the track-setter, because at the end they hid themselves and had to be found too and there were so many good spots to hide. Joe kept telling them to be careful of snakes, but Mrs. Edgar was sure they'd be alright and sent them off with some bread and cheese and told them to be home in time for their teas.

Ruth was telling Robin about the creek and the wondrous possibility of making a way to the beach by walking along its bed.

"When the creek starts to dry up, of course. Not now, it's too high and there's no room to walk in the creek-bed."

"We could walk along the side"

"It's too bushy and it would take too long. More than a day."

"When will it be low enough?"

"Don't really know. When we came to the block it was low but that was the middle of summer and I don't know how long it had been like that."

"Let's go and look anyway."

They slipped through the trees to the bank of the creek that ran through Ruth and Joe's block. It swerved away from Robin's block in its upper reaches which made Robin a bit annoyed and

Ruth didn't know about it up that way anyway as all her interest had been in tracing it to the sea. They pushed through the red boronia bushes that clothed the creek bank until it became too difficult and scratchy.

"See, it would take ages to get through this to the beach. Joe and I couldn't even get there walking in the creek bed for ages."

Robin was grumpy. Ruth had told him all about the beach and its wonders and they beckoned deliciously.

"Tell you what," said Ruth, "let's play tracking."

"Don't want to."

"Oh go on."

"Can't be bothered."

"Alright then, what about hide and seek?"

"Nuh."

"Will we make a little hut then? With branches?"

"Then we can play Robinson Crusoe!" Robin was at last enthused.

"Well, let's do it away from the house so that it really is like a desert island."

They waded through the undergrowth for ten minutes or so, the sound of the creek a constant babble as it grabbed at the sides of its channel, teasing the overhanging foliage that whipped in its current.

"Here?" suggested Robin.

"Looks alright."

Robin had a pocket knife that Ruth coveted passionately. It had two blades, one big and one small, and a pig-sticker. In spite of the knife's gleaming efficiency, it still took a good deal of effort to hack through the stems of the boronia and the bracken and it had no chance at all of cutting through wood, but it made easy work of the fronds of the little squat zamia palm. They worked hard at pulling the twigs and small branches off fallen timber and making a lean-to on to which they piled the zamia fronds. It was beginning to look really good, room inside for both of them and for the things that they'd bring when they were properly set up.

Ruth thought that a tin for some biscuits and a bottle of water would be good. And some cups. Thinking about water made her thirsty.

"Going to get a drink from the creek," she said.

"Me too."

They pushed through the undergrowth towards the stream, leant over and drank deeply from the rushing water, getting rather wet in the process.

"I'll bet we could get down to the beach if we had a boat," said Robin, considering the fast-flowing water and wiping his face with his sleeve. "And really fast."

"Let's make a raft!" Ruth jumped up and down in her eagerness.

Robin really liked to be the one who had the ideas, so he was slow to answer.

"I s'pose we could."

"'Course we can, 'course we can. We can get some branches and tie them together."

"What with?"

"Umm, I know—fencing wire! We have rolls and rolls of it, so Joe won't miss one. We'd better keep it a secret, though, don't you think?"

"Yeah, better had."

"Let's collect some branches now and tomorrow we can come back with the wire."

Their collection of branches was varied and, when they finally laid them out on a more-or-less square with two big branches on the outside edges, there were some big gaps in the middle bit, but perhaps it would be better tomorrow when they were tied together.

It was another whole week before Ruth and Robin managed to get back to their hut and raft; after-school visits had been impossible due to heavy rain, but the Saturday was sunny and mild and the bush gleamed after its week-long drenching.

Robin threw down the coil of wire and dragged the wire-cutters out of his pocket—it had been Robin who brought the wire in the end, and he had also thought of the cutters. Eager to start, they began to wind the wire around the logs. It immediately became obvious that this was not going to work. They could not make the wire bend any more than a gentle U-shape, and although Robin pulled and puffed he could not manage to pull the logs close to each other, let alone secure them. The wire was stronger than they were.

With smarting hands, they sat back and looked at the raft-that-wasn't.

"We'll never get it together." Robin was sulky.

"No." Ruth was hardly less so. She'd been looking forward to bobbing down the creek and ending up at the beach that she was so anxious to show to Robin. She had pictured it so vividly during the week—she could feel the raft grinding to a halt in the beach sand when it came to the end of the creek and could feel the salty wind in her face.

Dejectedly, they lay back on the carpet of fallen leaves and looked up to the tree-tops, the shiny leaves making diamonds in the sun. Ruth was feeling a bit drowsy when suddenly Robin jumped up.

"I know! I know! Let's hop on a log and float!"

"What if we fall off?" Ruth was doubtful.

"We won't, we won't. But I think I can wire those two big branches together with a big loop and you can sit behind me and hang on. We'll be fine."

He leapt up and dragged the two big branches together. He managed to get a piece of wire round them, twisted the ends together and cut them off. He did this in three places down the length of the branches while Ruth watched. The branches were not absolutely straight so there were gaps and the branches moved against each other, but it was beginning to look like something that would serve their purpose.

"Turn it over so that the joins are underneath so they don't cut you."

They dragged the twinned logs towards the stream, which was considerably higher, due to the rain, than it had been last week when they drank from it.

"Will we put the raft in first?" The two branches had been elevated to vessel status.

"I say we go in with it. We're going to get wet!"

"Take your boots off, Robin." Robin was sufficiently new to the country for his mother to still make him wear his boots. Ruth was barefoot. They stripped to vests and knickers.

"Take an end and jump on three," ordered Robin. "One…two…*threeeee!*

The creek, though high and swift, was still shallow enough for a precarious toehold to be had on its sandy bottom, and they hopped and bobbed downstream for twenty yards or so before Robin managed to straddle the raft, but he immediately fell off again as the logs turned over. Spluttering, he hooked his arm over the logs and looked back at Ruth who was clinging to the ragged ends of the branches.

"We're moving anyway!" he yelled triumphantly. "Hang on and we'll get there yet!"

Ruth struggled to pull herself to the side of the craft, behind and opposite Robin. This seemed to have been a sensible thing to do as the log raft became more stable and was making quite good progress.

"Kick!" Robin yelled back at Ruth, "Kick and we'll go faster!"

They did.

They came to a bend in the creek and the current pushed them against the bank. Without consulting, they pushed off again into the flow. Same with the next turn, and the next. Then creek suddenly quietened and widened into a small lake. On one side was a small sandy shore with overhanging trees and the creek seemed to continue on at the other end.

"I'm going to try to get on again," grunted Robin, flinging a leg hopefully over the logs. This time the logs did not flip over, but he fell back into the water with a cry.

"Bloody bugger, bugger, bugger!" His eyes were huge and his mouth twisted with pain and shock.

"What's the matter? What's wrong?"

"Tore me leg on the ends of the bloody bloody bloody wire."

Ruth could see that "bloody" was indeed the appropriate word as a red stain was spreading round Robin as he flailed in the water.

"Hang on and we'll paddle to the shore."

Despite his wound, Robin splashed and kicked his way towards the edge of the tiny lake, with Ruth kicking and splashing at her end of the raft. Robin hobbled up the little beach and collapsed. He looked at the pulsing wound in his groin, jagged and bloody, and at the blood soaking into the sand. He began to cry.

"Don't cry, don't cry. Look," said Ruth hurriedly removing her vest, "Hold this on your leg. I'll go and get help. Don't move."

"Hurry, please hurry. Get Mum or Dad or anybody you can. I'm cold."

"Oh Robin, I'm sorry, but I don't have anything to keep you warm." Ruth was almost in tears. Just sit in the sun and I'll be back as soon as I find someone to help."

"Go then! Hurry. Hurry, hurry!"

Ruth took off into the bush. She had no idea where she was, but she thought that if she followed the creek back from where they'd come, that would get her to one of the Group blocks. She wondered how far they'd come down the creek. Stumbling and really crying by now, she punctuated her journey with croaky little cries of "Help!" which didn't penetrate more than a few yards.

A small mob of drowsing kangaroos took off at her approach, skittering away through the trees with crashes and thumps. Her breath was red-hot in her throat and her face was running with tears and snot. He legs were cut by spiky undergrowth and the bushes and branches she pushed aside whipped back on to her face and chest. She ran until she could run no more, but still she ran, crying and babbling Robin's name.

There was a bend that she was sure she'd passed with Joe when they were trying to walk the length of the creek. She allowed herself to pause to study the opposite shore. Surely that was the rock they thought looked like a frog? If that were so, then to cut across away from the creek would bring her to somewhere near a Group block, perhaps even Auntie Alice's, and if it was dinner time the men would be home.

She plunged into the bush, away from the creek and its gurgle ceased abruptly as the deafness of the forest pushed into her ears. She had learned from Archie how to blaze trees to show you your route back to where you came from, and Ruth wished fervently that they'd been walking and blazing rather than sailing down the creek, uncaring of their route. These trees all looked the same. She tried to look for the sun and remember what Archie had taught her about that, but she didn't know where the sun was when they started out so that was no use anyway.

She ran. She ran, cried and cried out. It took her an hour to realise she was lost.

There was a small clearing. Not really a clearing, just a little bit of less-dense bush. The trees were spindly. It was the first difference she'd seen in the never-ending forest, but still she didn't recognise anything as she stumbled her way across to the other side. Or at least that was her intention.

At first she thought she was imagining it, that strange sinking of the solid ground under her feet. Something like Alice in Wonderland, a real thing becoming unreal. But before she could think about it, her feet were standing on nothing at all and there was a brief moment of whooshing darkness then a crashing thump, searing pain, and all the air in her lungs left her body.

63

Same day, late afternoon

Joe was not overly concerned at the lack of smoke from his chimney as he trudged back from his work that afternoon. True, Ruth usually had the stove re-lit by that time but he knew she'd been off with Robin on some secret thing they had concocted and it was such a pleasant day they were probably still playing.

He lit the stove and gathered some more wood, washed and considered the options for tea. Waited for Ruth. It was the rule that she was home by dusk.

The light weakened and with the encroaching darkness Joe's anxiety grew. He left a lamp burning, took another and walked the half mile to the next-door house. The children were obviously not there; Mrs. Edgar was trying to appear nonchalant. As Joe enlisted the help of her husband for a search party, her pretence of control was fraying and her eyes showed her fear. She whimpered quietly and the two small children clung to her skirt.

"Hush, love, come on, we'll find them. You know how Robin is—they could easily be lost and we'll just go find them." Jack Edgar patted his wife vacantly on the shoulder and said to Joe: "Can we get other men to help?"

"Yes, of course. They went in the direction of Alice and Stephen's I know, so we'll collect Stephen on the way. That'll have to do for a start. Bring a lamp and some rope if you've got some?"

They jogged quickly along the track to Alice and Stephen's block and the three men plunged into the bush, calling "Coo-ee!" at regular intervals. They spread out and were quickly joined by Len who'd heard their calls, and by Michael and Cec Smith a little later. Cec went back to gather more men, and the others spread out from the bank of the creek, inward into the forest, within earshot of each other but nearly always out of sight. The "Coo-ees" rang out like whip cracks in the night air. Blessedly there was a moon.

They were less than half an hour into their search when they found the palm-fronded hut. Joe and Jack Edgar looked at the strewn wire, the cutters and the spindly branches still placed together.

"Oh my God," Robin's father was ashen-faced as he put an arm out to support himself on a tree. "D'you see what they've been doing? Do you? They've been making a bloody raft! Oh no, oh no, oh no!"

Joe was already at the creek bank. He plunged in and began wading downstream. Jack followed him.

If the circumstances had been different it would have been a beautiful scene, the moonlight on the water and the slender vegetation leaning to brush the surface of the creek. But this beauty had a malevolence that threatened and mocked. Joe's breath was ragged and his legs burned with the effort of walking through the water and keeping upright on the pitted creek bed. Here and there the creek deepened so that he had to catch hold of bushes along the bank to drag himself along. He didn't want to think of examining these deep hollows because he was sure he was going to find the two of them huddled somewhere along the bank. Soon. Very soon.

He didn't know how long he'd been going, but he knew that Jack was behind him somewhere because he could hear him grunting with effort and he could see lights through the trees from time to time indicating that the others were keeping up on land.

Still they waded, scanning the banks as they rounded the curves, starting at bumps and rocks that appeared out of the darkness, teasing, taunting.

They came to the small lake and Joe cried out with anguish as he saw the two logs wired together floating in the middle of the water. A tormented cry behind him and Jack splashed past, throwing himself at the water and looking, looking, looking in its depths. Joe was too afraid to follow him. Too afraid of what he might find. What he didn't want to find, what he was terrified of finding. He stood like a statue in the middle of the lake, water to his chest, crying silently, afraid to his very bones.

In the moonlight he saw a pale shape on the little sandy beach. He grabbed Jack as he surfaced and pointed.

"There!" he said, "There!"

With an animal cry Jack stumbled out of the water with Joe following. Everything slowed down as Joe felt every step an individual effort and full of dread. He registered that there was only one little person on that beach and he knew it wasn't Ruth. His eyes razed the banks, still looking.

Jack Edgar had reached his son and gathered him into his arms, uttering a cry that sounded as if he was baying at the moon. Robin's blood had soaked the surrounding sand; his body was alabaster-pale and very, very, cold.

The other men crashed through the trees to the water's edge but each drew up and stood silently as they saw Jack Edgar keening over the body of his son. There was nothing to say.

Joe was charging around the overgrown bank, flailing at the matted vegetation until he was sure that Ruth was not tangled in it but failing to find her increased his panic. He dived repeatedly into the water, combing the muddy bottom of the little lake with dread, and the men on the bank went to his aid until they were sure that Ruth's body was not at the bottom of the river. Reasonably sure—the moonlight was helpful to their search but not bright enough to be absolutely sure that they were missing nothing.

Shaking the water from his hair, Joe shouted at the men flailing in the water:

"She's not here, she's not here, I'm sure. She must have gone through the bush to get help for Robin. Come on!"

He charged into the darkening bush, to be pulled back by Stephen.

"Hold it, old man, let's do this sensibly. And we need to help Jack here."

Joe forced himself to look at Robin's father bent over his body, racked with sobs, but he didn't want to see this ghastly reality which could have nothing to do with him because they were going to find Ruth, alive and well. He turned away as the men organised Cec to go with Jack as he carried Robin back through the bush, Jack refusing offers of help and clutching is son to his chest as if to consume him into his own body. The pair stumbled off.

Stephen quickly directed the remaining men into a wide band within earshot of each other and they set off as they had searched before, crashing and coo-ee-ing, their bobbing lights through the trees pitiful assistance in the darkness.

Their progress was slow but methodical and two hours later they came to the long track that led past Joe and Ruth's block and pulled up, uncertain.

If Ruth had reached this familiar track she would certainly have taken it to her own house, but an exhausted trot there by Joe confirmed that she had not. The other men had trailed after Joe in the same wan hope and it was Stephen again who suggested that they send men to enlist more searchers from the outlying locations, rest for the hour or so this would take and resume the search with a larger search party. It would be just about pre-dawn by then and searching in the dark, moonlight or not, was only half-searching. They needed daylight to see properly, especially if they were looking for an injured Ruth who was unable to call out, perhaps.

Joe groaned in anguish.

"Joe, it will be a better search with more men. That'll help. Look, we'll find her, we'll find her, don't worry."

Joe looked up at Stephen and gave a twisted half-smile.

"No, 'course I won't worry," he said.

"Sorry", said Stephen apologetically and patted Joe on the shoulder. "Put on some dry clothes and sit for a while, alright? Try to rest—you'll need it."

As the men trudged into the darkness or slumped on the verandah, Joe took a long drink of water, looped some rope around his waist, tucked in his small axe and a grabbed a compass that had been part of the kit that one of the handbooks had declared was essential for Australian pioneers and that he had not used till now, and holding his refilled lamp as high as he could, went looking again.

Somehow he felt more capable on his own. Stupid that, of course he wasn't—it took a lot of men to comb this monotonous bush where everything looked the same and it was so easy to go around in circles. But it was unthinkable that he could sleep or rest while Ruth was somewhere out there alone. He set out towards the west.

He heard crashing steps behind him and was joined by Len, lamp in hand.

"Not by yourself, Joe, not on your own."

Joe just grunted. The moon was gone now, clouded out. He called Ruth's name at what he tried to estimate were about one-minute intervals, trying to conserve his failing throat and not be rendered hoarse and useless. He crashed through the bush, the lamp swaying and casting its light in jerky waves through the undergrowth, Len on the same line ten yards to his left, keeping up with him.

"Ruth!" He stopped to strain his ears for a response.

"Ruth!" A minute later, some several yards further into the bush.

"Ruth!" Checking his compass and correcting his course. The light from Len's lamp grew a little more distant.

"Ruth!" Another minute and more yards of whipping bush pushed through.

"Ruth!" His ears rang with the answering silence. Len's lamp could no longer be seen.

"Ruth!" Desperation made his voice high and fluting.

It was when he fell over a half-rotted log and winded himself that he stopped to rest for a minute. He called out to Len to stop for a moment. Just a minute and then he'd get going again. Just a minute …

He started awake, amazed and ashamed that he'd fallen asleep, but certain that it had only been momentary. It was as he struggled to his feet that he heard the slight sound. He was beginning to be familiar with the animal sounds of the Australian bush, but this was a new one. It was probably Len, but ...

"Ruth!" His voice cracked and he tried again, more loudly. "Ruth!"

The slight sound intensified a little into a small wail and a muffled cry that might have been "Joe!"

Joe's heart leapt and he scrambled towards the sound, which was distant and to his right. He ploughed through the bush unheeding of the impeding branches cutting his hands, the whip of twigs on his face and catching in his hair. All the time calling, calling, calling.

He stopped. He could not hear her, and frantically he called again "Ruth!"

This time the sound, still muffled and incoherent, seemed to come from behind him. He swung around, confused.

"Ruth, where are you? Where are you sweetheart?"

The sound again, faint, unclear and directionless.

"Ruth, where are you?"

Nothing.

"Ruth!"

Nothing.

He cursed the darkness and begged God for the moon to re-emerge. He called and called until he was indeed hoarse but still kept up a cracked refrain of Ruth's name and an entreaty for her to tell him where she was. He knew that she was somewhere relatively close, he knew it because he had heard her, hadn't he? He tried to look up into the trees but most of them were too tall and too sheer to climb even for a nimble Ruth. He tore at dense undergrowth, calling, listening, calling, listening all the time. But the elusive sounds did not come again.

Joe found that tears were coursing down his cheeks. He rubbed eyes clear and dragged his sleeve under his running nose, pausing, panting and listening. Still nothing.

He began to see more clearly as his eyes became more used to the darkness and he thought the perhaps the moon had emerged although the trees were too tall and enmeshed for him to see the sky. But no, he realised with a start, it was emerging daylight. He could hear Len calling but he was some way away. He was grateful for the rapid emergence of the full light of day that was a characteristic of this new world and as the trees allowed slivers of golden sunlight to reach through their upper branches he stopped again. He was about to call out to Len to come closer when in the slanting sunbeams he suddenly saw a broken branch and some trodden plants. Someone had been through here. It might have been him, or Len, or the previous searchers, but he was absurdly sure that it indicated Ruth's path. He plunged forward, wading through the waist-high bracken that tangled his feet, slashing at it with his stick as the fronds waved like the surface of the sea. He still held his lamp high, unthinking.

Without warning his feet slipped from under him and there was no transition between striding through the bracken and sliding into blackness, down a steep slope of scree that rolled and skidded and scraped his back and bore him feet-first into inky blackness, buffeting and confusion.

His feet struck something solid with a body-wrenching thud that hardly stopped his momentum but now he was sliding sideways and he rolled, scrabbling at the loose rocks but unable to gain a hold. He felt that he was hurtling towards the centre of the earth with nothing to stop him and he was still not sure how it had happened.

Despite his animal panic his mind registered that he always knew it would end this way. Blackness and smothering earth had threatened him all his life and this was the one that would end it all.

But he fought against it. Only seconds had elapsed since he lost his footing but his whole body was writhing in the effort to stop his headlong descent. He had no idea what was around him, just what was under him, those sharp slipping stones at which he grabbed ineffectually. Nothing was solid enough to hold on to. Nothing solid enough to dig his feet into. Everything was slipping, moving, hurtling towards …

As suddenly as he had been enveloped by this black hole, he thudded against something that wrenched the breath from his body but thank you God, thank you God, thank you God stopped his descent.

For a while he didn't move. Didn't dare to, didn't want to. He was lying against something hard—a rock. Of course it was a bloody rock, what else could it be? Rocks under him rocks over him, rocks beside him. Bloody rocks everywhere. Rocks and nothingness. Darkness. He was huddled in a tangled heap on these rocks, gazing in what direction he didn't know. He had the irrational thought that not even his barely-used compass would help. There was a distant-sounding dripping of water.

Cautiously he raised his head and turned it experimentally. It hurt, but it worked. Tried his arms, one at a time. One worked, one shot pain through his body, his legs worked although he could feel the stickiness of blood almost everywhere. His head hurt a lot and his torn fingers throbbed. As he painfully turned his head again he could see a smudge of light way above him. It looked as small as a rabbit-hole but this was no rabbit-hole. It must be one of those caves that they'd been told about. Most of them undiscovered, they'd been told. Well, this was now one of the discovered ones.

He was surprised to realise that he was sleepy. Just have a snooze and then think about things. Yes. Maybe though, he was just getting unconscious. Maybe. Perhaps a snooze was not such a good idea, perhaps he should shout a bit.

"Help!" he tried. It was a pitiful effort.

"Help!" a little more loudly, but still ineffectual.

"Coo-ee!" Courtesy of the aborigines, they said, this was supposed to be the best-carrying sound in the bush, but he didn't know if it applied to caves. He tried it again, this time giving it a higher pitch.

"Coo-ee!"

There was a scrabbling at the patch of light and something—it must be a head because it spoke—thrust over the edge.

"Joe?"

"Len."

"Joe? Are you alright?"

Joe began to laugh, but it hurt so he stopped.

"Oh right as rain, Len, right as rain." He still wanted to sleep and his voice trailed off.

"Joe!" There was urgency in Len's voice. "Joe, talk to me. Where are you?"

Joe was stung out of his lassitude.

"I'm bloody well down here somewhere, you fucking fool."

"Alright, alright, Joe. The others should be here really soon and we'll get you out, don't worry."

Joe did not answer. There was time for a sleep before the rescuers arrived. He shifted slightly and his heart lurched into his mouth as the surrounding stones rattled and slid and fell into the void beyond his ledge, rattling and echoing. Newly alert, he froze and tried to concentrate his vision to see what lay around him. Could they rescue him? He strained his eyes; the thin wash of light that the distant entrance hole grudgingly allowed caught the edges of the rocks that lined the cave.

From where he had fallen in, there seemed to be an angled sloping slide of rocks that he had scraped on his descent and he was wedged against a large slab of rock at the foot of this slide. What lay beyond this life-saving outcrop he could not see and was not inclined to explore or even think about, except that of course not thinking about it made him do just that.

Events and pain and concern had crowded out the reality of his position until now. He had had a split-second thought about it as he was falling, but now he found that he was holding his breath with the dread that he was under the ground and that as well as all the mass of earth and stone above him he had nothingness beneath him, all the way to the centre of the earth for all he knew. Sure enough, the panic started even before he had fully formed these thoughts. The small entrance hole began to pulse—it was there and then it was not—and the walls kept time, rushing inwards and withdrawing. Even though they were invisible, Joe could feel them. With each pulsing movement, they loomed closer and they were not hard and flinty, they were soft and smothering and the light disappeared for longer and longer periods.

Joe whimpered and tried to curl his body and cover his head, but the movement not only hurt like hell, but dislodged more of the stones that skittered off his ledge and rattled into the void.

This physical immediacy brought back the light in the entrance hole and the walls withdrew and resumed their rocky character. Perhaps it was the pain and the movement, but perhaps it was the small sound that concentrated Joe's attention.

It was no more than a faint moan, but Joe was in a sitting position before he even gave thought to the action. Stones clattered.

"Ruth? Ruth? Ruth? Is that you sweetheart?" His eagerness quivered.

For long seconds there was silence, then a tiny sound of movement and another moan and something that was almost certainly his name. Joe's heart leapt.

"Ruth! Oh Ruthie, Ruthie darling heart, don't move, the men are coming to get us both, it's going to be alright, sweetheart, it's going to be alright."

There was another sound of movement and Ruth's voice came a little more strongly.

"Where are you, Joe? Robin's bleeding really badly. Have they found him? They've got to help him."

Joe's heart lurched at the pathetic little question. How long had she been laying here fretting not about herself, but about Robin, poor little dead Robin.

"Don't worry, my little love, the men will find us all. We just need to stay still and wait a little while, we can get lamps and things down here to let everyone see where we are. And we'll see as well then, won't we?"

"My leg hurts, Joe. It hurts such a lot."

"Oh sweetheart, I know you must be hurt, but just hang on a little longer and we'll be out of here and the doctor can fix whatever's wrong. It will be alright, you'll see. Just be brave."

There was no answer.

"Ruth! Say something, please darling girl!"

"Joe." The sound was faint.

Joe began to talk desperately. He talked more than he had talked since he came home from the war, or possibly even before the war. He talked non-stop as he had never talked before. He would pause only briefly to elicit a response—any response— from Ruth in her daze, before he would launch again into his monologue of stories and memories and repeated some of them in his anxiety to engage her.

He told the story she had always loved to hear—the happy and unexpected event of her birth and how it had delighted their parents. He spoke of their parents, old stories of his childhood and school days, funny stories of scrapes and jokes. He told of Sam's visit to the Place during the war, and he spoke of Sam, who spent so much of his war in places such as Joe and Ruth were in now—could she imagine? He spoke of Oak Tree Place and Dora and the Craggses, funny stories. Then more about Sam. He said that having fallen into this cave and being rescued was such an adventure that they would write a story about it when they got out. Miss Anderson would like to read that, wouldn't she?

Ruth managed a response to this. Joe's throat, scourged as it was by his searching cries of the previous day and now his non-stop babble, badly needed water. He croaked a call to Len and was rewarded by the sight of several heads at the hole.

"Ruth's down here as well!" he called. "Don't know where. Lower a lamp!"

Almost immediately a lamp was being lowered on a rope. It bumped on the slope of rocks and was withdrawn to be lowered from the other side of the entrance hole where it made a swinging descent, careening drunkenly and illuminating each side of the cave in turn as it did so. Joe was impatient for it to reach him but alert to what it revealed on its way down. The entrance to the cave was a hole at the top of what appeared to be a tube shape with a slight slope. The scree on which Joe had slid to his present position seemed to be where the earth originally covering the cavern had collapsed and allowed access from above.

The lamp reached Joe and he reached out to secure it. Gingerly he raised it above his head and looked around at his level. He was indeed wedged sideways at the bottom of the slope against a large craggy outcrop of limestone. Eight to ten feet wide and reassuringly solid, there was, however, a significant gap just beyond its extent and this was where the loose stones had rattled to.

It was easier now he could see where he was and what was around him. He struggled to a crouching position, cradling his injured arm, and tested the sturdiness of the rock that had stopped his fall. It was so massive that there was no doubt of its permanency. He raised the lamp high, wrapped his damaged arm across his body, wriggled to the end of the stone outcrop and peered round its outer edge.

It looked like something out of a goblin fairy-story. Where the top part of the cave was a simple rocky tube and slide of scree, the large rock was rather like a theatre curtain that once peered around revealed another world.

It was only a small cavern, but the lamp lit up a wondrous stage of leaping translucence, dripping stalactites and small pools glittering in the rare light.

But Joe had eyes for none of this as he sought out—and found—Ruth. She was huddled on the floor of the cave beside a small pool no bigger than a birdbath and Joe could see the path that her little body had taken, an extension to the slide that he had taken before his rock stopped his progress. He struggled to the edge of his protective rock and hardly felt the pain in his chest and his arm. He sat on the impermanent stones and dragged himself, heels, one hand and bum, zig-zag down the slope, tying not to dislodge too many stones and have them fall on Ruth.

As he came to her she raised her arms and Joe, using his one good arm, folded her into his body.

64

Four months later.
January 1927

On the outside Ruth was mended, Joe was mended. Bruises faded, cuts healed and broken bones knitted. And things had changed.

The property was slowly being gouged from the forest and in fact its progress had been modestly accelerated by the help given by most of the men on the Group at one time or another as Joe's arm and ribs mended. They had come singly, in pairs and in a goodly party on a couple of Sundays, felling and fencing and generally making sure that things ticked over despite Joe's incapacity. Joe's gratitude for the kindness, added to his relief that Ruth was safe, mending and would fully recover from her ordeal, made him a trifle maudlin. He tried clumsily to express his thanks to his fellow settlers but met with a universal shrug and "you'd do the same for me." Of course he would, he vowed to himself emotionally.

But things *had* changed. More than four months had passed since Ruth's fall and Robin's death. Nothing had been heard from the Edgars since they fled the Group with Robin's body. Cec Smith heard that they'd buried Robin in the Margaret River cemetery and the rest of the family had left on the train the same day. They really hadn't been on the Group for long enough to form strong friendships, so sometimes it seemed that they had never even been there, except for the indelible vision of the poor pale body of Robin being carried through the forest by his distraught father.

Ruth had taken the news of Robin's death badly. They had tried to keep it from her for as long as possible, but she kept asking, asking, asking. At first she thought that the search party had not found him and became almost hysterical in trying to tell them where to find him. When they had to confess that they had found him, it was inevitable that the fact of his death had to be revealed. Ruth cried for days, inconsolable. At this stage she was in the hospital with her broken leg in plaster, and Joe, with his arm likewise and his ribs taped, sat by her bed trying to comfort her. In the end Doctor Crawcour prescribed a sedative and Ruth spent days in a twilight of incomprehension from which she emerged wearily calm.

They tiptoed round her, everyone did. They tried not to upset her in any way, so never mentioned Robin or the ordeal she'd been through but spoke in soft bright voices of trivial matters like the weather, the birds in the trees outside the window, who was coming to visit, the gifts she'd received. She lay in the stiff white hospital bed, her cuts and bruises flowering darkly on her face and body, her leg stiff and splinted, and smiled vaguely at their attempts to amuse.

Joe had spent all his time in the hospital by her bedside, drowning in guilt. Guilt that she had come to such grief when she was in his care and guilt that she was in fact *here* and although battered and bruised, she lived, she breathed, she could be touched. It could so easily have been Ruth and not Robin …

Every time he allowed himself to think this way his stomach flipped and he felt an echo of the old days of daytime nightmares, whose dank horrors he had been sure had long been dried up by the hot Australian sun.

He had been trying to engage Ruth in a game of Snap when Helen Anderson came into the small hospital ward one afternoon after school. She brought some school work for Ruth to do and made a small joke about her not being able to get away. Ruth's worship of her "Miss Anderson" was well known so Joe was perturbed when the presence of her heroine, an occasion that would normally have had Ruth jumping through hoops, raised only modest enthusiasm.

Miss Anderson chatted to Ruth about school and her fellow-pupils and the things they'd been doing in class, the book she was reading to them—which she promised to bring to Ruth when finished—and the big fat bobtail lizard they were feeding every day. It was apparent that Ruth was trying to be engaged and it tore at Joe to see her effort to respond failing so dismally.

As Helen Anderson left he walked with her out of the hospital building where she was to be collected by Mr. Padman in his cart and taken back to the farm where she lodged.

They moved to the wooden steps of the hospital's verandah in the fading sunlight, Joe somewhat gingerly folding his body as he eased his ribs into a sitting position.

"Still hurt?" Miss Anderson asked.

"Yes, a bit." It was more than a bit and her expression showed that she knew that.

"Ruth is very quiet. Even more than usual. Do you think?"

Joe had never thought of Ruth quiet and said so, avoiding the question in Miss Anderson's remark.

"It's only to be expected," she continued, "considering what she's been through. Poor little lass."

There was a silence.

"She feels responsible, I know," said Joe eventually "that Robin died while she was going to find help for him. And she failed. When we try to reassure her she gets so upset that we have to stop. It's terrible," his voice almost broke "to see her so unhappy."

"I think that time might help, Mr. Barlow."

"Joe."

"If it's Joe then it's Helen," she smiled.

Joe smiled back absently. "They say time heals and I suppose it does in the end. But getting there is so painful. I just wish I could take on Ruth's hurt and confusion … "

Helen placed a hand on Joe's knee and shook it briefly.

"We all wish that impossible thing at some time or another if someone we love is in pain. And your sister is very precious to you, I know."

"She's all I've got."

"Yes I know."

"I just want to protect her."

Helen rested her elbows on her knees, hands supporting her chin.

"She's growing up." Then she added "Joe." The echo of his name hung in the air for a few beats.

It took a moment to sink in that he was having an easy and intimate conversation with a single woman and that this had not happened for a considerable time and he was out of practice.

Helen turned towards him with a puzzled air and Joe blushed to his toenails. He struggled to find a distraction. Before he could recover, Helen had said: "She's growing up, Joe."

She spoke again. "You do know that you're going to have to think about her future, don't you?"

"Ruth's?"

"Yes, of course, Ruth's future." Helen seemed amused by his vagueness and regarded him quizzically. He snapped back to the conversation.

"Ruth's future."

"This conversation is starting to sound like an opera!" Helen laughed. Joe had never come close to seeing an opera.

"Ruth will be finishing school here at the end of next year, you know Joe".

She smiled and turned to him. "I'll have passed on to her all of my wisdom and learning. What do you plan for her?"

"I don't know," said Joe honestly, still wondering about the opera. He really hadn't thought about it but the threat of another change suddenly loomed and he felt immediately anxious. "What do other families do?"

"Well, there's always the option of helping on the farm, of course, but I think Ruth's bright enough, if she works hard, to at least apply for a scholarship to the high school in Bunbury. I think every pupil who's got the ability should be put up for one, actually. It's such a waste to limit a child's horizons so early in life."

"Do you think farming is limiting?"

"No, that's not what I said, Joe. It's just that at fourteen … "

"Ruth's not yet twelve."

"Even more so, Joe. She either cools her heels at the Group school until she's of school leaving age, or gets a dispensation to leave early, or goes to high school and learns a bit about the world and the options open to her."

"Like what?"

"A job in an office, or a bank, or even University."

"University!" Joe didn't know anyone who'd been to university and hadn't actually realised that girls did. Could. The thought of Ruth in such a place made him laugh.

"Don't laugh, Joe. I'm serious."

"What would she do at university?"

"Anything she wanted!"

Helen was indeed serious, Joe realised, and her hackles were raised. Placatingly, he said "Alright, alright, good enough. I give in. But Ruth can take her own part and I promise I will talk to her. There's time, after all."

"Not that much, really, if we need to plan for a scholarship."

"I'll talk to her. But not just yet, not until she's back to herself again."

Mr. Padman's cart creaked up the track as he spoke and Helen stood, smoothing down her skirt and picking up her basket. She turned back as she walked away.

"Nice talking to you, Joe. Do it, though, won't you?"

He nodded. He had plenty of time.

65

Two months later.
March 1927

Alice poked languidly at the garden bed where, despite her lack of attention, a variety of vegetables more or less flourished. She pulled a weed or two and splashed water from the bucket that she filled from the well.

She wandered to the steps of the little house and sat on the top one, cupping her chin in her hand, elbow on knee. The day had been hot but it was blessedly coming to an end. Now that a good deal of the land was cleared around the house, the evening breeze was no longer impeded and it brought sweet relief. Alice sensed its coming, saw the tree tops shimmer with it and turned her face toward it, tilting her head and allowing her hair to lift gently. She sighed.

Stephen would be back soon. He'd been working with two other men on a location more than two miles away so he had not been back for midday dinner and had left soon after dawn. Despite the fact that she'd spoken to no one, seen no one, since he left that morning, Alice's stomach knotted at the thought of his return.

He'd be the same—anxious, accommodating, puzzled. Trying to work out what he could do to make her happy, when all she wanted to do was *go home!*

She let the yearning wash over her. Imagined the scene at Oak Tree Place when they'd all lived there, saw in her longing vision the comings and goings, the busy-ness and the casual, comfortable ordinariness of it all. Then her eyes ranged the scene that was in front of her. The sandy grey soil with its struggling pasture, dotted with the anguished leafless skeletons of the dead and dying ringbarked trees that had been too big to cut down. The fence posts fading to a silvery grey that got lost in the background tree trunks, that solid mass of trees that crowded the fence line.

She wondered how *anyone* could ever, ever, *ever* be happy in this ghastly place. It was so harsh and cruel and … foreign.

When they met from time to time, she studied Ellen and Ida covertly to try to see behind the facade that she was sure they had erected to please their men, dutiful and loving as they were.

Perhaps that was the difference, the loving part. And Ida was positively luminous with it now that she was expecting—they could probably even do without lighting the lamp these days she was so bright. Yes, there was no doubt that there was a lot of love there, she thought. Always had been of course, but Ida overlooked a lot of things in Len and Len had very much taken her for granted. This had gradually begun to change once they left Oak Tree Place, Alice realised when she thought about it. He'd had to work really hard to hide his wooden foot and perhaps it was succeeding in this that made him feel less sorry for himself and less useless. But why was she thinking about other people's happiness when it only made her more miserable? She needed to believe that everyone was secretly as unhappy as her because if she was the only discontented one that made her inadequate and the whole reason for coming to this God-forsaken place was to prove to herself that she could manage her life. Oh, alright, she needed to come to stay close to Ruth, but she'd cast Charlie aside and married Stephen and really thought at the time that she was not only clever, but was controlling her life, perhaps for the first time.

She hadn't bargained on missing Charlie so much. Ida said that Len felt pain in his foot that wasn't even there and that was what she felt, an aching nothingness. She was so ashamed of treating him so badly, yearned to be able to see him hold him, tell him she loved him. She'd never done that, but then again he'd never asked. She smiled; of course he wouldn't, she knew what made Charlie tick and revealing his needs and emotions was just not in him. Not at all, not ever. But if only she had the chance, she'd be so different. She'd tell him, she would really, and she could imagine the hardness in his lovely brown eyes dissolving and his big arms tightening around her. She wouldn't tease him any more, she wouldn't pretend indifference, she'd just love him.

She'd tell him everything. If only she could get out of here and back to England. Out of here, out of here …

On the powdery earth Stephen's footsteps were soundless and he was standing in front of her, empty billycan in his hand, axe over his shoulder, smiling tentatively, before she had time to shut off her daydreams. She started resentfully and the frown was back almost before Stephen had a chance to register the expression of pleasure that her fancies had smoothed on to her face.

She scrambled to her feet, irritated that he had glimpsed her unguarded, and Stephen followed her into the house that was cooling now as the breeze blew through from the front door to the back, sucking out the heat of the day. The fire in the stove had gone out, of course, and Stephen tried to make a joke of that inevitability as he re-stoked it.

Alice slumped at the table and regarded his bent back, his sweat-stained shirt, his dusty hair and felt a twinge of shame at what she had manipulated him into. It may have been the softening influence of her daydreams that had not let her quite free yet. But as Stephen went outside again, first to chop some wood for the stove, then to wash off the day's sweat and dirt in the tin tub outside the back door, Alice's mind would not relinquish its homing thoughts, but this time it probed further back.

It had taken a great deal of courage to confess to Jessie that she was pregnant. Jessie had begun to express pleasure at the news until she caught sight of Alice's expression and also realised—

"It's not Johnny's baby."

"Couldn't be. Johnny's been gone seven months."

"Oh."

There was a wealth of expression in that single syllable.

"Who is the father then?"

Alice had just shaken her head.

"As if it matters, although I have little doubt who it is anyway." Jessie was contemptuous. "What are you going to do? What are you going to tell your husband, away fighting for his country?"

"I don't know."

"Are you going to keep it?"

"I think I have to."

"Why?"

This was a surprise to Alice. Jessie was the last person she would have thought would approve an abortion. But then, she thought sourly, Jessie was always more about appearances than realities

She took a defensive satisfaction in shocking her sister-in-law.

"I had an abortion once and I nearly died. I didn't think I could have any more children after it."

Jessie had flinched at the word "abortion".

There was another one of those significant pauses. Alice had to fill the silence.

"I love Johnny, really I do, Jess. But you don't know anything about our marriage or Johnny or me or why he went to the war so early, even. You just don't know. But I wouldn't ever want to hurt him and now that he's a prisoner and suffering so, he can't be told I'm having a baby because he'll know it's not his baby, he'll know, and he's been so good to me that I don't want to hurt him, I don't!"

By this time Alice was sobbing. When she raised her head from her hands, she found Jessie looking at her speculatively, with a glint of avidness.

"You'd better tell me everything."

So she did, almost. She might have glossed over the early details, over-embellished others, but she took pains to be quite vividly accurate about the fact that her marriage to Johnny was as much a rescue for him as it was for her. That she and Johnny had never lived as a normal married couple and his precipitous enlistment in the army was caused by the only big row they'd ever had and that was because Alice had actually seen him with another man …

She was glad to see that she had managed to shock Jessie significantly this time, whose eyes had filled with tears. Alice didn't know who the tears were for at first, but Jessie, pale and now tearless, soon set her straight.

"Ned must never know about Johnnie."

"Did you know?"

"I'm not a fool. I suspected something, but it's still a shock to have it confirmed. So very disgusting. Very disgusting." She shuddered slightly and repeated "Ned must never know. He is very fond of his brother and such information would kill him."

She was looking differently at Alice, though. Not exactly with sympathy, but the contempt was a little less. Alice didn't have to be told that Ned loved his younger brother. Always in the background to his assertive wife, Ned Barlow was a gentle man whose demeanour belied a hard and difficult early life, a life in which he had protected his younger brother from a bullying step-father. Alice had observed the light in Ned's eyes when he looked at Johnny and had heard him say often how very good it was to have his brother living in Oak Tree Place alongside and how good it would be when Johnnie had a family of his own.

Jessie pulled herself upwards in her chair and took a deep breath, regaining her authority with the action.

"Let me think about this, Alice. Let me think."

That had been the beginning of the conspiracy.

As Alice prepared the rice pudding and Stephen splashed water everywhere outside the door, she thought about how it had evolved.

Jessie's idea had at first been shockingly bizarre. But as it sat there between them it became seductive, then possible to contemplate, then a resolution. It involved the utmost secrecy from everyone involved.

Ned was told a suitably limited version of the facts and Alice was forever tainted in his eyes, but she probably deserved that.

Jessie's mother was told the same limited version and Alice had to live with that, too, as she did for the duration of her pregnancy in Southampton in her care. She smiled grimly now as she remembered the endless months of pregnancy under that disapproving gaze.

It had, in the end, been remarkably simple. A succession of cushions and pillows tied under voluminous smocks had been quite enough to satisfy the gaze of all observers of Jessie's remarkable late pregnancy. Alice had left Oak Tree place to live with her mythical widowed mother while Johnny was away.

And when the time approached, Jessie simply visited her mother and Alice, assisted with the birth of Ruth, stayed a while and took her back to Oak Tree Place as her own.

Alice's expression was bleak as she relived the event. She simply hadn't counted on feeling the way she did. Her body had screamed for her baby, her engorged breasts throbbed and spilled the milk that should have been nurturing Ruth. She cried incessantly, wailed even, until Jessie's mother threatened her with a good shaking, but then unexpectedly, after all the months of disapproval, took her in motherly arms and let her cry.

She had thought that going back to Oak Tree Place and watching her daughter grow up as her niece would be pleasant and straightforward, but again she hadn't banked on her amazing sense of connection with Ruth. She lingered around Jessie and Ned's house, dumb with desire to hold, nurture, love …

In the end Jessie had to tell her to stay away, that she was too much around them, that she was not needed and had made her own bed.

In case she was disposed to revoke her agreed part in the fabrication, Jessie took pains to remind Alice that the official registration of Ruth's birth stated that Jessie and Ned were her parents. Jessie had insisted that the charade be carried through to its full extent, and it had been amazingly easy to effect the erroneous registration. Once that it was done, and set forever in official records, Jessie told Alice with relish that the fact that she had allowed this to happen, and taken an active part, made her a criminal. This criminality, Jessie said, if detected, always *always* resulted in the criminal going to jail. They would all of them keep the secret forever, wouldn't they, Jessie had said repeatedly, unaware of the dread she awoke in Alice's breast at the thought of an official investigation of any sort. But of course they would keep the secret from Johnny. Of course they would. Johnny would never know.

And Johnny had been dead all the time and they didn't know it. What a great joke it all was.

Alice had actually snorted softly and mirthlessly as Stephen came into the kitchen, glowing and scrubbed.

"What's that you're thinking?" he enquired lightly.

"Nothing."

"Oh."

Stephen's shoulders slumped as their familiar ritual of bright enquiry and taciturn rejoinder seemed likely to continue. Alice's brief surge of tenderness for him ebbed to nothing as she applied herself to putting the pudding into the oven. She could not afford to claim Ruth as her daughter, that was probably the fact of the matter. Fear of the inevitable further consequences had kept her cowed and silent for all these years. Complacent Jessie had thought that her silence was ensured by the threat of jail that she had waved in front of her, but little did Jessie know that it was much, much, more than that that had kept her quiet and amenable. Living for so long with the secrets that she had mentally classified as the big one and the small one had managed to blunt the menace that had so terrified her initially, and it had become background to her life, wrapped and buffered. Except when she let herself think about it, like now.

But if she were free to claim Ruth as her daughter, what would that mean?

Ruth herself would find it easy to adapt to being her daughter, she was sure. A pause here for the glow of delight at the picture, then she dragged herself back to the reaction of Joe, who to be sure was a loving guardian of the girl he thought to be his sister. But not always guardian enough, she thought quickly, not after the terrible series of events that he had allowed to happen to Ruth and that poor little Edgar boy.

People had been so sympathetic to Joe at his anguish over Ruth's accident and all that had gone with it, but Alice had not. He had insisted that Ruth continued to be safe and happy at their house on her own until he came back from his work and indeed Ruth herself had confirmed this—but then she would, she agreed with Joe in everything he said. She said she liked preparing tea, liked the silence. Liked being by herself! Of course she was just saying that for Joe's sake.

If Ruth had been directed to come to Alice and Stephen's house when Joe was working, where Alice could care for her, the terrible thing would never have happened. So it was actually Joe's fault. But nobody seemed to see it that was except her. She raked the fire with vigour.

Stephen was speaking.

"What did you say?"

"I said that Miss Anderson came by the Fox's place this afternoon where we were working. She wanted to see Mrs. Fox about Joanie. We all had a cup of tea together."

"And how is Miss Anderson?"

Stephen looked surprised at her tone.

"Well, I expect. She looked well."

"Oh, I expect she did."

"What on earth do you mean by that? There was slight annoyance in Stephen's voice.

"School teacher. Huh."

"Oh Alice."

"Don't you 'Oh Alice' me, Stephen Dent." Alice began to wind up. "School teacher, airs and graces, so clever, looking down on settlers' wives, so high and mighty—"

"Oh Alice," Stephen repeated "you are being a goose. Of course Helen Anderson doesn't look down on you."

"Ah!" Alice seized on the fact, "It's *Helen* now is it? Very interesting, very interesting." Her voice rose. "I do wonder why on *earth* she needed to speak to Mrs. Fox about Joanie when you just *happened* to be working on their place. Hah!"

"Oh Alice."

Stephen walked tiredly out the front door on to the verandah and leant against the rail, staring out at the surrounding, enveloping, forest.

66

The following month.
April 1927

It was a ridiculously warm Sunday in late April when a little party of Groupers made their way to the beach, trailing through the bush on what had become a fairly well-used track. The journey now seemed much shorter than their first few forays to the sea through scraping undergrowth and strange landmarks; familiarity had blunted the sights and shortened the path. The news of the planned outing had spread from family to family and a small party had gaily set off on what would certainly be their last opportunity before the cold and the winter rains set in.

"Funny how much shorter this trip seems now," said Joe to Stephen.

"Ah, the unknown is always more intense," Stephen laughed.

"And therefore longer?" Joe raised an eyebrow.

"Of course! When you're experiencing something for the first time you notice every little thing and storing up all those new things takes mind-time."

"Mmmm," said Joe, flicking the flies away from his face with a switch of leaves.

They crested the dune and, as usual, paused. It seemed automatic to take a deep breath of the sharp salty air before they plunged headlong down the loose sandy dune, laughing, always laughing, at their own awkwardness as the sand collapsed and skidded under the weight of their feet and they hurtled, splay-legged, spraying plumes of white sand sideways, towards the beach. Breathless, they reached the flat sand, smoothed and lightly crusted by a recent high tide. There was always a feeling of awe at the virginal sheet of untrodden sea-sand, only pitted with the claw-prints of a small bird they had been told was the hooded plover, a bird with a delicate vulnerability that seemed totally unsuitable to a littoral life where the breakers boomed and crashed and the next landfall was Africa. Joe felt that the settlers themselves were no less unsuitable and vulnerable; the nature that surrounded them was so overwhelming in every aspect—the wide sweep of the unpeopled bay, the far horizon of the sea, the endless dome of the sky, so unremittingly blue and cloudless. It could gobble them all up and no one would ever know they'd been here.

But this feeling dissipated as the party breached the untracked sand, spread blankets, settled bags and baskets, peeled off shoes, socks and stockings and made for the water's edge, to stand and gossip while the tiny waves lapped and sucked at their feet. But for the breakers beyond, the scene became almost suburban.

Being at the beach changed the dynamic of the Group. It was liberating to be away from farms and houses and animals and anxieties, even if the men often discussed Group concerns quietly between themselves, it was not like the serious meetings they held from time to time at the school. It seemed impossible that anything could be seriously amiss when the sun shone on such a scene and they were part of it.

"What would they make of us now at the Oak Tree?" asked Len as he and Joe sat at the waters' edge, Len with his foot unstrapped again, bathing his stump in the wash of the waves. "A bit difficult for them to imagine, a scene like this."

"Mmmm," said Joe.

"But then again, all you need is a grey sky, a cold wind, pebbles to twist your ankles on, a few donkeys and a Punch and Judy show, and it's a typical works outing, eh?"

"Mmmm," said Joe again, turning his face to the wind.

"Sad to hear that old Dora died last year,"

"Yes," said Joe, looking at the horizon. "Sad but not unexpected."

"No, she must have been well into her eighties, the old duck. Nice of Mrs. Craggs to let us know, though. She wrote to Ruth?"

"She's written to her a few times. Surprising, really, I never thought she'd keep in touch with us."

"She doesn't write to *us* though, Joe, just Ruth. Funny that. You don't really see her as writing letters to an eleven-year-old, do you?"

"I certainly don't see her writing chatty letters to any of us!"

"P'raps on engraved writing paper!"

"Oh the thrill of getting a letter from Mrs. Craggs! Just like from Royalty"

A small silence ensued as the water bubbled and eddied in front of them. Further out crashing breakers pushed a spray of foam into the air where they collided with the shiny black rocks in the bay.

"All that seems so far away."

"It is!"

"Yeah, can't get any further away, can we? Do you miss it Joe?"

"I'd sometimes commit murder for a pint at the Oak Tree."

"Oh yes, yes! And some fish and chips and a night at the pictures!"

They both laughed before Len continued.

"Do you dream of it, Joe?"

"What, you mean real dream, at night?"

"Yeah."

"No, can't say I do. Too damned tired to dream."

Joe thought of the beneficial effects of hard work. Blisters and backache, certainly, but a solid exhaustion that had him sleeping in a blissfully dreamless state until morning. He was almost afraid to think about the fact that he had not had a nightmare for months. Len was speaking again.

"I do, you know."

"Dream about Oak Tree Place?"

"Yes, funny really, it's all very mixed-up but the houses are all empty and falling down. And I'm always alone indoors at our house with no furniture and bits of the roof caving in on top of me."

Joe tried distraction from a description that he didn't want to hear. "Good job you left, then."

It worked. Len laughed, agreed, and changed the subject.

"Have you spoken to Alice recently?

"Yes, I mean, yes, I suppose so."

"She seems pretty fed-up to me. And Stephen's not very happy, I can tell. He's very quiet these days."

Len was such an old woman for gossip! Joe kept a deliberate silence, despite the fact that he had noticed too, despite himself, despite not wanting to notice. Alice was definitely edgy and nervous, belittling Stephen if the opportunity arose and generally putting down the other women. She scorned the Australians whom she considered uncouth, and closer to home, Ellen and Ida, who were getting on with being farmers' wives and making the best of things. That was as far as Joe could see, anyway. He could be quite cross with Alice for her unreasonable attitude, especially with what he knew about her. Someone with her history was in no position … Len was speaking again.

"Seems a shame that Stephen is getting on so well with his block—better than most of us—then to have Alice dragging him down like that."

"It'll blow over." Joe was not going to be drawn into this conversation.

"Doesn't always, Joe. Remember the Riggs and the Allsops and that other family, what was their name? Next door to the Cowpers?"

"No … "

"Healy! That's it, the Healys. They all left because the women couldn't cope. You could see it coming for a mile, the looks on their faces, the way they slouched around … "

"It's not for everybody,"

"'Course it's not, and sometimes it's not for me! Specially on those early mornings in the cold. And," he added, "the early mornings in the hot!"

"Early mornings generally, you mean?"

"That's about it!"

Len was so remarkably cheerful even when he was moaning. Joe remembered the prickly self-obsessed Len of Oak Tree Place and marvelled at the change. Perhaps it was Ida being in a certain condition. But no, it had started to happen almost as soon as they arrived on the Group. Funny that, he would have thought that Len was the one in their party least able to cope with the hardships, and there he was, seemingly happy as a lark.

He leant back on his elbows and idly speculated on who he would have expected to adapt best to the life here. Stephen. Yes, of course, no doubt, capable Stephen was cut out for challenges like this, but it could well be that a fed-up Alice could bring it all to a halt if she ever got around to insisting on leaving. That would be a terrible shame.

He looked up the beach to where Stephen and some of the other men were playing with the children at the water's edge. The game involved a ball and much splashing and shouting. The women were together further up the beach, beginning to prepare the picnic lunch. The breeze caught a tablecloth that Ellen was spreading on the sand and ballooned it softly into the air.

He must have closed his eyes and half-dozed because he did not see the two figures coming down the dune, only heard the shouts of surprise as they neared the beach. He and Len craned around and saw a slim young woman and a tall dark man, who even from the distance seemed to be dressed with an unsuitable formality for a beach visit. He shook his feet every few steps in a fruitless endeavour to empty his shoes of sand but ploughed on with dogged intent towards the group of women.

Joe recognised Helen Anderson as she trailed the dark stranger, and the dark stranger himself had a curious familiarity. His recent thoughts of Oak Tree Place made him wonder if he was imagining things. But no—it *was*, it was Charlie!

Charlie Craggs was in Australia, Charlie Craggs was forging through the sand with an intensity that was obvious even from a distance. Joe and Len scrambled to their feet, Len grabbing his stick and dangling his false foot on its straps as they made clumsy haste towards him. The previous residents of Oak Tree Place were dumbfounded, the other Groupers highly curious. They all came together as Charlie and Helen reached the women and their half-prepared picnic. There was a babble of voices, and men reached out to shake Charlie's hand.

Joe said "Charlie, Charlie, Charlie, what on earth are you doing here? How did you get here, why are you here?"

Helen was explaining, to no-one's interest, that she'd found Charlie just off the train in town and that she and Mr. Padman had taken him to Stephen's block where he'd wanted to go, and then on to here.

Len, Stephen and Michael crowded closer, "What are you doing here?" emerging as the most-asked question and the one that was patently going to take more than a sentence to explain.

Charlie was sweating and he dragged a handkerchief from his pocket to mop his face. He was pleased enough with the impact that his arrival was causing, shook hands with the men and was introduced to the settlers he didn't know. But his eyes were darting around the group, seeking a face that wasn't there. His intent was transparent and Joe feared ensuing events. It was going to get sticky.

67

The same day

Ruth felt her spirits rise as soon as she was on the beach. It was something about the air, the salt on the wind, the huge space of the sea and the sky that made her feel happy. But she never came to the beach without remembering that Robin never saw it. She always pretended when she came that he was with her, and she talked to him as she splashed along the wave-line. She was nearly always sad when she thought of him, but here at the beach it was really as if he was with her, as if the journey down the creek had actually delivered them here, where they were headed before the …

"Race you to the end of the beach!" She took off, leaving one set of higgeldy footprints to mark the race.

She loved to be in the water and could nearly swim now, but it was the lovely spooky little forest on the other side of the small headland that was an essential visit each time she came to the beach and she was intent on visiting it again today with Robin. She could talk out loud to him up there without anyone hearing. She had shown him each time the way that the sounds of the beach were cut off as if a blanket was thrown over them the minute they stepped over the top of the ridge and she pointed out again and again the twisted little umbrella trees and told him that she loved them more every time she visited because they were so spooky, like a story book.

She literally stumbled across Auntie Alice at the end of the beach. She had been sitting behind a huge rock on the soft sand, gazing out to the sea with such a sad look on her face that Ruth felt that she should stop with her for a while to cheer her up. Robin's presence dissolved.

Impulsively, she suggested to Auntie Alice that she show her the spooky gnome-forest at the top of the cliff. Auntie Alice consented with a sigh.

They were half way up the sandy cliff, concentrating on hand and foot-holds, when Charlie and Miss Anderson appeared on the beach below but Ruth did not glance backward as she took Auntie Alice's hand and pulled her towards her magical fairy wood.

"When we get to the top," said Ruth, "just you wait and see how it all changes."

"When we get to the top," laughed Alice, "I'm going to sit down and catch my breath!"

Ruth was pleased that she had made Auntie Alice laugh.

"No, it's really, really good, you'll see."

They crested the ridge and suddenly their footsteps were inaudible on the soft dust and the sounds of the beach fell away.

"See? See?" It's all different, isn't it? And do you see my fairy wood? All twisted and quiet and like out of my old fairy story book with those curly pictures."

"Oh yes, love, it's really nice."

Ruth thought that more enthusiasm would have been nicer but pressed on.

"You can go further than this and down into the next bay. Joe and me went on through the bush a little bit a few weeks ago but it got too hard. We saw the bay though. Joe thinks that maybe nobody has ever been there, isn't that exciting? When I'm older I'm going to get right down and be the first footprint on the sand, ever. And I shall name it Ruth's Bay!"

Auntie Alice was looking at her with a smile on her face.

"Or perhaps Barlow Bay?" Ruth rattled on. "Then we could all be in the name. Me and Joe—and well, you were a Barlow before you married Uncle Stephen, weren't you?"

"I was indeed."

Auntie Alice was still smiling at her with a smile that was familiar—she had always looked at her with a secret really loving sort of look. She didn't smile at anyone else that way and it used to make Ruth feel special.

"Tell you what. I'll hide and you see if you can find me."

"Oh no, love, no. I'm too big and out of breath to go playing hide and seek in this place."

"Oh go on! Alright, tell you what. I'll hide and you sit down and see if you can see me when I hide. I won't be far."

Before Auntie Ruth could complain or stop her, Ruth scudded off through the spindly trunks of the umbrella trees, calling out "Count to fifty!"

She darted a look back and Auntie Alice was sitting obediently and putting her hands over her eyes, counting slowly and loudly.

This was going to be so easy! The shallow little hollow that she'd fallen into when she and Joe first came up here was ideal for her purpose and she couldn't use it to trick Joe any more because he knew about it. But Ruth knew that it was invisible from the edge of the cliff where Auntie Alice sat, and she'd be amazed at Ruth's disappearance because the trees here were definitely not big enough to hide behind, or to climb, so she just wouldn't know where Ruth was when she was actually very close to her! She rolled into the depression and lay comfortably in the warm gritty sand, grinning broadly. Auntie Alice was up to thirty five.

It was forty-five and Ruth was giving a last wriggle when Auntie Alice's counting stopped dead and she screamed. Ruth's first thought was that this was a trick to have her show herself, so she raised her head slowly and carefully to just above the rim of the depression, smiling in sly anticipation and hoping that Auntie Alice wasn't looking in her direction.

She wasn't. She was looking an amazement at a strange man who was hauling her from her sitting position and hugging her tightly to him. Ruth sat upright in surprise, just as Uncle Stephen burst on to the scene and started to pull at the man. Ruth's first instinct was to scramble from her hiding place to help, but before she could, the big man pushed Uncle Stephen away with one hand and roared so loudly that Ruth fell back, terrified. She pulled herself into the far end of the hollow and peered around one of the skinny tree trunks.

They weren't fighting each other any more. The three of them were standing looking at each other, panting. Even Auntie Alice, and she hadn't been fighting. None of them were saying anything.

Then "Right!" said Uncle Stephen, "What's all this about then?"

The big dark man began to look familiar.

"Charlie?" said Auntie Alice shakily.

Charlie! It was Mr. Craggs! Mr Craggs from Oak Tree Place! Ruth stumbled from her hiding place towards the three of them. Mr. Craggs looked amazed.

"Is it Ruth?"

"Yes, it's me but I've grown!" she laughed at the delicious surprise of it all, more than happy to disregard the tussle she'd seen.

"Have you come from Oak Tree Place?"

"More or less." Said Charlie Craggs of Oak Tree Place. "Let me look at you."

Ruth obligingly turned around twice for his inspection. Auntie Alice was staring hard at Mr. Craggs, Uncle Stephen was staring hard at Auntie Alice and everyone seemed to want to say things but didn't. Uncle Stephen spoke first though, and to Ruth.

"Ruth, do you think you can find your way back to the beach?"

Ruth was scornful. "Of course I can, it's just down the cliff." She could sense the adult-ness of the situation and knew there was no way she was going to be allowed to stay. With some resentment she said "I'll go back to Joe and the others then, shall I?"

"Yes please Ruth."

They stood there in silence—she took a quick look back—until she disappeared over the crest. They continued standing as she quietly wormed her secret way back and into the same hollow that she'd emerged from minutes before. By the time she had settled within hearing distance they had all sat down, Auntie Alice on a rock, Mr. Craggs on another rock and Uncle Stephen on the ground. She heard Uncle Stephen say something about not needing to have it aired in public.

She thought she'd better not chance a look but she could hear everything quite well. She was still stunned by the sudden appearance of Mr. Craggs. She did so want to talk to him about his mother and all the other people in Oak Tree Place and maybe he had heard something of some of her school friends. She hoped he was not here just for a day visit. But no, that was not sensible, to come all this way and not at least stay for a while. Uncle Stephen was speaking again.

"So Charlie, what's going on here? Why the sudden visit?"

"There's things to sort out."

Mr. Craggs sounded surly, but then he mostly always had been.

"Perhaps you should just explain."

Mr. Craggs seemed to find it hard to speak. Perhaps it was the fact that he was hot and tired, or perhaps there was something really interesting to be told. Ruth strained to catch every word, as Mr. Craggs slowly began to speak.

The first thing he said was sad.

"My mother died three months ago."

Oh, poor Mrs. Craggs.

Uncle Stephen sounded confused when he said "I'm sorry to hear that."

Then he said "Is that why you're here?" in an even more puzzled voice.

"No. I mean yes."

"Go on"

Ruth noticed that Auntie Alice had not spoken at all.

"She left a will. And a letter."

"Yes?"

"I've got them here."

"If that's what this is all about, perhaps you'd better just tell us, Charlie."

Ruth could hear the deep loud breath before Mr. Craggs spoke.

"My mother never really showed herself to any of you. Most people thought she was a snob and well, she was that, I know. But she always lived up to her responsibilities and she was very good to me, I know that too. But she needed to be on top of everything, in all sort of ways, from knowing everything that was going on to being in charge of it all. I'm probably not telling you anything you didn't know."

No one spoke.

Ruth thought suddenly that she had heard the same sort of thing said about her own mother. Oak Tree Place must have been full of busybodies!

"Mother died suddenly," said Mr. Craggs. "she just left the bar and went back to sit by the fire for a bit, and when we came in, she was dead. Just sitting there looking as if she was asleep, but not really. She must have died suddenly and perhaps in her sleep, and that's always a good thing, isn't it?" He seemed to be asking for an opinion.

Still no one spoke.

"Well, I'm here about the will. I have letters from the solicitor that explain it all in detail, but the long and short of it is that half of my mother's estate has been left to me and half in trust for Ruth."

"*Ruth!*" said Stephen and Alice together, and Ruth herself almost joined in. She was not sure what an "estate" was, but if she was important enough to be in Mrs. Craggs' will, this was extremely interesting. She chanced a peek from behind the tree trunk, just a little one.

Mr. Craggs was side-on to her and she could see that he was staring hard at Auntie Alice. They were all still sitting in the same positions, so Ruth sank down again.

"Does half of the estate provide adequately for you?" Uncle Stephen asked Mr. Craggs quite rudely. "Or do you intend to contest the will?"

"No!" said Mr. Craggs loudly, "that's not why I'm here, not at all. You don't understand."

"What is it then, Charlie?" Auntie Alice's voice was squeaky.

"You know, damn you, you know! And you've kept it from me all this time! Does this husband of yours know?"

"Know *what*?" Once again Auntie Alice and Uncle Stephen spoke together.

"That I'm Ruth's father, damn you!"

Ruth dared not look, could not look. Mr. Craggs was quite mad. Fancy coming all this way to say such a stupid thing. She didn't really remember her Dad except as a shadowy warm presence and some photos in an album, but it certainly wasn't Mr. Craggs. *He* wasn't anybody's father.

"I think" said Uncle Stephen, "that I've changed my mind. This is no subject to discuss on a windy clifftop. Let's just calm down and go back to the others. You'll stay with us, Charlie? We have room in the house."

Ruth admired Uncle Stephen's calmness, but that was probably the best way to handle mad Mr. Craggs. You could not do much with a mad man way out here.

Ruth suddenly realised that she had to get back to the beach fast to avoid discovery. She wriggled and scrambled back to the sandy hill and ran down as fast as she could. Right at the bottom she almost fell into Uncle Michael and Auntie Ellen, who were wandering along the waterline collecting seaweed for their garden in a flour bag.

"Hello there, little Ruth!" said Uncle Michael, "where have you been?"

"Umm, I went to the cliff top with Auntie Alice but Mr. Craggs and Uncle Stephen came up too and they all wanted to talk so I came down," she said, feeling that she was not telling lies. Quite truthful in fact.

"What are they talking about?" said Auntie Ellen with bright eyes.

"I don't know." This was a lie, but unavoidable.

"I suppose there must be a lot to catch up on after all this time."

Ruth did not feel that she had to answer this, but joined in the seaweed collection, walking back along the beach until the bag had been filled.

Soon after, the three people from the cliff top climbed down and rejoined the party. Uncle Stephen and Auntie Alice did not sit together on the sand for the picnic lunch, and Mr. Craggs was in the middle of a little crowd of people who were asking him tons of questions about home and England and everything.

But as they all walked back, the three of them peeled off together at Uncle Stephen's block and disappeared into the trees.

68

The same day

Alice's mind was whirling, the possibilities beckoned through the confusion. Had she not been dreaming of this opportunity? Wishing it, yearning for it? But she'd have to be quiet and clever, needed to listen for the most part and hear what was to be heard. But she could not help the elation that surged through her as she felt the nearness of Charlie prickle like sunburn on her skin. She tried not to steal sideways glances as they trudged through the bush towards their house, aware of Stephen's stiff presence on her other side.

She couldn't blame him for being furious, but she really didn't care a fig. The presence of Charlie changed everything, no matter what he was going to say, no matter how puzzled she was about what he'd said already. What had Edie Craggs seen ... thought ... heard ... ?

The house came into view through the trees. Alice was looking at it through Charlie's eyes, seeing more objectively the little house dwarfed by the surrounding trees, the meagre cleared area dotted with dying ringbarked monsters, their bare upper branches stark against the sky. Goodness knows they lived modestly in Oak Tree Place, but this was something else again. She had been railing against it ever since she'd arrived, but familiarity had worn off the edges and now she saw it all afresh. All afresh and much, much more dreary.

Inside it was a bit better. Stephen's book case made their front room look quite nicely furnished, and the kitchen where they assembled, although frugal and basic, was pleasant enough. Still seeing it all through the eyes of a newcomer, Alice felt a small surge of pride at its adequacy. Oh yes, oh yes, here you go, Alice, contrary to the end you'll be. You hate the place, remember?

Their small back room was hurriedly cleared and a stretcher set up for Charlie. His suitcase, left at the station, would—or was that could?—be collected tomorrow. He had shed his suit coat long ago on the journey back from the beach, and now, in shirtsleeves, he sat at the kitchen table with his hands palm-down on the table in front of him as Alice, mute, boiled the kettle and made tea.

Stephen forced some casual chat, asking Charlie about the voyage, the ship, and finally, seeming to remember with a start, about Lily.

"She's looking after the pub. Mother left it to her. Of course." Charlie's lip curled. "Mother always looked after dear Lily."

Oh. That was rather nasty. Not that Charlie had ever made any effort to pretend affection for Lily, of course. Everyone had always known that she was the woman his mother had selected for him—married to take advantage of her experience of managing the pub. Well, she'd done alright, hadn't she? No longer the barmaid or the publican's wife, the *owner* no less. Alice scrubbed Lily from her mind and set the teacups on the table. She still didn't speak as she sat down. Let the two of them get on with it. She needed to listen.

Stephen—of course it would be—was the first to speak.

Drawing a breath, he said "Alright Charlie, let's hear it all." Charlie fixed his eyes on Alice, asking again, as he had on the cliff-top "Why didn't you tell me?"

Alice squirmed and contrived a look of guilty anguish. Listening. Learning.

"What did she tell *you?*" Charlie turned to Stephen belligerently.

"Not much," said Stephen.

"Did you know that Ruth was Alice's daughter?"

"Yes."

"Who did she say the father was?"

"She said she didn't know."

Alice bit her lip.

"When did she tell you?'

"Back in England. Just before we all decided to emigrate."

"Ah." A pathetic sound came from Charlie that was a cross between a sob and a moan. Alice felt such sympathy for him that she had trouble stopping herself from throwing her arms around him. She had never seen him so obviously vulnerable before. She blinked back a threatening tear.

"So Charlie," said Stephen in an even tone, "What is it that you've come all this way for? Did you want to tell Ruth that she was a young lady of substance? Or did you want to have it out with Alice for not telling you she was Ruth's mother?" Alice noticed Stephen's lack of reference to the identity of Ruth's father. A bit of a shock for him as well, that.

"The first thing I want is to know how my mother knew it all and I didn't! I feel such a bloody hoodwinked idiot!"

Alice's mind had been racing in the same direction. Mrs. Edie Craggs—and Mrs. Lily Craggs too for that matter—had always openly disliked her. Edie Craggs had constantly nagged and belittled her when she worked at the Oak Tree, tried many times to dismiss her until Charlie always stepped in, and had constantly made her life so unpleasant that indeed it would have been sweet relief to leave it all. Except that that was unthinkable.

Alice's thoughts cartwheeled around in her head. She was mystified that Edie had been able to keep the secret about Ruth to herself for so long, and it was also a mystery how she came to her conclusion anyway when the false details of Ruth's birth had been so elaborately and carefully constructed; they were watertight. There was only one answer: Jessie must have told her. Yes, that must be it, she could see it happening, those two stiff and proper old hens who had always been as thick as thieves, clucking away with each other, sharing the scandal over cups of tea, swearing each other to secrecy. Promising not to let Charlie know that he'd got Alice in the family way, promising to keep the true facts of Ruth's birth a secret. Edie trying against the odds to hold Charlie to the marriage that she had engineered. Heavens she was—had been—a determined woman.

So clever old Edie and Jessie had put two and two together, come up with five, and decided that Charlie was the father of Alice's baby, and that was that. Clever cluckers. So they both knew about her and Charlie all the time. And she thought they'd been so careful. Ha.

"You feel an idiot, Charlie? Let me join you!" said Stephen loudly.

"What sort of stupid game do you think you're playing with all your secrets and your lies and your using people for your own ends?" He had turned on Alice and was practically spitting the words. Calm, reasoned Stephen was very angry.

Alice's mind was whirring and it was too much to take in and take advantage of at the same time.

"Leave me alone!" she shouted, flouncing into the bedroom and slamming the door. She stood with her back against it, her breathing rapid and her mind racing. She needed some time alone to work this all out. But the voices continued from the kitchen, and she scrambled to press her ear against the thin internal wall.

"Look, Charlie," Stephen was saying in a controlled voice, "I understand how you must feel, and you've come a long way to try to get to the bottom of it all, but good Lord man, all you had to do was write a letter—or the solicitor would have done it for you. Such a lot of trouble you've gone to. Why was it so important to actually come out here?"

"I can afford it," mumbled Charlie, "and I want to really sort things out, once and for all."

"What do you mean?"

"Ruth is my little girl. In Oak Tree Place I didn't know it, and I wasn't able to be a father to her. I *want* to be a father to her. She's my child!"

There was a small silence.

"How do you propose to achieve that?" Stephen's voice was more puzzled than troubled.

"I want to tell the truth to everyone. Alice has got to stop pretending about it all. And I want," Alice heard the creak as he sat up straight in the chair "to take Ruth back to England."

"Oh."

"She's money for a good education now, and I want her to take advantage of it. Something that she can't do here, even with the money. Can she?" he added.

Alice was reeling. To hear Charlie talking this way was so foreign. He had never shown any interest in Ruth, or any other children. Nor had he set much store by education! Now all at once he sounded like the ideal father.

"I think," Stephen was saying, "that removing Ruth from Joe's care will not be easy. It will be very painful for them both if it happens."

"It's gone on for too long, and I don't give a damn! Joe is not her brother—in fact he's no relation at all, is he? I'm her father, Alice is her mother, and that's that."

"All of this relies on the fact that what your mother supposed to be true is actually true, of course, Charlie."

"Of course it's true! She'd hardly leave half her money to Ruth if she wasn't sure, would she?"

Alice burst out of the bedroom.

"Yes, yes, yes, it *is* all true and I'm the one who knows, aren't I?"

"Are you?" said Stephen coldly. "What if you're lying about it all? There's no one to confirm your story, is there? Ruth's birth certificate—you told me yourself—shows Jessie and Ned as Ruth's parents. How can you prove otherwise? And Alice," Stephen continued with steel in his voice, "do you not remember why you so wanted to come to Australia? Why you wanted to leave England behind with all its memories and happenings and people? Do you? Do you?"

Alice slumped into a chair by the table, suddenly deflated. She had had a plan and now Stephen was putting all sorts of barriers in her way. She massaged her head savagely, messing her hair without thought. She could not let Stephen's wretched commonsense ruin everything that had suddenly become possible. Could not. Fight, Alice! One thing at a time.

"If I tell Joe about me being Ruth's mother, he'll know it's true," she said. "I can tell him all the little things and he'll know it's the truth."

"So what about poor little Ruth?" said Stephen. "Loses her mother and father. Her *official* mother and father," he hastened to amend, "and now she's set to be taken away from the brother she adores—and who adores her—just after a terrible accident where her little friend died and she could have died herself. It's altogether too much to heap on to such a little girl."

"She's young enough to manage it all, and it's all for the best in the end." Charlie was surly again.

"If you really had Ruth's interests at heart you would not want to uproot her." Stephen was grave. "What's really behind it all, Charlie?"

Charlie stood up so fast that the chair overbalanced.

"Bloody hell and damnation!" he yelled "I don't care if you don't believe me! I just don't care, I tell you! But I am going to take Ruth back to England, by hook or by crook. And I might as well say it now, I want to take Alice as well."

At this point Charlie turned to Alice and stretched his hand across the table. Without hesitation, Alice grasped it and rose to her feet, her eagerness knocking over the chair which clattered to the floor. They stood there, hand in hand across the table, eyes locked, for several seconds.

"Well, now we have all the cards on the table," said Stephen grimly, "and a pretty mess it all is. I'm very sure," he rose and shrugged into his jacket, "that I have no wish whatsoever to be involved with the shameful events that are going to take place as a result of your arrival, Charlie. All I can say is may your chickens all come home to roost one day."

As he went out the door of the house he turned and said "I will be back in an hour. I want both of you gone from here when I get back and I don't wish to see either of you again, ever. Do what you are going to do—no one is going to stop two selfish people like you, but I do not wish you well. Goodbye." Stephen left without another word, with only a small stumble on the bottom step to indicate that he might not be as sanguine as he sounded.

69

The next day

Alice woke slowly that morning in the rumpled bed, slack and voluptuous with remembered sex.

The small guest house in the township was just adequate, but the beds were clean and soft and more comfortable than anything Alice had slept on since coming to Australia.

Full awareness and memory seeped slowly into her consciousness as the dawn light gradually outlined the furniture in the room, the window, the door, and the blissful awareness of the bulk of Charlie's body beside her. Her body was soft and loose but her spirit was soaring, despite the knowledge that a very difficult day lay ahead. Didn't matter, everything was going to plan, and much better than she could have imagined. All those knotty problems would be overcome somehow. With some hesitation, she mentally listed them.

Lily. She has the Oak Tree. Should be satisfied with that. Tick.

Joe. Well, he had no real right to Ruth, did he? She thought of all the times they'd fought over Ruth, all the times she'd been so close to telling him that he had no rights at all, so there. She wondered what might have happened if she had done just that. Leaving England, being in Australia, had blunted the old terror that she'd felt while living in Oak Tree Place and she felt a lazy acceptance that that danger must surely have passed. Must have done. So much time … Tick.

Next on the list was Ruth herself. She was attached to Joe, certainly, but once she knew that he was not in fact her brother, and that she, Alice, was her mother. And, and … and that Charlie was her father … *And* the fact of the money and the wonderful education available because of it. This education seemed to be important to Charlie even though Alice herself did not set much store by it. But if it was an argument for Ruth's return to England, then well and good. All this, however, did require careful handling. Cautious tick.

Also on the list would be living with Charlie without being married. This didn't worry her one bit, but if they had money now (Wheeee!) perhaps the proprieties should be observed. Alright then, Charlie would divorce Lily and she'd divorce Stephen and that would be that. Tick. Her assumed identity had stood up to scrutiny for both her marriage to Stephen and for emigration, so it should be perfectly fine for the divorce. There you are then.

Well, that was really only three things to overcome and they were all now overcome in her mind. She found it difficult not to squeal with delight and jump around at her changed circumstances.

As it was, she bounced gently in the bed, shifted slightly and pressed herself against Charlie's back, reaching around his chest to twine her fingers in his chest hair and graze his nipples. He grunted and turned on his back. Alice quickly threw her leg across his body to sit astride him, rocking and rubbing her body against his, eager and avid.

"Oh God, Charlie, I've missed you so much!"

Charlie groaned with pleasure.

Suddenly she stopped.

"Charleeee?"

"Uh?"

"Would you have come for me if it hadn't been for Ruth?"

"What?"

"If Ruth was not in the picture, if she didn't exist, and I'd come to Australia with Stephen like I did, would you have come to get just me?"

"Yes." Charlie's reply was strangled.

"You're not just saying that, are you Charlie?"

"No!"

Alice resumed her position astride Charlie and wanted to sing with happiness.

Several hours later they were bumping along the rutted track toward Joe's block, a chatty and enormously inquisitive cart driver shouting questions at them over the clatter of the spring cart.

"Are you a new Grouper then?" he asked Charlie.

"No, not me," said Charlie fervently. "I'm visiting."

The driver was impressed. "Groupers don't get many visitors," he said.

"Be gone soon," said Charlie. "I hope," he added sourly as the cart lurched through a particularly deep rut and a cloud of dust enveloped them.

"Where are you from then?"

"England."

"Yeah I know that, mate. I meant where from in the Old Country?"

"London, south of London."

"My Dad and Mum were from a place called Leeds. Dad was, anyway. Mum was from somewhere near there. Is Leeds anywhere near where you're from?"

Charlie looked at Alice and rolled his eyes. "No." he said.

"Dad didn't talk much about where he came from and I never really asked. All water under the bridge now, anyway—I'm never likely to go back there."

Charlie was intrigued in spite of himself. "Why wouldn't you want to go back?"

"Well, I was born here for a start. Dad worked in the timber, falling those big buggers of trees for the mills. That's the only life I know and I reckon I'd be pretty out of place in Leeds, wherever it is. Dad used to say it was a crowded old place, and I can't imagine me and crowds. What is it like to live in a crowded place like England eh?"

"It's not all crowded," chipped in Alice.

The driver cast her a doubtful glance.

"Dad said it was," he said. Mercifully this thought seemed to silence him and they jolted on through the forest.

It was a working day. They passed two parties of men at work on blocks who waved as the cart passed, leaning on their tools in the universal fashion of paused workmen, until the cart was out of sight. Alice could imagine the conjecture—the bush telegraph would have been working overtime since yesterday.

As the cart neared Joe's block, Alice's heart beat faster. There was so much to tell, so much to negotiate, and Joe and Ruth knew nothing yet, unless of course Stephen had made it his business to tell them.

Joe was at the house as they approached, descending from the verandah to return to his afternoon's work. He stopped in his tracks and watched as they came nearer. Alice could feel the cloud of conflict and drama surrounding their arrival as if it was real, and they were groping through it.

"Alice? Charlie? Good to see you, Charlie."

So Stephen had not told him.

"We need to talk to you, Joe."

"Do you indeed?" Joe raised his eyebrows at the portentous tone. "You'd better come inside then."

Once again they were around a kitchen table, just with one different character in the mix. Joe raked the fire and set the kettle to boil. Alice offered to make the tea, but Joe said curtly that he'd do it. The tension in the room was building.

Finally they were all seated at the table

"So?" said Joe. "What's all this solemn stuff then? Is there a particular reason that you've shown up here, Charlie? Not just a visit?"

"Yes, there is. I mean, no, it's not." Charlie quickly corrected himself. "I'm not here just on a visit, and there is a particular reason."

Charlie placed on the table two documents, smoothing them heavily with his hand. He turned them to Joe for him to read.

It took Joe a good five minutes because he read them twice. Alice watched his face the whole time, but it gave nothing away.

But when he finally raised his eyes, there was a bleakness in them that took her breath away.

"Why didn't you tell me, Alice?"

"She didn't tell me either, Joe." Charlie put his big hand on Joe's shoulder, which seemed to sink under its weight. "But it's true."

"How can it be true, how can it be true? It's not. It can't be. Ruth was my mother's baby—she told me herself that she was expecting and, and, and … " he was gathering his thoughts as he spoke "*and* she was with her mother when she had Ruth. Why on earth would she do what you say she did anyway? Why does Edie Craggs know about it? She's making it up," he said finally and with conviction. "It simply cannot be true."

"Listen to me Joe," began Alice.

"This is just a big made-up story so that you can take Ruth away from me, that's what it is, I know it." Joe pushed his chair back from the table and made to stand.

"Joe!" Alice pulled at his hand. "Sit down and listen, just listen."

Angrily Joe settled in his chair again and folded his arms tight against his body. "Go on."

"It is true, Joe, and let me just tell you. I didn't know that Charlie's Mum knew about Ruth, I never knew that, but it must have been that Jessie talked to her, because nobody else could have known.

"Listen, Joe, listen."

And so it all came out, Johnny's secret, Johnny the prisoner, Alice's pregnancy, Jessie's solution and the fact of Ruth. The threat that discovery posed.

"You remember how I told you and Stephen about how Johnny and I came to meet?" Alice glanced quickly at Charlie, but the remark seemed to pass him by.

"Yes," said Joe dully.

"Do you also remember asking me just after you came home about a spare cushion in Jessie's cupboard that had a tape sewn on to the corner? How I said I didn't know what the reason for that tape might have been? Well, I did know, and it used to have four tapes, one on each corner, and that was one of the cushions and pillows that Jessie used over the months to pretend that she was expecting."

Joe leant forward on to the table, massaging his temples furiously.

"I went down to Southampton and spent my expecting time there with Jessie's Mum, then Jessie came down when I was near to being due, and I had Ruth and Jessie took Ruth back to Oak Tree Place and—"

Joe raised his head.

"So you're her mother, and Charlie's her father."

Alice breathed out. "Yes".

"And you never told Charlie?"

"No." Some explanation seemed to be required. "Well, he was married, wasn't he?"

"But Edie knew and that's why Edie has left money to Ruth, because she's her granddaughter."

"Yes."

"How much money?"

"Quite a lot, Joe." Charlie was being quite gentle for Charlie. "Enough for a good education and a comfortable life."

"She'll have to go to boarding school in Bunbury or Perth. That will be hard for her, she won't know anyone."

"Joe," said Alice softly. She stopped and started again. "Joe … "

"Joe," said Charlie.

Joe's head snapped up. "What?" he said sharply.

"Charlie and me are her Mum and Dad," began Alice.

"No!" the word exploded from Joe. "No! No! *No!*" His clenched fist beat on the table so that it jumped. "You can't take her, you can't, you can't, you just can't!"

Alice had been through arguments of this kind with Joe so many times over the years. But this time she had all the cards in her hand. It would be these that would defeat Joe. Might take time, but she would do it. She felt powerful enough to overcome anything today.

"Joe," she said carefully, "listen to me."

"I've done nothing but listen to you since you arrived, you devious bitch."

"That's enough Joe!" Charlie held up his hand.

Alice felt a surge of loving pride.

"Joe," she began again. It was starting to sound like a chorus—his name repeated over and over. "Listen to me, please."

"I'm bloody listening, alright?"

"Charlie has come all this way and spent all that money to get here because he wants to be a father to Ruth, now that he knows about her. And you know that I've always been as much of a mother to her as you allowed me to be. We are going back to England—"

"You're going back with Charlie?" Joe was incredulous.

"Yes."

"Well, that takes the cake, that does. What a first-class cow you are, Alice."

"That's as may be, Joe, but please don't imagine that you know all about my marriage and how it's been for me, thank you. You don't know."

"Oh yes, oh yes, yes I do, Alice. I know that Stephen rescued you from being bashed about by Charlie and you were pleased to be rescued at the time, as I remember. You just used Stephen for your own ends, you nasty piece of work."

Charlie's face was blazing red and he was having difficulty breathing.

Alice tried to soothe the situation.

"Joe, think about it. Yes, I left Charlie, and that was the silliest thing I ever did in my life." She didn't look at Charlie. Joe snorted derisively.

"But at the time all I was thinking about was staying close to Ruth. That was really why I married Stephen and came to Australia—because you were bringing Ruth out here, to this horrible place that I've hated since I arrived, with a man who's so superior and so smothering and so damned *reasonable* all the time … "

"He's worth ten of you."

"Your opinion, Joe, your opinion. You've always hero-worshipped him, for some reason that I can't see. You should live with him and see how you like it."

"You really are a nasty person, Alice. Stephen has looked after you and cared for you and—"

"Perhaps I don't want to be looked after and cared for ...!" Alice suddenly realised that she was digging herself into a hole. She wanted Charlie to look after her, but in Charlie's way. She relished the thought of some spice in her life, some light and shade, some more of the thorough and demanding lovemaking she'd enjoyed last night. She'd had her fill of Stephen's sort of care—wrapped in cotton wool, him always gentle, but always knowing better, always telling her things as if she was one of his school pupils, bowed but uncomplaining of her calculated and deliberate rudeness.

She was allowing her thoughts to wander. At a time like this you need to stay on track, Alice. Concentrate now.

"This is about Ruth," she said firmly, "not me, not Charlie, not you."

"Oh, is it? It seems to me that it's very much about you, Alice, and always has been." Joe was standing now, stiff and angry.

"Joe, Joe, look at it. I have never regretted anything more than agreeing with Jessie's stupid scheme, just to save face—*her* face and not mine, really, when I had a chance to look back on it. It was Jessie who wanted to protect Ned and Johnnie from the truth—the two truths, that is. Ned from the truth about his brother being a ... one of *those* ... and Johnnie the truth about his wife. His wife who was so evil and wicked that she actually needed some love in her life—"

"Love!" snorted Joe.

"Joe, you're as narrow-minded as your mother. You really are a prude, do you know that?"

Joe snorted again.

Irritated, Alice burst out "And what's more you're a two-faced prude, Joe Barlow. Where was your high and mighty properness the night that your wonderful Lydia came to the Place and knocked so hard on your door? Where was your properness when she left two hours later? I'll bet her scanties were in her handbag!"

This crudeness made Joe blink and Alice immediately regretted her outburst. Joe was really such a delicate creature; she needed to reason him into her way of thinking, not shock him rigid. Damn. Start again. Keep on track!

"Joe," she said briskly, "I'm sorry for that remark, but you have to come to understand that Charlie and me, Ruth's *Mum and Dad*, have the right to bring her up and that she will have a better future in England than she ever would here. Particularly here on the Group—where's the future for her in that? Milking cows and looking after you for the rest of her life, her only prospect perhaps marrying another settler and working her fingers to the bone for the rest of her life?"

"I'm going to—*we're* going to—make a good life here, Alice. You just can't see it."

"Joe you know what I'm saying is true." Alice adopted a conciliatory tone. "You're right, and I know you probably will make a good life here in the end, but it will take a good deal longer than anyone thought it would, and you know that, don't you? Ruth could waste the best part of her life waiting for that good life. Charlie and I could make sure she has all the advantages, right now. At least," she added, "when we get back to England."

Charlie spoke. "Do you realise that it's not right to be living alone with Ruth, now that you know she's not your sister?" He sat back in his chair.

"Not right? Not bloody right? What sort of judgement is that, coming from you, Charlie Craggs? You talk about morals? You adulterer. You woman-basher. You wife-pincher. Pinch in both senses of the word," Joe added suddenly and meaningfully.

Alice, though vigilant, was bewildered by this oblique remark but she continued with an assumed calmness that belied her thumping heartbeat.

"If you have Ruth's best interests at heart, you know that it will be best for her to come back to England with us to take advantage of the good fortune that's come her way. You read Mrs. Craggs' letter, she wanted Ruth to come home and have an education and a good life."

Suddenly Alice saw Joe having a moment of indecision. The money made all the difference. Money had never been a factor in their arguments before and while Alice was barely able to grasp the fact that her promised future life with Charlie would now be cushioned by its presence, the thought fizzed at the back of her mind all the same.

"Ruth is out of the run of people here now, Joe", she said in a deliberately reasonable tone. "She has enough money to live a decent life, not scrape a living on a miserable farm like this."

"Shut up, Alice" Joe obviously wanted to defend his beloved farm but was taking care not to be sidetracked. He looked at her again.

"I'm not going to let Ruth go back to England with you and Charlie, Alice. I do have a right to some say in her life after all these years of her being my sister." He began to warm to his argument. "I just don't see you and Charlie as suitable parents, I just don't."

"What do you mean, Joe?" Alice squeaked in protest as Charlie shook his head. "What do you mean? I have been a mother to Ruth as much as I was allowed to be, first by Jessie and then by you. I have looked after her, fed her, read her stories, made her clothes, knitted her woolies and I've been there waiting whenever you needed her minded, you know that. I've never, ever, ever, let her down. Or you, come to that."

Joe remained surly. "The way that you and Charlie carry on together, it's not right. Now that's out in the open I realise that I've been seeing things without understanding them, for years and years. Since I came back from the war. You with bruises, cuts, limping, all that sort of thing. I can't let Ruth live in a house where that sort of thing's going on. No one would."

Both Alice and Charlie bridled. Alice was prepared to be dismissive of the importance of what Joe had just said, but Charlie, making an obvious effort, said "Joe, that's all in the past." It wasn't easy for Charlie to be humble, and Alice had never loved him so much.

"It's all in the past," he repeated. "I was miserable being married to a woman I didn't even like very much and it was always the drink that made me act badly. I never tried to limit myself. I used to tipple all the time, but since before you all left for Australia, I haven't had a single drink, and I intend it to stay that way."

"So you're a changed man?" Joe was sarcastic.

"Yes," said Charlie simply. "That I am. I want to do the right thing."

"And the right thing is abandoning your wife to take up with your fancy woman?"

"And my daughter." Charlie was keeping cool.

"And you expect me to believe that you and Mrs. Floozy here are suddenly going to be upright and proper and do things like go to church on Sundays? If any church would have you," he added ungraciously.

"Joe, I don't expect you to believe me, but it's true. I am a different man from the one you knew and I am going to do everything to make Alice and Ruth happy."

If it had not been for the robustness of their lovemaking the previous night, Alice might have been quite worried. As it was, she was not sure how much of this was the real Charlie and how much was being put on for Joe's benefit. There was going to be a lot to learn here, but taking advantage of the uncertainty that Charlie's revelations had introduced, Alice pressed.

"We'll do anything you like to prove that Ruth will be the best looked-after little girl in the world, Joe" she said, assuming a partnership that grew in her mind by the minute. "What can we do to show you?"

"You can't do anything, you stupid woman. It's not something you can stand up and demonstrate like a talk at the Women's Institute! I just don't believe you, and what's more I am just not letting Ruth go, so there!"

Any slight advantage sensed had been an illusion. Start again Alice.

"Joe, you can't keep Ruth here. She deserves the opportunity that's come her way from Mrs. Craggs. You would be really cruel not to allow her a good education, at least."

Joe did not speak.

"She could have four or five years at a boarding school in England and that would set her up for meeting the right people, getting a nice job in an office if she wants to and meeting and marrying someone much more suitable than anyone she'd find in anywhere in Australia, let alone on the Groups. Think about it from her point of view, Joe. She has no prospects here, and you know it."

Joe breathed deeply. "We are all taking about Ruth," he said, "as if she's a parcel or a puppy. She does have a mind of her own, and I think she should be told what's happening—what's happened. Mind you," he added quickly, "we can't just ask her to decide one way or the other before she's had time to think about it. She's had more than enough sadness and upset in her life recently and she's not to be bullied."

Alice saw the glint in Joe's eye and thought yes, you sneaky rat, you'll talk to her when we're not here, talk all night so that the poor little love won't be able to think for herself at all. You think you've given yourself an advantage, but you're not that smart. I can talk too.

But Joe had not finished.

"Alice," he said slowly, "what about your past? What about the men who came to look for you at Oak Tree Place?"

"What men?" asked Charlie sharply.

"Oh, Alice hasn't told you about that little part of her life then?" asked Joe with elaborate surprise.

"Alice will tell me later on if she wants to," said Charlie quickly, in his role of the changed man.

"No, I think it might be better if she told you right now, in front of me, so that I can see if her story is the same one that she told Stephen and me." Joe was warming to his advantage.

"When was this, then?" Charlie asked.

"A few years ago on Oak Tree Place two men came looking for—who was it again?—Violet Green. Turns out that good old Vi Green is none other than our Alice. Come on Alice, tell Charlie all about it."

"I'll tell him afterwards. It's got nothing to do with what we're talking about here," said Alice desperately.

"Nothing to do with it? Oh come come, Alice. What happens if you do get found, by those men, or some others, or by the police when you go back to England? You know what could happen. It's one of the reasons you were so pleased to come to Australia, wasn't it? It wasn't just Ruth."

By this time Charlie was alert and puzzled.

Alice was furious, her confidence slipping away. She gathered her thoughts again.

"I'm sure that's all over, forgotten and in the past with everyone, Joe. It was a long time ago." She tried to sound brisk and dismissive.

"You know that's not true, Alice." Joe had the upper hand.

Charlie's curiosity was obvious. "No secrets, now," he said with a smile that didn't reach his eyes, "let's hear all about it, can we?"

"It's Alice's story to tell. I'll just listen—again." Joe pretended to settle in his chair.

She had no choice. She was so furious that she had ever revealed it to Joe and Stephen in that single moment of panic and weakness that she almost choked and couldn't begin. Then she couldn't think of how to start. Joe was sitting there like a bloody judge and jury ready to contradict her if she changed one bit of the story he'd listened to all those years ago in Oak Tree Place. Oh Lord, what a stupid, stupid woman she was. What would Charlie think when he knew? Was she going to lose him again? No, it couldn't happen, she wouldn't let it happen.

She sat close to Charlie and wormed her hand under his on the table. It felt so good. Too good to lose.

"Charlie," she began haltingly, "I never told you about this … "

"Another secret as well as Ruth?" Charlie's smile was twisted.

"Different."

Under Joe's rigid stare she began. And it seemed that her careful forgetting had had no effect on her memory because it came out as vividly as if it had happened yesterday. Once she started, everything was there and Joe did not prompt or interject once. Indeed, he seemed to be listening as if for the first time, as spellbound as Charlie.

Alice almost lived it again in the telling. She shrank in on herself at the account of her early life, shuddered at the scene of Arthur's bloody death, shivered in the pile of rubbish and relaxed into Johnnie's care. And finished with their marriage and arrival in Oak Tree Place. The pretense of that marriage.

No one spoke for a long minute after she stopped speaking. Then Charlie cleared his throat.

"That doesn't," he began but his voice cracked and he began again. "That doesn't sound all that bad, Alice. The death of that man was an accident, wasn't it?"

Alice was flooded with relief. Charlie was on her side and he wasn't going to throw her over. Such sweet delight, all the sweeter for the fear that had preceded it. She looked at him with tears in her eyes.

"Oh Charlie, yes, but who would believe me?"

"I would," said Charlie stoutly.

She couldn't help it, she couldn't, the tears just flowed and she threw her arms around Charlie's heavy shoulders.

But Joe wasn't going to let it go that easily.

"That's as may be, Charlie, but you're hardly judge and jury, are you? What if Alice does get found out, that would change everything, wouldn't it? Innocent or not, what would that do to your precious new life, and more importantly, what would it do to Ruth? *If*," he continued, "she did happen to be living with you." He paused for a moment and then said deliberately "And what's more, you could be found guilty, couldn't you?"

Alice collapsed into deep sobs. Charlie banged his fist on the table.

"Enough, Joe, enough! You will not speak like that, do you hear? Alice has got enough on her plate without you sticking your six penn'orth in. Just shut up, you hear?"

Joe said nothing.

The back door creaked open and Ruth stepped into the kitchen with her schoolbag over her shoulder.

70

Later the same day

She was really pleased to see them there with Joe because she badly wanted to know why Mr. Craggs had come all the way to Australia and she wanted someone to explain why he'd said that stuff about being her father.

At first she didn't notice that Auntie Alice had been crying but as she threw down her schoolbag and sat eagerly at the table she did see and she felt a heaviness in her chest. She didn't like it when adults cried, and Auntie Alice had done quite a bit of it recently.

Then she noticed that Auntie Alice was holding hands with Mr. Craggs!

"Do you want something to eat, love?" Joe asked. "There's that cake in the tin that Auntie Ida made for us, why don't you get some out and make another cup of tea for us all?"

Eagerly Ruth jumped down and set the kettle to boil. By the time she'd made the tea and cut some pieces of cake, she was bursting with curiosity and she had noticed that none of the three people sitting at the table had said anything.

There had been a few murmurs and a bit of chair-scraping but nothing very much at all. It felt very much as if there had been some sort of argument or something. That would account for Auntie Alice's tears. Bother.

Although she could very well do it herself, she set the teapot in front of Auntie Alice for her to pour and took her seat at the table again. She couldn't contain her curiosity any longer.

"Why did you come to Australia, Mr. Craggs?" That was a simple enough question to start with.

"I wanted to see you, of course!" said Mr. Craggs jovially.

Ruth frowned. If she was going to be treated like a baby, she would not be told anything important at all.

"I heard you at the beach. I heard you say that you were my Dad—"

"How did you—"

"Where did you—"

"Why did you say that?" she continued. "You *aren't* my father, of course."

"Well, er, er, Alice, your Auntie Alice, that is, she … " Mr. Craggs was going red.

"How old are you now, Ruth?" Auntie Alice asked.

"You know how old I am. I'm eleven-and-a-half."

"I think you're old enough to hear the whole story. Don't you think, Joe?"

"She's not to be upset."

"No one's going to upset her. None of us want to do that, do we?"

"I think some of the detail might be, er, carefully handled," said Joe, looking embarrassed.

"I know that."

"What story?" asked Ruth. She was excited about hearing what must be an important story, but there was a little knot of fear in her stomach too.

"It's about you, and about me and Mr. Craggs too," said Auntie Alice.

Ruth didn't speak. She waited for the start, at the same time thought it an odd combination of people.

"Ruth, about twelve years ago, Joe was away at the war and so was my husband, your Uncle Johnnie who you never got to meet because he died in the prisoner-of-war camp. Well I was very lonely and I made friends with Mr. Craggs and we fell in love."

Ruth frowned. This was not right.

"But you were married to Uncle Johnnie and Mr. Craggs was married to Mrs. Craggs, wasn't he?"

"Yes, sweetheart, but it's still possible for married people who are not very happy in their marriages to fall in love with other people."

"Weren't you happy with Uncle Johnnie?"

"No, not very."

"Oh." The same must apply to Mr. Craggs, it seemed.

"Well, I found that I was having a baby."

Ruth's eyes were round with wonder. She did know how babies were made, improbable as the process seemed, but the thought that Auntie Alice and Mr. Craggs had actually done *that* was not just improbable, it was downright creepy. She collected her thoughts with difficulty.

"Where's the baby?" she asked.

There was a big quiet pause.

A flock of cockatoos wheeled over the house, squawking, then flew away. You could still hear them in the distance.

"You're the baby." Auntie Alice burst out. Her voice wobbled and she pressed her hand to her mouth. Mr. Craggs reached out and took her other hand in his again.

"What?"

"You're the baby. You're my baby." Auntie Alice was crying again.

"No, I'm not. How can that be right? My Mummy and Daddy were Joe's Mummy and Daddy and they had me and I lived with them and no one said anything about you being my mother, or even about you ever having a baby. I don't believe you!" Her heart was beating really hard and she turned to Joe.

"It's not true, is it, Joe? It's not true? It can't be true!"

Joe sat with his elbows on the table and his head in his hands, not looking at her. She began to be afraid.

"Joe? Joe?"

Joe abruptly raised his head and pushed his chair back, standing up.

"Alright, alright, enough for today, enough from everyone," he said roughly.

Auntie Alice and Mr. Craggs looked at each other but decided not to argue with Joe, even though she could tell that Auntie Alice wanted to stay and that she wanted to say some more. But they did leave, left without even saying goodbye, except that Mr. Craggs turned at the bottom of the verandah steps and said to Joe "We'll talk again, Joe. You know we have to." Joe didn't answer.

Ruth watched them disappear down the track before she turned and went into the house and to Joe; she'd been thinking hard in the meantime.

Joe was sitting at the table again and she took the chair that was directly opposite him.

"Joe," she began, and he looked at her with such sad eyes that she was newly afraid.

"Yes, sweetheart."

"Joe. Joe is it true?"

"I think so."

"You only *think* so?" she seized on this uncertainty.

"No, I'm sorry, sweetheart, I am sure it's true. It all makes sense when I think about it. Lots of things … But I've only just heard about it too, like you. It's a bit of a shock to us both, I think."

"A *bit* of a shock!"

Joe smiled a small smile. "Yeah, well, a big bit of a shock, right?"

Ruth started again. "Joe. Whose baby—whose girl—am I then, if Auntie Alice was married to Uncle Johnnie and Mr. Craggs was married to Mrs. Craggs when I was born?"

"You are the little girl of Auntie Alice and Mr. Craggs."

"Why didn't anyone know about me being their baby then?"

Joe sighed. "Sweetheart. My dear little sister … "

"Joe!" she sat bolt upright and her face crumpled. "I'm not your sister!"

Her eyes filled with tears and she hugged her arms to her body. "You're not my brother. You're not my brother." She felt a tearing inside her.

Joe came around the table and gathered her into his arms and they clung to each other. Ruth was crying and she thought Joe was too.

They couldn't cry for ever though, and they finally got up from the table. Ruth blew her nose and cleared away the untouched cups of tea. She put the slices of cake that she and Joe had had on their plates back in the tin but she crumbled up the other two and put the crumbs outside for the birds and the ants to eat.

She felt sort of floaty after crying so hard and her eyes and face were puffy. She went out the back door to pour some water into the dish and splash her face, and that made her feel a bit better. She was brimming with questions again but didn't really want to ask them because somehow she was afraid that the answers were important to something and she didn't know what.

Joe had gone to milk the cows and she went out to help.

She milked sometimes, but mostly Joe did that. She helped with the cleaning and now more often with the separator; she was quite strong enough now to manage it without the bell ringing too many times to tell her to speed up.

The two caramel-coloured cows were secured in the bails and Joe was just finishing with Edie. Her floaty after-crying feeling made her giggly.

"Joe, we'd better not let Mr. Craggs know."

Joe laughed with her as he walked round to milk Lily.

"Well, we never thought we'd have to hide them, did we?"

"No, never thought of Mr. Craggs coming here. He still looks out of place, though, don't you think?"

"He is," said Joe grimly and Ruth felt her stomach lurch again.

She picked up the first bucket and moved towards the little dairy but stopped in surprise.

Miss Anderson was in front of the house, just getting off Mr Padman's horse. She saw Ruth and walked towards her, brushing her skirt as she came.

"Hello Ruth," she said cheerfully. "You didn't think you'd see your teacher again today, did you?"

"No."

"Where's Joe?"

"He's milking Lily."

"Can I talk to him?"

Ruth was instantly gripped with guilty fear. She must have done something seriously bad that Miss Anderson needed to speak to Joe about, but she really couldn't think of anything. Perhaps her arithmetic homework… No, that was not a speak-to-Joe crime.

Miss Anderson was making her way towards the shed where the fat sound of milk jetting into the bucket indicated that it was almost full.

Ruth paused, uncertain whether to continue to the dairy or learn what was going on. As she scanned her memory for dreadful deeds and found none, she grew more confident that Miss Anderson's visit was not to discuss her behavior, so she hurried to the dairy and deposited the bucket, then returned to the milking shed.

"Ruth," said Miss Anderson. "I really want to speak to Joe in private, if you don't mind." Miss Anderson was a school teacher and was used to telling her what to do, but Joe looked a bit confused.

"We really need to do the dairy," he said.

"Alright, then I'll help you," said Miss Anderson and she turned up her sleeves and did.

Ruth was rather impressed and she could see that Joe was too. Miss Anderson knew exactly what to do. She turned the handle on the separator evenly and scrubbed the pails and the other equipment vigorously and set them along the dairy wall to dry. Then with a very efficient turning-down of her sleeves and buttoning the cuffs once more, turned to Joe who was just finishing washing down the floor.

"Now we can have that chat, I think?"

"Ruth," said Joe, "it looks as if you're the chicken and horse-feeder today."

At the top of the cliff at the beach Ruth had managed to squirm back to listen to a conversation that was supposed to be a private one too. But as Joe and Miss Anderson settled on the front verandah steps to talk, she knew there was no way she could eavesdrop on this one. Bother, she wanted badly to know what it was all about.

Joe was very quiet after Miss Anderson left. Ruth had heard a snatch of laughter from them at the beginning of their conversation, but then either they'd become serious or she couldn't hear them, one or the other.

Miss Anderson was still polite and cheerful when she left, but Joe was quiet in his goodbyes and stayed so.

Quite certain now that Miss Anderson's visit was not because of anything she'd done, she waited only a little while before she asked Joe why she had come.

"She wanted to talk about you, really," he said.

Ruth's confidence plummeted.

"Nothing bad, nothing bad, don't worry. You haven't done anything wrong chicken," Joe said with a smile.

"Then what … "

"Miss Anderson is interested in your future. She says that you have promise."

"I've promised?"

"No, love, you *have promise*. That means you are bright and intelligent and beautiful and you could do just about anything you wanted to."

"And Miss Anderson came all the way out here to tell you that?"

"Well, not exactly, sweetheart. It's a bit more complicated."

"Why?"

"Miss Anderson heard—and I don't know how, but it's hard to keep secrets round here—about Mr. Craggs coming here and … what he and Auntie Alice want to do."

"What do they want to do?"

Joe didn't answer the question straight away, just looked very sad.

"Because they're your Mum and Dad," he began, and bit his lip.

"And you think they really are?"

"Yes, love, I do."

"And because they're my Mum and Dad – Joe, I've *got a Mum and Dad again!*" The reality of that had just hit Ruth and she burst out with it.

"Yes," said Joe sadly, "but no brother."

"Oh Joe, you'll always be my brother inside. You know that."

But she was suddenly really excited to think she was just a normal girl with a Mum and Dad. Joe spoke.

"My Mum and Dad—and they were yours too, really, they loved you very much and brought you up and cared for you, you know what, don't you?"

"Yes."

"Well, they were good people and they must have thought they were doing the right thing when they pretended to be your parents, and I don't want anyone telling you otherwise, you hear?"

"I wouldn't listen, Joe." Ruth could feel herself splitting into many parts—a part that was a little girl to her newly-found parents, one that had to remember good pretend-parents but who in truth she found hard to recall, and yet another part had to stay loyal to Joe, who'd always been so kind and loving and such a wonderful big brother. She did think fleetingly that she should keep another part to be just Ruth.

"But that's not what Miss Anderson came to talk about."

"Oh." Ruth came back to the present and to her previous curiosity.

"She heard—and I don't know where or how, but she heard, like I said before, what Auntie Alice and Mr. Craggs want to do."

"And what's that?"

"I want you to listen very carefully to what I'm going to tell you and I want you to think about it before you say anything— anything at all."

Heavens, what could be coming?

"Auntie Alice and Mr. Craggs are going back to England to live together and probably get married or something. They want," Joe inhaled deeply, "they want to take you back with them and for you to live with them. They want to send you to boarding school to get a good education like Mrs. Craggs planned when she left a lot of money to you in her will." The last sentences were delivered quickly as if Joe had to get them out before he lost his courage.

From all of that, one thing struck.

"Boarding school? Like in 'Marie McLeod Schoolgirl'?" Ruth's favourite book of the moment, sent for her last birthday by Mrs. Craggs.

"I suppose so. A bit, anyway."

Ruth's mind had already run to chums and dorms and midnight feasts and hockey and crumpets; she dragged herself back with difficulty. The world of boarding school was full of unimaginable glamour and daring adventures, and previously as remote as the moon. But these thoughts dissolved as something else Joe had said pushed into her consciousness.

"Mrs. Craggs left me some money in her will?"

"Yes."

"How much?"

"I don't know. Charlie said quite a bit. Enough for your education and some left over."

"I wonder how much?"

"It's in trust, sweetheart. That means that the money is looked after by someone legal until you're old enough to have it all."

"Who looks after it and do they pay for boarding school and when am I old enough?"

Before Joe could answer, she added "And can I have some now?"

Joe looked at her gravely. "That's a lot of questions, my girl."

"I don't mean to sound greedy, Joe. I just want to know all these things. If I could have some money now we could pay to have the bottom paddocks cleared and fenced, down to the creek. And get some more cows."

Joe's face relaxed into a smile.

"Sweetheart, you don't have to worry about those things."

"But you do, all the time. So if I could get some of the money, that would help, wouldn't it?"

"What do you think then, about going back to England?"

Ruth tried to compose her thoughts, but they were racing. Already the glamour of boarding school was fading a little at the reality of what else was involved. What did she think? She didn't know, and that was the truth.

"Joey", she said, "I think I would like to go to boarding school, but I don't want to go back to England very much and I can't get my mind to understand that Auntie Alice and Mr. Craggs are my Mum and Dad. It just doesn't seem right somehow."

"Poor little one", said Joe. It's such a lot to take in, isn't it? You just think about it in your own good time and don't worry, there'll be no decisions made about anything until you are quite sure you want them made. We'll talk about it again tomorrow— you'll probably have lots of questions. Alright?"

"Yes", said Ruth thankfully.

She got ready for bed and climbed in, turning on her side and staring out of the window where the outlines of the trees could still be seen. There was one little patch, a rough triangle in shape, where you could see through the tree branches to the sky in the distance. Once the full moon had risen right there, and for a wondrous time beamed its full gentle light through this one small opening. Ruth always checked to see if it was happening again, but it never had. Not so far, anyway.

She thought that if she went away she'd miss the next time. By the time she came back the triangle hole might be grown over by the trees, too, and she'd absolutely never see the moon shine through ever again. Was this what was making her feel so sad? She wasn't usually sad except perhaps when she thought about Robin, but she thought that she shouldn't feel sad because everything that had happened was good—she now had a Mum and Dad, she apparently had money too (a circumstance never even contemplated before, so it took particular pondering) and there was the prospect of going to boarding school.

But that meant leaving Joe and their house and their farm and going back to England. She could remember England, of course, at least her little corner of it in Oak Tree Place, but the memories were fading and they did seem a bit unreal.

And leaving here would mean leaving the flies and the ants.

But it would also mean leaving Miss Anderson and her friends at school.

But she'd already left school friends in England when she came to Australia, so she knew she could do that, and anyway she could still write to them and Miss Anderson could read her letters out to everyone at school so they'd know what she was doing.

And it would be tremendously exciting, all of it.

But she was still not sure about Auntie Alice and Mr. Craggs being her Mum and Dad. That was the strangest thing and she giggled at the thought of calling Mr. Craggs "Dad". No, that was just not possible.

But she'd have to, wouldn't she? If he was her Dad, she couldn't call him Mr. Craggs for the rest of her life.

She dissolved into giggles and bit the blanket to stop Joe hearing.

She wondered if she counted up the "ands" and the "buts" and saw which side won, maybe that would make her deciding easier. She resolved to do this the next day and fell asleep.

71

The next day

Next morning Ruth was rather quiet as she readied herself for school and Joe put it down to all she had to take in. Rather a lot for an adult, let alone an eleven-year old. Eleven-and-a-half.

He stood on the verandah and watched her disappear down the bush track on her way, watching her out of view before setting out along the same track for Stephen's house next door. He was still amused at the thought of the difference between "next door" here and back in England. Borrowing a bit of sugar was not the casual affair it had been once.

He was unsurprised to find Stephen sitting in a deck chair on the verandah, moodily contemplating the surrounding forest and his few cleared acres where three mismatched cows, one creamy brown and two in different patterns of black and white, grazed with determination.

Despite Stephen's lethargy, Joe noted that the cows had obviously been milked and he was relieved that he apparently didn't have to cope with a total wreck. Stephen flicked a glance in his direction, then away.

"Morning!" said Joe heartily and flopped into the other deck-chair, making it squeak protestingly on the verandah boards.

"I don't particularly want to talk about this mess".

"No trouble there", said Joe. "I'd like nothing more than a nice quiet ordinary day myself." He stretched his legs out straight.

"But", he said, "it's all still going on and until those two get their own way I rather think it will stay on the boil."

"I *rather thought* that they'd got their own way already. You will notice that my wife is no longer here."

The adjacent deck chairs made it all but impossible for the two men to see each other. Clamped into their bulging canvas depths, the conversation had a peculiar remoteness for which Joe was quite grateful. He spoke to the distant tree tops.

"You're not going to thank me for saying this, my friend … "

"Then don't bloody well say it!"

"You and Alice were never rightly suited, and you know it."

The other chair remained silent.

"I think," said Joe with difficulty, "that you wanted to help her. I think you are the sort of person who likes helping people. Look, you were an ambulance driver in the war. And" this was something of a presumption and had only just occurred to him "your first wife, the one you told me about … "

"Louisa."

"Yes, Louisa. You told me how lovely she was, but how she'd been an orphan and—"

"Alright, alright, alright! So I'm kind to strays. That doesn't mean I set out to find deserving causes. I do have feelings for the women I marry."

Joe smiled. "You sound like Bluebeard. 'The women I marry', indeed!"

There was a soft snort of laughter from the other chair. This was better.

"Look," he said, "let's have a cup of tea, eh?"

They extricated themselves from the deck chairs and went into the house.

"Thank you," Stephen said, trying to be casual, "for coming over."

"Oh, you think I came for your sake?" Joe tried for humourous bluster. "Well, you think that and you've another think coming, I can tell you. You haven't heard the latest yet."

Sitting at the table in the kitchen, he told Stephen what had transpired the day before.

"You can't let them take Ruth away." Stephen was calm and adamant. "You cannot let her go with them."

Joe felt a rush of relief.

"I don't *want* her to go … "

"Then don't let her go."

"I want to do the right thing for her, though. Helen was there yesterday, telling me what a bright future Ruth could have with the right education opportunities … "

"Miss Helen Anderson thinks she knows what's best for everyone. She is indeed very sure of herself." Stephen's tone was, however, indulgent. "The point is, Joe, that Alice and Charlie, while they might well be Ruth's parents, should not have sole charge of that girl. I don't trust either of them to be consistent enough in their lives to be bringing up an impressionable little girl who's already coped with more upsets in her life than most people ever have to do."

"I know that. I do know that. I don't feel easy about it either. The fact is though that Ruth herself does not seem to be against the idea."

Stephen snorted. "What Ruth thinks is probably a kaleidoscope of feelings, mostly excitement, if I know Ruth, at the adventure of it all. She will not have thought it right through to the end—the bitter end, I might guess."

"I want her to make the decision."

"An eleven-year-old girl is not a fit person to make a decision that could so radically change her life and you know that, Joe."

His spirits began to lift. Until Stephen's practical voice pierced the jigsaw of his thinking he had been unaware of how wound-up he had been. Stephen continued.

"Remember, Joe, the way Charlie and Alice carried on in Oak Tree Place—carried on under the nose of Charlie's wife and mother? The way Charlie treated Alice—remember those bruises? Do you think Ruth would really benefit from living in that sort of household? People like Charlie don't change, you know."

"He says he has … "

"Rubbish."

Joe capitulated. He didn't want to speak up for Charlie, did he? All his old antipathy to the man came flooding back into his mind with the memories that had caused it and he wondered that he had so quietly sat at the table with him yesterday. Of course Stephen was right. Of course he was. He could not let Ruth leave Australia and go back with Charlie and Alice, no matter what the other advantages might be.

But they were her parents.

"Could they force me to give her up, do you think?"

"Don't really see how, unless they resort to legal means, and that's a pretty pickle if ever there was one. Look at it: an illegal birth registration that can't be proved really because the other colluding parties are … no longer with us. And even if it were provable, there's the other stuff that Alice is very keen to avoid a probe into. Her convenient name change would be a start for investigations in that area, I'd imagine. She definitely doesn't want to stir that pot."

"Yes, of course."

"So I think you're safe there—they won't want to rake things up."

"So I just stand my ground."

"Yes … " said Stephen slowly.

"What is it?"

"Just watch them, matey. Remember what Alice has done to stay close to Ruth all her life. No mother could have been more determined to be with her child. I can't see her going quietly, not without Ruth."

"What can I do?" Joe looked earnestly at Stephen, willing an answer. Stephen would know what to do, if anyone did.

"Buggared if I know, mate!" Stephen aped the accent and vocabulary of their Aussie neighbours.

Joe ignored the attempted joke. "I must be able to do something."

There was a silence, broken by the cruel cawing of crows in the distance. Joe thought there could not be a more desolate sound.

"You could … " Stephen started. "You could convince Ruth that she doesn't want to go. Show her that it's not the adventure she fancies—pull out all the organ stops and speak to her like an adult. Paint the picture."

Joe considered. "That's what Alice is afraid I'm going to do while I have her alone, but hell, it's the right track, isn't it? They can't take Ruth if she won't go, can they?"

"Can you convince her? Can you, Joe? You'd have to be truthful or they can argue against you and a confused Ruth will not be a convinced Ruth. Mind you, being truthful and painting a black picture are one and the same thing when it comes to those two."

"Would you talk to her too?"

"With pleasure." Stephen's eyes gleamed and Joe saw wryly that he would very much enjoy the role of discrediting his wife and her lover. Well so be it—if it was to his advantage.

"What do you say to breaking the ground for me, eh? Watch for her coming past on her way home from school today and have a word then. Sort of prepare her."

"Good-oh. I might well enjoy this."

You will, thought Joe. Good-oh indeed.

By the time Ruth eventually came home that day, Joe was more than ready to make his case. He had returned to his house to find Alice and Charlie sitting disconsolately in the kitchen, Alice having made a pot of tea which they were sharing; Alice looked very peeved. Charlie, still is his very inappropriate clothes, looked hot, dusty and fed-up.

"Where's Ruth?" demanded Alice.

"At school, of course," said Joe just as rudely as he poured himself his third cup of tea for the morning.

"You should have kept her home today, Joe. You know we need to talk to her."

"What you need and what you get is not necessarily the same thing, Mrs. Dent. You should know that."

Alice raised an eyebrow, trying for an irony she couldn't quite pull off.

"Have you been talking to her?" She was frowning now. "Turning her against us?"

Not yet, thought Joe, but give me time!

He said, rather pompously, that of course he had been doing no such thing, and pulled out a chair to sit down.

"I don't want *you* pushing her into a decision either," he said. "It's just as well she's not here because she really hasn't brought herself to understand everything, let alone decide to up roots and go back to England with you."

"Roots!" exploded Alice. "What roots does she have here in this dreadful country? None at all. She should be back—we all should be back—in civilisation where we belong."

"Oh, you were so civilised, weren't you? So civilised that you're wanted for murder!"

His anger and desperate wish to wound had brought it up again. Alice's face blanched to the colour of milk and she breathed a gasp of pain and anger.

"Stop it, Joe!" Charlie roared.

"Why should I stop saying what's the truth? You two are just thinking about yourselves, but stop a minute and look at things logically. You have to take into consideration the fact that Alice has been hiding in Oak Tree Place from the first minute she arrived there. She was nearly found by a couple of characters who came looking for her, and goodness knows the police are probably still looking too. It must only be a matter of time before she's found—and what happens then, eh? What happens to your daughter that you say you care about?" Joe was warming to his subject as the picture he painted became vivid. "So she's at some posh boarding school or other, and her mother gets arrested for murder—or gets beaten up at best by some thugs looking for revenge." Joe paused, then resumed. "And so we have a little girl who'll be expelled of course because your posh boarding schools can't have murderers' children mixing with their toffy students, can they?"

Charlie was puce with rage, clenching and unclenching his fists, but Joe felt invulnerable as he warmed to his argument. His imagination was fired.

"And then, and then, you've got Alice in jail, *or worse*, and Charlie, there you are with a little girl whose life has been completely shattered *again,* what do you do with her, eh? You're the husband—if you get that far—of a convicted murderer ... "

Alice screamed and put her hands over her ears. The sound, despite the fact that Joe's voice had been raised, was shrill and piercing. Joe stopped and Charlie stared.

"Stop it, stop it, stop it!" Alice rocked in her chair.

Charlie stumbled round the table and tried to comfort her, patting her shoulders with his big hands. He looked troubled rather than sympathetic, Joe noted.

"Alright, alright, I'll stop trying to show you the obvious, but I think you should have thought of it yourselves. Your lack of foresight is quite telling. Your thoughts are really only for yourselves, you forget that other people are involved, don't you? As long as you get what *you* two want "

Charlie sat down again and tried to make a case.

"Joe, that's not true. Look at it from my point of view. I know I've been all sorts of villain here, unfaithful to my wife, not at all kind to her or to Alice either if it comes to that, but once Alice left Oak Tree Place—once she said she was going to marry Dent actually—I saw what I really wanted, and it ... it tore my heart out to see her married, and then leave."

Joe had never heard Charlie speak in such terms or reveal so much. Alice was quiet now, and her eyes were on Charlie.

"Then when Mother died and I learned about Ruth, it was too much. I couldn't bear living there in Oak Tree Place with a wife who cares as little for me as I do for her, not for the rest of my life. I just couldn't. The thought of Alice over here with a daughter I had never known about but who I *knew* all the same—it was torture." He looked directly at Alice. "You should have told me, girl, you really should have told me. We could have worked something out."

Alice looked down at the table. "I'm so sorry, Charlie."

"Water under the bridge," said Joe briskly. He didn't want to get enmeshed in a maudlin Charlie-Alice exchange. "What is it exactly that you want to do—or plan to do?"

He saw the indecisions chasing themselves across Charlie's face. He'd got through then, with the grim picture he'd painted. Good.

Alice sat looking at Charlie, but her face also showed fear. Whether the fear was for the possibilities involved in a return to England, or for Charlie re-thinking his impetuous journey across the world, Joe could not tell. But one way or another, he'd put the cat among the pigeons. He waited.

Suddenly Charlie cocked his head as if an idea had come to him. He blinked a few times and something that could have been a very slight smile twitched momentarily at the corners of his mouth.

"What is it?" Alice asked.

"Nothing, nothing, just an idea. Look Joe," he said purposefully, "you talk to Ruth tonight, and then how about we come and collect her tomorrow and have the day with her in town, so we can talk to her too. Let her make the decision when she's heard both sides."

Joe was uneasy. Charlie had something up his sleeve. "No matter what Ruth might *think* she wants, I won't let her go, you know, not as things stand at present. It's too much to ask, to send her off into a future like the one I can see and where I can't do anything about it."

Surprisingly, this response seemed to please Charlie.

"Yes, yes, alright Joe, no need to go into that again. We'll come and get Ruth tomorrow. What time?"

"About nine," said Joe uncertainly. "And have her back by three," he said to assert himself again.

"Fine Joe, fine. Time for us to go now, Alice."

Alice was as confused as Joe by Charlie's sudden assurance, but she scrambled to her feet and followed him out the door.

"Did you walk here?" Joe asked.

"Heavens, no," said Alice with elaborately false brightness "we took a taxi." Her returned sarcasm curled her lip and Joe felt disinclined to ask further, or to offer any help. They probably cadged a lift to the main track turn-off and as for getting back, well, they could bloody well walk for all he cared. He hoped they both got blisters.

Joe waited anxiously for Ruth to come home from school, telling himself that the later she was the better—Stephen would be putting his careful arguments to her, helping to convince her that she didn't really want to go back to England. He'd be making a better case than Joe could ever manage.

Actually she was hardly late at all, and as she trudged up the track she was accompanied by Stephen; they were talking animatedly.

Joe was leaning against the verandah-post watching them as they approached, smiling fondly in spite of himself at the sight of Ruth looking so lively. He did wonder why.

Ruth waved excitedly at Joe as they got closer. "Ho, Joe!" she laughed.

Joe felt a surge of affection so strong that he wanted to reach out and hug her. But hugs and kisses were for goodbye and bedtime, and he felt slightly foolish as his arms, which had instinctively reached out with his thought, dropped to his side.

The afternoon was sunny but cold and they went into the warmth of the house. Ruth was dancing with impatience; she obviously had something to say. Stephen watched her with much the same fondness as Joe and waited for her to speak.

"Joe," she said importantly, "I have been thinking about everything and Uncle Stephen and I had a discussion."

Joe reflected her gravity. "Yes?"

"We've got an idea. Well, it was really Uncle Stephen's idea, but I think it's a very good one."

"Yes?"

"What if, *what if* Auntie Alice and Mr. Craggs don't go back to England? What if we ask them to think about living in Perth?

I could go to boarding school there and still come back here for holidays and it would be the best thing for absolutely *everybody*. Wouldn't it Joe, wouldn't it?"

Stephen was smiling and they were both looking at Joe. His mind whirled but his spirits lifted giddily.

"Do you think they would?"

"It's certainly worth a try, Joe," said Stephen. "I thought about it and it seems to me that Charlie would only be going back to a bucket of trouble and scandal if he does go ahead with divorcing his wife and he might well appreciate being out of the country! And Alice is only courting disaster if she goes back and she knows it. I know she says she hates this place, but I reckon she'd feel differently about living somewhere like Perth, especially with some money behind her as seems to be the case now."

"And I could go to boarding school and come back here for holidays!" Ruth repeated. Joe's smile spread.

"We'll talk to Alice and Charlie tomorrow when they come for you, pet. You're to spend the day with them and you will have the chance to convince them, what do you say?"

"Easy!" Ruth stood laughing with her hands on her hips in an attitude that was so like Alice that Joe wondered why he had never seen it before. He was damned if he could see Charlie though, not for the life of him.

◆

He could see it even less when Charlie and Alice presented next morning, this time on a cart with a driver that Joe didn't recognise but who exhibited a lot of curiosity about what was going on. Charlie looked huffy and irritated and waved the driver away in outraged fashion when he attempted to come into the house with them. Joe took him a cup of tea on the verandah and rolled his eyes in sympathy.

Inside Charlie was being soothed by Alice. Apparently Jim the driver had not stopped talking all the way from the township, giving his opinion on everything, up to and including England, which he'd never seen but knew everything about—more than Charlie, whom he thought to be ill-informed. After a few moments and a cup of tea in place Charlie settled down and was even able to smile ruefully. "And we've got to go back with the damned fellow!" he said, shaking his head.

Alice bustled in a proprietary way around the kitchen and Joe resented her familiarity. Again they were seated round Joe's table, but this time there was an air of excitement rather than hostility. Joe wondered if they'd spoken to Stephen and knew of his idea, but no, they wouldn't have done. He decided to wait to see what they were about.

"Joe, Ruth," began Charlie. "Ruth, Joe. I have had some thoughts about the situation we are all in and after discussing it with Alice last night, we would like your opinion on the idea of us—both of us that is—well—I mean—living in Perth with Ruth instead of us all returning to England."

There was a stunned pause and then Ruth banged the table with delight and nearly fell off her chair laughing. Joe laughed too, in spite of himself. Charlie and Alice looked dazed at their reaction.

"That's our idea too!" Ruth spluttered. "That was OUR idea!"

"What do you mean?"

"Uncle Stephen and I talked yesterday and we thought up that idea, too!"

Alice's eyes narrowed; she was obviously evaluating the idea in the light of Stephen's approval—Stephen's approval made it suspect. But Charlie was so pleased to find favourable reception of his plan so easily gained that the mention of Stephen hardly penetrated. He beamed.

"So what do you think?"

"Well, it's better than you all going back to England, anyway. Better all round, I'd say," said Joe.

"You want to marry Auntie Alice?" Ruth frowned in Charlie's direction.

Charlie flushed, but managed a brave "Yes."

"Are you going to divorce Mrs. Craggs then?" asked Ruth.

Charlie looked uncomfortable. "Er, yes, yes," he said.

"What about the Oak Tree?"

The sight of Charlie being quizzed relentlessly by an 11-year-old girl was quite captivating to Joe. He stood back and watched.

"What about the Oak Tree?" Charlie asked back.

"Will you sell it?"

"Umm, no, it's not … "

"If you do sell it, where will poor divorced Mrs. Craggs go?" Ruth was peering into Charlie's face. He recovered his ascendancy with difficulty and didn't reveal that Lily had been left the pub so it was hers to do with as she wished.

"Don't you worry about that, Ruth my girl, we grown-ups will deal with all that sort of thing," he said.

Joe watched Ruth bridle at the condescension and reflected that Charlie's fathering skills would need to be sharpened up and that Ruth was just the girl to do it.

"We would have to make sure that nothing bad happened to Mrs. Craggs because of us," she said.

Joe saw Charlie melt, charmed by his daughter. The shape of things to come, he thought, the shape of things to come.

Things had worked out well, but all Joe felt was a huge hollowness.

72

A few weeks later.
July 1927

The farewell party was in full swing and Joe and Ruth's house was bulging at the seams.

The weather was not kind to the festivities; a cold wind gusted rain against the windows and a few of the unplugged gaps in the walls let slices of cold slip inside.

All the Oak Tree Place people were there, of course, plus Miss Anderson and some of Ruth's school friends and their parents. Despite the weather, the feeling was warm and the mood congratulatory. For hadn't nice little Ruth Barlow suddenly become an heiress and not only that, but found a mother and father? It had after all been the talk of the Group, dissected and examined minutely and where facts were missing a spontaneous creativity supplied them. There were as many versions of the situation as there were families on the Group.

Buoyed by the occasion, Joe was busily refilling glasses with Len's home brew and Ida was dispensing cups of tea. A babble of voices overflowed the house and out on to the verandah where Stephen and Helen Anderson, together with Ellen and Michael, braved the cold and dodged the rain. Joe approached them, beer bottle held high.

"Another?" he asked.

"What are you going to do without her, Joe?" Michael asked with a smile.

"He'll be alright. He's got me next door!" said Stephen.

"Two bachelor boys, now there's a thing," said Michael knowingly. Ellen kicked him and he looked surprised. There was a small silence.

"For goodness' sake don't go pussyfooting around me just because my wife's left me." Stephen was determined to ride out the situation with bravado. He had spent most of his time on the verandah away from the main party and the warmth of the house, and indeed he was shivering now.

"Come on inside, get a bit of warm. It's a bit crowded but that raises the temperature!"

At that moment Charlie came out of the front door. Ignoring the others, he spoke to Joe.

"We'd better be going I think Joe. Time to go."

There were all three—the family—to leave Margaret River by train the next day and Ruth would spend the night with them in town. Charlie had borrowed, or hired, or somehow got hold of, a spring cart to transport them to and from Joe's house, and he heaved Ruth's suitcase on board. Her suitcase with her life inside, Joe thought. Ruth came running out on to the verandah.

"Oh Joe, I am really going! I don't know whether I'm sad or happy!" It did seem to be the former, as she had tears in her eyes as she hugged Joe tightly. She was breathing fast and shallow and hiccupped as she released him.

"Now then, Miss Ruth," boomed Michael, "None of that now, none of that. Come here and give us all a hug too. It's not as if you're leaving forever, is it now?"

Ruth laughed and ran towards Michael, who leaned down to hug her tightly, and then stood with his hands on her shoulders as he offered more words of wisdom.

Joe saw them both in profile and it suddenly occurred to him how like Michael Ruth was. The same dark curly hair, the same complexion, the same eyes, the same nose—they were mirror images. As they both laughed, they threw back their heads in exactly the same manner.

Something like a lightning bolt passed through Joe's body, head to toe. He could not take his eyes off the two of them. The more he looked the more obvious it became and Joe stumbled against the wall for support as he stared. How could he have been so blind for all this time?

Shaking himself, his eyes sought Alice. He saw that she, too, was looking at Michael and Ruth, her expression unreadable. Then a tiny sly smile chased across her face as she turned away and put her hand on Charlie's arm to speak to him.

Ruth had danced off to say her farewells to others, and Michael and Ellen stood side by side on the verandah rail. Michael's eyes followed Ruth for a moment before he resumed his conversation with Stephen. A gust of laughter. Joe felt a desperate need to get away from the noise and the people—he couldn't for the life of him process this new information and think about how it did or didn't affect everything that was going on.

But it was all rolling up like a coil of rope anyway. Ruth gave him one last breathless hug and climbed up on to the cart. Before Joe could really comprehend that it was happening, the cart was creaking off into the distance and Ruth was gone.

"Don't worry, old man, she'll be back for holidays before you know it."

"She'll do you proud one day, that girl."

"She's a very lucky little girl, Joe. I'm sure you're happy for her."

"She's a credit to you, Joe, you know that, don't you?"

The comments, the clumsy attempts at commiseration that determinedly denied the maudlin, all went over his head. Ruth was gone, gone to a future full of promise that he could never offer her. If he upset the particular apple-cart that Alice had constructed, he also upset that future.

Cows, even the scrawny specimens on the Group, need milking morning and evening, and one by one the guests left, Stephen being the last to go. He patted Joe on the back in wordless empathy as he left.

Joe had wondered how he would feel at this very moment, alone in the house for the first time, a solitary meal to eat and no conversation to spice it. But he had not anticipated the whirlpool in his head that the afternoon had created. He had thought he'd be sad, perhaps feel lonely, perhaps regret letting Ruth go. But there was no room for self-indulgence as he seethed with confusion and anger. Sort it out, Joe, sort it out.

Michael is Ruth's father, not Charlie.

Alice knows this. Of course.

Charlie doesn't.

Charlie's mother didn't, obviously.

Does Michael know? Perhaps? Did it look as if he did?

What would happen if Joe spilled it all? Charlie would reject Ruth, certainly, and probably Alice as well—there was surely a limit to Charlie's affections and he wouldn't take too kindly to being duped, knowing him.

Head buzzing, Joe went back over the events that ensued after Charlie's surprise arrival and Charlie's puzzlement—and his own—as to why Alice had never told Charlie of her pregnancy and his fatherhood. Now he knew why. Nothing to bloody well tell you Charlie Craggs, nothing at all.

Edie Craggs must have assumed, like Jessie, the apparently-obvious when she learned about Alice and Jessie's elaborate deception. Jessie would of course have confided in her as they were as thick as thieves and shared the same sense of superiority. For all these years Edie would have held the thought that Ruth was her granddaughter—the pearls that she gave her when she left Oak Tree Place were now explained, as well as her indulgence of Ruth when no other child came close to enjoying such benevolence. But Edie Craggs disliked Alice, that was obvious. Not surprising, they were like chalk and cheese. Edie had looked down on Alice and denigrated her for as long as Joe could remember.

But why did she not say something? Perhaps it was to protect Lily and the pub and the marriage of the two of them that she had, it was said, engineered. It would rather mess things up if she'd interfered with the tortuous cobweb of lies and deceits that had been set up and goodness knows what would have happened if she'd tried! Joe's mind whirled.

So Edie thought that Alice had led her boy astray. Well, that bit was right, but apparently she'd been leading Michael astray at the same time. Or before. Even if he'd been there, Joe doubted that he would have seen, suspected or even remotely wondered about his aunt's affairs, so to wonder about them in retrospect and all at once was rather overwhelming. And more than that, of course. It was Ruth's future that he had to think about as well. On the one hand it would give him a great deal of personal satisfaction to reveal what he now knew and just watch what happened, but Ruth, Ruth, Ruth.

So … what do? Speak to Stephen and seek his advice? Mmmm, Stephen might be just a little bit too inclined to want to bring Alice down. Perhaps he wouldn't, but still he needed someone more visibly impartial. Len? Ida? He couldn't imagine asking advice from anyone else on the Group, recoiling from revealing what seemed like family secrets to anyone outside the family.

But perhaps Helen Anderson? Intelligent, no reason not to be impartial and she would have Ruth's interests at heart, just like him. Yes, that was it. On the other hand, perhaps he'd think about it.

And tonight he would sleep, if he could, alone in the little Group house on his 160 acre farm with two cows, one horse and five chickens.

73

Two months later.
September 1927

Joe was early at the Margaret River station, looking shiny, clean and nervous. The train was only a little late, but there'd been time for a couple of dozen walks up and down the little station platform before it puffed into view around the curve, looking like a toy as it emerged from the tall trees.

Suddenly and unaccountably shy, Joe hung back as the carriage doors opened and several travellers emerged, dragging bags and parcels. Then she was in front of him, laughing and jumping with joy. His first thought was that she was most unsuitably dressed—overdressed—for her visit. Horrified at himself for such a banal thought, he reached forward and hugged her. Ruth laughed, gave him a brief breathless squeeze and stepped back.

"Bags" she said gaily, leading the way and leaving an awkward Joe to follow and collect them from the railway carriage. The reality of her presence was so sweet—he couldn't take his eyes off her.

The bumpy journey back to the Group did restore some of the old familiarity and ease, but it was still a little bit awkward as they reached the house. Joe was on eggshells and couldn't say why. Yes he could. Although it was a matter of weeks since Ruth had left, she had changed so much. She was not his little sister any more. In maturity as well as fact. He was stunned at how much difference could be wrought in so little time.

He carried her shiny new suitcase into her old bedroom and went to attend to the horse and the cart. When he came back into the house, Ruth had changed from her travelling finery and at least looked a little more like the girl he knew—had known. She'd also put the kettle on.

She leant against the table and folded her arms. (Oh, a picture of her mother!). "So tell me all about the Group, Joe. How are things going with Mr. Bannister?"

"Oh, he's gone," said Joe eagerly, happy to expand on a familiar subject. "We don't know why they moved him, but we're glad they did and the new man is much better although not as knowledgeable as Mr. Harris was. But we need less help these days as we've more or less learned the ropes. We know what we've got to do." He knew he was babbling.

"How much more have you cleared here?"

"Another five acres."

"Well done, Joe, that's good progress."

Joe thought Ruth's interest forced. Once upon a time every newly cleared acre was cause for celebration, and delight that that was another of the 160 of the damned things ticked off. But he ploughed on with the conversation.

"Five cows now. One of them is pretty useless; I think she's past her prime but she might come good. I haven't named the three new ones—I thought you might like to do it." He added the last bit with assumed diffidence, in denial of the fact that he had anticipated this naming as one of the large events that would occupy the week-long visit. Naming had been a responsibility that Ruth took very seriously and guarded jealously.

"Oh yes I would, thank you Joe. I'll have a look at them later."

The kettle had boiled and Ruth made the tea. They sat at the table and sipped.

"Well?" Joe broke the silence a little impatiently. "How are things in Perth, and how is school?"

"Good." Ruth's eyes had been downcast but she lifted her head and gazed straight at Joe with something like bravado.

"Really?"

"Yes, really. I told you all about school in my letters."

"You didn't say much about Alice and Charlie."

"No, well, they're well and happy I think. I only see them at weekends, of course. We live not too far from the school; I could probably be a day-girl if I wanted, but I like to board."

"Marie McLeod Schoolgirl?" Joe smiled.

"Not really. No midnight feasts but no Miss Dangerfields either.

"Joe's curiosity got the better of him.

"What do you call Alice and Charlie? Mum and Dad?" It hurt to say it.

"I call them Alice and Charlie." Ruth said flatly. "I could call Alice 'Mum' and get used to it after a while, I think, but I couldn't ever call Charlie 'Dad' I don't think, so I decided on Alice and Charlie. The girls at school think I'm very modern."

Joe reflected that her inability to call Charlie 'Dad' was discerning.

He still hadn't made any decision about the bombshell he held close to his chest. He had meant to ask Helen for advice, but in the end felt it too private, too important, to share with anyone. So he worried at it like a dog with a bone and it gnawed away at him in return. Could be have fancied the resemblance? Why hadn't he seen it before? Had he ever suspected it? Of course not; he saw again and again the perfect matching of the two profiles, and more tellingly, the look on Alice's face as she watched them together. He was quite, quite certain. He went back over Alice's reactions to Charlie's arrival and his presumption of fatherhood. He remembered little starts and silences on her part as it all unfolded, demonstrations he was sure—now—of her own surprise. But how quickly she had seen how the situation was entirely to her advantage. Alice was nothing if not adaptable.

Waking up in her old bed in her old room seemed to bring out more of the old Ruth. She quickly assumed the chores and duties that had previously been her domain, although her clothes were incongruously new instead of faded and threadbare and her hair, Joe realised had been cut rather more expertly than Alice had managed in her days on the Group. That had been part of the alienation yesterday—he hadn't been able to put his finger on it at the time.

"Stop looking at me, Joe" Ruth laughed but Joe imagined that there was an edge of irritation as she continued to sweep the floor, dust dancing in the shaft of sunlight through the open door. He blushed.

"Don't you have work to do?" she asked.

"Just the usual stuff, and it won't hurt to ignore it for a day or so. I thought we could have a picnic or something." He trailed off lamely.

"Oh Joe, the beach, yes!"

Her enthusiasm was sweet relief from the constraint.

"Will we get the others to come?" he asked. There was no need to define "others". "They're all looking forward to seeing you. Tomorrow's Sunday—will we ask Miss Anderson too? What about some of your friends from school?"

"Yes, yes of course the aunties and uncles and Miss Anderson, yes too. That's enough for tomorrow. When is Auntie Ida's baby due?"

Joe wasn't sure.

"How's Uncle Stephen?" This question was posed some hesitation.

"He's well. He's doing well."

Joe took Willoughby the horse (no one knew where that name came from except Ruth) and rode to the Padman's to deliver the invitation to Helen Anderson which was accepted with pleasure. Ruth made her roundabout way to the houses of each of the three remaining Oak Tree Place parties and delivered the invitation between cakes, biscuits, cordials, much affection and many "oh-how-you've-growns."

As evening approached Ruth seemed really reimbued with the atmosphere of the Group and it was almost as if she'd never left as she and Joe sat on the verandah in the rapidly-cooling remnants of the day. Joe was disinclined to spoil the moment with questions, or even conversation, and it was Ruth who eventually spoke.

"Is Uncle Stephen still my uncle?"

Joe said that he was sure that Stephen would be her Uncle for as long as she wanted.

Ruth sighed theatrically. "Life's very complicated, isn't it?"

The failing light concealed Joe's wry amusement as he said "Oh yes, love, it is." He wished to hell that he could decide what he should do about it.

◆

The beach picnic had almost been like old times, except of course for the absence of Alice. Stephen, however, had risen to the occasion and was in fine form. Joe thought that this was probably due to the presence of Helen and that this was a good thing too. He was aware that some hopeful matchmaking had been going on for some time linking Joe himself with Helen but it had never really taken off. Truth to tell, he was rather daunted by Miss Anderson and she was much, much, *much* better suited to Stephen. Jolly good luck to them both.

The couple in question had wandered off along the beach, ankle-deep in the edging waves, their bodies outlined by the sun. Joe watched idly, noting the laughter and the avid conversation that didn't need to be audible to be apparent. He felt a wave of envy that was not directed against Stephen or Helen but overwhelmingly personal. What a mess he'd made of his life—he'd never enjoyed that sort of easy banter with anyone. He snorted with derision at the thought of his relationship with Lydia. How artificial it had all been and what a dupe he'd been. This was all-too-familiar territory; he shook himself mentally. His blind adoration had been determinedly crushed but Lydia's memory still had the ability to leach the pleasure out of a day.

Ruth had been watching Stephen and Helen too.

"Uncle Stephen can't marry anyone else until he and Alice are divorced, can he?" she said reflectively.

"I don't suppose he can."

"Everyone who doesn't know them thinks that Alice and Charlie are married."

"Even though they're not." Joe could not keep the asperity from his voice.

"I expect they'd like to be, but that's two divorces needed before they could, isn't it?" said Ruth.

Joe didn't respond. Other people's marriage, divorces and goings-on were overwhelmingly boring. He flopped down on his belly in the sand and closed his eyes, letting the thin warmth of the September sun lick his shirtless back. Through his lashes his saw Ruth's feet patter past toward the water and the gentle bustle of Ida and Ellen as they packed up the remains of the picnic. Despite his best intentions, memories of Lydia percolated. It hadn't been all bad, he thought lazily. In the dark of the night in their big soft bed Lydia had often surprised him with her passion. Perhaps she'd been thinking of someone else, but he pushed that thought away, just reliving the sweetness of it all. No harm in that. He dozed a little.

It was Ruth prodding him in the back that woke him and he found the beach party all packed up and standing round, laughing.

"Come on Mr. Sleepyhead," said Ruth, "all the work is done so you can wake up now."

Sheepishly he stumbled upright and brushed the fine white sand from his body and clothes, the warmth of his dreams still in the forefront of his mind. Ruth took his hand and he allowed the dream to drift away as they plodded up the dune.

That evening over scrambled eggs Ruth took it upon herself to quiz Joe. She began with a strung out "Joooooh?"

"Mmm?"

"How old are you?"

"I'm 30, nearly 30, you know that."

"Are you divorced from bloody Lydia?"

Joe chuckled. Lydia's name had become double-barrelled it seemed and he didn't remonstrate. "Actually I don't know, chicken," he said. "Lydia said she'd arrange it and I just don't know whether you can divorce someone without them knowing it has happened. I might be and I might not be, just don't know."

"Can you find out Joe? I think you should try to find out."

"Why's that then?"

"You should find a nice person and get married again."

"Oh, I should, should I?"

"Yes, everyone says that you shouldn't be here alone all the time, you need someone to be with you and look after you."

"Oh they do, do they?"

"Yes and I think so too. I think you should try to find someone you like and marry her."

"Oh yes, and where am I to find this "someone"?"

"I would have liked you to marry Miss Anderson but I think Uncle Stephen's more likely to do that. And that's alright," she added quickly, "because everyone thinks they're very well suited."

"Oh, "everyone" does, do they?" Joe laughed. "Well, let "everyone" pick me a blushing bride then, lovey. They grow on trees round here."

Ruth looked at him seriously. "I know there aren't many girls or ladies to pick in the Groups, but there are some, Joe. Allie Chandler, perhaps."

"*Allie Chandler*? Oh my goodness, girl, she can't be more than fourteen!"

Ruth looked truculent. "Fifteen. That's old enough."

"The hell it is! There's laws against that sort of thing, love. I don't know what the minimum age for marriage is, but it's certainly more than fifteen!"

"How old do you have to be then?"

"I just said I don't know, but I think it might be 16 or 18 or something, it might even be 21 as far as I know. I've never had reason to enquire, and I don't need to start now, thank you!"

"I'll be 16 in four years".

"Yes. And …?"

"I could marry you then".

Joe laughed out loud. "Oh chicken, chicken, I have never in my life had a better offer, but I think you should concentrate on being a clever schoolgirl for the time being and let the future take care of itself. Will it make you happy if I promise to look around carefully for someone to marry?"

Ruth knew when she was being put off. She looked sideways at Joe and then got up from the table to wash the dishes without further comment.

The end of the holiday finally came and Joe put Ruth on the train. It had been a moderate success, this holiday. Joe was coming to recognise that Ruth was no longer his baby sister, neither baby nor sister, but a very discerning almost-adult.

She had been genuinely hurt by his joking rejection of her plans for him, which, with a delayed masculine realisation, he now saw as a loving and considered design for his happiness. He tried to bring the subject up several times in order to repair the damage he'd caused but it had never worked.

They now regarded each other gravely as they waited for the train to start.

"Thank you for a lovely holiday Joe"

"Thank you for coming."

"See you next holidays."

"Yes". Work hard at school."

"Yes I will."

"Write to me."

"Yes of course. You write to me too."

"Yes of course."

Then the guard's whistle sounded, the flag waved and the steam hissed.

As the train began to move, Ruth burst out laughing and called out

"And think about getting married!"

She leaned out of the window waving, still laughing.

74

*Three months later.
Early December 1927*

Despite the promises, Ruth's letters, which had been regular and weekly up to her September visit, quite quickly diminished. Since September he'd received just two, and none for the past month. He'd kept up his end of the correspondence, doggedly determined to ignore Ruth's comparative silence. The minutiae of life on the Group was spelled out to her each week, with Joe becoming more and more despairing of making it sound interesting.

But it wasn't interesting to him either. If it wasn't for the necessity of milking, his days would be completely unstructured and mostly wasted. His clearing activities dwindled to almost nothing and he spent long periods leaning against the verandah post gazing out on to the panorama of his farm with its tufted grass, bleak ring-barked trees and its perimeter of dark forest. Sometimes the bush seemed to encroach rather than retreat under his clearing operations and the immensity of his task was a glutinous blob that engulfed him from head to toe.

Without Ruth it all seemed pointless. It had started out, of course, as a grand adventure and a new beginning for them all—him and Lydia and Harry and Ruth and truth to be told he was glad that he hadn't had to cope with Lydia if she had indeed come with them. Her disdain for Oak Tree Place would have been trivial compared to the faults she could have found on the Group. Lord, he almost wished her here if only to observe her fury and frustration. Oh no, vengeance would have been on his head too, and he could do without that, thanks.

He thought about little Harry. Still found it hard to accept that he'd been so duped. He'd loved that little fellow so much, but nothing could change the fact that he had no real place in his life.

Harry would never even remember him and Lydia would make sure that there'd be no mention of him, ever.

But, he reflected, his time here on the Group with Ruth had been some of the best time of his life. Now even that was changed, finished and gone as Ruth seemed to have discarded him too.

Joe slumped to the boards of the verandah and threw an arm around the post. What the hell was he doing here? Why was he slaving his life away for nothing? His debt to the government was growing by the day for the cows, the equipment, the house and everything and he was damned if he could see a time when he could begin to repay it. This realisation had come to many of the settlers on this and other Groups, and the rate of "walk-off" was high. Initially Joe had thought these people soft and without backbone, but it would be so easy to walk away right now, so very easy.

The mail delivery was collected from town and left at the foreman's hut for collection by the settlers. Joe had given up being part of the eager little crowd that greeted the weekly delivery so it was Stephen who delivered the postcard on his way past.

Joe had been doing some desultory root grubbing and was trudging back towards the house when he saw Stephen arrive and sit on the verandah step to wait for him. He had something in his hand. As Joe came closer he saw concern on Stephen's face. Everyone showed concern these days when they looked at him and it was driving him mad. Even Stephen, who he had looked up to with admiration and respect, looked more like a worried old mother hen than his wise friend of the past. Joe was short.

"Stephen."

"Hello Joe." A hesitation and then "Got any beer, Joe?"

"In the safe."

Two bottles of Len's home brew sat in the cooling environs of the Coolgardie safe, and Joe opened one of them to pour two glasses before he sat down on the edge of the verandah, back against the post, legs dangling, scuffing the dirt.

"You got some mail?"

"Actually it's for you, Joe."

Strangely Stephen did not move to pass it over.

"Give it here then."

Joe turned and reached out, but Stephen twisted away from him.

"Joe ..." he began.

"Oh God," Joe paled. "What's the matter, what's the matter, it's bad news isn't it? Is it Ruth? Is it Ruth?" His voice had risen with each word. He lurched towards Stephen and grabbed the postcard from his hand.

Stephen was saying no, no, Joe it's alright, really it is. It's alright. It's alright.

Joe looked stupidly at the postcard that showed a bright black and white ocean liner sailing a bright blue sea against a bright blue sky. The caption said "SS *Oronsay*". Although it made no sense, the commonplace picture was reassuring. A picture of a ship.

Then the significance hit and Joe turned the postcard over to read the message.

Two hours later, both bottles of home brew and some brandy left over from Christmas found Joe and Stephen in maudlin brotherhood. Stephen had managed to calm Joe and stop him from charging off to Perth immediately although his determination had been strong and the open suitcase on the floor was testament to his initial impulse.

Not for the first time, Joe said "Bitch!" and added "Bastard" for good measure, again. He rubbed his face hard and tousled his hair until it stood up in spikes. He was past the shock stage now and was warming up to red-hot anger.

"That woman must the most evil and shifty person on earth. How could she lie like that to Ruth? How could she?"

"Pretty easily, I'd say," said Stephen, nodding heavily with the weight of experience on his head. "Pretty easily, given the lying she's been doing all her life." He nodded more forcefully. "Her whole life has been one big lie when you think about it. Yes."

"Why did I let her take Ruth away? Why was I stupid enough to let her take Ruth away?" Joe thumped the table.

"You thought you were doing the best for Ruth, Joe, we all did. You were acting for her best."

"I should have known."

"*I* should have realised." Stephen was definite, if a trifle slurred. "I should have been objective enough to see the danger of the situation, but I was so wrapped up in my own hurt pride … "

Joe picked up the postcard and read the message again, his voice cracking.

Dear Joe, it is such fun on the Oronsay and <u>much</u> better than it was on the Diogenes coming out. We arrive in Ceylon tomorrow and Charlie is going to buy me a moonstone. I have met some new friends. The food is delicious. I am so excited. Hope you are feeling better. Must get this postcard to the Purser's office to catch the mail. Love from Ruth.

"Obviously", Stephen said, "our devious friend Alice has been filling Ruth up with lies."

Joe kept staring at the message on the postcard.

"Feeling better? *Feeling better?* What am I supposed to be suffering from?"

"Whatever Alice decides."

"God she's a low sneaky cow."

"Don't malign the cows, Joe."

"Oh, what the hell can I do?" Joe thumped the table ineffectually again. "I have to get her back."

"That might be difficult, old man." Stephen looked at him seriously Legally it's complicated of course but you are only her … her half-cousin or something. No blood relation"

Joe sat back in his chair. "She may be Alice's, but I'm sure as hell Ruth's not Charlie's daughter."

"*What?*"

In fits and starts, Joe regaled Stephen with his observations, theories and conclusions. Stephen sat incredulous throughout, not saying a word until Joe had finished.

"So you're saying that Alice was playing around with Charlie and Michael at the same time? Whew. I knew I wasn't part of a very exclusive club, but that's a bit close to home. Whew." A pause. "Are you quite sure?"

"Yes, I am. Think about it; think how alike Michael and Ruth are—dark curls, a bit of a turned-up nose, blue eyes with those thick lashes, the same complexion. And there was the way Alice was looking at them that day—I just knew. And as I said, looking back, Alice was all over the place when Charlie arrived and it wasn't all to do with the surprise. She was calculating, even then. She would have done anything to get off the Group, you know that."

Stephen flinched but Joe was too preoccupied to notice.

"I didn't—couldn't—say anything at the time because I was too surprised and shocked and couldn't believe it, even though I really knew I was right. It'd been hard enough to cope with Charlie being Ruth's father, and there I was with another father for her! I must say I'm glad Charlie's not it though."

"Mmm yes." Stephen was thinking. "What say I telephone the shipping line and find how to send a telegram to the boat, or to their next port or whatever the best plan is."

"Telegram to Ruth to explain?"

"No, no, that'll come later. Telegram to Alice. Threaten her with exposure if she doesn't give Ruth up and let her come back."

"Exposure?"

"Think about it, Joe. Where would Alice be if Charlie knew the truth?"

"Oh God, yes."

"I rather think that Our Alice would settle for what Charlie can offer if she has to make a choice between that and Ruth. Despite all she's done over the years to get and stay close to Ruth, she's been happy enough to put her into boarding school in Perth and if I know anything she's taken to life with a bit of money like a duck to water. She'll think twice before giving it up now she's got it in her grasp, I'll guarantee." Stephen smiled with his mouth but his eyes were cold. "I'll also go so far as to guess that the adult that Ruth's growing into is a different kettle of fish from the baby or the little girl that she could play with—and control."

"Of course you're right, Stephen, with everything, as usual." Joe spoke with the first enthusiasm he'd shown for weeks. "Let's find out about the telegram first thing tomorrow. I'll pick you up in the cart on the way into town as soon as I've done the milking. I wish I could be there to watch when it arrives. I wonder how she'll explain it to Charlie."

"Huh," said Stephen bitterly, "that's for her to decide, but given her history, she'll find a way."

75

The next day

They were proud of their plan. The shipping company assured them that their cable would go straight to the *Oronsay* and be delivered to the passenger addressed. They were a little vague about how long it would take to arrive but were sure it would be very fast. Less than a day? Oh yes.

Composing the message was painstaking, especially as every word made it more expensive.

They sat on the bank of the river with pencil and paper for half an hour before they came up with a suitably framed communication.

Madam return daughter Australia immediately or Charlie will learn true father situation advise arrangements Joe

Joe was loath to waste money on the short words like "or" and "will" but Stephen was adamant that Alice needed simplicity and clarity. They had changed "paternity" to "father" and deleted a "please."

They were prepared to wait a week for a reply, allowing even then that it would not contain the arrangements made for Ruth's return as this would be difficult to arrange in the middle of the ocean. Just a notification that Alice had agreed and things were in train, that would be it.

Two weeks went by and half of another before a letter arrived for Joe. He and Stephen had somehow expected a return telegram, but this rather battered envelope with its exotic Egyptian stamps was bound to contain more detail than any telegram so the delay was excused.

The Group Settlers could be divided into two types on mail day—the eager impatient readers who ripped open envelopes and sat down under trees to devour their correspondence and those who tucked their post away in a pocket and trotted home to make a cup of tea.

Neither Joe nor Stephen received many letters, but they were both privately inclined and would normally read them at home. But today was different and they drew aside from the small crowd at mail collection and tore open the envelope. Alice's large round handwriting glared up from the paper.

<u>Dear</u> *Joe,*

We are on our way back to England and will be there before you read this letter and we are gong to stay there, far away from the flys, the heat and dirt of that awfull place you have berried yourself in.

You dont have the money to follow us I no and even if you did you woodent find us anyway because we havent even decided yet wear we will go. I will tell Ruth anything I please and she will beleve me, so there. You will be in the past and will soon be forgoten. By me as well.

Goodbye. For ever. Im shore Stephen is looking over your sholder, so goodbye to him to.

Alice (or perhaps some other name)

Both men were silent. Joe's hand shook slightly as he refolded the letter and his voice cracked.

"I thought we had nailed her."

"I fear we're just two blokes and not devious enough to cross swords with our Alice," said Stephen, "and obviously my lessons in basic spelling didn't have much effect either."

"Bugger the spelling. What can I do now?"

"You have no money?"

"No money. Just a couple of quid put away for emergencies but not enough for the fare to England, let alone the other bits and pieces that I'd need money for if I did try to follow them."

"Yairs," said Stephen, stringing out the word like an Australian, "and you don't want to go off on a wild-goose chase anyway if it's as Alice says and they're going to try to hide themselves. It'd be useless."

"But what can I do?"

Occasional laughter and snatches of conversations punctuated their mutual silence as settlers discussed news and happenings that their mail had brought. Stephen sighed.

"Sorry old man, actually nothing comes to mind at all. We thought we had the upper hand and that we were going to get Ruth back, but obviously now we can't do that, not at the moment anyway. I don't know … " Stephen's voice trailed away and he put his hand on Joe's shoulder. "Let's go back to the house. But let's go to Bill Blain's place first and get some more beer."

76

January 1928

Ruth thought that she should feel as if she were home again, but all she felt was strange.

She might well be back in the country she was born in and which she'd only left a few years ago, but she was back with new parents and a new future and what's more she was living in a part of London which was totally strange to her.

The house was nice though. Lots of rooms (many more than they needed) with a little garden at the back and lovely coloured glass in the tops of the windows and round the front door. When the winter sun shone through the glass it made coloured patterns on the floor or on her hand if she stuck it out. She had her own room, of course and it overlooked the back garden. Charlie said they'd probably move somewhere else in good time but she didn't know why because this was a very nice house.

School was … good, although the girls weren't all that friendly but Ruth knew enough about settling in to a new school to know that these things took time. Not at all like the Groups, where you knew everyone anyway.

Which reminded her about Joe. Why hadn't he written, why hadn't he replied to her letters? She'd been so anxious to let him know every detail of her new life and had looked forward to his reaction so much. She could hardly wait to tell him that they had a maid! Her name was Doris and if the truth be told she was a bit of a misery but Alice just *loved* telling her what to do, which Ruth thought was funny and she knew Joe would think so too. But Doris did work hard and seemed to cope with Alice alright, even if she did mumble under her breath sometimes. Goodness though, she had a lot to do each day, Ruth thought. She did most of the cooking, shopping and message-running and even helped

Mrs. Bishop who came to clean once a week. Such a hard-working person would do well on the Groups, Ruth thought sagely.

Why had Joe not written to her? When they were on the boat, Alice said he'd been ill but that he was getting better and that was why he hadn't written. But that was ages ago and she'd been writing to him for weeks now without a reply.

One of the things that Doris did each morning was to place any letters that had been delivered that morning at their places on the breakfast table. So far Charlie had had several, but neither she nor Alice had any at all. Every morning she hoped, and every morning she was disappointed.

Oh Joe, why don't you write to me? I miss you so.

77

Three months later.
March 1928

Nearly three months had passed since Alice's stinging response to their ultimatum, and true to her prediction, Joe had not taken any action. He plodded on with the never-ending clearing, the strident demands of the animals.

The end-of-summer days still dawned knife-bright over the bleached paddocks and every breeze brought showers of dead leaves, making dun-coloured drifts against the ringbarked trees and the chicken-pen fence.

Clearing was always sweaty work but it was worse in the heat. Joe and Stephen worked a contract with Johnny Douglas to clear five more acres on his land, then on Joe's. It was slow work and the heat was sapping to energy and thought. Joe stumbled home each evening too tired to do anything but wash, eat and fall into bed. Only a little time ago, his enthusiasm would have overcome his exhaustion. Only a little time ago, he had Ruth.

The feeling of loss was a cannon ball in the middle of his chest, always there, dull and heavy. Frustration and defeat ate away at his mind every minute of every day. He became surly with Stephen as they worked together, barely bothering to converse as they sat in the patchy shade at dinner time or smoko, grunting in response to attempts to engage him.

Stephen, on the other hand, was talking the leg off an iron pot. His spirit seemed undaunted and his enthusiasm as high as ever. He and Johnny chatted amiably as Joe gazed into space.

"What do you think, Joe?"

Joe started up and shook his head slightly. "About what?" His tone made it plain that he didn't care.

"They've stopped accepting Group Settlers. What does that mean for the rest of us?"

"Same as ever, I'd say."

"Well that's deep." Stephen was irritated.

"Well, what do you think? You're the thinker round here."

"Oh come on Joe."

"Come on where?"

Johnny was plainly uneasy at the hostility Joe was displaying. He shuffled to his feet and made to resume work, but Joe was not finished.

"Where do you want me to come on to, Stephen? Where the bloody hell is there to come on to? Around here? Come *on*? On what? To what?" Joe couldn't stop but his belligerence turned away from Stephen.

"Does anyone really believe that we're ever going to earn a living off this bloody land? Talk about hopeless! We'll just work like navvies forever and get deeper and deeper into debt and there's no way out because we owe the government for every damned thing we've got since we arrived."

Joe was dangerously close to embarrassing tears. His voice broke as he tilted back his head and seemed to talk to the trees.

"I've had my fill, really I have. You know, I've lost everything I ever had in my whole bloody life—my Mum and Dad, most of my friends, and my little sister." His lips twisted and he added "Oh yes, and my *wife*, of course, damn her to hell."

Johnny turned away, embarrassed, and Stephen put his hand on Joe's arm.

"Come on pal, sometimes it looks bleak, I know, but it's always better in the morning."

"No, I really mean it, I really am completely fed up. Had enough."

Without pausing to collect his tools, Joe stumbled off over the paddock towards his house. Stephen and Johnny wordlessly watched him go.

When they'd finished work—a bit early actually—Johnny made off to his block and Stephen went to check on Joe. He made a bit of noise putting the tools down on the verandah but Joe didn't come out of the house.

"There Joe?" Stephen called as he opened the door.

The front room was empty but one step brought Stephen to the door of the bedroom where Joe was in the process of vigorously strapping a suitcase closed. The room was in disarray.

"What are you doing?" Stephen's voice showed his alarm.

"What does it bloody well look like? I'm getting out of this place."

"Oh Joe, you can't give up now. Things will get better, you'll see, they'll get better."

"No they bloody won't. We've been thrashing a dead horse all along. We all should've turned around and left the minute we arrived. It's all been a total waste of everything. Time, money ... *life*." Joe choked on the last word. "And nobody gives a damn about us. We can all lay down and die for all anyone cares." He was trembling with emotion.

"Joe," Stephen began, "Joe, alright, you're fed up and you're leaving, but don't leave angry. Slow down a bit and let's talk it over to see what's best to do."

"I'm going, Stephen, no changing my mind, I'm going."

"I understand that, Joe, I just don't want you to leave like this. Where are you going anyway, at this time of day? Leave tomorrow and I'll take you to the train, I promise. Walking all that way with a suitcase wouldn't be much fun."

Joe grunted. "Fun!" he said "Oh yeah, my whole damned life's been a lot of fun. Getting funnier by the day."

"Alright Joe, alright, just promise me you won't do anything before tomorrow and let's have a bit of a talk tonight, yes? Get together a plan for you at least. You don't want to go leaping off like a kangaroo if you don't know where you're going."

Joe seemed to crumple. He slumped on the bed, folding up on himself like something deflated. "I've got to go. I've packed."

Stephen's eyes were moist as he sat beside him on the bed and awkwardly put a hand on his shoulder. "You can do that again tomorrow, mate," he said.

Joe was never quite sure how they got word around so fast, but in what seemed next to no time, the whole Oak Tree Place contingent was in his house. There weren't enough chairs, so a heavily-pregnant Ida was eased into one of them and kerosene boxes did for the men. Ellen fussed with cups of tea.

They were all obviously aware of Joe's intention and regarded him with sympathy and a certain unease. Despite all of them reporting immediately for this Oak Tree Council of War, no one seemed to know what to say.

Stephen cleared his throat and began. "What can we do to help Joe?" he asked, looking around at everyone.

Joe looked up, surprised. He had begun to steel himself for a mountain of arguments against his leaving. "I don't need help" he protested wanly.

"One way or another, you do, my lad," said Stephen. "For instance, if you're set on going you need money to get anywhere. I expect you'll be heading for Perth?"

"Umm, well, yes but … "

"We can give you a bob or two, Joe" said Michael.

"Us too." Ida had spoken before Len had a chance, but he just added a confirming nod.

"And me some too," said Stephen. "You'll need your train fare and a bit to get set up."

Joe squeezed his eyes shut and bit his lip. Hardship and opposition he could face with dry eyes, but kindness and concern brought him undone. He made several efforts to speak and finally blurted a shaky thanks. "I've only got a couple of quid myself," he said "so thank you. I'll pay you all back, of course."

Of course he would, they all agreed.

"But Joe," said Len "have you really through about this? I know you're fed up and you've every right to be with all that's happened, you poor old fellow, but you've done so much here, do you really want to give it all up? Look at your pasture coming through and the amount you've got cleared now and your cows will grow to a herd in time and … "

"I'm going, Len, I'm going. I've decided. I can't work myself to death here for no reason. What would I do with a herd of cows anyway? Just work harder. Work harder and come back of an evening to nothing. No one to talk to, no one to laugh with … " He kept his voice from breaking with great effort.

"Hey Joe, you've got me down the road for that!" Stephen tried to lift the mood. "And there am I sitting on my verandah looking at my own trees and my own personal stars listening to my own skinny cows and loving it all—I never realised how bleak it all was!"

"It wasn't always." Joe was too emotional to say more and felt that there was nothing more to say in any case.

"'Course not, boyo, and we understand." Michael spoke softly.

Joe looked at Michael's face, the dark, gentle face looking at him with such sympathy. This was Ruth's father. He was flooded with the desire to share the knowledge with him. He deserved to know. He deserved to know that he had a beautiful daughter who was in fact being more or less abducted by her mother and her lover.

"Michael," he began, "there's something … "

Stephen jumped up and slammed his mug on the table, interrupting anything that Joe was going to say, at the same time flashing him a warning glance.

"Well, if this man here is decided," he said loudly and jovially, "we need to send him off royally, don't we? What can we do?"

"What were you going to say, Joe?" Michael asked mildly.

"Oh, nothing really. Forget it."

"No come on Joe, what was it?" Michael was looking at him keenly.

Joe gave an anguished glace to Stephen, his impulse to confront Michael totally gone. But Stephen was no help. He was looking hard at Michael, who in turn was leaning forward, seeming to urge Joe to go on. After a few seconds of silence he spoke.

"Is it about Ruth?"

Joe's silence was assent.

"I saw it happen, Joe, I saw you realise, the day she was leaving. It took you a long time, boyo."

Len and Ida were frowning with incomprehension. Ellen's eyes were downcast and Joe and Stephen were both stunned.

"What on earth … ?" said Len. He was ignored.

"So it's true," Joe managed to croak.

"You know it is. I'm just surprised it took you so long."

"Why … how … ?"

"Not a long story at all, Joe. Just a mistake in the beginning that has got a bit complicated over the years with nobody actually doin' anything." He turned to Len and Ida, who were sitting close to each other at the end of the table. "You're the only ones who don't know yet, so I'll tell ye the story, and a sober tale it is to be sure." He paused. "Ye see, it's me that's Ruth's daddy."

He ignored the small gasps.

"In me defence I have to say that I didn't know meself for a long long time; that part of the story that we've all just learned about Alice hiding that she was having the babby and Ruth being born like Joe's sister to Jessie and Ned—I was taken in like everybody else and it never once occurred to me that it was a slew of lies and made-ups. Well, it doesn't, does it?" He asked the question of everyone, but no one answered so he drew breath and continued.

"I'm not proud of meself, don't think I'm anything but ashamed. Except." He raised his head and ran his fingers through his hair. "Except that one sound thing has come out of it and that's Ruth, the grandest little lass you ever saw." There were tears in his eyes.

"There's no excusin' me o'course, not at all. No. Except that me lovely wife has done just that. More than I deserve, yes it is." Ellen's drooped head shook denial.

Michael continued. "When I came to Oak Tree Place I was on the run. I was trying to lose meself so that I wouldn't be found. I'd tried to do just that in Liverpool and in London and I was tired of running but I had to keep going until I could find a bolt-hole that was safe. On that night when I walked into the Oak Tree the weather outside was fierce and I had nowhere to sleep and I was tired, so tired. The pub was warm and the beer was good and when Alice started to talk to me she was like a little bit of sunshine in it all. Truth to tell, just talkin' to her cheered me up no end. If you're wondering" he paused to survey his friends, "if you're wondering where our good friend Charlie was, given his habit of takin' to anyone who Alice looked at, well then, I learned later that he had a chill or some such, so he wasn't on the scene at all. And o'course I knew nothing about him at the time.

"I didn't have anywhere to stay that night and Alice was mighty invitin'. I'm not proud of meself for taking advantage but I'd hopped off the train just because the railway station up there had a soft name, sounded country-like. Then I'd walked, just hopin' and hopin' that all this walkin' round would get me lost. If I was lost, I thought, then so would the couple of chancers who were lookin' for me. I'd got away from them at Victoria by jumping on the train at the last minute and I hoped they'd think I went right on to Brighton."

Michael paused, leaned back on his rickety box and regarded the faces agog and waiting on his next words. He smiled ruefully.

"And ye'll be asking what it might be that caused me to run away in such a manner from two men. Sure an' I don't want to talk about that at all, no I don't."

"Why, Michael?" asked Joe with exasperation. "Don't you think there've been enough secrets round here to last a couple of lifetimes? I'm sure you couldn't surprise any of us much more even if you'd committed murder!"

There was a silence that was too long and too heavy.

"Well, there's the thing," said Michael eventually.

"No love, don't!" Ellen was out of her chair and around the table to Michael, her arms around his neck, cleaving to him desperately. He reached up and held her awkwardly until his kerosene box rocked dangerously and they had to disentangle.

Normally everyone would have laughed, but a realisation was dawning and there was sober silence.

Michael regarded them all with a small smile.

"Well then, Joe lad, hit the nail right on the head, right on the head. And you're right, I might as well make a clean breast of it all here and now because I can't run any further away sure I can't. It's a short story and a sad one."

Now that he had started, Michael seemed anxious to get on with it.

"See, me young brother Sean an' I never did see eye to eye even though we had no one but each other in the world and that's the sad truth. Sean was always up to some mischief or other and as we got older the mischief became more and more serious. Still it was a shock when I learned that he was hangin' about with the hard lot—the IRA. I tried me big-brother-talkin' to him but he didn't take too kindly to that and it was, as a matter o' fact, the last time I spoke to him at all.

"Sean sort o' disappeared from sight, but I did hear of him from time to time as being involved in this and that, but at the time I was a bit wrapped up in meself and me own sorrows as me own darlin' wife and our wee babby had both died together, poor sweet souls, and I wasn't in a carin' state o' mind."

Joe looked quickly at Stephen, thinking of his similar experience, but he was intent on Michael's story as he continued.

"But it was still a deep shock when people, me own people, started lookin' sideways at me and the rumour reached me that Sean had turned Judas and informed on his mates.

"To be sure, the rumours flew thick and fast in those days and I was not o' the mind to accept this one meself right off and I tried to find out the truth of the matter but the more I asked about, the more the shutters went up and I was treated like a traitor meself so I was. No one would speak to me about Sean because I was Sean's brother and so I was a suspect too.

"I was sore depressed and no matter how I tried I could not see any sort of future in me own country at all, so I decided to move over the water and try for a new start. And o' course when the news of me plannin' to leave got around, things got even worse for me. I was visited, I was, I was visited. Told that I was on no account to think of leavin', that I was the cheese in the mousetrap that was goin' to bring Sean back from wherever he was hidin' so they could mete out due punishment for his treason.

"Useless it was for me to reason with these eejits, so sure of themselves and so, so wrong in their reasoning. Sean would as likely fly to the moon as call on me for help, so this cheese would moulder and die long before any trap was sprung.

"Even after weeks of them watching my house, when they had reduced the watchers to just the one, they were still determined that what they fancied would come to pass and that Sean would obligin'ly present himself one dark night.

"O'course he didn't. But on one of those dark nights when I was feelin' totally fed-up and angry, and to be honest after I'd had a drop to drink, I decided suddenly that I would get away no matter what, so I just put on me coat and walked out me back door. Sure and I hadn't even bothered to check where me watcher was lurkin' I was so fed up and unthinkin', so o'course he tackled me as I was swingin' over the back fence. There was a tussle and he had a gun. I was so angry, so determined to get away or die, that when the gun went off I truly thought I was dead. But when the poor lad fell down on the ground it only took me a second to turn tail and run."

The assembly had been silent throughout Michael's storytelling, but the silence that followed its climax had a denser quality. It was broken by Ellen, who pushed back her chair and stood behind Michael again with her arms around his neck. She pressed her cheek to the top of his head.

"This man," she said "is the gentlest, sweetest man in the world. He told me his story years ago and it makes not one tiny bit of difference me. He's my husband and I love him."

Michael covered her hands with one of his and spoke again.

"I'm luckier than I deserve to be, indeed I am. As I'm being honest for the first time with you all my good friends, I will also say now that when I married me lovely wife—and she knows this—I thought her sweet and gentle but she was a bolt-hole for me to get lost in and away from the line of men who've searched for me and followed me over the years—oh it remained a task for them and probably does to this day. And after all it's true that I killed a man in cold blood and that's on me conscience forever, so it is. I hope for forgiveness every day in spite o' the fact that I've lost me religion somewhere along the way.

"But," he continued with a rush, "I want to say now that I have come to love my wife very, very dearly." There were tears in his eyes. "I was so lucky, so I was indeed, to meet her and have her look at me even … "

It was Stephen who spoke first although when he did it was to mutter that he didn't know what to say. Joe stood up.

"It's a sad story more than anything else, Michael," he said, "and I for one am glad you told us. As for what happened in Ireland, it can stay there on the other side of the world as far as I'm concerned."

"I don't mean to burden you all with me story," said Michael. "It just seems to me that over these past years we've all become so close with all we've done together an' all … "

No one else spoke but the silence was one of acceptance and acquiescence. Stephen wordlessly put his hand on Michael's shoulder.

"And ye'll be wondering why I stayed quiet-like on the subject of me bein' father to young Ruth," Michael suddenly said, returning all eyes to him again. "The fact is that it never even occurred to me for a long time. We were all in the dark now, weren't we, and then young Ruth started growin' up and lookin' more like me every day and I was thinkin' about how quare that was to be sure but I still couldn't work out how it could have all come about. But then when in me heart I felt I had the truth of it, suddenly there was Charlie sayin' that it was him who was Ruth's daddy. And Alice was sayin' he was too and surely Alice would be the one to know … "

He shook his big head slowly. "And then with little Ruth gettin' the money from Mrs.Craggs an' all, I just thought it better for her for me to be leavin' it all alone … "

"Completely understand, Michael, completely," said Stephen.

There was a general shuffle of movement as people rose from the table, except for Ida, who remained in her chair, her eyes wide and one hand groping the air for her husband who had been sitting beside her but was now halfway out the door to the verandah. Ellen saw her distress first.

"What is it, love? Is it …?"

"I think so. Yes. It is. It is."

"Whoa everyone, we need some help here!" Ellen didn't have to elaborate.

Len rushed to his wife's side and began to chafe her hands while gazing into her eyes. Ida's eyes remained wide and vacant, all interest gone from her immediate surroundings, concentrated on what has happening to her body.

78

Still March 1928

It was a little boy. Ida had been conveyed to the hospital over the rutted tracks that led to town in a Group spring cart with an accommodating mattress and had thankfully been able to give birth in relative comfort and safety of the hospital. She and the baby were both well and Len was elated.

Joe was remote and although he knew that he wished Len and Ida and their baby well, everything seemed to be happening at a distance. He calmly packed his bag again—with less content than he had originally included—and walked to the railway station without a word to anyone except for the short note he left tacked to the door for Stephen, who he knew would call that day. Stephen could distribute the animals as all the settlers were used to doing when people walked off the Group.

The journey to the station took him three hours and he transferred his bag from shoulder to shoulder and from hand to hand as he made his dusty way there.

Although he was tired and dishevelled, his journey and its attendant silence had buzzed in his head and brought an idea that grew in rightness and suitability so that it was a burning mission by the time he slumped on the seat on the railway station platform. During the wait for the once-daily train Joe did reflect that in his haste to leave without goodbyes he now had no additional money and although he could manage the fare to Perth, there was precious little left after that. Not much could be done about it now, so better get on with it, Joe.

In the end it was not too difficult.

79

Still March 1928

Ruth wanted so much to talk to Joe and she had no idea why he should be ignoring her.

Sometimes she thought that Miss Anderson might have become his girl friend and perhaps they'd even got married and not bothered to tell Ruth about it. She knew that a few people on the Group had thought that this would be a good idea and even though Miss Anderson might be a bit better suited to Uncle Stephen, actually Ruth had thought that this would be good too. One-up to have Miss Anderson really living with them in her and Joe's house, one-up on her schoolmates who thought they were lucky just to walk home with Miss Anderson …

But she wasn't there, was she? She was on the other side of the world and didn't know anything about what was really happening in Margaret River. Poor Robin's grave was probably not being looked after and her old schoolmates had probably forgotten her. She felt empty. She'd written so many letters to Joe, in fact Alice made her write every Saturday when she came home from school for the weekend and she'd told him *everything* about St. Margaret's and Miss Macrae and Miss Copinger and her new friends Jean and Frances.

Jean and Frances were full boarders, not a week-day boarder like she was, and that was something that made her a bit different from them. They'd been friends for a long time anyway when she came to St. Margaret's. She knew that they found her different and interesting because she'd been to Australia but they didn't know the more personal (and probably more interesting!) parts of her life. Sometimes its complications bemused her too.

That was another thing she'd like to talk to Joe about but she only hinted at it in letters because she didn't want him to be worried about her. The fact was that Alice and Charlie were fighting a bit. Probably more than she saw, with only being in the house for two days in a week. It was more boring than upsetting though and she just went up to her room when they started. She thought that Charlie should get a job or buy another pub or something— that would give him something else to think about and surely he had enough money. It might make him less cross with Alice, who was always trying to make him calm down but Ruth thought if she spent a bit less money then perhaps Charlie wouldn't be so angry.

She was thinking all these thoughts as she finished her weekly letter to Joe and passed it to Doris to put the stamps on and post. Then she just went to her room.

80

Eight months later.
November 1928

Eight months later Joe stepped off another train on to another long, bare railway platform. The air sang with dry heat as he went with the crowd towards the exit where the town of Kalgoorlie— Sam's Kalgoorlie—lay spread-eagled under the baking sun.

Stiff from the hours of inactivity on the train, Joe nevertheless strode with purpose down the wide street, tipping his hat over his eyes as the pavement glared up at him and perspiration trickled from every pore. He had studied a street plan of the town before he embarked on this journey and he made his way with outward confidence towards the hotel he had chosen.

He had thought the streets of Fremantle wide when comparing them with those he had known at home, and they were undoubtedly so when compared with the Margaret River tracks. But the broad expanses that were the streets of Kalgoorlie eclipsed anything he'd ever imagined. He squinted across to the shops on the other side and in spite of his half-concealed uncertainty, smiled a little at the proliferation of hotels. He crossed an empty intersection where there was a hotel on each corner, a wrought-iron balcony decorating each one and affording some shade, as did the awnings on the adjoining shops, to wandering shoppers and hotel customers.

It was one of these hotels that Joe had chosen, with the unexotic name of "The Australia" and he was so relieved to have located it easily that there was an extra spring in his step as he entered and was shown to his room in the cool stone building. He stripped off his clothes, kicked off his boots and lay on the bed, feeling warmly complacent that he had negotiated these last months and actually achieved the goal he'd set himself. Work in Perth had been scarce but he'd managed to score a job by the enormous good fortune of being in the right place—outside the pub—at the right time, when the yard man had been thrown out drunk. Joe was taken in on the spot and also scored a modest little room above the stables which suited him well as his intention, formed on the Margaret River railway station, was to save enough money to get to Kalgoorlie.

His work at the pub was hardly onerous when compared with the exertions required on the Group and he marked time for a while even after he had enough for his purpose and a bit to spare.

But here he was now, in Sam Curtis's wonderful Kalgoorlie. Joe felt warmly disposed towards the town simply because of its association with Sam, but additionally it represented something that he had initiated and executed on his own account and as he lay looking up at the plaster ceiling rose from his supine position on the big, soft bed he felt a sense of achievement that he couldn't remember feeling before. A simple achievement, untrammelled by the needs, wants, or accommodation of anyone else.

He woke later as the night became cooler, and tunnelled under the covers.

Next morning, after a hearty breakfast served in the sedate dining room of the hotel, Joe approached the landlord to ask if he knew of the Curtis family. He was directed to the Town Hall, an unmistakable and amazingly imposing building, towering on a corner that for once didn't support a pub, and was able to obtain a list of the Curtis families in the district. The clerk was interested and helpful although he couldn't say which of the list of four families might have been Sam's. He was amazed that Joe had come all the way from England to find them, and Joe didn't contradict him as it was almost true.

He chose the nearest address to walk to and felt the town settle down on him, a sense of unreasonable familiarity imbuing his step. It wasn't that Sam had described his beloved town in any detail for Joe to follow—it had been all snips and snatches—but the sense of Sam's presence was strong and Joe smiled crookedly as he thought of how Sam would have loved to show him around, just as Joe himself had done for Sam in London and Thornton Heath. The inevitable sadness pervaded and the smile faded.

The Town Hall clerk's directions were good and twenty minutes later Joe found himself hesitating before knocking on the door of a modest house built entirely of corrugated-iron. Joe thought of the humpy back on the Group, but this house was a lot more substantial – why, it had a door and windows and curtains. His heart beat fast as he waited for the door to be answered.

It suddenly swung open and Joe's jaw dropped.

"Sam …" he whispered, taking a step backwards.

"Nuh" said the young man calmly, "Bill."

"Sam's little brother."

"Yairs …"

He looked so much like the Sam that Joe had known, and when he said "Yes" in the drawling way that Sam had always done, Joe was almost undone. With difficulty he collected himself and cleared his throat.

"Hello", he managed, "my name's Joe Barlow."

Bill regarded him without expression.

"I was with Sam during the war."

Bill turned and yelled back into the house.

"Ma!"

He moved aside in the doorway to make room for a small grey-haired woman in a worn print dress covered by an enveloping apron, wiping her hands on a tea towel. She regarded Joe warily.

"Yes?" This time the word was a little less drawn out. In fact it was quite clipped and there was a surprising foreign accent as she continued. "I help you? We don't want nothing if you selling." This last was delivered quickly to prevent a sales spiel. Joe smiled uncertainly, still surprised by the accent.

"Oh, no, no, I'm not selling anything, I just came to see you because I was with Sam in the war." This was abrupt; he had practiced other introductions but they failed him as he faced Sam's mother and brother in the flesh.

Sam's mother sagged slightly and put her hand against the door frame.

"You know Sam?"

"Yes."

"Come inside. Please come. Come." Mrs. Curtis made beckoning motions with her hand and Bill moved aside, his eyes still fixed on Joe. Joe stepped inside.

The house was a ramshackle version of a Group house; four rooms and a verandah back and front. They stopped in the front room and Mrs. Curtis indicated that Joe should sit on the miner's couch while she and Bill faced him on the two chairs Bill had fetched from the kitchen. Another figure followed Bill into the room, also carrying a chair.

"Hello," said Sam's sister, "I'm Biddy." Joe nodded. "Joe Barlow" he said.

"Yes, Sam write about you," said Sam's mother, "but I thought you in England."

"Not for some time now, I've been trying to farm the south-west. But I left."

"And you came to Kalgoorlie?" Biddy's expression was comical, and Joe smiled hesitantly, glad of the glimpse of humour.

"Sam always talked so much about Kalgoorlie that when I left the Group I just thought I'd come and have a look at it."

"Mmm, Sam probably forgot a lot of things about the place once he was away from it," Biddy mused.

"Oh come on Bid, it's not that bad." Bill frowned at his sister. Biddy pulled a mocking face at him and turned again to Joe.

"Long way to come just for a look," she said.

"I did think, too, of visiting Sam's family," he said defensively.

"Why?" said Biddy insolently.

Joe was taken aback. He began to stutter a reply when Biddy cut in again.

"I mean, it's years ago, isn't it, and it's not as if we need to know any secrets or anything. We know that he died of the 'flu after the war was finished and that he's buried in some cemetery in London somewhere and that we'll never see him again."

Mrs. Curtis raised a hand in distress and said weakly "Bridget, Bridget."

"Quiet Biddy," said Bill, "you're upsetting Mum."

Joe fervently wished himself somewhere else. Biddy's antagonism was wounding and totally unexpected. Sam's description of his family had been one of gentle and fond memories—his twin siblings a pair of joyous frolicking puppies, his mother warm, loving and happy in this wonderful place called Kalgoorlie bathed in sunshine and humming with industry.

And here he was, sitting in front of an unreadable young man and a very rude young woman and their sad, tired, foreign mother. He reflected that he'd only been in the town for a day or so, and that would probably be a disappointment too in the long run. He wished he hadn't bothered to come, but then he immediately felt as if he was standing on a clifftop with nothing in front of him but space and air and emptiness. He'd set so much store by this visit. He hadn't thought of anything beyond being here, meeting Sam's family and seeing Kalgoorlie through Sam's eyes. He blinked quickly, just in case he had tears in his eyes.

"Joe, where do you stay?" asked Sam's mother, and before Joe could answer she said "You should stay with us, here, you stay here Joe."

"Oh no, no, that's not necessary, not at all," blurted Joe in embarrassment at the thought of sharing the house with these total strangers.

"Yes, yes, you share Bill's room, is not any bother, we like you to visit with us and let us know you. Sam said much about you in his letters and he told us that your family look after him in your house, so we will do same for you here in Kalgoorlie. It is right thing to do."

"That's unless you snore," said Bill. It could have been Sam speaking.

It took Joe a moment to acknowledge that this was a joke and it got tied up with his attempt to extricate himself from the obligation of staying with the family.

In this he failed miserably and found himself promising to return with his bags the next day. Bill amiably accompanied him halfway back to the hotel to make sure he didn't get lost.

As they crunched dustily down the street, Joe looked sideways at Bill and said "You're very much like your big brother, you know. Looks, way you speak, everything."

"I was too young to really remember him except as a sort of picture in my mind of someone big and grown-up and a few little bits of stuff that I remember him doing. Shaving, polishing his boots on the back verandah. Biddy and I were only six or so when he went away."

"Sam used to talk about you two, though."

"Yeah, s'pose he would've. Long way from home he was. And is."

Bill slewed a long glance at Joe and said "Why'd you come all this way, mate? Seems a slog for you just to meet the family, all this way."

Joe searched for a responsible reply, one that would make sense.

"Well," he began, and stopped.

"Well," he began again. "Well, I s'pose I always meant to visit with Sam, even though we never got to plan it definitely. It was always in the air, me visiting so Sam could show me round. He talked about "Kal" all the damned time and I wanted to see the place."

"Took you a long time to get here."

"Yes, you're right. There were some things that sort of got in the way."

"You married?"

"Why … why do you ask?"

"Lot of blokes come to Kal to get away from wives and stuff. Most of them think they can still make their fortunes here, bloody fools."

"I'm not married," said Joe.

81

*Four years later.
September 1932*

Joe found it moderately surprising that he had taken to life in Kalgoorlie—after a bit of settling in—almost like a duck to water, as his mother might have said. Not that it was a suitable comparison, ducks and water both being in short supply in the town. Rainfall here was minimal and avidly collected, waste water always utilised on the pitiful plant or two that some determined townspeople nurtured and the main source of the life-giving liquid was a pipeline, a 30-inch diameter, 330 mile long engineering marvel of a pipeline that sucked water from Perth to deliver to the thirsty and thankful goldfields.

He hadn't had many ideas about the place, to be sure, no expectations. Before he got to Kal he'd really always imagined Sam being with him to flesh out the places he talked about, the people, the work ... but he'd had to find those out for himself although he often felt that Sam was beside him. But he'd had to find his own feet and he'd surely benefited from *that* journey, even if four Kalgoorlie years had sped by without him noticing their passing. Good and bad experiences along the way, surprises. Such a mixture of people—Italians, Germans, Greeks, Dutchmen, Slavs as well as English, Welsh, Scots, Irish, so that nationality should have had little meaning. But, usually after a few drinks, arguments seemed to erupt with monotonous regularity and sides were quickly taken along national lines; men who'd been working amicably side by side that very day were likely to be in a bruising street-fight.

One of these seemed to be coming to a boil by the bar. Joe was adept at keeping out of such fights and quickly sidestepped as it was expertly kicked out of the pub by the landlord and continued as a thudding melee in the dusty street.

He plodded homewards, just drunk enough to be in maudlin mood. The September moon was full and bright in the cloudless sky, the stars so numerous they looked like arrested snowflakes. He lifted his face and could feel them cold on his eyelids and lips and wondered if he would ever feel snowflakes in reality again. His mind slewed to Oak Tree Place and a world that was so far away that it had taken on a dreamy quality. But he could still feel the cobbles under his feet, uneven and slick with rain, still smell the pub's unmistakable fug, hear the creak in the stairs to his bedroom. Drifting memories of his parents were fond but blurred and were dredged from the innocent times of his early childhood. His adult years in Oak Tree Place suddenly wrenched at his gut with their brief false contentment and breathtakingly spiteful resolution. It was all gone, gone, gone, the imagined happiness with Lydia, the fact of little Harry—and Ruth.

He swerved into another hotel, suddenly needing one last drink. Flopping into a corner seat, his thoughts would not be drowned by the beer. All too familiar, they played again like a reel of film.

As from a height, he looked down on his life. Yet again he assured himself that he had demonstrated well enough that he was really and truly cured of Lydia and the pathetic fantasy that he had built around her, feeling only embarrassment that he could have been duped so easily and contempt for her selfish manipulation. Dear blameless little Harry was harder to dismiss and Ruth was still an open wound.

Ruth would be seventeen in November. Joe could picture her growing into womanhood, slender, dark, agile and laughing. When he thought of her she was always laughing. He had stopped writing to her years ago when he learned that addressing letters to her at the Oak Tree was pointless and that Ruth could not have been receiving them. But surely she would not have just stopped writing to him? He told himself that this could not be so but still the worm of doubt was there. Perhaps Alice and Charlie had managed to poison her mind against him. With their access to her, and she such an innocent, it might not have been that difficult.

The pointlessness of travelling back to England to try to find the three of them had been explored and glumly acknowledged. He had fruitlessly written to Lily Craggs at the Oak Tree in an effort to trace her until he learned of the sale of the Oak Tree. A desperate letter to old Mrs. Keily down the road from the Oak Tree had been returned, after several months, marked "Deceased". Stilted letters to several acquaintances and old school friends had eventually provided the information that Lily had sold up at the Oak Tree and gone to live on the south coast somewhere, no one was quite sure where. Neither Charlie, Alice nor Ruth had been seen at the Oak Tree.

Joe dreamed though. He pictured Ruth walking towards him, skipping with excitement at their reunion, still the same lithe laughing twelve-year-old who'd waved so excitedly through the clouds of dust that the departing cart had created five years ago. The imagined reunion was always at the Group House because it was there that he'd seen her last; if she hadn't left they'd still both be there.

Or would they? He never had the money to support her at school in Bunbury, even if she did get a scholarship but that too-clever Helen Anderson might have found some way to organise it, who knew? But face it Joe, if Ruth was forced to stay on the Group, much as she had loved it then, her future was severely limited. Grow up and marry a Grouper or a Grouper's son ... It wasn't a bad life or wouldn't be once the farms were properly established and the cows were all producing. Not bad at all. His fancies swerved back to the Group House. He could see Ruth as the young woman she must have now become, standing there on the verandah waiting for him. The picture was so vivid that it was a physical jolt to bring himself back to his seat in the Kalgoorlie pub. He sat up from his slumped position and blinked.

He'd had a couple of letters from Stephen and a really lovely one from Ida that had made him very nostalgic for the Group for a while. He really should get round to replying one of these days. And perhaps he should check at the Post Office to see if he'd received any letters lately.

A little blearily he raised his eyes to take in his surroundings and his drinking companions. The pub was similar to most others in the town, geared for drinking hard and fast and although the hotel building itself was solid, ornate and quite elegant, the public bar was fairly desolate. Most of the customers clustered noisily round the bar and Joe was one of only two men sitting in the room. His counterpart was seated in the other corner, slumped in his chair morosely regarding his empty glass, his demeanour and his worn and dirty clothes suggesting strongly that he lacked the means to buy himself another. Joe was about to leave when he checked himself and walked over to the man and offered to buy him a beer. He didn't know why he did it but there was something about the man that reminded him—of home, was that it, or was it himself … ? As he came back from the bar with the two dripping middies and the man looked up at him, it struck him like a blow.

"Bloody hell, you're that Martin Addison bastard."

Joe sharply turned away, reeling from the shock of seeing the man yet again—London, Fremantle, and now Kalgoorlie. Damnation, was he attached to him by a string?

A cracked little voice behind him said "Wait, stop!"

It was probably because of the two beers he held and indecision about what to do with them that made him pause, but he swung round to Martin Addison again and slammed the glasses on the table in front of him, further slopping the contents.

"Have them both, you look as if you could use them, *mate*" he said, curling his lip on the last word sarcastically.

He was about to turn away again when Martin Addison looked up at him and Joe's furious gaze faltered. The bright blue eyes were bloodshot and puffy, the tan was still there but it was not the healthy glow that looked so glamorous in the pub by the clock tower; this tan was parched, wrinkled and dirty. As Joe hesitated, he was horrified to see tears welling in the man's eyes.

Embarrassed, he flopped down in the chair opposite, at the same time irritated at himself for staying.

"Looks as if life's not too clever at the moment, Mr. Addison-Wilson-whatever," he snapped. "Run out of gold mines?"

Martin Addison wiped his sleeve across his eyes and reached for the first beer, draining it in a few gulps. His hand shook as be replaced the glass on the table.

"What's your name?" he asked in the same cracked voice.

"No I wouldn't expect you to remember my name with all the people you have met and fleeced over time," said Joe, "but it's Joe. Joe Barlow."

"Where … ?"

Joe snorted. "Would you believe, two places, *two* places I've come up against you before. London and Fre—"

"Fremantle!" Martin Addison's head shot up. "You were at the Freemasons' in Fremantle!"

"And afterwards" said Joe.

"You had me nabbed and I never knew why. Didn't remember anything about meeting you in London. But I obviously did." This was added with a sage nod of the head, nodding that continued while Joe regarded the man contemptuously.

"What happened to you?" Joe asked in spite of himself.

"Nothing. Absolutely nothing at the time. You never came back to make a statement and they couldn't find you so they had to let me go."

"Oh." Joe had difficulty remembering what made him let the matter slide. Then he suddenly recalled the brutal sounds of the arrest and Martin Addison's ashen face and wide eyes and the certainty that he didn't want to have anything further to do with that sort of anguish, deserved or not.

"But I pushed off from Fremantle, of course. Came to Kal, thought it was far enough away, did some bits and pieces of work around the place, made some money, lost some money and then … "

"Then what?"

"My guts got crook."

Martin Addison's easy use of the Australianisms of speech were just as easily translated by Joe.

"How crook?"

"Pretty crook." Martin looked into his beer for a few moments before adding "Pretty *bloody* crook, actually." He leaned forward on his bentwood chair and pulled his shoulders back, a pitiful attempt to deny what he'd just intimated.

Joe cursed himself for yielding to the urge to stop at the table. He couldn't leave on that note, could he? Oh bugger. After due pause he asked with an obvious lack of warmth whether he could be of any help, transparently hoping to be refused. The irony of Joe offering help to this man was not lost on either of them. Martin Addison smiled wryly.

"Another beer would go down well."

"There's another one there."

"It's yours."

"You're welcome to it."

With that beer's rapid dispatch, Joe went to the bar and ordered two more but as he turned back into the room Martin Addison was lurching out the door into the street. Abandoning the glasses on a nearby table, Joe followed him to find him leaning on a verandah post and vomiting helplessly into the gutter.

In a town like Kalgoorlie this was not an unusual sight and it was one that Joe had seen a hundred times and even been the subject once or twice. But as he leaned against the pub wall and watched the man finally straighten up and shakily wipe his mouth with a grubby handkerchief he compared this wreck with the smooth and confident Martin Addison of the Prince of Wales pub all those years ago, and the expansive Dick Wilson of Fremantle. A sense of justice finally prevailing was quickly overtaken by something that might have been pity. It was one thing to wish for punishment in the abstract but very different when you were facing it in the flesh. It was this very same pity that had spared this man in Fremantle. Still reluctantly, Joe supported a limp Martin Addison and they stumbled together up the street.

"Where d'you live?" he asked.

"Where ever I can find somewhere to sleep."

Martin Addison's groan alarmed Joe more than the response. The man was very ill, not just drunk, and he had obviously reached rock-bottom. Nothing for it then. Oh damn and blast it, how he wished he'd never stopped in at that pub.

82

The same evening

Kalgoorlie's inland situation meant that the nights were invariably cool, but Joe was sweating freely by the time he arrived at the Curtis' corrugated iron house in the landscape of scattered dwellings that was one of the town's suburban dormitories.

Martin Addison's real name appeared to be George Bowler, if that could be believed, but given the state of the man in question Joe thought the truth was more than likely coming out.

Newly-named George had tried to disentangle himself from Joe's support at various stages of their walk from the edge of town, but each time his feet seemed unable to point him in a forward direction and he fell back again on to Joe's less-than-eager embrace.

It took some time to get to the house but not much conversation took place. George's speech was slurred and his words garbled but he punctuated the journey with thanks to Joe at regular intervals.

"Don't thank me, Georgie, I don't know what I'm going to do with you yet," said Joe through gritted teeth.

"But I do thank you. You're a good man and no one can say different."

"Huh."

"Not many good men in this world, Joe."

This time the silence prevailed until Joe pushed open the door of the little house. Light from a kerosene lamp spilled from the kitchen and Bridget, who'd been sitting at the table, jumped up in alarm as Joe slung George from his shoulder into a chair across from her.

"What in the name of … "

"We've got a visitor I think," said Joe

"Hello," said George hollowly.

"Who on earth is he? Where did he come from? What's he doing here? What are you going to do with him?" Bridget backed off from the table in alarm and confusion.

"Calm down Bid, he just needs a bit of rest," said Joe placatingly.

"Why, who is he?"

"A sort of old friend," said Joe unconvincingly, as George looked up at Joe with adoring eyes.

"Yes, an old friend," he said with a choke in his voice that developed into a sob.

Joe patted him briskly on the back as Bridget stood uneasily by the stove.

"There's not enough for four," she said distractedly.

"I'm sure there is, the way you cook," said Joe with a smile.

Bridget turned and added another plate, knife and fork to the table with undisguised distaste and began to ladle out the steaming ragout. She put some on a plate and covered it for Bill when he came in.

"This'll do you good, George, Bridget's a great cook, her Mum was Italian—you've never tasted anything like her cooking."

George slumped in his chair. "Just some water," he said wanly, "please."

Bridget began to bristle until Joe quickly interceded.

"He's not well, Bridge, upset stomach."

"Oh." Bridget was mollified and they all proceeded to eat. Joe talked too much but evaded Bridget's pointed questions, too edgy to explain and not sure that he could. He was still not certain what made him pick up this sad piece of ex-manhood and bring him home. What on earth was he going to do with him anyway? Decisions did not come easily to Joe, he knew this but the knowledge of this deficiency didn't make him any more able to make them.

"What?" He was brought back from his reverie by Bridget. "What did you say?"

"I said I expect that friend George is staying the night?"

George was swaying in his chair, whether from drink, weariness or his illness Joe didn't know. Staying the night was inevitable.

Joe and Bridget made him up a bed on the miner's couch in the front room and sat across from each other in the kitchen again drinking tea, Bridget full of questions. They spoke in low voices.

"He was a friend of a friend back home and I met him once or twice," Joe said evasively. "And I just bumped into him in the pub tonight after work."

"He's not well."

"No, looks a bit sick."

"Expect he'll be better tomorrow?"

"Mmmm, yes, probably."

"Kind of you to bring him back here." Bridget's prickliness suddenly dissolved and she looked across the table with a smile. "I didn't know you were a good Samaritan inside. You are a quiet one, aren't you?"

"Not sure about that. But I could hardly leave him."

"It's good that you brought him. What does he do for work?"

Joe almost smiled. "Not sure," he said lightly, "something in one of the mines I think. But he might be out of work right now, I don't know."

"What a surprise!" said Bridget ironically. "A grimy miner in Kalgoorlie!"

"There are some other occupations. Look at me. A grimy market gardener and part-time shopkeeper instead."

"Mmmm," murmured Bridget vacantly as she leaned back in her chair to check on George.

83

Kalgoorlie

Although they came from different countries, the Italian, German, Dalmatian, Croatian and other women of Kalgoorlie applied a universal strictness that Joe found almost quaint. Their minimal housing, often just of corrugated iron like his own, was immaculate and any small touch to soften the grim edge was eagerly sought. Joe was reminded strongly of the days in the humpies before the Group houses were built, and the lengths to which those women had gone to keep up standards. That scrubbed front step might not be there in fact, but it still existed symbolically. He had even seen a crocheted antimacassar on the back of a deck chair.

Morally—here *and* there—the situation was similar and it was only Bill's presence in the house that permitted Joe to live in such close proximity to Bridget. If only the vigilant watchers knew how far from intimate was his connection with her! While they enjoyed an easy relationship for most of the time, Joe was intimidated by her assertiveness and her quick temper, not to mention her string of burly miner boyfriends. The disproportionate balance of males and females in the town made for a busy social life for the young women there and Bridget gaily took advantage of the situation. She made no secret of the fact that she was "off out of here" when the mood finally took her and her circumstances allowed. These circumstances were never articulated and whether it would ever happen was a moot point. Joe had had enough time to observe the boyfriend roundabout to make him realise that Biddy was having a great time playing the field.

And good luck to her. He himself had been assessed in the early days as something a bit exotic and with possibilities, but he'd obviously been found wanting, which suited him well even if it did rankle a bit to be found so, but that was just his pride.

Joe had been drawn into the market garden and shop business simply through being in Kalgoorlie at the home of Sam's family, and without a job. Sam's mother had not so much embraced him as taken him by the scruff of the neck and dragged him into the family circle. The family's business had been set up by Sam's father when he lived and comprised a small market garden and a shop in Hannan Street to sell their produce and that of a few other market gardeners. The town's existence owed itself to gold mining and most of the employment opportunities were in that field, a field that Joe would never think of considering, so the work in the market garden and sometimes in the shop had the advantage of being above-ground and would do for the time being anyway, Joe had thought.

His presence in the business suddenly allowed Bill to go off and work at Hannan's, the most developed mine in the area with a 600-foot deep shaft, the thought of which made Joe's stomach churn. Bill laughed at his phobia and took him to see his workplace from above-ground but even the open-cut pits on each side, worked out and now with walls collapsing, made Joe very uneasy. Green-grocery suited him fine. But Bill had been hankering to work as a miner for years and gleefully quit the business for the more manly and more lucrative employment. He was seen less and less around the community as he spent his leisure hours with his hard-drinking mining mates. He rolled home to a disapproving mother and sister to eat and to share the small second bedroom with Joe.

Market gardening was demanding work and it was even more so in Kalgoorlie. Water, that scarce commodity, was rationed and had to be used sparingly. Natural rainfall was sparse, except for the chance in late summer that there may be a cyclone up north whose edges dumped a deluge on the town, turning the streets into rivers for a day or two before they resumed their normal dustiness as if the rain had never happened. Kalgoorlie's water pipeline from Perth was literally life-saving for the population and the vegetables as well.

The town's desert location meant hot days and cold nights, with frosts that could destroy a crop of valuable early tomatoes in one night unless the plants were covered and protected—and uncovered next morning. Soil preparation was by horse and plough—very hot, hard work. Joe often compared his life with the similarities, yet the differences, from the one he had so precipitously left in Margaret River and wondered often how his friends were faring.

How much land had been cleared now, had they all stuck it out, had it got any easier and were they flourishing? The early letters from the group had dwindled to nothing over time, due, Joe ruefully admitted, to his non-answering. Last communication he'd undertaken was during his first year or so in Kal. Lord, that was four years ago. Len and Ida probably had a brood of children by now, Michael and Ellen too, perhaps. He did wonder what Stephen might have done. Had he stayed? Had he left? Maybe they'd all left! Suddenly it was imperative that he should know, that he not lose contact. He resolved to write to Stephen—write to everybody—that night. He didn't, but the idea of doing it remained to nag him.

There was a division of labour, him on the land and Bridget in the shop, that he and Bridget had fallen into after the death of Mrs. Curtis. Maria Curtis died suddenly and without fuss one day while working in the market garden, her death as modest and unremarkable as her life, except to her family whose lives changed forever without the moral and social conventions that she had enforced. Her authority had been both absolute and loving and Bridget and Bill were lost without it. Joe was glad to have been there to help them through and gladly took on the extra duties and responsibilities that Mrs. Curtis' absence created. Actually, he was pleased to observe—to himself—that the business was actually growing a little under his stewardship. The addition of George in the shop was a good thing.

The morning after Joe had brought him home George had asked diffidently if he might rest there a little before leaving. He was still there that evening and the following day he had chopped some wood and lit the fire and was chatting with Bridget when Joe came home from the shop. Three days later he asked, again with diffidence, whether he might board with Joe if he could get a job and pay his way. Bridget had answered before Joe could say anything and assured him that that would be an ideal arrangement. So George became a fixture, sleeping each night on the miners' couch. Then he had sort of floated into helping in the shop.

His cadaverous pallor had cautiously bloomed into something resembling the man Joe knew from London and Fremantle. He remained lean but not the bloodless scarecrow Joe had found in the pub's bar; Joe actually began to enjoy his company. As George had become strong enough, Joe employed him in the market garden but more often in the shop, where he was in fact better suited—his easy chat with the customers was actually good for business. It seemed that life and work with Joe had slowed the progress of his physical ills but although Joe was careful not to overtax him by working him full-time, he sometimes found him in bed in the late afternoon "getting himself back" as he put it, as Biddy prepared their evening meal in the kitchen.

It was only when Joe came in early one afternoon and saw George scuttle out of Biddy's bedroom and a flushed and flustered Biddy come out some minutes later that Joe realised what had probably been happening for some time when he thought about it.

None of his business really, he tried to tell himself, but of course it was. He was responsible for introducing George to the household and he had covered up the man's criminal past as well. Bridget was vulnerable to George's stories and clever repartee; he should have noticed how raptly she had listened. Oh, he did now! George represented to Bridget exactly what she had been looking for—someone to show her the world beyond Kalgoorlie. Was George taking advantage of her innocence? But then, how innocent was Bridget? How would Joe know? And what did they plan to do, if anything? If they didn't plan to do anything, it wasn't any of his business, was it?

He decided to think about it. After all, George seemed to be reformed character, he told himself.

Joe was a paid employee in the market garden and shop as was George. Bridget and Bill were joint owners and that was fine by Joe who had no aspiration to anything more. But occasional dark thoughts began to pervade; what-ifs danced across his vision. Bill was less and less attendant at the house and had little part in day-to-day business. With his increasing stamina, George and Biddy could easily run the whole operation even if not quite as efficiently as it was being run now—quite acceptably though. He really was quite redundant, and feeling more and more irrelevant each evening as he coolly watched the relationship between the two lovebirds develop. He wondered if he was jealous but put the thought aside as unworthy.

There is, he reflected, little that's more boring than watching other people fall in love.

84

Four months later.
January 1933

He had been meaning to write, really he had. But because he hadn't done so, he hadn't checked at the Post Office for mail for himself either.

On the other hand, George presented himself there regularly and more than once had received mail that Joe did wonder about, but only fleetingly.

It was a benign January evening when George mentioned to Joe that he'd noticed a couple of letters addressed to him while the young man at the Post Office had been looking through the Bs for letters for George. He had offered to deliver them to Joe, but that was against the rules and Joe would have to collect them himself.

The thought of hearing news from the Group made Joe's step light with anticipation as he strode to the Post Office the next afternoon and collected two letters when the mail was checked. One was a bulky envelope addressed in Stephen's clear handwriting and the other letter was contained in a stiff and expensive-looking envelope addressed in a hand that he recognised immediately with a lurch of the stomach. He had thought that he'd treat himself to a beer while he read his mail, but when he examined the two different envelopes he changed his mind and squatted unsteadily against a shopfront to tear them open and devour the contents with increasing and obvious anxiety.

He stumbled to his feet, stuffing the letters into his pocket. He ran towards the shop, then stopped and ran instead towards the railway station. He stopped again and ran raggedly homewards, reaching the empty house breathless and panting. Dragging his suitcase from under the bed he hurled clothes and belongings into it with abandon. Bridget came in from her morning's work and paused in the doorway of the bedroom.

"What on earth are you doing, Joe?"

"Have to go. Have to go," he babbled without stopping his frantic packing.

"Go where, why?"

"Don't know, don't know, but I have to."

"You have to go but you don't know where or why?" Bridget's inclination to laugh at such a preposterous statement was tempered by Joe's obvious anguish. She moved into the room and laid her hand on Joe's arm.

"Stop it Joe, stop it. You can't just leave. This is not like you. You've got to tell me why you're like this and maybe I can help. What's happened? Tell me!"

Joe paused and regarded Bridget with wild eyes. Then suddenly he crumpled and sat heavily on the edge of the bed. "Oh Biddy," he said.

Bridget crouched in front of him and took his hands in hers. "Tell me."

"Before—"began Joe. "before I came to Kal, there was a lot … "

Bridget remained silent, folded her legs underneath her and waited.

Haltingly, Joe started. He started with the Group but doubled back to the war and then Alice's presence in Oak Tree Place. His parents, Ruth, Lydia, Mrs Craggs, Charlie, Stephen, Lily, Ellen, Michael, Len and Ida. Then again, bitterly, Charlie and Alice and Ruth.

"Then today I got some letters from the Post Office. You should read them while I finish packing and you'll see why I have to go. Have to do something."

"Joe, I'll read the letters and try to sort out all that you've told me, but slow down, you can't leave until tomorrow morning's train anyway. Come and have a cup of tea and calm down now."

Suddenly docile, Joe trailed into the kitchen behind her. He sat with his hands clamped around the enamel mug of tea and tried to stop trembling. Bridget smoothed out the crumpled pages and read intently. She raised her head once and observed that Stephen seemed like a nice man. Joe agreed vacantly.

"Well. So what are you going to do?" she said finally as she finished reading and pulled the flimsy pages into a pile.

"Have to go to her, have to find her. Have to go."

"I gathered that," said Bridget dryly, "but these letters were all written months ago and you can't even be sure where Ruth is right now let alone what her situation is. It certainly sounds as if she needs some help but you can't go charging around the countryside unless you have some idea of who is where and when and what they actually need."

George's entry went almost unnoticed as he came into the kitchen with an arm full of slightly-wilted vegetables from the shop.

"What's up?" he asked in surprise when he saw the intensity of the huddle at the table.

"We-ell," said Bridget "I think it's like this. You'd better sit down, it's a long story."

She sketched the story that Joe had just recounted to her, with Joe interjecting occasionally to correct or embellish, looking at the same time like someone hearing the story for the first time, but when Bridget came to the matter of the recent letters, he took over.

"Got this letter from Stephen … "

"Stephen being?" asked George with a bemused look.

"My neighbour. My friend. In Margaret River."

George nodded. "Oh yeah, go on."

"And a letter from Ruth."

"Ruth? Long-lost Ruth?" George's eyes widened. "That's good, isn't it?"

"Yes of course but … and a letter from Lydia as well."

"Lydia?" asked George, "Remind me?"

"Wife" said Bridget brusquely.

"Oh. Which should I read first?" asked George. "Assuming I'm allowed."

"Ruth's," said Bridget and Joe in unison.

Dear Uncle Stephen," began George, *"I'm writing to you because Joe doesn't write to me any more. I don't know why he stopped writing but I hope it wasn't something I did or said because, as I hope you know, I would never, ever want to hurt or displease him in any way. But I've said that before and I'm sorry to bother you with it all, but I really don't have any other real friends I just hope that you can help me now.*

Joe groaned out loud and gouged his fingers through his hair. "How could she think … ?" George continued.

But you will be wondering what the matter is and I have to tell you. The first thing that happened was that Charlie found out that the solicitor who was managing Mrs. Craggs' estate stole and lost all of her money, along with money of other people as well. So I was no longer the lucky little rich girl and Charlie and Alice suddenly had no money either.

The news of this happening made Charlie so angry. I have never seen anyone so angry. He dragged all of Alice's clothes out of the cupboards into the back garden and tried to burn them – he even got her shoes and put them on top of the pile and her hats and her fur coat on top of them, shouting all the time so loudly that the neighbours came out to see. He was yelling that Alice had wasted all their money and that she was the cause of it all, which was silly because it was the solicitor who was the bad person and I know that because the true story was in the newspaper and I read it. But he also yelled that I was an opportunist and that was a cruel and wrong thing to say too.

Alice was trying to calm him down and hanging on to him to stop him from throwing more things on to the pile to burn, but he roared and shook her off and pushed her so that she fell and hit her head on a rock on the edge of the garden path.

Oh Uncle Stephen I was so frightened. Alice's eyes were closed and her face was white and she was bleeding all over the path and

Charlie just looked at her, puffing like a train and with his eyes and face all red. Then he made me even more frightened when he stood and yelled and yelled at the sky. Then he fell down on the ground and the neighbours came in from both sides and the police came and took Charlie away and the ambulance came and took Alice away but they covered her up so I knew she was dead even though Mr. and Mrs. Foxholm were very kind to me and took me next door and gave me cocoa and said they were sure she'd be alright.

Oh dear, Uncle Stephen, I'm telling you all this because I so need you to understand my situation. Goodness I do miss you all so.

"Poor little lass," said George with surprising tenderness.

"Yes, poor thing," said Bridget.

George took a breath and resumed reading.

I could tell that after a little while Mr. and Mrs. Foxholm were rather uncomfortable having me in their house with all the trouble I'd been involved in so I went back to our house try to sleep and decide what to do. I was afraid that the police or someone would come back and take me—somewhere—I didn't know where but I couldn't be sure they'd leave me alone.

I thought I should get away but I couldn't think where. I thought of some of my school friends but I wasn't sure what their parents would think. Oh I did want Joe so much! I thought of Oak Tree Place but there's no one living there any more that we know.

Then I remembered a newspaper clipping that I'd kept. I had been surprised to see a photograph in the paper of the lady that Joe and I had come to call "Bloody Lydia" and you might already know this because I told Joe in a letter some time ago. Her name is Lady Curthoys now and she was attending a charity luncheon with her husband—who is apparently a member of Parliament—and his father Lord Burnside.

This is turning into a very long story, so I'll get to the point as quickly as I can. I found Lydia's address in the telephone directory, took a deep breath and knocked at the door. A long, very long, time after this I had told my story to Lydia and to her husband that evening and I was tucked up in bed in their house. I have had to change my opinion of Lydia you'll be surprised to learn, she's a lot different from the Lydia we all knew in Oak Tree Place. She's very grand of course but a lot ... calmer ... than Oak Tree Place Lydia. That being said, she was very keen to hear what everyone was doing and the story of Alice and Charlie being my mother and father made her laugh with disbelief. And some delight, I think.

Of course the biggest thing was what had just happened to Alice and to Charlie and it was only when I was telling Lydia about it that it really started to become real to me and I realised that I'd never see Alice again. Charlie either, probably. My new parents were gone, just like my old ones, Joe wasn't my brother and never had been so I had no one, no relations in the world. I felt so alone and I'm afraid that I cried rather a lot in the first few days. I eventually stopped crying but I still felt terribly lonely.

The horrible facts of what Charlie had done were in the newspapers the next day and also the fact that the police were seeking "the couple's daughter" who had disappeared. This is where the lovely Marcus got involved. (He is a very nice man). He dealt with the police and calmed everything down. He was rather curious about how Lydia knew me, let alone the other people of Oak Tree Place, but Lydia told him that she lived nearby when she was young and I thought it a good idea to keep quiet. He seems to be very fond of Lydia and rather indulgent and I think she takes advantage a bit. But then, she always did, rather, didn't she?

Poor Uncle Stephen, you're getting this long letter because I hardly know how to stop babbling. But I will, and just ask that you please speak to Joe and tell him about everything and ask him to please please write to me? If he's no longer on the Group, could you please tell me, and if possible, also tell me where I might find him to write to? Lydia and Marcus say that I can stay with them for as long as I need to, but that obviously doesn't mean "forever" even if I wanted to, so I do need to make some plans and I think you know what I'd really like to do and where I would like to be.

There was a small silence as George finished reading, a silence punctuated with small groans of anguish from Joe.

"Other letters?" asked George.

Wordlessly Bridget pushed another letter towards him.

"Who's this from?"

"Lydia. His wife." Bridget enjoyed the impact this had and smiled. "Or perhaps not … "

"Not from his wife?" George was bemused.

"No, perhaps Lydia is Joe's *ex*-wife, not his wife. They *may be* divorced, Joe's not sure."

"Uh," George shook his head in bewilderment but began to read the letter. This time he didn't read aloud and when he had finished he pushed his chair back and widened his eyes. "Well," he said. "Well. You're a deep one my lad, aren't you? More to you than meets the eye, isn't there?"

"And I'm sure there's more than you've told me, too, eh Joe?" Bridget patted Joe's arm. "But this Lydia is a hard one, eh?"

"Lydia knows what she wants and then goes about getting it," said Joe dolefully, "always has. And it does appear that she's got pretty much what she was aiming for when she left me."

"Story for another day perhaps Joe," said Bridget briskly. "Your Lydia is married to a Lord who seems to be as rich as anything so I'd say, among other things, that you and she are definitely divorced, wouldn't you? But that's not the subject at the moment."

"So," said George pulling the letter back towards him, "she seems to have come up trumps taking Ruth in and looking after her."

"Yes," said Joe, "I have to be thankful for that." He shook his head rapidly. "But this letter—these letters—are weeks, no, months old. While I've been messing around here, Ruth's been waiting to hear from me, Stephen's been waiting to hear from me, even Bloody Lydia's been waiting to hear from me!"

The unexpected swearing caused both Bridget and George to look up in surprise.

"That's Ruth's and my private name for Lydia," he said a little vacantly, "but I suppose I'd better think again now that she's turning into a guardian angel. Against all odds," he added.

Joe pushed back his chair and began to pace the room but was defeated by the room's size and the furniture in it. He stumbled and sat down again.

"I think the first thing I need to do is go back to Margaret River," he said with conviction. "I have to go back."

"The first thing you have to do, my lad," said Bridget firmly, is write some letters. You need to find out what's been happening since these letters were written and you need to let the people who wrote them know you've got them—finally."

"Yes, yes, of course." Joe ran his hands through his hair again. "But better, yes better than that, I'll send telegrams to them to let them know that my letters are coming."

"Good idea," said Bridget. So, first things first, off you go to the Post Office and do just that. Then come back and write your letters. Go on now, hurry up." She was speaking to the space Joe had left as he ran out the door.

85

Late January 1933

Two cables and a telegram sent, three letters in the process of being written the next day found Joe at the kitchen table, chewing the end of his pen and gazing distractedly at the ceiling as George came hesitantly into the room.

"Got a moment, Joe?"

"Oh yes. Glad of a break from wondering what the hell to write," said Joe, putting down his pen.

"Joe, I just wanted to say … " began George. "I just wanted to say that you know better than anyone what sort of man I've been in the past."

Joe didn't respond, and George went on, still hesitant.

"I want you to know though, that I have seen my life for the worthless thing it was, and that's because you rescued me in the first place when I was so low and so sick, and Biddy, God bless her, rescued me for good. I will never ever go back to the life I used to lead, and I will never ever do anything to hurt or distress Biddy, I swear."

Joe regarded him levelly but still didn't speak.

"I just wanted you to know that Biddy will be in good hands when you leave. I promise. I know you might think that my word is not all that dependable, but I swear—*I swear*—that I will do everything I can to protect her and make her happy."

"Including …?" Joe asked with raised eyebrows.

"If she'll have me, yes," said George, colouring slightly under his Kalgoorlie tan.

"Well if you don't look after her, first you'll have Bill and his mates to contend with and then I will personally come back from wherever I happen to be and personally beat you to a pulp. Alright?" Joe was smiling and he held out his hand. "That's all good to hear, George, and I wish you all the best. She's a very special sort of girl."

Joe suddenly frowned as a thought struck him. "Just a question though George mate," he tried to sound casual, "I noticed that you get letters at the Post Office from time to time. If you don't mind me asking in my position of protector of Biddy's future, who are they from? Do you still have one of your old swindles going on?"

George looked uneasy, then outraged, then contrite, then a picture of honest rectitude. There was a significant period of silence before he spoke.

"I said I was a reformed man, Joe, and I am. But there were a few things still happening in a small sort of way when we met up and it took some time to cut them all off. Look, I was a crook and a spiv I freely admit to you and you know it anyway, but I am not that man any longer, really I'm not. I am too old for the game for one thing—" here he checked himself before adding in a rush "and I am really sorry for all those crooked schemes I pushed and it's all behind me now I promise. I've really come to love this place and the work in the shop. And Biddy."

Joe felt that he'd pushed as far as he could and dammit, the man seemed genuine enough. And Biddy wasn't exactly help-less, was she? She had chewed up and spat out bigger men than George and Joe had seen her do it. He could actually leave with an easy mind. That was a situation he could be grateful for; at least one thing was falling into place satisfactorily.

As George put the kettle on to make a cup of tea, Joe turned again to the difficulty of the letters he was writing. Trouble was that he still didn't know what was best to do. He could rejoice with Ruth on being in contact again and make a fairly shrewd guess as to how their letters never reached each other. He could plan for the future; ask Ruth what she wanted him to do. He could travel to England, she could come to Australia again … possibili-ties, possibilities, possibilities.

But if Ruth were to come to Australia, what would she do, what would he do? Where would they go? The same questions loomed: should he travel to England? Should he just hurry back to Margaret River? Circular thoughts. Leave that one for a while, Joe.

The letter to Lydia was much easier, all he had to do was thank her for her care of Ruth and apologise for the delay that had been caused by his lack of attention to incoming post. And send his good wishes to Harry who Lydia had assured him was well, apparently happy and at boarding school. He did wonder if Ruth had been able to see him. Something else to put in the unfinished letter. He was suddenly overwhelmed with a mental picture of him and Ruth sitting by the kitchen stove in the Group house, talking, talking, about everything in the world. She would tell him all about Harry—if she'd seen him—and all about the school she'd been to, where she'd lived, oh, and everything!

But the Group house was somebody else's now, of course. It would have been taken up by another eager family anxious to have a farm and as Ruth used to observe, the later-comers benefited from the hard work of the original settlers who felled the first overwhelming trees and fenced the first raw paddocks. Despite the rejection of the Group Settler lifestyle that saw him come to Kalgoorlie, he still felt a strong ownership of that little Group house and he almost grieved to think that the present owners wouldn't know the significance of the little oak tree behind the house that would now be on the way to becoming a significant landmark.

However, nostalgia—if that's what it was—was not achieving anything. What should he do?

Visitors were not common to the little house beside the market garden in Kalgoorlie, so the authoritative "rat-tat" on the door made Joe jump.

Opening the door, he was confronted by a dusty telegram boy waving something in his hand and asking if he was Mr. Barlow? Joe snatched the yellow envelope with a grunt and slammed the door, shuffling back to the kitchen as he tore it open.

It was from Stephen and it said briefly: Come back to Margaret River.

86

The next month.
Early February 1933

Joe felt a twinge of shame at the relief he felt at having at least one decision made for him. With renewed impetus he completed his letter to Ruth by asking her what she wanted to do and assuring her that he'd help her in any way he could. Not exactly masterly, but it would do until he could speak to Stephen. Stephen would know the best to do.

He packed with considerably more care than he had the day before, feeling calm and elated at the same time; he was at last taking some action.

The tedious train journey to Perth and then to Margaret River was spread over three days with a sleepless stay in Perth in the middle. He watched the countryside wax and wane like the phases of the moon, from the terracotta dust of the goldfields with their determined, sparse vegetation through featureless forests and glimpses of the sturdy water pipeline on which they had depended in Kalgoorlie. Then the train to Margaret River, initially quite domestic with a cleared farm or two spotting the forests then the reversal to the grey-green leaves of the eucalypts and their seemingly endless panorama of sameness. Stopping and starting, this part of the journey reminded Joe of the first time they'd made it, hot, confused, frightened ...

He dozed intermittently but was awake and eager as the train pulled into the Margaret River station. He stumbled out on to the platform, dragging his bag behind him, stopping for a minute to inhale the scent of the surrounding forest. He smiled— almost laughed—at the sheer joy of it. He mentally apologised to his surroundings for having been so dismissive of them when he left. More than dismissive, he remembered. Those thoughts were distant memories now as he ambled up to the main street,

455

noting with proprietary pleasure the small changes and several new buildings which had risen since his departure. More motor cars too, which was good because he hoped to get a lift out to Stephen's block, or at least some of the way, to take the edge of the long walk. At a pinch though, he could walk it if he had to. He had a bite to eat at Cosy Corner which was not on a corner and not cosy but the sandwich was good and the tea hot and strong. He asked about transport towards Group 19 but drew a blank and decided to walk after all.

Despite the increase of motor vehicles in the town, it was an old Group cart that picked him up and conveyed him to within half a mile of Stephen's house, the driver avid for details of his visit. Joe was evasive.

He was smiling broadly by the time he was within sight of the little Group house as he could see the enormous progress that Stephen had made in the past five years. The house looked settled into its environment, creepers softening its outline, and within the confines of a small fenced area a kitchen garden flourished. Milking shed and dairy stood at a distance from the house, looking neat and trim and the cleared and fenced paddocks stretched to a distant tree line. He dropped his bag and gazed in admiration.

The front door opened and Joe began to raise his hand in greeting when he saw that the figure framed there was not Stephen but a woman. A pregnant woman, what's more, who was as startled to see him as he was to see her. She recovered first.

"Joe?" she called, "Joe?" and began to run towards him. It was not until they were almost facing each other that Joe realised who this pregnant woman was.

Comically, he said "Miss Anderson?" then correcting himself quickly he said "Helen?" He barely registered her quick hug and her laughing rejoinder.

"Both, Joe, but there's been a bit of a change to my status since you left us, a change of status and of condition, as you can see!"

Joe's mind was working fast. "You and Stephen … ?"

"Yes, Joe, me and Stephen. And in due course I shall be Mrs. Dent. As well as Mr. Dent's child's mother!" She laughed happily. "Come on inside and we'll talk. Oh my goodness, how we'll talk! Stephen will be back soon—he's just gone over to help Will Halloran fix his cowshed roof, don't know exactly what the problem was, but Will's making heavy weather of a lot of things since he came so Stephen's trying to make things a bit easier for him. Oh my goodness I've just realised that of course the Hallorans are living in your house. There have been two families there since you left, the Hallorans are the second and quite frankly I don't know how long they're going to last, even with help. It's a bit strange really because it's a lovely block with the stream an everything but Stephen will be so glad to see you. Why didn't you let us know you were coming? You will stay of course, won't you?"

Helen Anderson was running out of puff but she managed to reiterate "Why didn't you let us know you were coming?"

"I don't really know. I think I was going to do it at some stage, but I just kept not doing it until I was here … "

"Oh Joe, you don't change, do you?" Helen was laughing indulgently. "There's such a lot to tell you but it must all wait until Stephen's here. Do you want to have a wash and get yourself settled?"

The smell of baking bread wafted through the house as Joe half-unpacked in a room that was obviously being prepared to house a baby but thankfully had a single bed against one wall. The bassinet gleamed with new paint and he carefully shifted it out of the way of his boots and his clumsiness.

"Joe," called Helen excitedly, "Stephen's coming. Sit at the table here and surprise him as he comes in!"

It seemed an age before Joe heard Stephen's voice, asking playfully what Helen was looking so pleased about.

And as he came in the door it was not surprise or shock that he registered, but sheer delight. "Joe!" he said, "Joe, Joe, Joe." A wringing handshake was not enough, they hugged roughly and both men were blinking hard as they sat at the table. Helen was conspicuously teary.

A cool bottle of home brew ("My own!" said Stephen proudly) was pulled out of the well and a second bottle quickly followed. Conversation began at the table, followed Stephen on to the back verandah while he washed, continued during a tour of the block that was conducted with pride on Stephen's part and admiration on Joe's, and back to the kitchen table. Joe was just finishing an account of his Kalgoorlie life.

"So I think I left it in good hands," he was saying. "Isn't it amazing how things sometimes work out?"

"Sounds as if you've rather enjoyed it all?" said Stephen with a smile.

"Yes, I did, rather. I think it was being able to see a result for the hard work—those vegetables grew quickly and were into the shop and sold and you had the money in your hand..." he paused apologetically, "I was too impatient when I was here. Couldn't see the forest for the trees."

"Literally!"

"And of course I also walked into a going concern—Biddy's dad and mum did the hard work in setting it up and everything."

"Rather like the latecomers to the Groups."

"Yes, you're right, exactly like that." Joe smiled and added "But there was still a lot of hard work to be done every day, I have to say in my defence."

"'Course there was, always is," said Stephen, stretching. "But can we turn to the subject that we've been avoiding since we started to talk? It's been hovering there … "

Joe's face betrayed his eagerness. Stephen was going to help him with the problem of what to do about Ruth. With Ruth. For Ruth.

"I just can't think what for the best, for her that is," Joe blurted. "I think of the possibilities and every one has its drawbacks as well as its good points. I need to write to her and I need to give her some sort of solution to her situation that can only be temporary, living with Lydia and her husband and everything but I can't think of what's best," he repeated.

"I did send a cable to say that I had seen her letter to you and that I'd be writing, but I've done nothing … "

"Well, Joe my lad, I think things have gone a little bit beyond letters and cables and going round in circles trying to think of a solution. Your Ruth is not so little any more and she has proven to be quite a resourceful young lady."

Helen had been at the stove stirring a saucepan and she broke in. "Oh Stephen my love, stop stringing it out and tell the poor boy!"

"Tell me what?" Joe looked from one face to the other.

"She's here. She's back in Margaret River."

87

The same evening

"Where?" Joe's gaze swerved around the room as if Ruth could be hiding somewhere. "Where?"

"She's safe and sound and in town, Joe, staying at the guest house."

"I have to see her!"

"Of course you do, of course you do, but you can't go anywhere tonight in the dark and you don't want to go haring off anyway until we've had a bit of a talk about things, so calm down, eh?"

"She's really here? Oh my God, I can't believe it Stephen, after all this time!"

"Yes, she's really here," said Stephen, patting Joe's hand paternally.

"How … ?"

"Quite easily in the end, mate. When Ruth wrote to me I sent her letter off to you and then we didn't hear a word from you so had no way of knowing whether you'd received the letter, whether you were still in Kalgoorlie, whether you were even alive … you weren't the best of correspondents, Joe my boy."

"I'm sorry."

"Water under the bridge. So, with no word from you, I replied to Ruth's letter and asked her what she wanted to do and said that we'd help if we could. Seems she'd decided in the meantime that she wanted to come back to Margaret River and had already booked her passage. Even when she learned that you'd left here and that you had apparently dropped off the edge of the earth she was still insistent on coming although I admit that I did try to dissuade her. Well," Stephen said defensively, "I didn't know what she would do out here, where she would live or anything at all really. It didn't seem a sensible thing for her to do.

"But apparently your Lydia's husband has been extremely helpful in smoothing the way and overcoming all sorts of problems that a rich and titled Lord-MP can overcome. I would imagine obtaining a passport without his intervention would have been well-nigh impossible, for instance. But that's for Ruth to tell you all about. Just know that your Lydia has at long last—somewhat accidentally and a bit sideways—come up trumps."

"Bloody Lydia," said Joe distantly.

"Mmmm. Ruth told me in her letter when she'd be arriving and I met her off the train here. You'll find her different Joe, from the girl who left five years ago."

"Different? How? I know she's older of course, and she's been through a great deal, but has it all changed her so much?"

"No, no, of course she's still a lovely girl, but she's grown up a lot. You will see changes, that's all."

"How early can we go into town?"

"As early as you like, but there's one more thing you need to know before you do. Two actually. The first is that Marcus—Lord Curthoys—also apparently managed to lever some money out of the mess that Charlie left behind and your Ruth has a small amount of capital."

Joe's head snapped up. "I'd forgotten about Charlie! What's happening to him? Do you know?"

"Not much. He's being held pending trial which is as much as any one seems to know. Not a bad thing for Ruth to be out of the country when all that happens and possibly that was another one of Lord Curthoys' manipulations. But the other thing you need to know is that Ruth has a friend with her.

"A friend? Who? Someone from England?"

"Yes and no. Someone she met on the boat coming out here."

"That's good that she had a friend. But why has she come here to Margaret River?"

"It's not a "she" actually Joe.

"Oh. Why are you looking like that? What's going on?"

"The young man's name is Rupert and he's romantically involved with Ruth. He wants to marry her."

"Bloody nonsense!" Joe banged the table with the flat of his hand. "Bloody nonsense! She's far too young to marry anyone, and certainly not some nobody she met on a boat!" He jumped up from his chair and went to the open door, clutching the door jamb speaking into the darkness.

"What does Ruth think about it?"

"She seems to be quite amenable to the idea, actually, Joe."

"Does that mean she wants to do it?" Joe asked belligerently.

"Umm, yes probably."

"Well she can't. She's too young and she would need her parents' permission. Now there's a minefield—poor little thing doesn't have any. Or at least any capable of giving her permission to marry. So there, she can't."

"I don't think that's an insurmountable obstacle, Joe." Stephen almost smiled, but thought better of it.

Helen had stayed quiet for most of the conversation since Joe had arrived, but she took his arm and guided him back to a chair at the table.

"Wait until you meet Ruth tomorrow, Joe, and meet Rupert too. See what you think. We found him a very nice young man, just so that you know. And you'll find," she added, "that Ruth has grown into a very sensible young woman and one who knows her own mind."

With difficulty Joe dragged himself back to his immediate sur-roundings as Helen and Stephen regarded him with sympathy.

"You look as if you need a decent sleep, my boy."

"Yes I do, I do. I haven't had a decent night's rest since I left Kal but hell, Stephen, I don't know if I'll be able to sleep, with the prospect of seeing her tomorrow. I can't believe it, really I can't. After all this time…"

But he slept like a felled log.

88

The next day

Nervous, oh so nervous. The steady tread of the horse pulling the cart was funereal compared to his heartbeat.

Joe had insisted that he didn't need Stephen to drive him, that he was perfectly capable of doing it himself. He was glad of the small concentration that this involved because his mind was skittering all over the place as he approached the edge of town.

For the life of him he couldn't imagine what Ruth might look like after five years of separation; his mind was determined to keep her twelve years old despite his efforts.

But then, when he saw her standing outside the guest house, he suddenly couldn't see the twelve-year-old at all and this real Ruth smoothly took her place.

She was beautiful, of course, laughing with delight and waving excitedly. She began to run towards the cart and her dress billowed and pressed in the breeze. Joe threw the reins down and jumped down to envelop her in an embrace that was so strong, and so strongly reciprocated that they stumbled and almost fell. Finally they drew apart and began, laughing, to observe each other at arm's length. Joe's eyes were bright with tears and Ruth regarded him fondly.

"Joey, Joey, Joey."

"Ruthie, Ruthie, Ruthie." He tried to make a joke of it.

"We have quite a lot of talking to do, don't you think?"

"Rather a lot, yes."

"Will we go back to Stephen's?"

"If you like."

"But can you come inside for a moment first, would you mind? There's someone I need you to meet."

Forewarned though he was, Joe's stomach did a little lurch and an immediate antipathy rose in him towards this fellow—no matter who he was—who he was about to meet and who wanted to marry Ruth. He most definitely didn't want to meet this person. But he had to, of course he had to. He composed his face to what he hoped was bland acceptance and followed Ruth into the empty lounge of the guest house. Ruth bustled a little self-consciously as she found a suitable chair for Joe and bade him wait a moment as she disappeared, appearing again almost immediately, followed by a slight, well-dressed young man.

"Joe, this is Rupert Hoghton, Rupert, this is Joe Barlow." Ruth looked on anxiously as howd'y'dos and handshakes were exchanged between the two. They all settled uneasily into chairs and there was a small and very awkward silence. Joe reluctantly concluded that, as the most senior person present, he should take the initiative. He cleared his throat.

"So, you met on the boat on the way out here?"

"Yes," chorused Ruth and Rupert in unison. Ruth continued "we just met on the first night of the trip. Both of us travelling alone."

"And that led to a shipboard romance?" asked Joe, trying to smile.

"A little more than that, I think, Mr. Barlow," said Rupert with an authority that Joe immediately resented.

"Time enough for that discussion," he said as firmly as he could. "Ruth and I have a lot to talk about, Rupert. Would you mind if I took her away for a bit and we had some private time together?"

"Of course, I do understand. But what time do you think you will you have her back here?"

So that was to be the game, Joe thought, establish a superior claim. Well, he had the seniority and the history, so he should be well-placed for the competition. He hoped he was hiding his thoughts as he said "Later this afternoon, Rupert, if that's alright with you?"

Rupert smiled disarmingly. "Have a good time then, don't hurry back," and he waved them off in the creaking cart.

"Did you like Rupert?" asked Ruth anxiously as Joe guided the cart along the main street.

"Nice young man," said Joe noncommittal, "but where will we go? Let's decide that first, eh?"

"Somewhere peaceful."

Without a word Joe steered the cart back towards the old house, but turned off to link up with the track to the beach.

An hour later they were sitting on the wet sand at the edge of the sea as the tiny waves broke over their bare feet.

"Well then, who's to start with the story of their last five years?" asked Joe.

"You start."

"Alright then."

Joe's account of his removal to Kalgoorlie left out the feelings that had caused his departure, concentrated on the adventure that it had been, the wonder of finding Sam's family and his entanglement with it, left out most of George's past history, emphasised his pleasure and success in the market garden and ruefully acknowledged his lack of contact with the Oak Tree Place contingent in Margaret River.

"You should have written, Joe. It would have avoided so much confusion and worry."

"I know. I'm sorry."

"With all that happened and with all the thinking that I had to do, I just knew that I wanted to come back to Margaret River no matter what, so I did."

"What are you going to do here?"

"Now that you're back I thought we could think about that together. Are you back, Joe? Are you staying or are you going back to Kalgoorlie?"

"I think I'm back, lovey."

"You think?"

"Well yes, but with all this thinking going on, I need to take a bit of it to consider how to earn a living."

"You could take up one of the abandoned Group blocks. Or a new CP block."

"Oh, *you've* been thinking, have you?" Joe laughed indulgently. "But old Group block or new Conditional Purchase, I'm beginning to think I'm too old to start that all over again."

"Old? *Old?* Joe my lovely man, you're not *old!*" Joe smiled at Ruth's vehemence, and looked sideways at this half-girl-half-woman, growing into all-woman almost as he watched.

"But what about you? Your turn now." Joe turned towards her. "I can't imagine how terrible it must have been for you with Charlie and all that happened in London. I wish that I had been there to help you."

"I managed, Joe, I managed. A lot of thanks to Marcus and Lydia. Bloody Lydia … " she smiled, "bloody Lydia no longer, I have to say. She's changed a lot, Joe. Even though—" she stopped.

"Even though?"

"Even though I sometimes thought that her interest in it all was a bit morbid. I also think she was a little afraid that I might reveal something to Marcus that she didn't want him to know. About Oak Tree Place, and her father, and even you …

"She did actually ask me not to talk too much about Oak Tree Place so of course I tried not to, it was sometimes hard. After all, nearly everything that we knew about each other was from that time and that place. But Marcus is a very nice man and very fond of Lydia, you can tell, so he didn't really want to know anything that Lydia didn't want him to. I think he might be afraid of upsetting the apple cart in some way. He likes his peace and quiet and his life with Lydia and Henry."

"Henry? He's Henry again now? No longer our Harry?"

"Oh Joe, he's a lovely boy, you'd be so proud of him. I only saw him for a little while but he is lovely, very polite and well-mannered."

"Not mine to be proud of, unfortunately."

"He didn't remember me though. Or you, Joe." This was delivered sadly, but Ruth quickly added "But you'd probably be happy to hear that he was in trouble for flicking inkballs in class." Joe laughed, also with a tinge of sadness.

He shifted as a tiny wave invaded their space and retreated. "Do you know anything about how Lydia and Marcus met?" He tried to sound casual.

"No, nothing at all. The conversations we all had together tended to be about me and my situation and what to do about things."

"Yes, and poor Alice," said Joe tentatively, "It must have been terrible for you, poor love."

"It's still not really real, Joe. I know it all happened and every-thing but it's almost as if it happened to someone else and not me." She smiled. "I'm not very good at keeping parents, am I though? I've managed to lose two lots of them, more than most people I'm sure." Her lips twisted, belying the wryness of her remarks.

"Alice was a good mother to me, Joe. She always took care of me and I feel Joe reached out and drew her to his side.

It was so sad that she had to pretend to be my aunt for all that time. It was am awful situation for anyone to be in but I think … I really knew, that things were going to get … difficult, more dif-ficult … between her and Charlie. The feeling in the house wasn't good. Oh, there were times when it was all fine and dandy, but more and more there were times when Charlie would drink too much and Alice sometimes would too and it was just horrid. I'd mostly just go to my room but it was hard not to hear it all—and see it sometimes too. Charlie hit her, you know. If I was there I tried to stop him and mostly I could, because he never ever hurt me, but when I was at school … poor Alice." She was sobbing quietly.

"Joe, it's probably not a good thing or a right thing to say, but I really hated my father."

Joe squeezed her tightly to his side. "No, my sweet, it's per-fectly understandable that you feel that way about Charlie. It's not wrong at all." Hell's bells, Joe mentally rolled his eyes, she thought that having two sets of parents was rich. What about three fathers? Well Michael-father had stayed a secret for this long, so could stay secret for a while longer, he thought. Couldn't bring himself to add more complications to the situation and besides, was that secret his to reveal?

There was a long silence, punctuated at first by Ruth's diminishing sobs. After some time she said "Joe, all those letters that I wrote to you, when I was writing them I would imagine you getting them from the mail delivery and reading them and thinking about me and what I was doing and I wondered why you didn't write back to me. I was cross at first, then worried, then really sad. I wrote to Stephen to ask him if anything was wrong, and when he didn't write back either I just thought that you'd all forgotten about me. Alice insisted that I write every Saturday though and I never ever suspected that the letters weren't getting posted. How silly I was not to see what was happening. I should have known—and deep down I think I did know—that you would never abandon me, even if I was over the other side of the world. I feel so silly."

"All over now, chicken, all behind us now. I'm just glad that you wrote to Stephen again when … " His voice trailed off.

"Joe," said Ruth in a small voice, "what will happen to Charlie?"

"Don't know, sweetheart, don't know." He was anxious to avoid discussion of the subject. "I'll write to Lydia's husband and ask him what's happening, shall I?"

"Don't worry, I can do that. I just thought you might know what was likely to happen. Oh, and I kept the magazine clipping that I saw with Lydia in it so that you could see what she looks like now. Do you want to see?"

"Yes, of course."

Joe looked at the glossy magazine page and saw a very different Lydia from the Lydia who had once ruled his life. He smiled and was about to pass the page back to Ruth when he caption caught his eye and he laughed out loud.

"Oh Lord!" he said.

"Yes they are both lords, Marcus and his father. I only met Marcus' father once but he was a nice man too, kind and gentle. Lord Burnside."

"No doubt about our Lydia," said Joe, still chuckling, "she knows what she wants and it seems that she gets it, however she does it."

Ruth let the comment slide over her and said again, "Yes, I'll write to Marcus about Charlie."

"Good idea."

"Marcus will know."

"These legal things take time,"

"Yes, I know, but although I don't like the fact that Charlie is my father, I can't avoid it, can I? I really should know what's going on."

Oh, father discussions again. Joe changed the subject. "Tell me about Rupert, then, my girl. Was he heading for Margaret River when you met him?"

"Oh goodness no, not at all!" Ruth giggled. "He was—still is, really—headed for his father's cousin's sheep property somewhere out from Sydney. He was sent out by his parents to work and help out there but he knows that they really want him to experience another way of living from the one he's been used to. He seems to have had quite a privileged life so far, from what he's told me." This last was delivered with a combination of pride and indulgence.

"So he's still going to Sydney?" Joe brightened.

"He's talking about staying here and finding a job instead."

"Oh. What sort of job?"

"Anything that means he can stay here."

"That he can stay where you are, you mean."

"Yes." Ruth blushed. "Do you like him, Joe?"

"Ruthie love, I have only exchanged a couple of words with the boy," he said with deliberate vagueness. "Much more to the point is whether you like him, and—" he held up his hand as Ruth attempted to interject, "you must realise that you are very young and not very experienced."

"Joe, I've had more experiences in my seventeen years than most people have in a lifetime!"

"That's probably true," Joe acknowledged soberly, "but they're not the sort of experiences that equip you to judge a maybe-husband."

"Joe, I do not agree. I believe that they are exactly the sort of experiences that equip me to judge whether a man will be a good husband or not. And," she said hotly, "Rupert is a sweet, kind boy and I know that he will be good to me."

"You say a sweet, kind, *boy*. That's one thing. A *boy*. Not a man, a man with a strong back, a good brain and experience of life. Who will be good to you, *of course*. But when has 'he will be good to me' been a declaration of a love strong enough to sustain a marriage for the rest of your lives? Don't you want more than that? Don't you want a passion that makes your scalp tingle and the hairs on your arms stand up? Don't you want the sight of your lover to turn you weak at the knees? His touch to melt you?"

Ruth looked at Joe with astonishment. He gazed steadily out over the sea but was flushed with the vehemence of his outburst.

"Joe … " Ruth said cautiously, "Joe." She stopped, then began again.

"Joe, I've never heard you speak like that before."

Joe shook his head dismissively. "I just don't want you throwing your life away."

"That sounded like experience. Did you leave someone you loved in Kalgoorlie?"

"No, nothing like that."

"Who, then?"

He wished fervently that he'd kept his stupid mouth closed. It had just come out, those memories of the passion he had felt in his distant youth. Hell's bells, he couldn't let Ruth know that his passionate memories were of bloody Lydia, that would be altogether too embarrassing.

"No one, no one. Come on, let's get back."

Ruth was silent for most of the journey back, but as they approached the town she put her hand on Joe's arm and said earnestly "Joe, dear Joe, I know you want the best for me and you always have, but there comes a time—and I think it's now—that I need to be making my own decisions and deciding what's best for me."

"And Rupert's best for you, you have decided." Joe spoke more roughly than he intended but Ruth chose to ignore his tone.

"I think so. He's shown how much he cares by coming back with me to Margaret River and … and … I care too!"

Joe digested this for a few minutes as the horse clopped, the cart creaked and his heart hammered. He was about to lose Ruth, when he'd only just found her again.

89

The next day

Yesterday he had left Ruth on the proprietary arm of Rupert and made his way back to Stephen's house for the night. That morning he had helped with the milking, chopped some wood and lent a hand with some fencing in the far paddock. He and Stephen were walking back to the house at midday.

"Right then, what are you going to do, my good friend?" asked Stephen, breaking the silence that had been punctuated only by their footsteps.

"Damned if I know," said Joe. "As usual," he added bitterly.

"No ideas?"

"Not really. Not really. I told Ruth that I'd come back into town this afternoon and collect them both, but that's as far as I've got."

"Look, take a load off your mind for a while. Let's get this evening's party over with then, and we can apply ourselves to thinking of something after that. Agreed?"

Joe gratefully pushed his dilemmas aside and helped prepare for the evening's gathering which was to be a joyful reunion of the "Oak Tree Place Mob", as they now apparently called themselves.

As he approached Stephen's block again in the late afternoon, with Ruth and Rupert jammed on the seat beside him, he smiled again at the sight of the neat little house with light spilling from all the windows and an air of welcome. Perhaps he was just being sentimental; what it represented was a tremendous amount of sheer hard work. But it still looked welcoming.

Ruth had seen Ida and Len in the couple of days she had spent staying with Stephen before she took a room in town at the boarding house to keep Rupert from being lonely there. She had yet to see Ellen and Michael, and they now came running from the house to help the cart passengers down, followed by the others that made up the party. There was a hubbub of exclamations and greetings, hugs and laughter as they made their way towards the verandah where chairs were waiting in the light of the lamps in the windows.

Already seated there were two small children, somewhat wide-eyed at all the noise and fuss. Len scooped them up, one on each arm and presented them to Joe with glowing pride and a smile that threatened to split his face in two.

"May I introduce Master Richard and Miss Margaret Dawson," he said breathlessly. "Two of Margaret River's very best products."

"My God, Len, what a lovely pair of … products, to be sure. Congratulations to you and Ida on a job very well done!" Joe held out his arms to the little girl, but she buried her face in her father's shoulder. "Give her time," said her father, "she'll be all over you in half an hour."

Joe's smile was almost as broad as Len's as he regarded the assembled company. "It's so good to see you all again," he began, then stopped as his emotions threatened to overcome his ability to speak.

"Oh Joe, it's so good to see you too. Michael and I have often talked about you and wondered how you were faring, haven't we love?" Ellen looked towards Michael, who Joe now saw clearly and noticed that his dark hair was surprisingly streaked with grey and his handsome mobile features were a little blurred and softened. But his smile was wide and his eyes still deep and clear as he agreed with his wife.

Joe looked round at his other friends. He saw changes in them all, changes that were inevitable considering the work they had had to do, the challenges they had faced, the drudgery they had overcome, and indeed the time that had passed. But by God, they looked … they looked … *settled*. Even allowing for the pleasure they were all feeling at meeting again, there was a deeper glow there, and it emanated from all of them. A sort of contentment. Maybe it was skin deep, or my sentimental imagination, Joe thought. Oh, relax and enjoy the reunion. Think deeper and more constructive thoughts tomorrow as you said you would.

But this was not to be allowed, it seemed.

"Are you back to stay, Joe?"

"What are you going to do, Joe?"

"Are you going back to Kalgoorlie, Joe?"

"Whoa, whoa," Joe raised his hand protectively, "enough, enough! I really don't know what I'm going to do but I don't think I'll be going back to Kal. Not because I didn't like it there or anything like that, but I came tearing back to Margaret River because of the arrival of Miss Ruth here—" he reached over to Ruth and ruffled her hair, "and there are things to be talked about before I can even think about what I'm going to do."

Thwarted, the inquisitors turned to Ruth and Rupert.

"So what are *you* going to do, then, you two?" asked Len.

"I heard you were on your way to Sydney before our lovely Ruth waylaid you!" Michael directed his jovial remark to Rupert, who shifted uneasily in his seat under the gaze of the entire party.

"Umm, yes, umm, yes," he managed.

"And? Are you still going?" Len asked, not unkindly.

"Umm, I did think that I might be able to get some work here for a while until Ruth and I marry, then we'll go to my uncle's sheep farm, er, *station*, and then of course we'll go back to England to live. My family has quite a large estate in Gloucestershire, you know." Rupert's confidence had grown as he made this little speech, but unfortunately he finished with a very inappropriate ring of privilege, given the assembly present. The atmosphere frosted despite the balmy evening.

"Oh, and what does our Ruth have to say about all this?" asked Stephen with entirely false bonhomie. "How will she enjoy living on quite a large estate in Gloucestershire, then? Mmmm?"

Ruth bit her lip and flushed.

"I expect I will enjoy our life very much," she said as she slid her hand into Rupert's, "wherever we are."

The ambiguity of her answer was not lost on anyone present but it did allow a lightening of the atmosphere, and the party drifted into diverse groups and general conversations. The children, yawning, said their goodnights and were put to bed by Ida in the cart where they would —hopefully—sleep until they got home.

Careful not to let go of Richard's hand, Ruth led him towards Michael and Ellen and confirmed the introductions which had been so perfunctory when they arrived.

"Rupert, this is my Uncle Michael and my Auntie Ellen," she said.

"Ah," said Rupert expansively, looking at Michael, I can see that this is a real relation and not an honorary one. The family resemblance is very marked."

Fortunately not everyone heard this exchange, otherwise the silence would have been total. Helen, who had heard, shot an anguished and questioning glance at Joe. Was this the time? she seemed to be asking. Time to tell? Joe turned his gaze to Michael, who was looking at his wife so didn't see Joe's half-questioning stare. Ellen was looking at Joe though, and it was she who spoke.

"There's a story to tell here, to be sure, but I'm not sure this is the time or place," she said in a clear voice that cut through all other conversations "but it should be—needs to be—told before too much longer, I think."

Ruth and Rupert both looked puzzled, and the rest of the party seemed to draw a huge breath, in unison. Rupert continued to look bewildered, but Ruth's eyes darted around the room and she frowned.

"Nothing for you to worry about, chicken," said Joe gently. "Come and sit down and listen to it all. Who's going to tell?"

"It had better be me," said Michael, gravely.

Ruth's frown deepened and she sat forward in her chair.

"You see," began Michael "the first thing you have to know is that Charlie isn't your Daddy."

Ruth's face quickly registered shock, puzzlement, relief and amazement in turn. "Then why did Alice say he was? Why did Charlie say he was? How do you know? Why didn't you tell me before? Is it true?"

As Michael opened his mouth to speak again, Ruth's eyes narrowed and she said "Who is my father then? Do you know?"

"Yes," said Michael simply, "I am."

His last two words were uttered at the same time as Ruth cried "You are!" and burst into tears.

Joe moved forward to comfort her, but Rupert was there first, proprietary arm about her shoulders and handkerchief in hand. Joe backed away awkwardly.

Ruth quickly steadied and looked up at Michael unemotionally. "I need to hear the whole story, please, all of it, all of the secrets that everyone seems so determined to keep from me. Don't leave anything out, I need to know everything. No more lies, no more concealing, no more pretending. I am tired" she added heatedly "of people keeping things from me. This is my life that I'm living and I have a right to know about it!"

Michael was having some trouble controlling his voice, so Joe started.

"You know the story that Alice told about hiding your birth and Charlie not knowing he was your father," he began.

"Yes, yes, that's what they both told me at Stephen's house when Charlie first arrived. Charlie said he hadn't even known that Alice was my mother with all that pretending and hiding that went on. So was Alice really my mother?" she added plaintively.

"Oh yes, that's something that's true and has always been true," said Joe.

Ruth turned on Michael. "Why didn't you do anything then, when you knew you were my father?" Ruth's voice cracked. "When Alice and Charlie were taking me away? Why didn't you do something?"

"Oh, me darlin' girl, I didn't know at all that I was your Daddy, not for all the years you were growing up in front of me in Oak Tree Place. One day I did notice that you looked a lot like me own mother, and even then I never suspected, with everyone being taken by Alice and Jessie's tricks. When we all learned the truth about all that I began to think hard and realised that it could be true, that I might be your Daddy indeed. But right then it was that Charlie was here with his story of Ruth's inheritance and if I'd thrown a spanner in the works at that stage it would have meant robbin' you of a lovely education and a bright future.

"And," he added desperately, "Charlie seemed such a changed and a sober man and Alice actin' so certain that he was your Daddy and I was not absolutely certain-sure of meself at all, so I just thought it would be better if I kept everythin' to meself, so I did," he trailed off miserably.

Ruth turned to Joe.

"You knew, you knew."

"Not until that last night when you were leaving with Charlie and Alice. I had absolutely no idea up until then, when I suddenly saw the resemblance between you and Michael. It was like a bolt of lightning and I was so dumbfounded that I couldn't even think, let alone do anything."

"What about after that though, Joe? You had time."

Stephen spoke for the first time, cutting into the exchange.

"It seemed to be the best thing at the time, Ruth. Joe and I talked about it, and with you in Perth, going to school and coming here for the holidays seemed like he best way to handle the situation. To take advantage of the situation, I mean. Until Alice and Charlie spirited you away to England, of course and all those clever plans went out the window," he added ruefully.

Rupert still sat beside her, his eyes widening as the story unfolded.

"So," said Ruth quietly as Stephen concluded the account, "thank you all for your care and attention over the years, thank you for doing what you all thought was right." She became vehement and concluded loudly "But as I said before, this is my life and I am taking the responsibility for it from now on and *I don't need protecting*." She was plainly on the point of tears again.

An awkward silence was cut by Rupert saying "I shall do all the protecting that's necessary from now on!" in ringing tones. The remark hung in the air, far too portentous for such a slight young man.

There was an embarrassed shuffle but Ruth bounded to her feet and said "Thank you Uncle Stephen, thank you Auntie Helen, goodnight everybody, we'll be going now. Come along Rupert." She didn't look at Michael.

Their exit was compromised however; they had no transport of their own and they were forced to wait until Len and Ida hurriedly gathered themselves, said their goodbyes and drove them back to town, assuring them that the deviation was hardly out of their way at all. Michael and Ellen left quietly and suddenly the house was empty but for the three of them. Helen said goodnight and went to bed.

"How do you think that all went then?" asked Joe, looking at Stephen.

"I think it went quite well considering how damned complicated it all was—is. At least it cleared the air and all the secrets are out now"

"How do you think she'll cope with having Michael for a father?"

"She needs time to take it in, but she could do worse, he's a good man."

"We all thought she *had* done worse for a while there."

"Mmm. Hard to feel sorry that she's managed to shed Charlie. Wonder what's going to happen to him?" Stephen looked into the darkness outside and shivered slightly. "We'll hear soon enough I suppose."

"Do you think Rupert's up to the job of looking after her?" Joe said suddenly.

"He's an earnest young chap and seems set on doing so."

"I have my doubts. He's too young, for one thing. And inexperienced."

"Experience can be acquired fairly quickly Joe, as you and I both know."

"He's still too young. And his background … "

"Afraid of meeting the family, huh?" Stephen laughed.

"Go to bed, you silly beggar."

Why would he ever need to meet Rupert's toffy family, anyway? It wasn't as if he was a relation.

90

Two months later.
April 1933

Things had moved on since that evening of revelations at Stephen's house. Stephen's and Helen's house, Joe corrected himself as he languidly flicked the reins and guided the cart down the dusty track. Very much their joint house; he was really glad to see his friend so obviously happy, contented and very much in love. Stephen certainly deserved it. But he couldn't—and wouldn't if today went well—sponge off the pair of them for too much longer, especially with the birth of the baby imminent. Besides, he sometimes felt like a damned gooseberry.

He pulled his wandering thoughts back to the cart and its destination, smiling slightly at the prospect of the final arrangements that were to be made when he arrived at the Mundy's farm. It was such a good plan that he and Stephen had cooked up.

Autumn was well and truly in the air and although the land was still bleached by the desiccating days of summer, the air was sweet and balmy and a feeling not unlike happiness welled in him as he meandered along. Even the thought of Ruth was not the stabbing pain that it had been. More of an empty ache. Activity was the key, that was it. And he was getting older; maybe those anguishes he'd once felt belonged to a more youthful version of himself.

Rupert had received a cable from his father in England, the contents of which were not revealed to anyone, but it somehow leaked that Rupert's presence was required, as planned, in Tingaloo on his uncle's property and that his dalliance on the way was not appreciated.

Ruth had not spoken to anyone since leaving Stephen's house, and that was weeks ago now. Joe, and then Stephen, had attempted contact but she adamantly refused to speak to anyone and the messages of rejection had been carried by Rupert, who adopted a superior and world-weary attitude that draped incongruously over his boyish shoulders.

Joe felt irritation at Rupert's assumption of authority and equal irritation at Ruth's intransigence, but was nevertheless shocked to hear that the pair had left town without farewells. According to Mrs. O'Farrell at the guest house, they were off to Sydney and beyond, information that she was delighted to relay to anyone who asked. She nearly always added a "tut-tut" at the idea of a young unmarried couple travelling together, but did add that the proprieties had certainly been observed while they were under her roof. The ripple of surprise, pleasure and curiosity that had flowed through the town at Ruth's re-appearance diminished as its subject retreated into an unknown landscape.

Joe hoped that Ruth would write in time. She couldn't—surely she couldn't—be so cruel as to cut him out of her life completely. But enough of this, Joe, you are almost there.

Bill Mundy's farm was an old one, not too far out of the town that had hardly existed when Bill and his wife Doris arrived before the war. Bill had tried a few things on his considerable acreage but had now settled into dairy farming and keeping pigs, more or less like the Group Settlers who had come to the district after him.

On his property there was a wide swathe of swampy land that was a danger to the animals, so Bill had fenced it off. Joe knew of this unused portion of Bill's property from a well-known local story of how the pigs got into it at one time and loved it, loved it so much that they were virtually uncatchable and it took days and days to actually find the mud-covered animals and then to recover them all. Some had bolted out of the other side of the swamp and were found in various places around town over the next week or two. Stronger fencing was installed.

Joe and Bill were now regarding the swamp, still damp at the end of summer and looking lush and green.

"Reckon you can do this?" said Bill, tipping his hat back on his head.

"Think so. If I can grow stuff in Kalgoorlie I reckon I can do it here."

"It's a bloody good idea if it does work, mate, that's all I can say."

That wasn't all he could say though. He continued. "You do know how swampy this bit of land gets, don't you? Can you manage it? But God I hope you do, mate, this place could do with some fresh vegetables. Me and the wife, we do alright with the stuff we grow ourselves, but we could do with some bloody variety, I'll tell you that. And some people," he added in wonder, "don't even grow anything themselves, silly buggers. They'll be grateful, I bet.

"Tell you what," he said expansively, "you could talk to Jimmy Tickner about that Group house that's on the location he took over to add to his land. It's going begging as far as I know. Not too big a job to take it down and rebuild it down there. It'd be just the thing for you."

Joe's excitement notched higher. He had been prepared to live in a tent on his prospective market garden until he could manage something more permanent. He went back to the house with Bill, had a celebratory cup of tea with him and Mrs. Mundy, signed the rental agreement that he and Bill had drawn up together, dropped off the fence posts that he'd brought from Stephen's and clopped back there at a steady pace.

The plan, which he'd thought of mainly by himself, was simple. He had come to actually enjoy growing vegetables in Kalgoorlie, come to enjoy the planting, nurturing, the harvesting and even the selling. Learned to enjoy the science of growing. He had never articulated this in Kal, never really realised it until he was back in Margaret River and found himself worrying (vaguely, it must be said) that the Kalgoorlie market garden was being operated properly and the crops were being harvested in timely fashion. This realisation quite amused him for a while, until the blinding idea came to him. He wanted to stay in Margaret River. He didn't particularly want to dairy farm, or pig farm, or cut timber, and he was nostalgic for the simplicity and the labour of growing vegetables. Well then … and the rest had followed.

He had cautiously told Stephen about it and with his enthusiastic support had sought out Bill Mundy.

He would have liked to tell Ruth.

Stop that, Ruth is making her own way and isn't interested.

And he had fencing, building, draining and planting to do.

91

3 years later.
April 1936

The little re-built Group house had initially been disorientating for Joe. Identical to the house that he and Ruth had lived in on their own block, his mind expected the farm to be there when he went out of doors. He had to adjust his thinking every time for the first few weeks, but the years had brought a deep familiarity to the scene that now greeted him.

Not for the first time, he thought of his father's allotment and reflected how gratified his Dad would be to see that his reluctant pupil had graduated to such a spread. Not that it was huge, just three acres of planting, but big enough. When it got a bit much for him he got some lads in from surrounding farms and it worked out well, as did the little stall on the roadside with its piles of produce and its honesty box.

He stretched his back muscles and swung his arms as he made his way toward the day's work before remembering that he should collect the bacon that Bill had told him about yesterday, fresh from the little smokehouse he'd built. Joe's mouth watered at the thought. He'd make some bread today too, even though it wasn't a bread-making day because he suddenly found that he badly wanted a bacon sandwich and that had to be with fresh bread for the salty fat to soak into. He smiled in anticipation. The last of the potatoes could wait to be dug, and the planting out of the cabbages was best done later in the day anyway.

It had been three years since Joe began his market-gardening enterprise and a year since the land became his own. His ten acres had been officially sliced off the farm and was now in Joe's name, a present from Bill and Doris. Their only son had been a casualty of the war, something that was never talked about, but Doris, in particular, fussed over Joe with an intensity that he accommodated with understanding. He was extremely grateful for the gift of his land and felt a loving and almost familial attachment to the couple.

He strode through the dry paddock towards the farmhouse but could not resist pausing and looking back towards his own house, admiring its place in the landscape, overlooking the rows of vegetables bright and lush in the morning sun. With the help of the Oak Tree Mob and sundry other farmers, Jimmy Tickner's Group cottage had taken only a day to dismantle and cart to "Joe's Swamp", as it was jokingly christened, and another few days to re-erect it. Joe reckoned that it looked as if it had always been there, but smiled as he remembered the party they'd thrown when the operation was finished.

In the winter following, a covert operation was launched by the Oak Tree Mob. As predicted, the settlers on Joe's old block had walked off, a sick wife and an overwhelmed husband unable to cope. Early one morning they had driven a cart to the block and dug out the thriving oak tree that had grown into a sturdy sapling from the acorn that had been planted all those Christmases ago. A combination of tarpaulins, ropes and muscle had loaded the tree and they hurriedly made good the hole and pretended to be robbers galloping away with the loot as they trundled to Joe's new location where they ceremoniously replanted it. The tree survived the operation with the stoicism attributed to oak trees everywhere. Much merriment all round, and a feeling of satisfaction that things were now in their right place.

Joe called out as he made the small jump on to the verandah of Bill and Doris's house. "Anyone home?"

This house had become quite familiar to him over the past three years; he had spent a number of soft summer evenings on the verandah with them both, enjoying the ease that comes after a hard day's work. On these evenings they often sat in silence but once or twice Joe had been unguarded—and relaxed—enough to tell them something of his past. Their comfortable acceptance of everything he said was soothing and Joe reflected that talking about it all, from the war and the death of his parents through the Lydia business (as he now dismissed it) and the losing, regaining and losing again of Ruth, had sort of helped him clear his head and perhaps, just perhaps, put it all behind him.

But for now he sat at Bill and Doris' kitchen table, cup of tea in front of him and the bacon, tickling his nose with its seductive smoky perfume, wrapped in a tea towel beside him.

"Going to enjoy this, Doris," he said patting the parcel of bacon possessively.

"Of course you will, love, it's a nice bit of meat and that smoker does a good job." Doris sat down at the table opposite him and said enquiringly "Did that nice young lass find you yesterday?"

"What nice young lass?" he said warily. There had been several nice young lasses thrown in his path over the past three years but Joe thought the local supply had been exhausted. He was just more suited to living alone, he said—to himself and to anyone else who asked.

There had been no trace of any young lass about the place when he came back from town yesterday. "What nice young lass?" he repeated.

"Oh she said she'd be back if she didn't find you. She said she was visiting and staying on one of the Groups with some friends. I think that's what she said." Doris frowned with concentration.

Joe's skin prickled. It was Ruth. It could only be Ruth. Draining the last of his tea he kissed Doris on the cheek and jogged back to his house, determined not to miss her again.

Even so, his feelings were mixed. There had been two letters from Ruth since her hurried departure from Margaret River. The first had been a half-hearted apology for leaving without farewells, but it included a waspish rebuke to him and the rest of the Oak Tree people for what she perceived as over-protectiveness and "thinking you know what's best for me."

The second letter had come two years ago now and included a clipping from the local paper at Tingaloo giving an account of the wedding of Ruth and Rupert. The letter had been spare in detail but sounded happy, they'd all thought, and it assuaged the concern that they held for her wellbeing. They did wonder how it had been managed though, with Ruth just 17 and no parental permission. Joe thought that Marvellous Marcus probably had a hand in it.

Since then there had been nothing, despite the fact that Joe had, contrary to his normal practice, written three times to Ruth over the two years that had elapsed since her marriage. Although the letters had not been returned, he couldn't be sure whether they were being received or whether Ruth and Rupert had gone back to England to his "considerable estate" and his family.

Perhaps they were on the way back there now, Joe thought, and were dropping in to say goodbye. It would be a significant undertaking to pay a fleeting visit to Margaret River though—perhaps Ruth needed to mend her friendships. If she and Rupert were going back to England it would be doubtful that she'd see the Oak Tree Place Mob again. That sounded like the affectionate Ruth of old. Having decided that his conjecture was in fact the reality, Joe set about finishing the bread for his bacon sandwich, trying to ignore the hollow feeling in his chest that had actually overtaken his enthusiasm for bacon sandwiches. He was alert to every sound outside but determined to be casual about the impending visit.

Bread rising in the tins, he swept the floors and the verandah (determinedly not looking towards the track to the road) and wiped down the dusty surfaces inside the house. He considered washing the windows but dug those last potatoes instead. The bread was baked and dusk was falling before he realised that Ruth would not be coming today. He began to revise his previous confident scenario.

His bacon sandwich somehow lacked the flavour he had anticipated.

92

The next day

Joe had a sleepless night and the following morning he was red-eyed and tetchy. If Ruth was in Margaret River surely he should have been her first port of call. And what were she and Rupert doing staying with someone on the Groups? That is, if Doris had got it right, of course.

Who would it be though? Stephen and Helen seemed the obvious choice, but perhaps Michael and Ellen? Len and Ida seemed an unlikely choice with their two little ones, their house was bulging at the seams.

Why hadn't they come to him?

He had to almost physically stop himself from setting out to the blocks where his friends lived and it was only the embarrassment he would have to endure that prevented him. But then, Doris may have got it wrong and they were probably staying in town. Yes, that made better sense.

Joe was digging with more than usual energy when the lone figure came walking up the track from the road. He pretended he didn't see her, turned his back with schoolboy truculence and continued digging. She was standing in front of him before he looked up.

"Those shoes will be ruined in this dirt," he said.

"They already are. They're not designed for walking."

"So where are you staying?"

"With … with Michael and Ellen."

"For how long?"

"Not sure. Look, Joe, are you going to offer me a cup of tea? I'm freezing."

Joe shouldered his spade and they made their way to the house without speaking.

As they entered the house, Ruth broke the uneasy silence.

"Joe, I'm sorry that we didn't say goodbye properly when we left last time," she said "but I was hurt and confused and quite angry that my life seemed to be being managed by everyone but me. I'm not—I wasn't—a baby."

Joe brought his hostile gaze back from the distance and looked at Ruth properly for the first time. No, she wasn't a baby, she glowed with young womanhood. He gulped, disconcerted.

"How are you then?" he said awkwardly.

"I'm well, thank you." Ruth smiled. "And I can see that you are too."

"Yes. This place keeps me busy."

"Is it hard on your back, all that bending?"

"Yes, a bit."

"Do you have plans for any more cultivation?"

"Not at the moment. It's as much as I can handle."

"Do you manage to sell all you grow?"

"Mostly. I supply the two boarding houses as well as sell on the roadside stall."

"Captain of Industry then?" Ruth laughed.

Joe shook his head and smiled slightly; the strained conversation lapsed.

Ruth jumped up suddenly, startling Joe. "Shall I make the tea, then?" she said brightly.

"Oh, sorry, sorry, I forgot." Joe lumbered to his feet and stoked the fire in the stove as Ruth filled the kettle. She seemed to know where the cups and saucers would be kept, and the teapot, tea caddy, and sugar bowl.

"It's nice to be back," said Ruth as they sat down again. "I've missed this place so much each time I've been away from it. I really loved our little house, Joe, and the block and the cows and everything." She paused. "And you." Joe didn't seem to notice the hesitation.

"Oh, then," he said with the first animation he'd shown since her arrival, "I must show you something that you'll certainly like."

Ruth gasped at the sight of the oak tree, a beautiful specimen now, full of health and the promise of a splendid maturity.

"Oh Joe, it's wonderful. What a lovely thing to do. This makes it really your home, doesn't it? Mrs. Craggs would be so pleased to see how her acorns have flourished."

The reference to the past was light and fleeting, but Joe looked anxiously at Ruth to see if other more recent memories intruded. It seems that they had.

"Did you hear about Charlie?" she asked.

"Yes, we did."

"Lucky him."

"Yes."

"I was there and it wasn't an accident, Joe."

"The coroner decided that it was though. Better that way, don't you agree?"

"Oh yes definitely." Ruth sighed. "I'm just glad it's all over now. All of it."

Joe missed the emphasis of the last words and tried to change the subject as they resumed their seats at the kitchen table.

"So how long are you staying?"

"As I said before, not sure."

"Are you on your way to England?"

"No."

"Oh? So this is just a special visit to Margaret River then?"

"Yes."

"And you're staying with Michael and Ellen?"

"Yes."

Cautiously Joe said "Have you sorted things out with Michael?".

"If you mean have I come to accept that he's my father, then yes."

"That's good then."

"We have been writing to each other."

Joe was stung. He didn't know this, Michael hadn't mentioned it and what's more, Ruth had only written to *him* twice over the years.

"Writing letters must have helped," he said stiffly.

"Yes it did. I came to know him, I think. To be honest," she blurted, "I've actually come to love him." She laughed self-consciously.

Joe was contrite. "That's wonderful, love." The casual endearment came naturally. "You couldn't wish for a better man for a father."

Ruth giggled. "You can't say I didn't have choices!"

Joe joined her laughter and a lighter atmosphere prevailed.

"So how are things in Tingaloo, and do you have your own property yet or is Rupert still working for his uncle?"

"Rupert's back in England, Joe."

"What?"

"Our marriage was a mistake. Rupert's parents were furious when they heard and cut him off completely—I was so dreadfully unsuitable, you see. Uncle Peter suddenly had us on his hands and really, we were such a burden. Rupert was never cut out for life on the land here, and I was just useless, no matter how hard I tried to be helpful. Rupert quite quickly realised that the life he'd always thought he'd have was gone from him. So I became the point of his disappointment and frustration. Just six months into our marriage I was regretting it every bit as much as Rupert was. Oh Joe he was such a *boy*; I felt ages older than him when he was so spiteful and hurtful and childish. It was awful."

Joe looked on speechlessly as she continued.

"I felt that I had burned all my boats, Joe. Or is it all my bridges? Both I suppose. I had left Margaret River in high dudgeon, but quite certain that I had a safe future and a loving partner. That quickly became a false prospect, and that was when I began to write to Michael and more than once I was sorely tempted to just pack up and come back here, but I did feel responsible for Rupert in a way because he had spoiled his life simply by marrying me.

So we bumbled along there with things becoming more and more impossible, until one day Rupert sensibly decided to pack up and go home, certain that he could mend things with his parents if he didn't have me in tow.

"Then of course it wasn't possible, as Rupert's rejected wife, for me to stay on with Uncle Peter on my own, so here I am." This was relayed in a matter-of-fact tone.

"So Rupert just upped and left you out there alone?" Joe asked incredulously.

"With his uncle and his uncle's family and the other workers, yes. He and I had just had a big, big argument and I went for a long walk to try to get over it. When I came back Rupert was gone. But Joe, all I felt at first was relief. Peace at last! It was only a few hours later that I began to look at the situation I was in—depending on the kindness of people who were virtual strangers to me, with absolutely no prospects and very little money. You can see why Margaret River looked like a haven? It was the only place I knew—the only place that held people I knew, people I ... Someone I ... So ... "

"So you came back."

"Yes." Ruth looked at Joe enigmatically.

"What are you going to do here?"

"Well I should be able to get some sort of job I thought." She held Joe's gaze, then dropped her eyes.

"And you'll live with Michael and Ellen?"

"For the time being, yes. They both say I can stay as long as I like and I am enjoying getting to know my actual father."

"What do you call him?"

"Well, listen hard," Ruth laughed. "I jokingly called him Three because I said he was my third attempt to nail down a father. That sounded like Tree when Michael said it, so he's Tree. It sort of makes it a secret name which is nice."

Joe looked at her, sitting there so confident and happy, and marvelled at her ability to cope with all she had had piled upon her over her short life. She was quite remarkable. At the same time he felt a sense of exclusion—she was being absorbed into Michael's family and he was standing on the side, just watching. But wasn't that right and proper? Michael was her father and he was a good man. He and Ellen were childless, so …

Ruth left soon after, perched easily on the broad back of Michael's horse as it plodded homewards.

93

*Three months later.
September 1936*

Ruth was working at the tea rooms in Margaret River's main street. Her duties seemed to range from waitressing to washing-up according to what she relayed to Joe on her visits. These visits had become fewer after she began working but still regular and Joe thought they were good friends again and at ease with each other. Once or twice she had helped him with some planting and they had worked together in amicable silence.

Joe had a nagging concern that Ruth was employed in just the menial capacity that they thought was going to be avoided by allowing her to leave with Alice and Charlie. Then, it had been the prospect of a limited range of options for Ruth's future that had been one of the tipping-points, and it looked as if this had come full circle. Educated she was now and confident she appeared to be, but what did the future offer to her? Assuming that Rupert instituted divorce proceedings, which seemed entirely likely, it would still be a matter of years before she was a free woman, and in the meantime she was unable to obtain a position befitting her. Joe would have liked to see her working for the Road Board in a nice clean office, or be a teacher or something. But teacher training would take her away to Perth so he quickly put that aside.

For the moment at least, Ruth seemed perfectly happy to accept the limitations that Joe was concerned about and cheerfully regaled him with funny little stories about her days at the tea rooms while he watched for traces of regret or sadness that just didn't seem to be there. For now, Joe thought with foreboding, for now.

In spite of her doubtful marital status, Ruth gained quite a retinue of admirers in a very short time after her return to Margaret River. Joe knew many of them, or knew their parents, and was able to disregard them quite readily as too young, too gormless, too cocky or too old. Why, one was even older than him—what a cheek! Thankfully, Ruth seemed impervious to their various charms and regaled Joe with comical accounts of their shortcomings. She seemed to want to impress Joe with her rejection of them; Joe thought that her failed marriage was responsible for her caution but was happy about it, whatever the reason.

It was after one of Ruth's afternoon visits, as she was walking down the track to the road with Joe watching from the verandah and hating to see her go, that it happened. She turned for a last wave, walking backwards, then Joe saw her stumble, scramble, skitter to the side of the track and fall, throwing up her arms and screaming shrilly and he knew at once what had happened. The dread of everyone on the Groups had always been the deadly snakes that lurked in the bush. Easy to say that they were more frightened of you than you of them, but if they were surprised or felt under threat, they damned well bit you. And you could die, easily you could die.

Joe was off the verandah and running to where he could see Ruth hopping on the track before he thought of collecting the snake bite kit from the kitchen cupboard. He paused to turn, then thought better of it and continued to gallop down the track. Ruth was clutching her ankle and Joe scooped her up and almost without changing his headlong pace ran back towards the house.

"Joe, Joe, it was a tiger snake. I saw it."

"Where did it bite you? On the leg?"

"It didn't bite me!"

"What?"

"It didn't bite me."

"Where?"

"What do you mean?"

"Where did it bite you?"

"It didn't bite me! *It didn't bite me!*"

Joe stopped, still clutching Ruth in his arms.

"What did you say?"

"Oh Joe, it's alright, really it's alright. I think I might have sprained my ankle or something jumping out of the way of the snake as it slithered away, but it didn't bite me."

Joe's strength drained from him and he almost dropped Ruth but he immediately recovered and drew her to him even more closely.

"My God, oh God, I thought you'd been bitten."

"I thought I was going to be bitten! It was such a big one."

"Back to the house now."

"Sorry I'm so heavy."

"You're not heavy."

When they got back to the house Joe deposited Ruth on his bed and went back into the kitchen to make the inevitable cup of tea. His chest felt cold and empty.

Examination of Ruth's rapidly-swelling ankle determined that a visit to the hospital was necessary, so Joe made her as comfortable as possible in the cart and took her there, casting anxious looks over his shoulder as they trundled down the bumpy tracks, looks that held confusion as well as anxiety. Ruth smiled back at him.

The nurses at the hospital decided that the ankle was badly sprained but not, in fact, broken. She was duly professionally bandaged and redelivered into Joe's care.

Once more back at Michael and Ellen's, with Ruth languishing (as she put it) on the couch in the front room, Joe stopped for a drink. Michael joked that they'd had two pieces of good news and was it true that things came in threes? No bite and no break. What would be the third?

They wanted to know how it had all happened. Where had the snake come from?

Ruth laughed. "I was walking backwards without looking. Just as everybody tells you not to do. I was waving to Joe so of course I didn't see it."

"Well Joe will have to do without the waves from now on, won't he?" Michael smiled.

"Not at all, I'll just wave backwards while walking forwards and keeping a sharp look-out," Ruth giggled.

Joe had been somewhat quiet and withdrawn until Michael asked him about his vegetables.

"You've got a good thing here, Joe, it's a credit to you," said Michael. Ellen murmured in confirmation.

"Yes and I am enjoying it. Still learning though." Joe seemed distracted.

"And that's a good thing, me boy, makes life interesting. But what about your private life here?" Michael leaned back in his chair and chuckled. "You are considered a catch around town, don't you know, good looking fellow like you? Don't you think, ladies?" He darted a look at Joe.

"The matron at the hospital thought I was Ruth's father," Joe blurted.

Ellen laughed and Michael made a jovial remark about fighting Joe for that privilege.

"You're not my father, you're nothing like a father!" said Ruth hotly.

There was another small silence. Joe still seemed preoccupied. Finally he said, almost to himself, "I suppose I could be, couldn't I? Oh, not in reality!" He hurried to correct himself. "I mean in age. I am quite old enough to be your father, Ruthie, I just never thought about it."

"But you're no relation at all," said Ellen.

94

Later that month

It was two weeks before Ruth visited Joe again, and Michael brought her in the cart. He protested that he was driving to town anyway and Joe's place was just a bit further. He'd collect her later.

They walked around the market garden together, with Joe walking ahead with a stick, riffling through the green growth of the vegetables to disturb any reptile that might dare to be hiding there. Ruth wore snake-impervious wellington boots as well. She seemed serious and distracted.

"Oh dear. I'm so sorry love, you'll probably be very wary of snakes for the rest of our life, I should have thought about that."

"No, it's not that, Joe, but I would like a cup of tea."

"That's easily done," Joe smiled at her nervously as they walked back to the house. He raised his arm to encircle her shoulders but lowered it again.

Ruth was quiet as Joe made the tea. Joe's awkward and hesitant conversational gambits fell on stony ground.

"Joe," said Ruth solemnly as he finally sat down, "please do be quiet because I have something very important to say."

Joe's stomach flipped with anxiety.

"Do you remember," Ruth began in a low voice "when I came back to Margaret River with Rupert and you came back from Kalgoorlie? Do you remember talking to me about marrying Rupert and warning me that the reasons I gave for marrying him were not good enough?"

"Yes."

"You were right, of course, as events have proven."

"Yes."

"Do you remember what you said?"

"Sort of."

"I said at the time that I'd never heard you speak like that before and I've remembered your words ever since because I think they showed a side of you that you keep away from everyone. I've been hoping that you'd show this side of yourself to me again but it isn't happening so it seems you need a push."

Joe tried to speak but failed. Ruth went on. "You asked me if Rupert's touch made me melt, whether his presence made my scalp tingle and the hair on my forearms stand up."

"Yes, I remember," Joe croaked.

"Well *look!*" Ruth thrust her arm across the table.

In truth Joe could see nothing but her arm. The most beautiful arm in the world. He tried to speak but couldn't, his heart was in his throat.

"And take it from me, my scalp is tingling and I'm damned well melting too!" Ruth's voice was breaking and she stood up, almost defiant. "So are you going to do anything about that or do I have to do it all myself?"

Joe appeared to sag for a moment, then there was a mighty splintering crack as he threw the table aside, overturned his chair and gathered Ruth's willing body into his arms. There was a kaleidoscope in his head as her body bent to his, closer than they had ever been. He sought her mouth and felt a searing desire combined with a sense of bursting *rightness*. This was so right, it was meant to happen. Had always been meant to happen. It was fate, it was destiny, it was…Ruth. Ruth, Ruth, oh Ruth.

95

Same time, same place

Half an hour later Joe and Ruth sat on the edge of the verandah, close and entwined, arms wrapped, hands moving, stroking, pausing only to kiss deeply.

"Oh Joe, what a lot of time we've wasted."

"I think this was worth the wait."

"You've been very slow, I have to say, my lad."

"I didn't know I was waiting—or slow—until recently."

"When, my darling Joe, when, when did you know you loved me?"

"I've always loved you—of course—but when did I realise that I wanted you so completely and would want you and love you forever? When I was running back to the house with you in my arms and thought the snake had bitten you and for just a few moments there I thought I might lose you, that you might die. The thought was so dreadful and then the relief was so wonderful. And holding you felt so good and so right and suddenly I wanted to kiss you, really kiss you. I was really shocked at myself at first, but by the time we reached the house my whole perspective had changed and I knew I would never look at you the same way again. Couldn't. It was that fast."

"You actually wanted to kiss a woman with snakebite who was in all sorts of delirium?" Ruth laughed merrily. "You were thinking of taking advantage of my defencelessness?

"Yesssss!" Joe made a monster face.

They were clinging together and laughing when Michael came round the corner of the house. He stopped as Joe and Ruth looked up at him, flushed and still laughing.

"Oho!" said Michael.

"Oho to you too, Father Tree," said Ruth. "We have something to tell you."

"I don't think you need to tell me anything, daughter mine, nothing at all."

Joe and Ruth had clambered to their feet and were standing in front of Michael, hand in hand and dazedly beaming.

"Nothing at all," Michael repeated, looking stern. "Except," he said with a breaking smile, "what took you both so long?"

"Could you see it?" asked Joe. Were we the only ones who couldn't?"

"I could, for ages," said Ruth. "Joe was the slow one."

"When did you know then?"

"Probably ever since I left with Rupert. So many things were mistakes that I made and kept making and all the time all I felt or wanted to do was come back to Margaret River and be with Joe. My lovely Joe. *My* lovely Joe."

With obvious difficulty they refrained from kissing, but became more closely entwined.

"Well then," said Michael, "I've come to take you home, my girl. Let's spread the news, shall we? Or is it too soon? I'll have to tell me lovely wife, o'course, but why don't we ..." he paused "yes why don't we, why don't we, have a small party and invite the rest of the Oak Tree Placers and make a big announcement then?"

"Oh yes, yes, that would be wonderful, Tree. Don't you think, Joe?"

Joe's indulgent gaze indicated that he'd happily agree to any damned thing.

96

The following day.

Sunday was technically the day of rest for the town, the farmers and Group Settlers, although the Group Settlement Scheme itself had long since been abandoned. The remaining Settlers were now entrenched in the landscape, if they had had the tenacity required to continue with the eternal toil that was their lot. Some, of course, had little option but to remain but many had left over the years and the Scheme was not considered to have been a success. Brave try, but …

Still, the Scheme did leave enough productive dairy farms dotted round the landscape to justify the erection of a butter factory to take their cream, and a grand Road Board hall and office had just been opened in town. An even more grand hotel was nearing completion on the main street and the shops were multiplying.

The Oak Tree Place Mob had prospered modestly. Both Len and Stephen had each managed to acquire (and would own, with luck, in years to come) adjoining Group farms to their own that had been abandoned by disillusioned Settlers so that their landholdings were now large enough for viable dairy farms. The work was still unrelenting but they had a future.

Michael and Ellen still lived in the Group House on their original 160 acres but only farmed in a limited fashion. Ellen had revealed a talent for hairdressing and on three days a week she cut, set and permed the hair of the ladies of the district, renting space behind the barber shop.

They all came to Joe's house, slightly puzzled by the invitation but happy enough to socialise which they all agreed that they didn't do often enough. The house vibrated as Len and Ida's two ran and tumbled with Stephen and Helen's pride and joy, a sturdy three-year old called John. Amongst the adults, one or two wondered why they had been summoned with so little notice and an air of slight mystery pervaded.

Joe busied himself with dispensing home brew and Ida, as usual, directed the heating and serving of lunch. The kitchen table wasn't big enough so they left that to the children and the adults balanced plates on their knees in the front room. The meal was almost finished when there was a sound of a crash from the kitchen. As the adults crowded through the door they saw three little faces rigid with guilty disbelief with a collapsed table at a crazy angle between them.

"Look, this is the culprit," said Len, waving a table leg in the air, "it's come right off. Goodness knows how that happened, these tables are as sturdy as rocks usually. Looks as if it's had a bad accident. Did you know about it, Joe? Can you fix it?"

"Joe?"

"Joe? What are you laughing at?"

"Let's get the little ones out of this mess."

"Don't worry, lovey, it wasn't your fault."

"Let's get you another drink of water, shall we?"

"Here then, take an apple and you can go outside and play. Don't go far."

"Richard and Margaret, take care of little John, won't you?"

Ida had begun to stack the plates and dishes and had put a kettle on to boil when Joe, unable to contain himself any longer, called a halt to all activity and summoned the adults back into the front room, where they perched, puzzled. Michael and Ellen looked a trifle smug but no one noticed.

"Ruth and I have something to tell you all," he began, as Ruth stepped to his side and he put his arm around her.

"Hooray! About bloody time!" cried Len immediately.

"I should think so!" echoed Stephen, "it took you long enough."

Ruth looked up at Joe; they both looked confused.

"You could see … " said Joe in wonder. "You could all see what I damned well couldn't see myself. Oh my God, Oh my God I was so blind."

"Just as long as you can see it all clearly now," laughed Helen. "That's the main thing."

They clustered round Joe and Ruth, shaking hands, patting backs, kissing and hugging in a whirlpool of well-wishers.

"Will I tell them how the table leg came to be broken?" whispered Joe to Ruth.

"No, my darling, that's ours, that story. Like the hairs on my arm!"

Joe had melted at the sound of Ruth calling him "darling" and he gazed bemusedly at her. All around there were broad smiles, huge goodwill and a little nostalgia.

Michael produced a bottle of sherry to drink toasts as he revealed his and Ellen's slightly prior knowledge of the situation.

"So Joe," Len said eventually as the front room settled down, "what are you going to do about Ruth being married then? And are you divorced yourself? Bit of a muddle there, eh?"

"Steady on, Len, that's none of our business." Stephen frowned.

"I've wasted too much time already to worry about things like that," said Joe airily. "And I'm divorced, by the way, that's a start."

"Anyway," interrupted Ruth, "we'll just live in sin, won't we Joe?"

"In the meantime."

"And in due course I will expect you to marry me, Joe, I warn you."

"It's manners to wait till you're asked, you know," Joe laughed with indulgent pride, pulling her even closer to his side.

"I have an idea!" Ida stood up, excited. "Let's have an Oak Tree Place non-wedding!"

No one had to ask for an explanation.

97

One week later

More than ten years had passed since they had left Oak Tree Place and embarked for Western Australia and they had all been changed by these intervening years.

Len, from being more than a little selfish and unthinking to a loving husband and father of two! Change had settled lightly on Ida; she glowed with motherhood and still adored her husband.

Stephen, dear, good, clever Stephen, was now father of a lusty son and very happily married to a woman who was his equal and his sanctuary.

Michael, casting off his dark past, had gained a beautiful grown daughter and lived serenely with the love of his life, who loved him deeply in return.

Joe's introspective thoughts meandered on.

The transplantation of Oak Tree Place had been more successful than anyone would have imagined, even considering the enthusiasm with which they had set out. Even their oak trees had all flourished!

It seemed like another world though, now, that place. Joe tried to recall the feeling of it, the sights and smells, but it remained insubstantial. It was, however, hard to imagine even that ghostly place being occupied by a completely strange and unfamiliar set of characters. It was, Joe supposed, the knowledge that strangers now lived there that helped the sense of disassociation. But the knowledge that he was never likely to see it again caused him some semi-sweet regret. Never another pint at the Oak Tree, never another whiff of trodden grass from Oak Tree Field, never another night at the flicks with his mates, never again feel the uneven cobbles of Oak Tree Place …

Joe had been awake for ages but now he went to open the front door of his house and stand in the doorway, relishing the cold air. His retrospective thoughts vanished immediately.

A wispy mist hung over his market garden and as he watched, the rays of the rising sun caught the tops of the surrounding marri trees, turning the tiny new leaves to shimmering crystals. A feeling of such wellbeing flooded over him that he felt warmed by it.

His place.

Later today he would make his way to Michael's house where he knew that a mock wedding ceremony had been devised that would be fun and ridiculous and nevertheless he would consider himself officially married to his own beautiful Ruth. The party would be full of joy and celebration by people who loved them both and afterwards they would come home to this house and start their lives together.

This house.
This place.
Their place.

* 9 7 8 0 6 4 8 9 2 2 3 0 8 *